W9-AJQ-212

'Because of the rare combination of a spotless style, the sympathy for the dangers that the protagonist faces, the suspense and, despite it all, the hero's undiminished ability to put his situation in perspective, this year's Golden Noose goes to *Mr. Miller* by Charles den Tex'
JURY REPORT, GOLDEN NOOSE AWARD

'An action thriller with brains'
Het Parool

'Clear, compelling prose. A must'
Vrij Nederland

'An incredibly exciting, tightly written story'
De Volkskrant

'Den Tex does not write a single line unthinkingly. His language continuously sparkles and surprises. *Mr. Miller* is witty, fast, exciting, adventurous, somewhat strange, and above all a stylistic masterpiece. In the work of Den Tex there are no futuristic concepts, only espionage-like computer techniques that are possible with the current state of affairs. He creates a universe full of managers, mergers, and opaque negotiations, and with that a new genre: the corporate thriller'
NRC Handelsblad

'A fast-moving thriller: the pace is perfectly judged, the writing astute and perceptive, both economical and expressive'
Euro Crime

CHARLES DEN TEX is the Netherlands' leading thriller writer. His work has been translated into several languages. He was born in Camberwell, Australia, in 1952, and moved to the Netherlands in 1958. He studied photography and film in London. He is three-time winner of the Dutch annual prize for the best thriller. His novel *CEL* ('Cell') was longlisted for the prestigious Libris Literature Prize. *Mr. Miller* and *CEL* were made into a ten-part mini-series for Dutch television and have been sold to Netflix. His work is often compared to that of John Grisham, Michael Crichton, and Michael Ridpath.

NANCY FOREST-FLIER is a New Jersey-born translator who moved to Europe in 1982 and has worked in the Netherlands since 1988. Her literary translations include *The King* by Kader Abdolah, *Dissident for Life* by Koenraad de Wolf, *Gliding Flight* by Anne-Gine Goemans, *We and Me* by Saskia de Coster, *Departure Time* by Truus Matti, *Hex* by Thomas Olde Heuvelt, and most recently *The Story of Shit* by Midas Dekkers. Nancy also translates children's literature and has translated for numerous Dutch museums and institutes, including The Anne Frank House and the Kröller-Müller Museum (home to the world's second largest Van Gogh collection).

Mr. Miller

Charles den Tex
Mr. Miller

Translated from the Dutch
by Nancy Forest-Flier

WORLD EDITIONS
New York, London, Amsterdam

Published in the USA in 2019 by World Editions LLC, New York
Published in the UK in 2015 by World Editions Ltd., London

World Editions
New York/London/Amsterdam

Printed by Sheridan, Chelsea, MI, USA

Library of Congress Cataloging in Publication Data is available
ISBN 978-1-64286-015-3
First published as *De macht van meneer Miller* in the Netherlands in 2005
by De Geus

The publisher gratefully acknowledges the support of the Dutch
Foundation for Literature

N ederlands
  letterenfonds
dutch foundation
for literature

Twitter: @WorldEdBooks
Facebook: WorldEditionsInternationalPublishing
www.worldeditions.org

For Rudolf: for almost as long as I can remember.

With thanks to Jeroen Kodde.

1

Bellilog, June 13

Kurt today. Tears in my eyes every five minutes. Didn't know I was so sentimental. Maybe it just means more than I'm aware of. Or want to admit. And with no more than half a day free. Even then it's a squeeze, since I have no idea how I'm going to make up for all those hours. Life on the margins. That's all I've got. Everything counts. Fuck it. Jess in S.F. at least until the end of the week, probably longer. So no sex, except in my head. Living for the future, the eternal now. Now, now, now, so much now. Anyway. Three and a half hours, three if all goes well. Going back in time. Wish me luck.

2

Hyperventilation

The end of my life landed at Schiphol four weeks ago. Since then nothing has been the same. On a Monday morning, eight-eighteen, it came in on a Boeing 747 flying non-stop from Atlanta, and I even went to meet it. From the minute the plane landed—seven minutes early, in fact—I was lost. Robbed of very bit of control I thought I had—if I had ever had it in the first place, of course. But as long as nobody tests you, you can think what you want.

At the gate there was that sense of expectation of people doing something for someone else that they'd never do otherwise: being part of a crowd staring through a glass wall at an area they cannot enter, where there's always less to see than what they had expected. Yet there I was, standing on tiptoe, struggling to see someone I wanted to recognize. Preferably a face with a probing gaze, with the same expectation, searching for emotional release. Arms and hands waving, men and women jumping up and down, children running all over the place, straining eyes that are sending signals past every obstacle to the other, THE other, the one they've come to meet.

I was waiting with my parents for Kurt, my younger brother, who had left five and a half years before and hadn't been back since. He was twenty-two at the time. He had gotten stuck in some course of study that changed its name every year, and meanwhile I had charged ahead on my way to a job that would cut me off from my past forever. Kurt and I are just over two years apart and we're not in any way alike. He's blond and I'm dark, but that may be the least of our differences. Our tastes always ran in opposite directions: flavours, colours—it didn't matter. If I wanted sports, he wanted music. And vice versa. If I felt like a burger, he campaigned for pizza. There was always a certain something, though, and we were always together, inseparable. Because with Kurt I knew who I was. He was my brother, I was his brother. It was as easy as breathing, as spontaneous as walking. Except he had signed up for an exchange programme in theoretical mathematics, a field he ended up in because it came easy to him. What he himself wanted was never entirely clear. He went to America, and five years later he still hadn't come back. After a couple of months he stopped answering his e-mails. The phone number I had for him was cut off overnight. I just didn't get it. There were things that drove my parents crazy, things they wouldn't talk about. Screaming behind closed doors, breathing so shallow that the air hardly had a chance to get down their throats and built up behind their eyes.

But they said nothing.

By the time Kurt left, we had both been out of the house for some time. I had gone from the outskirts of Dordrecht to study in Rotterdam and ended up in Amsterdam. The fact that I could move from the Bible Belt to the heart of international commerce just like that, without a passport or vaccinations, strengthened my trust in the things I had been unaware of in the austere religious world of my parents: the business community and the enormous amounts of money, drink and expensive clothing that go with it. Men and women competing at every conceivable level: status, position, relationships, power and property. Nothing is certain, except for the fact that you have to fight for it. Before the end of my fourth year I had a job in Amsterdam as a communications consultant with a large consultancy, HC&P. The economy had an insatiable hunger for young, recently graduated individuals with a high hormone level and a higher than average IQ. More than four hundred consultants and staff worked at HC&P in a gleaming glass tower in Amsterdam's southern quarter. It's the Dutch branch of a firm of consultants that operates worldwide. So there I was, on the ninth floor, with a hot desk, a complete array of modern equipment, a leased car and more money in my bank account each month than I had ever seen in my life.

I can talk to anybody, anytime, under any circumstance. That's what I do. I live by talking, e-mailing, phoning and meeting. Sixteen hours a day. I train other people so they always know what to say: how to be more relaxed on camera, better in meetings, more effective in consultations. That's my job. To a certain extent I've learned it, but mainly it's a natural gift. My clients are directors, chairmen and politicians. I saw the Minister of Justice every week, sometimes more than that, to teach him how to introduce tough policy with as little public resistance as possible.

I did that—for years—and during those years Kurt disappeared. Little by little he receded from my memory, where all the things we had done became happier but also less prominent.

Until that Thursday morning, as I stood with my nose pressed against the glass wall and projected images from the past onto the hesitating crowd of people shuffling around the conveyor belt in search of suitcases and bags. There I waited, lips dry and breathing too fast. Without thinking I pulled a chapstick out of my pocket and spread it around my mouth. Force of habit. Nowhere did I see anyone who looked the least bit like Kurt.

My parents, who were standing next to me, were just as surprised as I was when our gaze was finally reciprocated. A waving arm, first hesitant, then full of conviction. My parents waved back. I did not. For some reason I couldn't even raise my arms. My limbs felt as if they had been screwed onto my body. My lungs were bolted onto my back, full of air that was far too heavy. My heart was pumping panic through my veins. Kurt waved at me, and looked at me with eyes that seemed to suck me through the glass.

Soon the sliding doors of Gate 3 opened. Kurt dropped the bags on the floor and ran up to me—arms around my neck, pulling me close without uttering a word, pure physical contact—and finally said, 'Jesus, I missed you!'

That was the moment when I lost myself. Right there in the arrivals hall, Kurt in my arms. I knew what I was seeing, but I didn't see what I knew. Something fell apart somewhere and slowly I felt my knees go slack. The arrivals hall at Schiphol grew darker and darker, and it wasn't until later, much later, that I was aware of an unknown man tugging and pulling at me.

'He's come around,' the man shouted. I saw my parents in the midst of the crowd. And Kurt. And right after that everything went black. The next thing I saw was a man in a greenish yellow outfit in the back of an ambulance. He slapped me on the back, listened to my chest, shone a light in my eyes and moved his right forefinger slowly from left to right and up and down.

'Hyperventilation,' he said, and gave me a small bag to breathe into if it should happen again.

What did he know.

3

Bellilog, June 14

I'm not here. Okay?

4

Exclamation points in the void

Yesterday my flow of words was brought to an abrupt halt. After getting out of the ambulance, filling in forms, answering questions and being given a clean bill of health, I found myself standing alone in front of the terminal at Schiphol. Without parents, without Kurt. Between the attacks of hysteria I had made it clear to my father that they were not to wait for me. Best not to wait. In my hand I was holding the little bag and the instructions, 'what to do in the event of another attack.' I had nothing more to say. No matter how hard I tried, I could find no answer to the questions that kept coming at me, bigger and bigger and increasingly aggressive.

Except for drink. That's what I wanted. Lots of alcohol, and with no one else around. Especially no one I knew, no consultants or clients. Leeches. I went to the closest bar and asked for a double vodka on ice. After a third glass I didn't want to see anyone any more, not even the bartender. His professional cheerfulness had the opposite effect on me. Half drunk and half unhinged, I went back home. I couldn't go back to the office in that state, and I certainly couldn't meet with any clients. Nor did I want to. But with all that alcohol in me I didn't even have to think about it.

I closed the door to my apartment and started in. A little while later, as I was smashing the empty bottle to bits against the wall, I felt a total blockage of uncontrollable thoughts and disordered emotions raging in my head. The three hours I had taken off to pick up Kurt had turned into five. The first appointment came and went as I poured myself another drink and was unable to suppress a sense of victory. The phone rang, my cell. The office, I saw on the display.

Otherwise I ignored it. Alcohol had taken control of all my systems. My schedule disappeared as the hours passed. Meetings dissolved into thin air. The weekly session with the Ministry of Justice. The preparations for the European Summit on Security and Integration would have to take place without my input. Ethnic tension and religious claims were leading to increasingly sharp differences of opinion throughout most of Europe. The EU had to come up with a joint policy, but sensitivities were so acute that progress seemed impossible. For HC&P it was the biggest assignment ever. The firm was working on the conference from ten different countries. So was I. The counselling I was providing the minister was an essential part of the entire project.

But not now.

The endless peeping of my cell phone was only the beginning of a frenzied barrage of phone calls between the office and clients who were waiting in vain in various conference rooms. They didn't disturb me in the least. Nothing but irritating noises from another world, signals that were trying and failing to make any kind of connection.

Trembling from the drink, I picked up the phone and turned it off. Put it back on the table. It was silent now, a solitary object. A thing among things. I wanted to grab the bottle, which was just out of reach, but I lost my balance. Nothing unusual, except I could no longer remember how to stop myself from falling. My arms and legs still had some of their reflexes, such as swaying and groping for things, but the vodka gave me no control.

I went down with one enormous crash. Flat on my back. Nicely done, I thought, until my head hit the wooden floor with far too much force. Stabs of pain fought their way through the drink and helped me carry on, since the pain now convinced me that what I needed was more to drink. Lots more.

In the middle of the night the electricity went out. Everything. All at once. From one minute to the next the apartment was plunged into darkness. With half of me hanging onto the couch, I tried to figure out what was going on, but I didn't get much further than the circuit breaker. Why that had suddenly stopped working was beyond me. Stumbling and tottering, I made my way to the front hall, propping myself up against a doorpost or a wall with every step. At the halfway point I had to stop. My head was spinning. My limbs were slack and unreliable. I leaned against the wall, panting. The contents of my stomach became more and more agitated. Eyes closed. Breathing deeply. Slowly. Until calmness returned and I was able to continue walking. Four or five steps to go. No more.

The fuse box was located in a corner of the closet, right next to the front door of the apartment. Feeling my way, I searched in the dark for the shelf above the fuse box. That's where I kept my passport. Always in the same place. Right by the door. With my coats. Handy. Next to it were a couple of reserve fuses and a flashlight. Groping uncontrollably, I found the flashlight and flicked it on. Then I stared at the fuse box—for minutes, it seemed, because I hardly was able to grasp what I saw. And what I saw were buttons. It took a long time before I realized that all the switches were fine, and even longer before I came to the conclusion that the electricity in the apartment hadn't gone out after all. I sank backward into the coats.

That's where I woke up. My eyes opened and came to rest on familiar forms that I didn't immediately recognize. The light in the apartment was on again, and it took a while to recall what had happened earlier on. How much earlier on was no longer clear to me. My head was rebelling against the alcohol but my tongue and my throat wanted more. My body was in need of hydration. Physical demands slowly began to suppress all thought, although the images remained. Undiminished. Kurt with outstretched arms. Warm body pressed against me. Eyes that saw everything. Even now. Even here. This is what I was thinking, so I still did have thoughts after all.

Nausea suddenly overcame me. It spread from my stomach, and before I could reach the bathroom the contents of my insides had been squeezed outward. The potent smell of vomit rebounded through my entrails, and soon I was hanging powerless over the edge of the toilet bowl. Reflex heaving continued until there was nothing left to heave. Then the thirst intensified. In a burst of virtual sobriety I went to the kitchen and found everything I needed: two microwave hamburgers, a can of Coke and a bottle of rum. As the microwave did its work, I gulped down the Coke and uncorked the bottle. The rum had no trouble finding its way into my system and mixed readily with the alcohol in my blood. I was left to the mercy of a union of liquid compounds that only wanted the best for me. The fat and salt in the hamburgers provided no protection whatsoever, but what they did for my convictions more than made up for it. Junk food is the modern world's only real contribution to cooking. A hundred percent processed, treated, modified and flavour-enhanced, with a best-before date issued by a multinational. That's all I needed.

The floor was never far away. Crawling, glugging. Halfway through the rum there was little reason to get back on my feet. I leaned against the couch, bottle and cigarettes in hand. Daylight came far too early, with its ruthless optimism. A painful cheerfulness that I had absolutely no need for. More than ever, I missed someone to belong to. I missed Jessica.

The rest of the rum brought silence, unconscious silence. Time suddenly accelerated. An hour passed in the blink of an eye. The sun disappeared from the window. The rum became triple sec. The TV was on, broadcasting word games I didn't understand. Laughing faces, surprise, incredibly lively colours and people asserting things with utter conviction. Images flashed past, as if the TV set was full to bursting and everything flowed out as soon as you made an opening for it. Men with beards and women with headscarves looking at the smouldering remains of a building, their eyes filled with injured piety. And hate. That was something I recognized immediately. Hate that didn't yet have the room it needed, that was being kept for future use, imperishable, stored in the genes. The voice of the news presenter suddenly sounded strained, with less space between the syllables.

... fire broke out last night at the nearby Islamic school.
The fire started at several points and spread very rapidly.
The walls of the school were covered with racist slogans
and offensive texts. After the earlier disturbances, the
situation appeared to be under control, but the peace was
illusory. Local Muslims are speaking of an attack, and ...

I zapped away to MTV. Thundering music. Sound off. Swimming through the room on the last drops of triple sec. The orange flavour began to grate on me. I washed the sticky sweetness away with white wine, which I had more than enough of. I was past the alcohol, past drunkenness. I had landed in a transcendental state where I saw and heard everything but registered nothing. I stared at my computer screen for minutes at a time without any questions occurring to me, without the will to do anything. I was sitting there to work on my blog, that much I knew. Somewhere in the far recesses of my mind a habit was thrashing around that was stronger than any drink I could consume. I had to write in my blog, even if it was just a couple of words, because without my blog I was no longer in touch with the world. So with limp fingers I began punching at the keyboard. For a moment it surprised me that the computer was running. I couldn't remember having turned it on. An unwarranted conviction settled in my head, even though I knew I could no longer be sure of anything.

The e-mail icon flashed. Incoming message. I read the mail from Jessica. Sent an answer. Ignored all the frantic messages from the office. Exclamation points in the void. Christ, was I sick.

5

Bellilog, June 15

Intense mad-cow feeling, spongy synapses with signals disappearing and reappearing in entirely different form, subdued, distorted. Aggressive.

Mail from: Jess
Subject: sf
work hard play hard, 24-7, in shape in gear. very cock-centered place, this. regenerated protozoa with egos. maybe something to it. far from finished. everything ok on the amstel? miss-u.

jess

Mail to: Jess
Subject: Re: sf
youre not cheating on me, are you? more than I could handle. floundering here. lots of xxx and everything else ive forgotten. belli

6

Man is the information he carries

I had been receiving some fat bonuses in recent years. For every follow-up assignment I managed to bring in I was given a percentage of the returns, even more if the assignment was brand new. Sometimes this amounted to tens of thousands of euros. And suddenly now my future was uncertain.

No one had heard from me for two whole days. No colleagues, no clients, no one from management. Understandable for me, perhaps, but lethal for my job situation. It was a form of corporate suicide. HC&P gave its employees very little leeway, and I had gone way over the line. I was in the elevator, waiting for the doors to close. Clean underwear, clean shirt, white, no tie, dark blue suit with a narrow stripe, and enough gel in my hair to keep it in a state of high-spirited surprise. It wasn't real, but it worked. I was still up to my eyeballs in alcohol. I looked neatly pressed, but inside chaos reigned, more than I could suppress. I needed all the help I could get, and until I got it I was shutting everything out, beginning with my family. Talking to them was out of the question, especially with Kurt. Not because Kurt didn't say anything but because I couldn't trust my own words. Everything I wanted to say meant something different than what I actually said, so I kept my mouth shut. Much better that way.

That strategy probably wouldn't work at the office, since HC&P saw information as the firm's primary concern. Not the people, not the equipment, not the building or the clients, but the information. People were no more than the information stored within them and made accessible by them.

Man is the information he carries.

That sentence is engraved on a polished, dark granite pillar in the reception area of each of the company's seven hundred and twenty-three branches. It's a small, stylish object, not garish or gaudy. On the contrary, if you didn't know it was there you'd have to look for it, and that's part of its attraction. It's the company slogan, but perhaps more than that, it's the basic principle behind its dealings in the world. Job applicants have to fill out long questionnaires and go through endless interviews.

'If we don't know what you know, then we'll never know what we can do for each other.' That's how the leadership thinks at HC&P and that's how the company works. Openness, and the sharing of knowledge and information: that's the basis of collaboration. The company knows everything about me. It knows who I am, where I come from, where I live, my bank account number, what my favourite music is, what my strengths and weaknesses are, how high my IQ is (applicants with IQs under 140 are rejected out of hand), where my family lives, what illnesses I've had and when I last visited the dentist.

IQ is important. Partner IQ is 180 and higher. Partners are the men with the ability to see through extremely complex situations and facts and to formulate new possibilities. Jessica is the first woman in the company to think and work at that level. What she lacks in experience she makes up for in untamed killer instinct. She's faster and more accurate than the best of them. She can be totally concentrated and still remain accessible to others, as if her brain had two separate functions, just like breathing and seeing. Jessica is an IQ tempest in her own body, and there's nothing HC&P would rather do than make use of her fearsome capacities. All within the rules of the firm, of course.

The sliding door of the elevator was stopped by a strong, tanned hand. Dries van Waayen stepped into the gleaming, polished compartment.

'Me too,' he said. Partner-director, fifty-six, his watch cost more than everything I was wearing put together. His expression was solemn but happy. Everything he did was important, and therefore serious. He enjoyed his work so much that he simply radiated satisfaction. Always, under all circumstances.

'Bellicher,' he said. He had the ability to sound friendly in the chilliest way. 'Is it just the two of us?'

'Looks that way.'

As the door slid closed for the second time, Van Waayen placed a hand on my shoulder and gazed at me with a look that revealed nothing but the shameless pleasure he took in being himself.

'That's good,' he said, 'because we have to get together some time and talk about the future, don't you agree?' He pushed the button for the fifth floor with his forefinger. For a moment it looked as if the only effect of the elevator's upward movement was his eyebrows, which rose to unprecedented heights. The smile disappeared from his face. 'Because you understand, of course, that your future looks quite different than it did a couple of months ago.' He did not expect an answer. The bad economy, the plummeting stock market, the encroaching silence with regard to mergers and takeovers, the collapse of telecommunications and the draining of the IT sector, along with my recent two-day hiatus—all this was reason enough to discuss my future at the firm.

I nodded, pursed my lips a bit and attempted a vague smile. It made little difference.

'My office,' said Van Waayen. 'Around lunchtime, I thought. That work out for you?' This was not a question. Make sure it works out.

'About twelve-thirty,' I said. We both knew what this was going to be about.

Van Waayen nodded. 'Fine,' he said.

The elevator came to a halt with a sigh. The gentle electronic imitation of a gong and a blinking number indicated that we had arrived at the fifth floor.

'This is me,' Van Waayen said. 'Last in, first out. Goes for me, too. You see?' He laughed and vanished down the corridor. His corridor. Distinctions are made to be drawn. And just as the elevator began moving again it hit me: I was going to be fired. Even the last dregs of alcohol were no solace. In point of fact I was already out. Virtual, maybe, but what were a couple of hours in the big scheme of things?

The elevator shot upward, pressing my throat down into my heart. When I swallowed, it squeezed the rhythm out of my chest and my body stiffened into a dry cramp. This was more than I could take on. I couldn't get fired. It was impossible. My body seemed to resist the very idea. Being fired meant I'd be cut off from everything I had: the technology, the profession, the systems. Cut off from the assignments that had brought me to the heart of every major development. Mega-assignments that I could easily work on twenty hours a day, driven by the commitment to find solutions where often no solution had been found before. Where the solution didn't even exist until I found it. Until we found it. Racing through the country for every client, every assignment a different team. Connected. With everything. If I no longer had that, then all that was left was the content. And content is for losers. The prospect alone took my breath away.

Panting discreetly, shallow panting, not too fast, I got out of the elevator on the ninth floor. My lips were so dry I was afraid they'd crack. Briefcase in one hand and chapstick in the other, I rushed to my hot desk. Gazing out over Amsterdam I spread the balm over the tiny, sharp flakes of skin and the stinging fissures in my lips. It relieved the taut dryness around my mouth, but no matter how I looked at it, the morning only grew shorter. Twelve-thirty was arriving as it had never arrived before. Inevitably. Twenty-five more minutes. Twenty. Fifteen.

I can't let this happen, I thought, no matter what.

'I've had more dissatisfied clients on the phone in two days than in the past fifteen years ...,' Van Waayen said. He looked at me in silence.

I didn't respond.

'... your clients,' he went on. 'Erik Strila from Justice has never called so many times before. If you leave a minister high and dry without letting him hear from you, you're doing something wrong. And I'm putting this very mildly. I've had to spend two days tying myself up in the most awkward knots to make sure it didn't get any worse. But don't worry, all the clients have been reassured and they're all sticking around. Which is more than I can say for you.'

My own problem was only third on the list, if that. The client came first and the firm came second. Rightfully so, perhaps, but Van Waayen exaggerated. The power of the client is that he can walk away and go elsewhere. That may be true, but in real life clients aren't so quick to walk away. That wasn't a factor here, either, but his having to come up with excuses for me was galling for him. Worse than I could have thought.

'That's not what I hired you for,' he said. 'Seriously. Yesterday I had to send Peter to The Hague at a moment's notice. Preparations for the EU summit are continuing, whether you show up or not. I also discussed it with the other partners, and we can't act as if nothing happened, you understand?' He wasn't laughing. The interests of a satisfied client were more important than ever. 'The EU summit is our biggest assignment. Coordinating European security and integration policy puts us squarely in the middle of all the relevant ministries. Justice is crucial. And what do you do? Apparently this kind of responsibility is not in reliable hands in your case. So if I don't step in now we'll have no end of trouble, and what will we have to show for it?'

It was a conversation with lots of logical conclusions drawn from indisputable developments, but it wasn't about having a conversation. It didn't even look like a conversation. It was an offer of three months' salary and a promise to spend the next six months helping me find a new job. In concrete terms: a good eighteen thousand euros, five interviews with an outplacement advisor and not the slightest prospect of work, since dismissed consultants are an almost unemployable group. Especially communications consultants. I'd be turning in my car, my cell phone, my laptop and my clients, knowing only too well that the combination of mortgage and flexible credit line would be ruthlessly pulled out from under me within four months.

I did not respond to the offer. I had already decided that. Subconsciously. Instinctively. I pursed my lips, shook my head slightly and raised my eyebrows.

'Maybe,' I said. 'Maybe.' But I didn't go along with it, for the simple reason that I didn't agree with it.

'Take your time,' Van Waayen said. There was an obligatory sort of reasonableness in his voice. 'Then we'll talk further. I always have time on Friday.'

'Today is Wednesday,' I said.

'Whatever. You get what I mean. You don't have to leave before lunch. That's not how we treat each other here. But one way or another we have a conclusion to draw. You know that as well as I do.'

Twenty minutes later I was back in the corridor. I hadn't agreed to anything, hadn't admitted anything, and I hadn't eaten any of Van Waayen's sandwiches. All there was in my stomach was a corrosive pool of coffee and acid. Nothing was left of what I had once been so sure of. The immense HC&P building, which last week had still been the foundation of a rock-solid future, was now anything but. One decision would put me on the other side of glitter and security. If I let go now, I'd never get back in. That much was certain. So I didn't go anywhere. In fact, I stayed.

After lunch I called my contacts and rescheduled all my appointments. With plenty of apologies and placation I managed to charm my old clients one more time. Why I don't know, but there was nothing to it. I called Erik Strila, who seemed surprised to hear from me. Word of my departure had apparently gotten around. He listened to my excuses but skirted around them, as if he had heard other ones already. Better ones. And he had.

'Erik,' I said, 'how often have we seen each other and talked over the past year?'

'Too often to mention.'

'And all those times I always showed up. I was always perfectly prepared. True or not?'

'True, yes.' He agreed, but it sounded like a forgotten memory. A consultant is as good as his last achievement.

I said it to make sure it got said. I wasn't gone yet. Erik Strila was the client with whom I had the best working relationship. He was my contact at Justice. I had embarrassed him in front of his minister and he wasn't going to forgive me easily.

'We'll talk sometime,' he said. He even avoided saying goodbye.

All by itself, and almost imperceptibly, my subconscious came to a decision. My head was making assessments that I wasn't even aware of. What I knew, what I had done, what I had heard—everything lined up in neat rows, vertical and horizontal, compared, tallied up, subtracted, weighed and turned over one last time before being approved or rejected. While I was making my phone calls and talking it struck me: somewhere behind my eyeballs, along the finely branched nerve cells in my head, among the hundreds of millions of contacts there was one that stuck out.

Clear as glass.

Hard as war.

7

Bellilog, June 16

I am a communications consultant and I wouldn't want to be anything else. I can't even imagine being anything else. Being a consultant is a state of mind. In the meantime this is how things are stacked up: vw is a partner and I'm a junior—not anymore, actually, but that has yet to be confirmed, so until then I am—and partners never have to be right because a junior is always wrong. Life may not be fair, but that's no big deal. That's power. And because HC&P is a respectable company, a junior will always make sure that a partner never has to exercise his power. Because you just don't do that. Having power is chic, but exercising power is vulgar. And vulgar is a no-no. A vulgar consultant is an oxymoron. A vulgar consultant does not exist. He cancels himself out.

That's how things stand, and the only chance I have is to pass something on to the partner that will make him more important than he already is. Not in my eyes, because I don't even count, but in the eyes of his colleagues, the other partners, the chums. That's where the points are tallied up.

Take your time and keep on walking, the door shuts by itself.

Mail from: Jess
Subject: Re: Re: sf
cheating? floundering? excuse me? what's this about? hot and thinking of you. does that help? love u

8

The remains of able-bodied comrades

At the end of the afternoon I put my things in my briefcase, stuck my cell phone in my pocket, zipped my laptop into its bag, took the elevator to the third floor and locked myself in the canteen.

No one was there. All the tables were cleared, the floors swept. A salutary peace reigned. I walked coolly to the back as if I knew what I was doing and put my stuff in the farthest corner, the one closest to the kitchen. I pushed the swinging door open and looked inside. No one there, either.

Excellent.

I turned the latches on the entrance doors to lock them from the inside. They were swinging doors without keyholes. Nothing could have been simpler. No one had ever considered the possibility of a person wanting to ensconce himself in the canteen. Why would they?

Now I was sure that tomorrow I'd be able to get into the building, if only because I had never left. It was thinking and acting at the very lowest level, but there had been instances of a person's building pass failing to work the day after a candid evaluation talk. The person never got any further than the downstairs reception area. There was always a reason for immediate refusal of entrance. The most common was confidential company information about the client. Information was sacred and everyone accepted the need to protect it. Exaggerated? Perhaps, but in the consultancy world everything is exaggerated. People said goodbye from a distance, never in each other's company. That only muddied the waters. It was as simple as that, and I was not about to end up on the street in such a childish way.

With every move I made I became calmer, more convinced

that I was right. I made coffee, turned off the light and withdrew into the corner I had made for myself. Laptop on a small table, cell phone off. I didn't want anyone to call me. That would be too bizarre. I clicked through the documents in my computer and stared, sometimes for minutes at a time, at the memos and reports I had written for clients. A lot of the most recent work was for the Ministry of Justice. Media training for the minister, communicating the security policy. That was my work. What made it fascinating was the scale of the assignment, knowing that tens of thousands, hundreds of thousands, sometimes millions of people would be affected by the results. Amplifying small suggestions until they became noticeable changes. That's what I was staring at, and the waiting came naturally.

All around me the building grew quieter and bigger. Fewer telephones rang, fewer people walked through the corridors, the elevators went up and down only now and then. There were always a couple of midnight oil burners. HC&P had deadlines and interests that sometimes kept consultants at their desks until deep into the night. Even that was normal. I knew I wouldn't be really alone in the building until two or three o'clock in the morning, and even then I couldn't be sure. Because of the extreme working hours the alarm system was almost never in operating mode. It was there, all right, but no one ever turned it on because someone was always busy somewhere in the building. There was a night watchman downstairs armed with a battery of video cameras who kept an eye on the most important places. The canteen was not one of them.

I got hungry. In the kitchen I found well-stocked supply closets. I could hold out for a week here if necessary. There was plenty of bread and sandwich makings in the refrigerators, and salads of every shape and size. With a plate full of everything and a can of Coke to quench my unremitting thirst, I turned the light back out. I ate by late daylight, drank another can of Coke and waited for the rest of the evening. And the night.

I woke up on the floor. The Coke had done its work and was ready to move on. I stood up, my limbs stiff, stretched and looked around. It was dark. The only illumination was the small exit light above the door, a little white man running against a green background. It was ten past two.

Cautiously I unlocked the doors. The latches slid slowly back, and in a few seconds I pushed the door open a crack. The bathrooms were on the other side of the hall in one of the corridors on the left. Maybe fifteen metres from the canteen, no more than that. I stood with my hand on the door and listened.

All was silent, and here, too, it was dark except for the emergency exit. I heard no one and saw no one. The need to go became more intense. Quickly I slipped into the hall and shot across to the other side. Covering the floor with great strides, I rushed around the corner when suddenly my feet got caught up in something, first the right and then the left, and I fell headlong, flat on my face. Shocked and surprised, I looked around, almost laughing at my own stupidity for not seeing whatever was lying there, a bag or a ... what was it? I crept closer on my hands and knees, and my hand pushed against something that felt suspiciously like an arm. I pinched it. No reaction. Coming even closer I suddenly found myself looking into the blank, staring face of a woman.

She didn't respond. She was lying there on the floor in the middle of the night. I had no business being there, but she far less than I—certainly not like this. I pushed her shoulder again very gently.

'Hey,' I said.

Nothing happened.

'Hey!' I said again with a bit more conviction, and I pushed harder. She rolled over from her side to her back, and her eyes kept looking at me with a bewildered and reproachful gaze. She didn't see anything. She didn't even blink.

I withdrew my hand warily and leaned back on my haunches, my eyes fixed on the woman. On the body of a woman. A woman I didn't know was lying here dead in the corridor. I stood up, dizziness spinning through my head and tugging at my stomach. It lasted no more than twenty seconds in all, maybe a bit longer. The shock of the past few days, the excessive amount of alcohol I had polished off, the confrontation with Van Waayen, and my dismissal. And now this.

Who was this woman? And why was she lying here? Did she just collapse on her way home after a night of work, her bag over her shoulder? Even before she could reach the elevator? Or did she sprain her ankle, topple over and hit her head against the wall? One of her shoes had come loose and lay a little further down the corridor. It was possible. Except there was no sign of it anywhere. She was lying straight across the corridor, her head at least a metre from the wall. So how did it happen? If it wasn't just some kind of crazy accident, or cardiac arrest, what was it then? Had she been murdered? And if so, by whom? There was no one here. I held my breath and listened, trying to distinguish different sounds, but all I could hear was the building. Indeterminate ticks and clicks, a gentle hum and murmur of the climate control and the other systems tucked away behind the ceiling and walls, mechanical sounds produced without human intervention. Quite normal under any other circumstances, but not now.

How long had she been lying here? When was the last time I had heard sounds in the corridor? Before I fell asleep. Way before. It had grown quiet after about ten o'clock, at least on this floor.

I looked at the woman again. I walked around her, dropped

to my knees, picked up her bag and zipped it open. Bending forward awkwardly in the semi-darkness, I tried to see what was inside. It was a big bag with long, rigid handles that kept getting in the way. I saw a wallet, a pack of cigarettes, a lighter and all sorts of other little things. I rummaged through the contents, took out a set of house keys and was about to continue searching when I noticed a waving light approaching from one of the side corridors. The beam swerved back and forth from left to right, and almost immediately I heard the sounds of subdued whispers. Two, maybe three different voices. My breath caught in my throat, and in a flash I realized that being here was not a good idea. Not at all. These men were not from security. They were walking through a dark office building with flashlights. People who belonged here would simply turn on the lights and speak at normal volume. Suddenly I laid my hand on something, a flat plastic card. I pulled it out. It was her company pass, and in a split second I read her last name. Radekker. That was it. That's all I had time for. The men had almost reached the corner of the corridor. I put the other things back in the bag and was about to lay it down, but my hair had gotten tangled in one of the strange raised handles. With a single fierce tug I pulled the bag loose and could just barely suppress a scream. In four quick paces I was out of the corridor. I let the door of the canteen close gently behind me. Panting, and with a pounding heart, I leaned against the wall behind the door. I felt the place where I had pulled the hair out of my head and waited, listening to thumping and lugging sounds, to remarks that I could only half understand at best.

'... doing this? Do we take the elevator?'

'No, idiot!'

Laughter. More thumping.

'Yeah, the other side!'

'... get the stuff?'

Mumbling.

'What do you think?'

'What I think is what I'm asking. Otherwise I'd ask something else.'

There was a sound of dragging, sighing and groaning.

'Jesus, bitch is heavy.'

A dull smack.

'Hey, watch what you're doing!'

My head was a jumble of thoughts. I knew too little, and what I did know did not appeal to me. It was threatening. Overlooking the city from an office tower of glass, steel, stone and concrete, I was literally too far removed from everything. In a neighbourhood without houses and without shops, where people in suits travelled to make plans, attend meetings, write reports and do other abstract things, all high above the ground, the only manual work had to do with operating computers and telephones, keyboards and buttons. Everything else was verbalization. A communication consultant has no idea what manual work is. I was not the right person to run into dead people. Not on the street, not in the train and certainly not in this office building. Yet I did want to know what had happened in the hall, what those men were doing there. And I had to call security. Two things at the same time.

Call first.

Preferably as soon as possible. The only way I could do anything was by contacting someone else. I ran into the kitchen, found a wall phone next to the swinging doors and snatched the receiver from the hook. The number! I looked on the inside of the receiver and on the phone itself, but there was no list of internal numbers. Security had its own number that everyone was supposed to know in case of emergency. Except there never were any emergencies, so I had no idea.

Nine?

I pressed the key and listened. Nothing happened.

One?

Again nothing.

Zero?

Outside line.

I slammed down the receiver with a curse and ran back to the canteen entrance. Then I warily pushed one of the doors open a crack and looked out. And listened.

Silence.

No sound. No movement. Hesitantly I left the canteen. The corridor was empty. The woman was gone, her bag was gone, the shoe was gone and the men were gone. There was nothing to indicate anything to anyone. Still uncertain, I walked further down the corridor, toward the elevators. The doors were shut and the little lights next to the buttons were dark. The elevators had stopped running and were standing still somewhere, anywhere. I began racking my brains. The office was built in the shape of a wedge, with a central column and two curved wings. The elevator shafts were in the middle section and the emergency exits were at the far ends of both wings. Both exits were about equally far from where I was standing, except the men had come from the left wing. So logically, it seemed to me, they would follow the same route back.

Every choice counted, and no choice meant doing nothing. I ran into the corridor, not at full speed but at a strange, slow-motion pace. Inhibited by caution. By fear. I wanted to hurry, but at the same time I didn't want to make any noise. As a result I succeeded in neither. I didn't hurry and I made more noise than I had to. At the last turn in the corridor I stopped, leaned against the wall and peered cautiously around the corner. No one. The emergency exit sign was shining forlornly between the dividing walls. Now I ran to the doors at the end of the corridor and pushed one open.

Behind the door was a bare concrete stairwell, where every sound reverberated and boomed as if it were being produced by a cheap amplifier. I didn't hear a thing. Not a single sound. With great caution I stepped into the open space and tried to look over the railing and into the stairwell, but it was too far away. If I were to let go of the door, it would close and lock behind me and I wouldn't be able to get back in. All my things were still in the canteen so I had to go back, no matter what happened. I kicked off one of my shoes, placed it at an angle in the door frame, and let the door close on it. The powerful door-closer squeezed the soft leather all out of shape, and with faint, unexpected pain I stood there watching the compression of three hundred euros worth of footwear.

Taking two steps at a time, I stormed down the stairs to the exit on the ground floor three floors below, and soon I was standing in the parking garage beneath the building. I had jammed my second shoe into the heavy steel door leading to the garage, and it was even flatter than the first. No one was there. In that whole immense, bare, concrete parking level there were only three cars, and one of them was mine. Outside in the street I heard the sound of a passing motorcycle. A siren wailed in the far distance. Just for a moment. Then silence. There was nothing to see, nothing to detect.

Slowly I walked back upstairs to the canteen. I had seen something, but I had absolutely no proof that anything had taken place. None. If I were to call security, the man would want to know what I was doing in the building at the very least. And in the canteen at that. My place of work was six floors higher, so what was I doing there? What was I doing here? Calling the police would produce the same results, the only difference being that the police probably wouldn't even show up. No body, no people, nothing. All I had were my own thoughts, my ideas, and my trust in them was minimal. I was thinking things that paralyzed me, things that kept me from seeing who I was, or who I thought I was. As if you had always loved chocolate and suddenly, from one minute to the next, the smell alone made you sick, made you break out in hives. As if you had become allergic to the one thing you loved the most. Like that, only worse.

It was all because of Kurt, that was clear. Kurt had turned me inside out. My whole body had risen up in protest against my mind. A war was being fought inside me on the molecular level, and on that battlefield my self-confidence was the first casualty.

In one of the refrigerators in the kitchen I found a bottle of wine, and before I knew it I had polished off more than half. I was totally oblivious to the flavour. The alcohol found the remains of its able-bodied comrades with convincing ease.

Maybe half an hour had passed since I had first left the canteen to go to the bathroom, and I still hadn't been there. High time. I took off my jacket and hung it over the back of the chair, putting my hands in the pockets to take out my cigarettes. Pack, lighter—and there was something else in the right-hand jacket pocket. The woman's keys. And her pass. I looked at the pass and read the name: I. Radekker. Reading her name brought back the image of her dead body. Alone, dumped in the corridor, lifeless on the indestructible office carpeting.

I put the keys in my pocket, walked to the bathroom and retreated into one of the cubicles.

Goose bumps on my arms.

Bellilog, June 17

Adrenalin dreams, fingers on the computer keys, tools for making symbols, contact with the contact points, no one to reach, signals to myself ... slept very badly.

First look, then think

Daylight came. Finally. I had been waiting almost three hours. Awake, restless, uncertain as I was, it took much longer for the time to pass than I was used to. I made coffee, and in the kitchen I listened to the little radio that was always there. Music. Talk shows. News. Reports that flitted by: emigrating farmers, protesting health care workers, financial setbacks. I heard it, but the details had no impact on me. Except for that one item.

> ... at the mosque yesterday, Dutch youths came to blows with youths of foreign origin after the windows of the mosque had been smashed in. The police managed to separate the two groups. Seven people were wounded and taken to the hospital. Things remained tense until long after midnight ...

The reports you don't want to hear always sound the loudest. Every day provided new reasons for harsher decisions to be made at the upcoming European summit. I was haunted by images of escalating conflict, thoughts I had no room for. My own situation had priority.

The first employees began arriving at six-thirty, the consultants well before the office staff and before the clients could start calling. Often the early morning was the only part of the day you could work in peace without being disturbed by the phone, by ad hoc discussions, by colleagues popping in or by meetings that got out of hand. I packed my things and waited in the corridor until someone below got into the elevator going up. Only when the elevator began moving did I press the button, so no one below would notice that I was still in the building.

The elevator stopped and almost noiselessly the doors opened. Two men were inside, young consultants who, like me, had to find their hours where others left them. Frans Stutman and Thomas Ridden. Showered and shaved, they both looked at me, their eyes still heavy with sleep.

Frans was the first to speak. 'Hey, Michael, another all-nighter?'

'Can you see it?'

'And smell it,' said Thomas.

'Thanks a lot.'

'De nada.' Frans opened his briefcase, took out a designer bottle, aimed the atomizer at my jacket and pressed down. A cloud of fresh male scent descended on me. Thomas waved his hand back and forth and coughed.

'Good Lord,' he said. 'What kind of garbage is that?' He grabbed the bottle from Frans's hands. 'Three litres for ten euros? Or did Shell make this? Aerosol unleaded? I can't release this product anymore. Public health comes first.'

The door opened on the eighth floor. Thomas sprinted out with Frans right behind him, into the corridor, out of sight. With them went the fun of the job, the passionate desire to have an opinion about everything, to add an insight or throw in your two cents. One floor higher I got out, walked into the right wing of the building and headed for the large work area where the hot desks were. A consultant's place is with his client and not at the office behind a desk. Desk work is a waste of time, which is why an advanced form of musical chairs had been introduced. We had ten work stations for fifteen people. Ten desks that belonged to everyone, and therefore to no one. There was nothing on the desks: no plants, no photos, no postcards. Nothing. Ten virginal working surfaces that gave the impression of an unused office. Everyone had his or her own cart, a kind of glorified shopping trolley made of fashionable brushed aluminum and high-quality plastic with a place for files and folders and a small lockable compartment at the bottom. It was as if you had arrived at the ward for terminal patients and you were allowed to keep a few personal things next to your bed. Not too many, because before too long all your junk would have to be cleared away anyway.

At the door I grabbed my cart, walked with it to the farthest work station, next to the window and plugged in my laptop. While the computer was starting up I took out my cell phone. It was still off. I had been unreachable since the previous afternoon. The HC&P office had almost no land lines. Even the secretaries walked through the building with cells. Everyone was always available. Everywhere. Unless you turned your phone off, but that was only permitted during conferences with clients or higher-ups. The first was company policy, the second was an unspoken rule.

As soon as the phone found the network it began peeping and the voicemail symbol appeared in the display. I called, and the computerized voice from the phone company told me I had seven messages. Three were from Dries van Waayen—personal, no less.

'Bellicher,' the manicured voice said. 'On second thought, maybe we ought to work on reaching a point of clarity for both parties. Let's do it soon. I understand you're on the road, meeting with a client, and that's great, but once you start something it's a good idea to grab the bull by the horns. That's what we advise our clients and it's what we do ourselves. Call me,' he said.

End of message.

In the next one he elaborated his idea. 'Now we have to be careful that we don't turn our attention to the wrong things, that we don't lose sight of the difference between effectiveness and efficiency. Focus is the goal. That's important. That's what it's all about. I know it and you know it. So I think it would be good if we could come back to this as soon as possible. Call me. I'm available.'

End of message.

The third voicemail was less nuanced. The cultivated smooth edge of his voice was gone. I wasn't with a client at all, and now he knew it, too. 'If you don't mind, I'd like to know what IN GOD'S NAME you're up to! Whatever possessed you to make such a stupid decision, especially now? Not only is it at odds with the interest of the client, but it also jeopardizes the good name of HC&P. I expect to see you tomorrow morning at ten-fifteen in my office.'

A play in three acts. Announcement of the idea, confrontation with the principle and the immediate execution. All my own fault. Of course. Management doesn't make mistakes, and certainly not the management of an international consultancy.

That's why he was so eager to get rid of me. As soon as possible, before my behaviour could have any negative consequences. On that point he was merciless. You could make mistakes in your analysis, you could miss things in your research, you could forget to ask the right question. All signs of stupidity, of course, but it was permitted. People make mistakes. It happens. The seniors and partners made sure you knew what you had done wrong. All fine—in moderation, of course. But leaving a client in the lurch—a client—that was not done. That was cardinal sin number one. Even illness was hardly an excuse. As long as you could walk, sit and be present, you dragged yourself to the appointment. You might not utter a word all afternoon, but even that was better than not showing up. The only acceptable reason for cancelling an appointment with a client was to make room for an appointment with a more important client. A wholesale office supply company, for example, could be pushed aside for a ministry, but even then it would have to be absolutely unavoidable. But standing the client up, just like that, without offering any reasons and without even calling, was unthinkable. And that is exactly what I had done. For Dries van Waayen I had become intolerable.

I listened to the rest of the messages, and the only one that actually got through to me was the last one. It was Kurt, chatting alone in the digital storeroom.

'Hey, Michael, it's me, you're not there … or you are and you don't want anybody on the line … and that means me, too, whatever, and that's fine, I mean, that you're not talking to me, I can just imagine … so just for a minute, not long, of course, because … I really want you to talk to me again, because … Jesus, how can I say this … it's me, I mean, you know that, right?'

There was silence. The only noise was the faint hum of the connection, running for a couple of seconds. I sat behind the desk, staring out the window in a trance, the cell phone pressed to my ear. The message—ended, disconnected and stored quite some time ago—would be saved for another twenty-four hours. No longer.

I had arrived in a foreign land, in hostile territory. I didn't want to be there. And to tell the truth, I wasn't really there yet. All my suits were still hanging in the closet, shirts at a hundred-and-fifty euros apiece, silk ties. My consultant's pitch was still in my computer, which I always had with me.

If I had to report to Dries van Waayen at ten-fifteen, I wanted to know what to ask, not only about myself but mainly about Ms. Radekker. I'd find out soon enough when I was going to be fired. I knew exactly how that would go. HC&P let it be known in no uncertain terms that loyalty was the highest good. You were never to abandon each other, to let each other down, but if you did you'd be out the door before the end of the day. I had absolutely no faith in the loyalty of the firm. Apparently it was my time to go, and this was how I'd make my contribution to maintaining the profits. Fine.

But with Radekker things were not fine. She was dead and her body had disappeared. Something had happened within the walls of this office building that no one knew anything about except me. If I didn't do something fast, I wouldn't be able to do anything at all. Once I was outside the firm it would be impossible to make contact with anyone, so someone from management had to be informed. Dries van Waayen was the first. After all, he was responsible for personnel. If I was going to tell Van Waayen, I'd have to know who Radekker was, what department she worked in and whether she had been reported missing. Those kinds of things. Simple things.

All the names, telephone numbers and workstations of the firm's employees were available through the HC&P network. Within two minutes I knew that only one Radekker worked for the firm: Ina Radekker, debt analyst in the Finance & Control department with an assigned workstation, room 3-026. She had her own phone extension, but I had little use for that now. I clicked through the phone book, looking up Radekker in Amsterdam. Two hits. H.K. Radekker on Van Breestraat. Didn't seem like the right one to me. Wrong initials and much too upmarket. My lips were so dry they hurt. From the air conditioning or from something else, maybe the radiation from all the cell phones. I pulled on the loose bits of skin with my teeth until one tore off. Without chapstick I had no life. I looked at the second name: I. Radekker, Admiraal de Ruyterweg. That sounded more like a debt analyst in her early thirties. I wrote down the address and phone number and called. Instinctively I held my breath. What if someone answered, what was I supposed to say? I could hardly just blurt out what I thought: that someone had been killed here last night and I thought it was Ms. Radekker, and was she missing perhaps, or ... After twenty rings I hung up. No one was home. Logical. Or not logical, that was possible, too. Everything was possible.

One by one the others came in. New smells jostling with each other. Coffee, eau de toilette, leather and wax from polished shoes and chic briefcases. Snatches of conversations could be heard left and right, sometimes faltering, then pierced with an unexpectedly loud laugh. Beginning of the day, an ordinary day, Thursday, not even the end of the week. Outside a watery morning in June, inside enough collective ambition in one room to supply the Netherlands with its own aeronautics industry.

'Here, you look like you could use this.'

From the corner of my left eye I saw a steaming cup of coffee appear on the desk.

Gijs dragged a chair from another desk and sat down across from me. He was holding an old plastic bag, from the Albert Heijn supermarket. Gijs was not one for luxury briefcases. A waste of money. Especially if you could pick up a perfectly good bag every week for ten cents when you did your grocery shopping. Gijs was my age, a little more than ten centimetres taller—one metre ninety-three— economist by training, mathematician by nature. Set him down in front of a complex calculation and he'd simply see the answer, as if the numbers and symbols were exactly the same as the colours and lines in a painting. It was like me looking at a photo and saying, 'Oh, right, a car,' except he'd look at a complicated math problem and say, 'Oh, right, twenty-one.'

Where it came from he himself didn't know. 'Can't you see that?' he'd ask. 'It's right there. You can see that it's there, can't you? How can you not see it?' He saw sums as compositions, tables as visual constructions. For him, annual reports and balance sheets were the simplest of cartoons. During his college years he once failed an exam because although he knew the answer he couldn't explain how he had arrived at it. In fact he didn't arrive at answers; they were there already.

But not for me. I saw the world in terms of relationships, of positions and interests. If someone said something to me, I saw his words like a river flowing across a landscape. From his tone and pronunciation I could hear the relative importance of what he was saying and see where the dikes were strong and where they were in danger of giving way. I could sense exactly what a person ought to say, when and to whom, in order to preserve the unity of his words while remaining within the banks. Gijs couldn't see that. When Gijs listened to someone, all he heard was what had been said.

'If someone says twelve, then what he means is twelve, right? Or am I being stupid?'

Sort of like that. And we were both colour blind, he a bit more than I, but we both thought there were an awful lot of metallic green cars riding around.

'Report done?' he asked.

I shook my head.

'Not done?'

I shook my head again.

'Worked all night and still not done? Bad planning, Bellicher.'

I nodded.

'Can I do something? Help? I have an hour.'

The hot coffee spread slowly through my body and produced a relaxation I hadn't felt in hours. Gijs's phlegmatic attitude did the rest. Suddenly I realized that I was taking myself for a ride, and doing it big time. I was hiding behind the events of the previous night and acting as if my future in the firm didn't matter anymore. My own problems were nothing in comparison with a murder. At least that's what I thought. But if I was brutally honest with myself, things were exactly the opposite.

HC&P was an unusual collection of people, full and partial geniuses with audacious talents and bizarre gifts. People like Gijs van Olde Nieland, who saw the world as a pallet of numbers, values and codes, who looked at everything other people regarded as abstract and saw it as concrete—and found that perfectly normal. There were many more like him in the company, attracted by the work, by the sometimes absurdly convoluted problems that were dumped on the consultant's desk with increasing frequency, because this was the perfect place for people who could see straight through the most complex questions. It was a self-sustaining process. That explained the incontestable position of the big international consultancies, and with just over a hundred thousand consultants in more than seven hundred branches in a hundred and twenty-four countries, HC&P was among the biggest. Consultants from the firm exercised influence over the policies of governments and the business community throughout the world. As modern *consigliari* they had the ear of the rich and powerful. Behind the scenes they guided the decisions of governments and companies, decisions that affected the lives of hundreds of millions, billions of people wherever they happened to live: in Amsterdam, London, New York or Paris, but also in villages like Rijpwetering, Lurcy la Ville, Pleasant Hill or Wexford. With their far-flung network, consultants were not only aware of developments wherever they were taking place, but in some cases they set that policy themselves.

In the Netherlands I was part of that network. I belonged there, with people like Gijs and Thomas and Jan, and with Jessica, who saw everything as an expression of strategy and tottered on the brink of perversion. You could see that by the way she moved her body, sometimes with barely controlled little jolts, almost undetectable, because she managed to gain control over herself at the very last second. At inconvenient moments she would come and stand so close to me that I could hardly speak. Every movement could be a form of assault. She would do those kinds of things and then look as if she were in a meeting, talking about the strategic difference between a brand and a product.

Jessica and I did not live together, but that didn't really mean anything. She had an apartment on Gerrit van der Veenstraat. I lived on Deurloostraat, a hundred square metres on the top floor. The two addresses suggested more of a difference than there really was, because without her I wasn't the man I wanted to be. Gijs was the first person I had met at HC&P, but it was through Jessica that I came to love the firm. I belonged with these people.

And I belonged with Sandra and with Marja, who could see the religious background and upbringing of everyone she had ever met as if it were wrapped around them like an aura. She could reduce the most complicated conflicts to manageable proportions within three minutes. 'One Protestant among four Catholics,' was her observation after having been merely introduced to the five members of a completely gridlocked board of managing directors. 'The Protestant always loses, of course, except you know Protestants, they never give in.'

I belonged there, with all the other goofballs who couldn't tell a grey car from a green one but who could study a collapsing public service, learn about the strategy, the economics, the sociology and the communications and tell them all apart, list the priorities and explain it all to boot.

First look, then think. That was rule number one. Otherwise you wouldn't know what you were talking about. All around me I could see the people I belonged with. If I couldn't belong with them anymore, I couldn't belong anywhere.

Dries van Waayen wasn't finished with me yet.

11

Black or white

'You know anybody at Finance & Control?' I asked.

Gijs nodded. 'Of course,' he said, 'they're the only people in the building who know what a number looks like, although most of them are hopeless. Who are you looking for?'

'Radekker.'

'Mr. or Ms.?'

'Ms. Debit analyst.'

'Never heard of her. Something going on? You want me to call somebody for you?'

I thought fast and saw how my words would make their way through the company—via Gijs to the department and from the department to the manager of that department, and on and on.

'No, not necessary,' I said. 'I just can't find her.'

'That's because you don't know who to ask, Mr. Communications Specialist. Leave it to me.'

Before I knew it he was sitting there with his phone in his hand, glancing at me with an expression that was something between surprise and complacency. Nothing ever bothered Gijs. It wasn't just because of his mathematical way of thinking but it also had to do with the kind of family he was from. Gijs van Olde Nieland was raised with the manners of the old nobility, which was still manifestly apparent. If you had to fart or burp, you went ahead and did it; if you wanted something, you asked for it; and if you thought somebody else ought to be doing something, you said so. Gijs possessed an enthusiastic ease and a natural aloofness. The simplicity of privilege was still in his blood, and that was just the quality that I could use right now. If I had any hope of averting my approaching dismissal when I met with Dries van Waayen later on, I needed good arguments. Convincing arguments.

'I need a client,' I said.

'A client? Any old client?' Gijs slid the cell phone back into his pocket.

'No. A client who makes an impression.'

Gijs thought a bit. In his eyes I could see him making an assessment. That assessment was me. Gijs had an imposing circle of relatives, friends and acquaintances. He was part of a network of people in good positions, through his father's family as well as his mother's. There was no multinational or ministry that didn't include some member of his family. Decades of democratization and equal opportunity had made fewer changes in this picture than you would expect. Only if you worked directly with someone like Gijs would you notice his easy powers of persuasion and his matter-of-fact way of getting otherwise inaccessible people on the phone. But he never flaunted it. Never.

That's why my question was so unusual. I was asking him to mobilize his contacts in order to help me. Here. Now. I was asking him to dig up some uncle or second cousin who would come asking for me—specifically for me, whether they were actually interested in my services or not. For Gijs the question was whether I was worth it. A simple question, but one he would never ask me himself.

'And you'd like this to happen fairly quickly, right?'

I looked at my watch. It was eight-fifteen.

'Um, what's quick?' I said. 'If I can't bring in a new account within the next hour and a half, I'm out of here.'

Gijs said nothing. He stood up, rubbed his lips with his hand, waved a finger at me and walked away. After three steps he turned and came back to my desk.

'An hour and a half?' he asked.

'More or less.'

'So that's ...' now Gijs looked at his watch, '... about a quarter to ten?'

'If possible.'

'And what happens at a quarter to ten, if I may ask?'

'I'll be sitting with Dries van Waayen.'

'Right.'

Neither of us spoke. Gijs stood up and picked up his cup. 'You want more coffee?'

Without waiting for an answer he picked up my cup as well and paused for a moment at my desk, a cup in each hand, his mind God knows where. A subservient genius. He bowed toward me and whispered a question. Always quite correct.

'This doesn't happen to have anything to do with that ... uh ... Ms. Rakker from Finance & Control?'

I shook my head. 'Radekker is something entirely different.'

'You sure?'

'Don't worry.'

Gijs laughed and leaned in a bit closer.

'Is it something I should know?' he asked.

I laughed too but said nothing.

Gijs slammed the cups down on the desk. 'The basics, Bellicher! Come on! You're still capable of that, I hope? Without the basics I can't get anywhere with you.'

It was one of the company rules. The ability to stick to the basics was one of the preconditions for working at the higher advisory level. Anyone who got caught up in the details would find himself in some dead-end job as assistant or researcher without any hope of escape. Details were important, of course, but the devil is in the details. Everyone knew that. Everything has to tally up, no one is ever to allowed to slip, but there comes a point when the consultant trusts that all the aspects, even the smallest, the ones that are still invisible, will ultimately be dealt with. The senior trusts that the junior will close up all the leaks. The partner trusts that the senior has his juniors working in all the right places. That's how it goes. Everything focused on advancing the basics. Gijs was right. In a world where the normal pace was three steps ahead, I was hopelessly behind. If I didn't take care of myself first, I could forget the questions about Ina Radekker. No one would listen to me.

'Okay,' I said. 'I left my clients stranded for three days.'

Gijs burped. 'Excuse me?' he said, and not out of politeness but to show his surprise, although it did smell like his last meal. 'You left your clients stranded, without calling them? Without e-mailing? Just like that?'

I nodded.

'Because?'

'Personal,' I said.

'Circumstances beyond your control?'

'Way beyond.'

Gijs smiled. 'Say no more. I'll call someone.'

Van Waayen was in consultation. Essentially there was nothing unusual about that, since Van Waayen was always in consultation. That was his work and he was exceptionally good at it. Of the nine partners in the firm, Dries van Waayen was far and away the best talker. He could think and talk at the same time. It was a quality that made many clients trust in him implicitly, because he sometimes would come up with the solution to a problem while they were literally sitting there. Once people worked with Dries they never left him. He had a cast-iron reputation which he protected in every conceivable way. And rightly so, since a good name is the basis on which every new client walks in the door. Without a good name the river ultimately dries up.

I waited, sitting in a chair in the waiting room with his secretary, Rachel, who looked over at me every now and then and smiled in a way that made me suspect the worst.

'I'm afraid he's going to be a while,' she said, and she pointed to the door to his office. It was going on ten. 'He's in there with Mr. Breger, and ...'

The phone rang, cutting off the little contact we had. Behind the door were the sounds of bumping and laughter made by people who had come to the end of a conversation. The door handle went down, and soon the door was resolutely opened. A big man came out of the office. Tall and broad, with rough features and a voice that was much too loud. Dries van Waayen followed on his heels, still laughing at something that had been said earlier. The two men walked through the secretary's room and out to the corridor. They didn't even look at me and acted as if there was no one else in the room. The secretary gestured to Van Waayen and pointed to the phone.

'One moment,' she said, and she pushed a button to put the caller on hold. Van Waayen and Breger were now standing in the corridor.

'Huib, we'll see each other the day after tomorrow at Kolf's farewell party. You're coming, too, right?' Van Waayen was backing into the secretary's room.

Huib Breger?

'You bet,' said Breger. His voice could be heard from the corridor, and with every word he spoke I thought I recognized a certain sound, a tone. 'And you'll talk with the States, okay? I can count on that?'

I knew I had heard that voice before, but I couldn't remember where.

'What do you think?' said Van Waayen, and he laughed. He waved and turned around. To me. To his secretary.

'What I think is what I'm asking,' said Breger from the corridor. 'Otherwise I'd ask something else.'

I stiffened in my chair. It was the same remark I had heard in the corridor the night before, pronounced in exactly the same loud, flat way. Breger was one of the men who had removed the body of Ina Radekker from the building last night.

Breger and Van Waayen?

Questions flashed through my head, none of which I could ask here. I tried to concentrate on the upcoming conversation, but no matter how hard I tried I kept hearing that voice. And every time I heard the voice, I saw Ina Radekker lying there. First dead and then gone.

One of the men who had done it had just paid a visit to a partner of the firm. Coincidence, perhaps (everything in life can be a coincidence), but it could also have meant something quite different. What I really wanted to do was stand up and run away, but Van Waayen was coming toward me. On his face was the unmistakable expression of a manager who's about to do some managing and is really up for it. His secretary, gesturing in the background and frustrated because she wasn't getting the attention she wanted, slammed her fist down on the desk just as Van Waayen was about to say something to me.

'WHAT?' he asked irritably. 'You know I've got an appointment now with Michael and that ...'

'I have the Secretary-General of the Ministry of the Interior here on hold,' Rachel said. She was imperturbable. 'Shall I ask him to call back later?'

Van Waayen quieted down. The Secretary-General of the Ministry of the Interior was a client with a capital C. 'Eberhuizen?' he said.

Rachel looked at her watch. 'Three minutes so far,' she said. 'If he hasn't already hung up.' She pressed the button and put on her professional voice. 'Mr. Eberhuizen? Yes, I'm sorry you had to wait, but Mr. Van Waayen had to step out for a moment ... yes, we don't mention those kinds of things, you understand ... exactly ... you're so right ...' She laughed. 'I'll put you through.' She pushed a few more buttons and the phone rang in the inner office.

Van Waayen reacted immediately. 'Just a minute,' he said to me. 'Really, this won't take long.' He hurried to his office and shut the door behind him.

'What a pain,' said Rachel, and she laughed again. 'The old bathroom trick. Works every time. Can I get you a cup of coffee? "Just a minute" is a euphemism, you realize. In fifteen minutes you'll still be here. Black or white?'

'White,' I said, and I was glad there was at least one simple answer I could give that morning.

Van Waayen was looking at me from the door to his office. Defiant. Scowling. He didn't beckon and he didn't move. He just stood there—legs slightly apart, one hand in his pants' pocket, the other playing with his cell phone—and looked at me. It was as if he were seeing something he didn't understand, something that was beyond his expectations, something he wished he could dissect simply by looking at it to see what was inside. I couldn't tell whether he loathed me or whether he didn't. I just waited, heart pounding, to hear what he had to say.

He didn't say anything.

With far more effort than necessary I succeeded in standing up and taking a couple of steps in his direction. I am not tall. Not as tall as Gijs. Not even as tall as Jessica, certainly not when she's wearing heels, and Jess loves a good pair of heels. I'm one metre seventy-nine, dark curly hair, dark eyes, heavy eyebrows, straight forehead, little conviction. I'm not much good at anything, but I don't give up easily. My muscles were stiff and my hands and feet tingled because I had been sitting too long in a cramped position. Nerves. I gave my limbs a shake to try to get the blood circulating until I realized how unutterably stupid I must have looked, flapping my hands around like that.

Van Waayen ignored my performance and took a couple of steps toward me until we were standing eyeball to eyeball.

It was a few seconds before he spoke.

'Is this some kind of campaign, Bellicher?' he asked. 'If it is, it's a doozy.'

Without waiting for my response he turned around and walked into his office. Soon he was back with a piece of paper in his hand.

'Because guess what? The Ministry of the Interior—no, wait a minute, what am I saying—the Secretary-General of the Ministry of the Interior wants a communications consultant, and of all the communications consultants walking around in this country (and there are quite a few), the good secretary has his eye on one in particular. Just one! A thirty-one-year-old consultant is what he wants. Yes, indeed! Can you believe it?'

He pushed the slip of paper in my face.

'Tomorrow morning, ten o'clock, in The Hague. One false move and you can keep on walking.'

I took the paper.

'Have you got that?' he asked.

I nodded.

'Good. Until you bring me that client, I don't want to see you again,' he said, and he kept his eyes on me until I left the room.

12

Bellilog, June 17

Gijs is hanging over my desk. He puts an old plastic shopping bag on top of my papers, this time an ordinary red-and-white one from another supermarket, the Edah. He always does this. His big hands fiddle with his glasses. He makes movements that I associate with him, that I see almost every day. I know he's going to fold the arms of his glasses in and out three times before he puts them in his inside jacket pocket. I know it and he does it. Just like putting that bag on my papers. And I know that he'll start picking on the cuticle of his right middle finger. And he does. The more he picks, the more problems he has with the skin above the nail. I know this, just as he knows things about me that I'm not aware of. And as he stands there waiting before he says anything, I wish I felt as comfortable with myself as he does.

If you ask the right person, you can be saved. Maybe it's only for a moment, but that's already a lot. At least it is for me. I'm an ICT orphan. My parents are so out-of-touch they don't even live in the same dimension anymore. Technology makes you lonely, and we've only just begun. Without Jess, without Gijs, I'd never make it. Look mom, no hands! Better yet, don't look.

Mail to: Jess
Subject: family
you still there?
things here falling apart
kisses,

m.

13

0.17 seconds

Sometimes a plan works too well. Like now: suddenly I wasn't out on the street at all but working under even greater pressure. All the clients I had called the day before to postpone their appointments, thinking I would never be seeing them again, were now firmly inscribed in my date book. Every one of those clients would expect me to make up for lost time. That was normal. In a week I'd be up to my eyeballs in meetings and deadlines. But before then I'd have to manage to ingratiate myself with the Secretary-General of the Ministry of the Interior. How Gijs had been able to enlist the aid of such a mega-client was beyond me. Gijs had his own reasons for doing what he did, and what he had done for me today was invaluable. I realized that, just as I knew that someday I'd have to make it up to him in an appropriate way.

Not now, though.

Now I had to make the best use of the time I had. I didn't even want to think about clients and assignments until I found out what had happened to Ina Radekker, until I knew what had taken place on Wednesday night and who had been involved. And the simplest way to get started was to go to her department and ask who Ina Radekker was. And where she was.

The name Finance & Control had a militantly financial ring to it, as if money were the measure of all things—which it is. In the west wing of the third floor, however, there's little of that in evidence. You can always find somebody in the staff areas, which are generally off-limits to clients. There's a staggered lunch hour, although the vast majority of the employees head for the canteen at twelve-thirty.

Which makes it the most peaceful time in the building. A deep silence prevailed in the department. Three-quarters of the rooms were empty. Here and there someone was staring at a monitor with great concentration or had a phone to their ear. No one asked me any questions; I don't think anyone even saw me. I kept on walking unhindered, in search of Ina Radekker's desk.

Number 3.026 was a spacious room with three desks, all of them unoccupied. At two of the desks the computers were on and there were obvious signs of work going on. The third desk was straightened up, almost empty except for a couple of papers. The computer was off and there was no indication that anyone was working there today. If Ina was gone, then this was her desk.

I thumbed through the papers: a couple of internal memos on the use of the photocopy machine and amended instructions concerning the safeguarding of documents and administrative data. There was a desk date book with appointments in it. Nothing this week, nothing next week either. Ina Radekker didn't have the kind of job that required conferring a great deal with others. She had no clients and she had no suppliers, she didn't have to keep track of her hours and she didn't have to drive fifty thousand kilo-metres a year to always be where the client wanted her to be. She did her work at one place, at one desk. Her work was not billable, her hours were her working hours. If she worked longer, that was overtime, a concept unknown to consultants.

I opened her desk drawers. In the first drawer there was nothing special. Paper clips, stapler, staple remover, some pens and pencils, ordinary office supplies. The next drawer contained a box of blank computer disks and a stack of CD-ROMS. I flipped quickly through the CDs. Each and every one was a software CD with extra programs, all for the processing of administrative data. In the bottom drawer were some folders and a couple of large, thick envelopes. I took them out and examined the contents. They contained print-outs of financial accounts that, at first glance, had nothing to do with the company. I saw the abbreviation 'MF' somewhere with a great many names and numbers that meant nothing to me. Probably a private job she was doing on the side along with her regular work. I put the papers back in the folders and envelopes and took everything with me.

Two doors further on I saw a woman concentrating intently on her work. I knocked briefly and walked in. She was about forty, small and spindly. She had short, straight, blond hair and a look of grim determination on her face, with only the occasional flash of a smile. She looked up from her work and asked me what I wanted.

'I'm looking for Ina Radekker,' I said. 'Do you know where she is? Or is she just on her lunch break?'

The woman laughed.

'Well, she may be having lunch, but not here. Ina is gone, so, uh ...'

'Gone?'

'On vacation.'

'Huh?' It came out before I was aware of it.

'Yes. Try Crete,' she said. 'Otherwise she'll be back at her desk in three weeks. If you can wait that long.'

'Crete?'

Apparently Ina's departure for the Greek island was entirely in keeping with the department's vacation sched-ule, which everyone had known about for months. Five-thirty a.m. flight, four o'clock check-in. No one expected to hear anything from her until she returned in mid-June. Except maybe a postcard.

'And if that's too long for you, you'll have to make do with me,' she said, tossing me another grim-faced look.

'Are you angry?' I asked.

'Because you're here to complain about Ina, right?' she huffed. 'To grovel with that little smile of yours. You're all like that. Consultants. Butter wouldn't melt in your mouth. Most people come here to tell us there's a problem with the figures, and of course it's our fault. But we're just auditors, and if things don't add up we let them know. It's almost like no one can count anymore these days.'

'And we can't,' I said. 'Any self-respecting consultant knows that one plus one is three, so there's no hope for us.'

I tried to reach Gijs, but he was busy, tied up in meetings. I left a message on his voicemail to let him know that I'd be at Vak Zuid between six and seven. Vak Zuid is the pub behind the Olympic Stadium. It was usually packed and noisy, but it was also close by and easy to get to. Everybody went to Vak Zuid and had been for years, and the more the southern quarter of Amsterdam grew the busier it got. There weren't that many other places around.

I took the laptop out of my cart, re-connected to the network and checked my e-mail. Twelve messages. Clients, clients and more clients. Every day they sent entire packets of information. Reports, plans, research, measurements, Power Point presentations, spread sheets, folders, annual reports—everything got dumped into the e-mail and sent off. It often made things needlessly complicated, because nobody knew what was important and what wasn't.

The last e-mail was from Kurt. 'I see you,' it said. And there was an attachment: a photo of Kurt, a portrait with eyes full of expectation and a smile that could bring you to your knees. Literally. I knew all about it.

Irritated, I clicked the photo away and saved it on my hard drive. The irritation itself stuck with me. I could feel it in my body, my back and my neck. I was angry at myself more than at Kurt. I opened the e-mail again and sent a reply: 'I see you too. I need a little space right now.'

I began searching the HC&P network for Huib Breger but I couldn't find him in any of the company's departments. Not a single one. That surprised me. I thought about the encounter that morning, about the way Van Waayen and Breger talked to each other. It was clear that the two men were well-acquainted and spent a lot of time together. No one accompanied Breger out of the office, either, neither Van Waayen nor his secretary. They didn't even attempt to do so, which meant that he wasn't just a visitor. Or at least that he was part of the company, since it was a strictly kept policy that visitors were to be accompanied on their way out until they had passed through the security gate. Too much had been stolen from the building in recent years—not just computers and equipment, but the contents of entire rooms had been removed, including desks, chairs and cabinets. It wasn't long before the building passes and security gates came along, as well as the policy that unknown persons were no longer allowed to roam through the building alone. And this included guests of management.

So Breger was not a guest, not an outside visitor, and that meant that he had to have a building pass and that somehow he had to be registered in the company's hierarchy as an employee, high or low. But he wasn't. Stranger yet was that he could be in the building and leave it in the middle of the night. That, too, meant that he and the other men had to have passes in order to get in and out of the building. You couldn't even get out of the parking garage without a pass.

In silence I gazed at my screen, mentally following the computer's exasperating logic. If the computer gave an answer that didn't make sense, it would have to be correct nonetheless because the computer's answers were always correct. In that case it would have to be the question that was wrong, a fact that it sometimes took a long time to grasp.

No matter how hard I looked at the screen, I couldn't get any further. It might mean that not all the people with a pass were registered with the company. That was a simple conclusion, and once I had come to it I could understand it. There were all sorts of people in the security service, the cleaning service, the canteen and the maintenance services who were not employed by HC&P but by the firm's suppliers. You'd never be able to find those people in the HC&P network. Logical. But if Huib Breger worked for one of those companies, why was he so friendly and buddy-buddy with Van Waayen? Dries van Waayen detested the cleaning and canteen staff. Their vulgarity offended his dignity. He could make the occasional joke with such a person, but usually no one laughed because they rarely understood his jokes. Dries's sense of humour had to do with vested interests and positions, which was completely lost on the janitorial types. They wiped the floor with that kind of pretentious crap.

I clicked the icon at the bottom of the screen and surfed to Google. The name 'Breger' brought up thousands of hits. Far too many. I tried the last name and first name together, 'Huib Breger,' and 0.17 seconds later I had the complete results of my search operation: seven hits, all seven for the same Huib Breger, student of computer science at the University of Johannesburg, member of the rowing team and bearer of the suggestive title 'Man you would most like to have ice cream and chocolate sauce with in a public sauna.' He even had his own website: Huibbreger.sa. I clicked on the link and browsed through the blog of a nerd and a sports freak, an endless collection of brief messages, observations, comments and photos that he posted as a report of his life. Just like I did on bellilog.com. In the upper right-hand corner of the screen was a large button: mail me. So I did. I wrote that I had bumped into a man here of about fifty years old with the same name as his, and I asked him whether this person happened to be related to him.

You never know. The internet is the medium by which you can track down coincidences and make contacts that are seemingly impossible. People who don't know each other, who will never get to know each other, exchange messages as if they were neighbours. And they *are* neighbours. In the digital world, everyone is your neighbour.

Van Waayen wasn't there. He had slipped out for a talk. Rachel, his secretary, was busy dealing with reports and notes and answering the phone, which rang every couple of minutes. She gave me the address of the Ministry of the Interior, right next to Central Station in The Hague.

'Taking the train at rush hour is a disaster,' I said.

'That's ridiculous,' she answered without looking up from her notes or slowing her typing speed. 'An earthquake is a disaster. Famine is a disaster. War is a disaster. Taking the train at rush hour is work, so watch your language.' She turned to a stack of papers, pulled out one sheet and gave it to me. 'Here, the briefing for tomorrow morning.'

It was a short report of the conversation that Van Waayen had had with the Secretary-General of the Ministry of the Interior, A.W.J.M. Eberhuizen. Van Waayen had reduced it to a row of key words and supplemented it with standard advisory sloganizing to fit it into a recognizable context. The 'complex environment' had already been added as well as the 'redefinition of strategic principles' and a few other concepts that were meant to secure the work of the consultant at the highest level.

I smiled. This was something I knew.

'Thanks,' I said, and began walking out of the room. When I reached the doorway I turned around. 'Oh, yes,' I said. 'Something else I wanted to know. That man who was here this morning ...'

'Which man?'

'That guy who was with Van Waayen when I was scheduled to meet with him.'

'Oh, him. Mr. Breger, I think. What about him?'

'Do you know who he is?'

Rachel glanced at me with a look that could raise the ante to astronomical heights at a poker table.

'No idea,' she said. 'Never saw him before in my life.' She turned to her computer screen, and the next minute her fingers were flying across the keyboard.

Our conversation was over.

14

Ruud

Munching on a cheeseburger, I looked from the car to the building diagonally across from me on the other side of the Admiraal de Ruyterweg. It was a large house split up into apartments. The home of Ina Radekker was on the second floor. Here, on a busy street in Amsterdam-West, was where she had lived. I had no idea how long she had lived there or under what circumstances, whether she had rented the apartment or had owned it. All I knew about her was what I wished I didn't know. Drops of grease ran down my chin. The flavour and juice from the burger swam in my mouth. The instant gratification of food with global brand recognition.

I had to find proof that she wasn't on Crete, that she hadn't just gone on vacation, because only then could I call on other people to do something about it. I was hoping that somewhere in her apartment I could find the name of her travel agent so I could call someone to ask whether she really had booked a flight, or a whole vacation package. And if she had, whether she had actually shown up. Or had cancelled the trip. Or not. Those kinds of things. I had to get started, I had to do something, because if she really had booked a flight and hadn't appeared at Schiphol that meant she was missing and the police could be called in. That's what I wanted to accomplish.

I crumpled up the paper wrapping, wiped my mouth and hands and called her number one more time to see if anyone just happened to be there. The phone rang endlessly, but no one picked up. Finally I got out of the car and walked back and forth a few times in front of her building, looking at the front door, at the windows two storeys up and at the windows of the floor below. I didn't see any movement anywhere. I walked to the front door and went up five steps, a bunch of keys in my hand. The door had two locks, a standard one and a deadbolt. First I opened the deadbolt, then I stood there fiddling awkwardly until I came to the right key for the standard lock. Finally I pushed the door open and soon found myself at the bottom of a narrow stairwell with a steep set of Amsterdam stairs going up to the first and second floors.

There was a second front door that separated the residence from the rest of the building. I chose one of the remaining two keys, which turned out to be the right one. When I reached the top floor I cautiously entered the apartment. This was where Ina lived. This was where she had lived. Technically it was still her apartment. It was full of her stuff and her past, even though she herself would never live anywhere again. Detached thoughts about someone I didn't know gave me an unpleasant feeling of emptiness.

Once I got inside, the hesitation and fear vanished. As soon as the door shut behind me I felt safer, and my natural urge to stick my nose into everything rose to the surface.

There was a bedroom at the back and a small bathroom. At the front of the apartment, the front room and a small side room had been combined to form a large living-dining room with an open kitchen. That was all. Opposite the front door, on the landing, was a narrow hall table with a large mirror above it. On the table was a small basket containing a number of items: a card for the video library, another couple of keys (probably for a bike), a bus and tram card, some hair elastics and some change. Next to the basket was a stack of envelopes, three blue ones from the tax authorities and some advertising leaflets. At the front of the table was a small drawer, not the place where someone would save information about their vacation, but I opened it anyway. Two pairs of gloves and a folded up scarf. Nothing else.

I closed the drawer and went to the large front room. Near the kitchen was a round dining room table with four chairs. At the other end of the room was an arrangement of two two-seater sofas, a small coffee table and an enormous wall unit with space for a sound system, television, DVD player, books and much more. The wall unit covered a wall and a half, from the door through which you entered the room to the corner, and half the wall opposite the door. At the end of the cabinet was a sliding extendable desk. On the desk was a closed laptop: Datwell, the same model as mine. I quickly searched through the cabinet. I didn't have to identify everything in it. I just needed to find something having to do with her trip. I could skip everything else. Someone who has booked a trip doesn't usually store their travel information between literature and cookbooks.

I opened the computer, and while it was starting up I continued searching the cabinet. It had everything in it—and nothing. Ina Radekker had drawers full of CDs (hundreds, mostly classical), lots of books, vases, candlesticks, dishes, a couple of porcelain figurines and photos in frames. Too much for such a small apartment, but too little to provide any kind of picture. I pulled over a dining room chair and sat down at the laptop. This was her home computer. It didn't go to the office with her, and the log-in name and password were filled in by default. Here at home, the chances that someone else would look in her computer were so small that she didn't need to keep her password a secret. I took a pen and a piece of paper from my bag and wrote down her log-in data.

Then I quickly clicked to the web browser and the machine began connecting. As I waited, I looked under the desk. On the ground were two small dumbbells weighing two kilos each. They were made of one solid piece of metal: a bar in the middle and a small, massive steel ball at each end. I picked one up and did a few exercises with it. It was too light for me—I could hardly feel the weight—but for someone who sat behind a computer day in and day out and only moved her wrists, hands and fingers, it was just the right weight to give the muscles something to do every now and then.

The computer made a faint noise, indicating that it was connected to the internet. I put the dumbbell back and clicked to the web history window in the hope of finding the site of a travel agency.

A long row of websites appeared in the window. The names meant nothing to me, except for HC&P's own site. I copied the list and mailed it to my own e-mail address. The computer was busy for only a couple of seconds, and during that time I tried to imagine where I might find information about Ina's trip. If she had booked it using her office computer I'd never be able to find it. I was deep in thought and was unaware of what was going on. It wasn't until the lock of the front door clicked that I realized someone else was in the apartment.

Too late.

There wasn't a single place in the room to hide, so I went for the only defence left to me: offence.

'Hey,' I called out. 'Who's there?' And with a look of indignation on my face I walked through the room towards the hall. But I never got that far. Before I could reach it, the doorway was filled with the frame of a stocky man in the ugliest shell suit I had ever seen. Gleaming yellow, orange, black, green and silver absolutely spattered from his arms and legs. His trainers were bright white. Hanging around his thick red neck was a gold chain with a gold nameplate— Ruud—written in cursive letters.

Just what I needed.

Ruud didn't speak. He just stared. Not in order to understand but to make himself perfectly understood. He looked me straight in the eye without blinking. Then he glanced quickly to the left and to the right to make sure there was no one else in the room. From that moment on he only had eyes for me.

I tried bluffing.

'Did you hear what I said?' I asked, taking one step forward. Whenever I find myself with a group of men who feel the need to play Who's Got the Biggest, I always play along. It's what we do. It's part of the male code.

Ruud saw things differently. His immobile right hand suddenly shot forward and grabbed me by the throat. With no effort at all he pushed me backward over one of the sofas. I rolled and tumbled, and at no time did the pressure on my windpipe diminish. Ruud had a hold on me like a cat biting down on its prey. Flexible and strong, he slid across the sofa. I fell, he dropped to his knees. I rolled, he turned. I kicked and flailed with my legs, clutching at the hand around my throat. The less air I got, the more I panicked. Ruud was not playing a game. Ruud wasn't interested in male codes. Ruud didn't need to make an impression.

He picked me up off the ground, let me go and pulled his hand back. Breath came shrieking down my throat. I saw nothing and I heard nothing. All I could feel was the overpowering need for air. Then, in an almost leisurely fashion, Ruud punched me. His fist hit me right in the middle of my chest. The air I had just inhaled with such difficulty was knocked out of me again with one well-directed blow. I doubled over, wrapped my arms around myself and tried to find a way out. More than the pain, it was the shock that paralyzed me. This was something entirely new. I had known bullies, assholes, ordinary fitness club types, street-corner delinquents and frat rats who were always up for a little rough and tumble, but this was new to me. Ruud was a different species altogether. He wasn't interested in being educated or entertained. Ruud was out to show who was boss. Once and for all.

He placed one hand under my chin, pulled my head up and tossed me back over the toppled sofa. I landed against the bookcase. Books and figurines and vases and knick-knacks rained down on top of me. Ruud grabbed one of my ankles and dragged me from this mess to the centre of the room. There he placed a second hand around the same ankle, and I felt the two hands close in an iron grip. He set his feet wide apart, crouched slightly, bent his back and waited a few seconds. He groaned and exhaled. Then he took a deep breath, filled his barrel of a chest with air, pumped himself up, and with a rough jerk he dragged me through the room in a rotating motion like a windmill. My shoulders and head banged against the furniture, knocking over the dining room table and chairs. I felt a sharp stab in my cheek where the skin of my face was being scraped. In a panic, I stretched out my arms and grabbed the first thing I came across, the edge of the cabinet. My fingers found purchase on one of the legs of the wall unit, and I pulled with all my might, arms and legs together. Ruud threw his weight backward in response, and at that moment I let go and kicked along with him. With no counterforce Ruud fell backward, slammed against the doorpost and let go of my ankle.

I was lying flat out on the floor. I scrambled away from him as fast as I could and tried to stand, but I wasn't fast enough. Ruud sprang from the door to the sofa, pushed against the sofa back and dove on top of me.

I blindly groped for something—anything—to defend myself with. I didn't stand a chance with bare hands alone. Not only was he much stronger, but he also knew what he was doing. Ruud had experience, that was patently obvious. You could even see it in the way he moved. His body was his most important instrument. Not in my case, though. I was a brain worker who did a bit of fitness for the fun of it. My survival instinct was all in my head. If I couldn't think better and faster than the next guy, I was done for. I could swoop and spin, sprint and strike, I could trip people up, back them into a corner and finish them off. With words. Ruud could too, but he didn't have to open his mouth to do it.

He kicked me to the edge of the room. I curled up tighter and tighter to ward off the jolting blows. The toe of his shoe pounded against my chest and stomach and grazed my face. Now there was a second wound, on my forehead. Blood ran across my eyes and down my cheek. Ruud paused for two seconds to take a breath, just enough time for me to roll under the extendable desk where the laptop was. He had to stoop down to drag me out, and just as he bent over I grabbed one of the little dumbbells and started flailing it around like a club. The massive steel ball struck him right across the jaw, and in an instant of unexpected silence I heard the bone crack. Ruud straightened himself up with a scream, striking the back of his head on the desk top above him. The impact sent the laptop flying through the room. It smashed against the bluestone windowsill. Ruud came stumbling back. Toward me. I took another swing, and this time I hit him in the middle of his forehead.

Once.

The steel ball left a dent just above his eyes and his gaze became glassy. I held the dumbbell with a trembling hand. Ruud twitched a couple of times. His eyes closed and opened again. He looked at me as if he no longer knew where he was or who he was, and then he collapsed. I lay on the ground, panting and shaking. I could hear my own frantic breathing in the sudden silence.

I looked at myself in the bathroom mirror. I had two large swipes across my face. There was blood everywhere. I dabbed myself clean with a wet towel, carefully wiping off the blood stains. It didn't seem too bad. The wound above my eye bled the most, and it took a while before I managed to staunch it. I found band-aids in the medicine cabinet and used one to bind the wound as tightly as I could, so tight that it pulled my left eyelid up in an expression of permanent bewilderment.

I put another band-aid over the first one to make sure the whole thing stuck, cleaned up the mess in the bathroom, rinsed all the spatters of blood from the sink, stuffed the dirty towel in a plastic bag I found in the kitchen and left the rest as it was. Ruud was still lying motionless under the desk. Cautiously I knelt down beside him. His broken jaw could be fixed, but the dent in his forehead was probably there for good. It was hard to tell, given the position he was lying in. His power of speech wouldn't be affected at any rate. Every other side effect was a bonus.

I staggered down the stairs to the street and threw the keys to the building in a glass recycling bin further on. They fell among the shards with a jingle. I crossed the street and got into my car. For a moment I thought about calling 112 to report a wounded man at 753 Admiraal de Ruyterweg, third floor, but decided against it. Ruud certainly wouldn't have called if it had been me. A son of a bitch with a dent in his head is still a son of a bitch.

Vak Zuid was packed. The combined noise of people and music was intense. I was late but Gijs wouldn't mind. In Vak Zuid everybody hung around until they found the person they were looking for. Somewhere in the middle of the cafe was a large group from HC&P. I squeezed my way through the crowd until I reached them. A glass of beer appeared out of nowhere, then a glass of white wine. I passed the wine on but polished off the beer in one long draft and sent the empty glass back through the crowd to the bar. Thomas was the first one to see me. He asked with gestures whether I wanted another beer. I held my thumb and forefinger five centimetres apart and made a brief tossing-back motion. Thomas nodded, and soon a double vodka on ice appeared before me.

'And?' Gijs screamed suddenly in my ear in an effort to be heard above the pounding music. The bare concrete interior at Vak Zuid was an acoustic assault on every customer.

'And what?' I screamed back.

'Has Uncle Walter called yet?' Gijs leaned toward me and spoke almost directly in my ear. 'I figured you have to have somebody who knows Dries, and he said he'd call, and usually when Uncle Walter says he'll do something, he ...'

'Uncle Walter?'

'Ministry of the Interior.'

'You bet he called,' I said.

'Great.' Gijs looked around absently.

'Thanks,' I said.

'Easy peasy,' he said. Only then did he notice the band-aids above my eye. In the semi-darkness of the cafe, with such a tightly packed crowd, it was easy to miss the most conspicuous things. He pressed a finger carefully against it.

'Difficult client?' he asked.

'No big deal,' I said. 'But it bled as if I had undergone some ritual treatment.'

Gijs nodded. If I said it was nothing he'd believe it immediately and wouldn't press me on the subject. That was fine with me, because I had no desire to explain. This wasn't the place for it either. Vak Zuid was the neighbourhood's corporate club, the place for hard-working and well-paid high potentials, account executives, product managers, marketing managers and consultants of every shape and size. Ambition and competitive spirit kept the energy level high until deep into the night. The acquisition of new assignments was celebrated here with gusto, and people anticipated the procurement of clients who didn't even know they were about to be approached. Success was the magnet that influenced every compass. North, south, east and west were replaced by one almighty direction. The wind blew from only one quarter, and whether it was a headwind or a tailwind was carefully monitored here.

At two-twenty a.m. I was standing outside on the sidewalk, laptop in a carrying case over my shoulder, car key in my hand. A moonless night. Hundreds of stars in a cloudless sky above the apartments on Stadionweg. I didn't know why, but that night was different, bigger, the stars seemed further away, the cars seemed closer. A plane glided past noiselessly high in the sky on its way to some remote place on earth. All you could see were the blinking lights. Red and white.

I was dying for a cigarette. I patted the pockets of my jacket with my hands, found a pack and pulled it out. Empty.

15

Bellilog, June 18

Would you be able to kill another human being? How often have you heard that question? And how often have you responded with some glassy-eyed, theoretical, hypothetical answer? Sure, if I had to. If I were being attacked. If someone wanted to harm me. If that's what it came down to. Then I think I could beat the shit out of someone. Or if they went after my girlfriend. If they went after Jess. Then, too.

But they're just words, until you really start hitting. And keep on hitting. I've been walking this earth for a good thirty years now and it's finally happened. Now I can answer the question. But it doesn't make me feel any better.

And then suddenly there's HB2. Huib here and Huib there. Two names exactly the same. Cloned sounds. Names that know each other, that have more in common that the letters from which they are constructed. The questions are piling up.

> Mail from: HB2
> Subject: All the Bregers
> Hi Michael,
> All the Bregers are related. Even the Bregers I don't know, but there aren't too many of them. The Huib Breger you mean is probably my 'lost' uncle. Doesn't live in South Africa anymore. Hasn't for a long time. What do you want to know? Just ask.
> All the best, and in haste,
> HB2

Mail to: HB2
Subject: Re: All the Bregers
HB2!
I certainly didn't expect this. Never. Maybe I thought so for
a second, or dreamed it, but I never took it seriously. Really.
This is really very good. And I hardly know what to ask.
Anything you can tell me about your uncle: PLEASE! What
he does, where he is, and all the rest.
The more, the better. And the sooner, the better. And not to
be rude, but time is an issue. Of the urgent variety.
Thanks in advance and all the best,
Michael

Mail to: Jess
Subject: Bad
Not going well here. Missyoumissyoumissyou,
Belli

16

The system wins

Barely rested, I found myself at the entrance to the Ministry of the Interior, my hair stiff with gel and my nerves stiff with coffee. My head filled with the tattered remains of the previous day, which was distressing since they threatened to undermine my concentration at any moment. Reminders of the fight in Ina Radekker's apartment were in evidence all over my body. Unexpected movements were painful. There was a new band-aid over the wound above my eye, smaller than the last one but still clearly visible. I stomped on the paving stones and drew the smoke from my cigarette deep into my lungs. Pollution helped. Tar and nicotine provided tangible support. The arrival of Dries van Waayen did the rest.

'You look like you'd been run over by a truck,' he said.

'Don't worry,' I said. 'It feels that way, too.'

'That's justice for you.' With these words he entered the building and announced us at the reception desk. We were given passes and told to wait until we were called. Van Waayen made every effort to demonstrate the difference in position between us. He lost himself in endless remarks about developments in the organization of the Ministry and the importance of communication in those developments, and I kept hearing what Gijs had told me: 'When Uncle Walter says he's going to do something, he does it.'

A secretary came through the security doors wearing her welcome face. She nodded, smiled and extended her hand. Just as Van Waayen was reciprocating her greeting his cell phone began to peep. He pushed me forward at the first possible moment, pulled his phone out of his pocket and excused himself.

'They always know where to find me,' he said, and laughed the laugh of a man who knows he can't be missed and likes to apologize for it. 'But after this, off it goes.' He answered the call with a short 'Yes?' Professional. Then for several seconds he was silent. His eyes grew wider, his mouth dropped open and the concentrated energy suddenly vanished from his body. 'What?' he finally said. 'Wait a minute, but ... What ...? That's not possible!'

He turned away and began walking in circles, shaking his head. He no longer seemed to know where he was. The blood drained further from his face with every step he took, and in one minute he was as white as a sheet. The self-confident volume in his voice was entirely gone.

'... no, of course I'll come ... yes, right away ... yes.' He ended the call and stared vacantly into the distance. The secretary and I walked up to him, but before either of us could say anything his phone began peeping again. He looked at the screen, pushed the button and listened.

'Yes ...' he said. 'Yes ..., do whatever you have to do, it doesn't matter what. I'll be back in the office in three quarters of an hour ... yes ... till then.' He ended the call and grabbed me by the shoulder. In a corner of the entrance hall I heard what I already knew, except I didn't yet know any of the details. The body of a woman had been found in a dumpster in the parking garage under the building. The police were already there with a team of detectives. The entrances and exits were all cordoned off. Van Waayen was in shock.

'Because the corpse—the body, I mean—is inside. You see what I'm saying? It's inside.'

I nodded. Van Waayen had no idea how well I grasped what he was saying. Shivers ran down my spine. My fingers tingled.

'The body is inside our security system, and that means ...'

His phone began peeping again. He accepted the call automatically and almost immediately his face became rigid.

'No comment,' he said. He tried to remain polite, but every word he spat out reverberated with doggedness and rage. 'I said no comment and I mean it!' He cut off the call with an ill-spirited gesture and a curse. 'I think the TV cameras have beat me to the scene,' he said. 'You'll have to manage here alone, I'm afraid. Is that okay? I'll talk to you later.'

He turned in his pass and vanished. I watched him through the glass wall of the building and knew exactly what he had been talking about. Better, in fact. Ina Radekker was back, at a place where no one had expected her.

I didn't know what to think. On the one hand I was glad her body had been found. Now I wasn't the only one who knew what had happened to her. I wasn't walking around with disturbing information that I couldn't share with anyone because no one would believe me. On the other hand, I knew that now all sorts of questions would be asked, questions that I couldn't always answer. Or didn't want to answer.

Walter Eberhuizen was a tall man somewhere in his fifties with blond, greying hair, a high forehead and blue, restless eyes. He did three hours' worth of talking in fifteen minutes and hardly let me get a word in edgewise. That worked out fine for me. I took notes, asked questions and tried to direct the conversation as quickly as I could to the firm's first standard conclusion: an inventory. As soon as I had the assignment I could leave.

But Eberhuizen wouldn't let himself be won over so easily. He wanted to play the whole game from start to finish, and the longer he took the more I wanted to go. Nothing helped, so I switched over to automatic pilot. I listened, laughed if it seemed appropriate and made a joke when I saw the opportunity, and much to my relief Eberhuizen laughed, too. From that moment on it all went smoothly. I was given a tour, introduced to managers, assistants and staff members, and served even more coffee.

'You've got time for a sandwich, I hope?' Eberhuizen asked. 'Because we've counted on it.'

No, I thought, but that's not what I said. 'Of course. What's a man without a sandwich?'

It wasn't until halfway through the afternoon that I got back on the train to Amsterdam, with a follow-up meeting scheduled and the prospect of a first assignment. It should have been a perfect afternoon, because there's no better way to travel than in a half empty train. Big and spacious, as if you were riding with time in abundance. A carriage the size of a nice little apartment to deliver you somewhere. And all for less than twenty euros.

But my lips were drier than ever. There were nine messages on my voicemail. Between applying chapstick and rubbing my sore muscles I listened to them all. Three from clients who wanted to postpone appointments that had already been postponed. One message was from Jessica. Her return from San Francisco had been put on hold. The project she was working on was taking longer than expected and could go on for another week. Or longer. A message from Gijs, wanting to know how it had gone with Uncle Walter, and that back at the office the shit had hit the fan. One from my mother: where was I, that the police had called and had tried to reach me at home but I wasn't there, either. And two messages from the police with the urgent request to contact Inspector Pletting. As soon as I could, please. It was important.

I gazed out the window mutely as the meadows raced past. The view from the train between The Hague and Amsterdam is not very exciting. On the contrary, it's intensely ordinary. The landscape is both familiar and strange. I looked at the straight irrigation ditches, the straight plots of land, the straight fences and hedges, the straight houses and straight streets, and I wondered whether such a high degree of organization was even tenable.

Probably not.

I didn't understand what the police wanted me for. No one knew that I had been in the building that night. Even Breger didn't know.

The urgency of the summons didn't really sink in. My head felt as if it were somewhere else. With my laptop in a bag full of documents and papers, sitting in a train on my way to the office. That's where I was. On my way back to Amsterdam, where less than twenty-four hours before I had struck a man between the eyes with a massive piece of steel. Hit him so hard that his head had cracked. And no matter how often I told myself that I had no other choice, that I had done what I had to do under the circumstances, it didn't feel good.

I called Gijs, and before I could say anything he started to whisper. 'Don't come here!' he hissed. 'Whatever you do!'

The first investigation had yet to begin, but HC&P had immediately made a print-out of the automatic pass registration from the night that Ina was murdered. The print-out clearly showed that she had never left the building. But it also showed that I was the only other person in the office that night, so everyone was looking for me. Especially the police.

'They've been to our department twice already. There's a cop stationed out in the corridor and four more downstairs at the entrance.'

'But Van Waayen knew where I was,' I said.

'Of course he knew,' said Gijs. 'But give it some thought. Do you think he's going to have the police drop in on the Secretary-General of the Ministry of the Interior because he's sharing a couple of sandwiches with a consultant suspected of murder? Really? Where's your head at, man?' He fell silent.

I cursed.

'Maybe you didn't do anything, but ...'

His caution felt like betrayal. 'Maybe?' I asked. 'What do you mean, maybe? If that's the attitude you're taking, then I know right away what I can expect from the others.'

'I mean maybe you didn't do it,' he said, 'but no one knows that. You were the only other person in the building, so what are people supposed to think?'

'Nothing,' I said.

'Exactly.'

'I wasn't the only one.'

'No, of course not. I'd say the same thing.' Gijs cursed. 'Anyone would say that. Jesus, man, can't you hear what that sounds like?'

'No,' I said. 'I have no idea what that sounds like.' I was furious. 'There were at least two and maybe three other people in the building. You tell me what that sounds like!'

Gijs said nothing.

'For God's sake, what happened?' he asked.

I turned off my phone to avoid getting an unexpected call from Inspector Pletting. When we got to the World Trade Center station I stayed in my seat because I didn't know whether the police were keeping the station closest to the office under surveillance. If I got out they'd just pick me up off the street, and I couldn't let that happen. Not now. If the HC&P building pass system had registered my presence alone, I was lost. My word, without witnesses, against a fully automated system. No one would believe me. The system wins. Always. Now that Ina's body had been found, the police would investigate her apartment, and suddenly I realized what they would find there. Ruud would be long gone, I was convinced of that, but the interior of the apartment was in chaos and my fingerprints were everywhere. If they found any blood stains, it would be my blood. Wherever they looked, it all led to me. Communication is the art of conveying the most complex or unpleasant information as clearly as possible so the other person fully understands, agrees and knows what it means for him.

I had just been communicated with.

In the two minutes it took for the train to get from the World Trade Center to the RAI Convention Center my options dropped away one by one. Everything I did could be followed or found by the police. From one minute to the next I'd have to disappear. That's all there was to it.

Instinctively I looked around at the other passengers—people like me, people with briefcases and papers, problems and dreams, family and friends—and suddenly I realized that they were very different. They didn't look like me at all. Not anymore.

17

Bellilog, June 18

Okay, anyone can read this, and that's the whole point, but in the meantime the world has become a mirror image. I'm stuck, on the wrong side of the facts, and the facts are not cool. They're Old World, but they're tough as nails. The facts dictate, and those who dictate the facts have it all. I don't dictate anything. I have what I have, and that's all that I have. Wanted for murder, with no defence. Can't go to my office. Can't go to my apartment. Can't go to my parents. Can't name any more names. Can't go to G. J. isn't here. Can't drive my car. So what's left?

E-mail and money. Bank: 900, savings 16,700, stocks 28,300.

And the rest of the city. Of the whole country.

> Mail from: HB2
> Subject: Uncle
> Can't just reveal all. My family wants to know more about you. Who are you? What do you do? Why are you looking for Uncle Huib? Okay?
> Let's have it.
> HB2

> Mail to: HB2
> Subject: Re: Uncle
> I am Michael Bellicher and I'm on my own—1 MB, that is—consultant with HC&P Amsterdam (look it up on the internet), suspected of murdering a colleague thanks to your uncle.
> Your turn.
> MB

18

Welcome?

I didn't have to worry about money right away, as long as I could get at it. I had no idea how quickly my bank accounts could be blocked, or even whether it would happen at all, but I knew it was a possibility. And that was enough. If I were to run out of money, I'd be done for. This realization made me think. I had to look for a place to stay, and I had to prove that I wasn't the only one in the office that night. In that order. Not to mention the smaller problems: that I didn't have the slightest idea why Ida Radekker had been murdered or how I could find Huib Breger, that I had nothing to pin on the man, and that I had no clean clothes.

I got out of the train at RAI station and took a tram to my bank. There I withdrew all the money from my account and arranged to have all my savings paid out and to sell my entire block of shares. Everything would be available the following day. My own efficiency amazed me. As soon as I knew that I had nowhere to go, a strange sort of detachment came over me. I did what I had to do. Clinical and desperately calm, mainly in an effort to keep from losing my self-control. That would only make things worse. I accepted the fact that I could no longer return to my own apartment as a temporary anomaly, but as soon as I began thinking about it I broke out in a cold sweat. I was confronted by my own powerlessness, and that cut deeper than I ever could have imagined. I missed Jessica.

I went to the telephone shop on the corner and bought a new cell phone, prepaid and with tons of credit and a full battery so I could start calling right away. At the local H&M I bought underwear, a couple of t-shirts, socks, two pairs

of pants and a jacket, and at the v&D I purchased a back-pack, one big enough for my laptop, my clothes and more. Dark red and grey. Black shoulder straps. Before leaving the store I bought a bag of liquorice drops, almost a pound, to give me something to chew and suck on if I suddenly ran out of ideas.

At Rembrandt Square I took a taxi to a car rental company on the edge of town and rented something small and incon-spicuous. Then I sat in the parking lot for several minutes behind the steering wheel, staring at the traffic racing past. I had done everything I could think of. I had money. I had clothes. I could make calls and I was mobile.

But what now?

When I got to the RAI I drove under the ring road and took a room in the Novotel, as if it were the most ordinary thing in the world. Man in a suit, with briefcase and back-pack. Step by step I was disappearing into the no-man's-land of the travelling businessman. A parallel universe, one of many, that hundreds of thousands of people passed through every day and in which I slid in effortlessly.

'Will you be paying by credit card?' asked the man behind the desk. Friendly, inquisitive eyes.

I shook my head. 'Cash,' I said. Car rentals and hotel rooms could be traced, so I'd probably have to change hotels every other day.

Without even giving it a moment's thought I had slipped into the next phase, that of self-preservation. Now I needed time to figure out what to do next. More time than I would want.

In the hotel room I set up my laptop on the desk and plugged it in. As it was starting up I zapped through the channels on the TV. Games, music, happy people dressed in happy colours. News. The Minister of Justice, my minister, out on the street in front of the Ministry, Erik Strila in the background. My people, my clients. The minister was

speaking to three or four microphones that had been thrust in front of him. In that strange, pinched, distant tone, as if none of it fazed him in the least, he made assertions that seemed to come from the realm of the absurd. The lack of counselling was now audible. Without blinking an eye, he said that the number of Muslim extremists in the Netherlands appeared to be much higher than anyone had suspected, and I knew that wasn't right. I was familiar with the report on which he was basing his statement. I had received it under embargo a few days before my debacle, and the conclusions it drew were quite different. And here were these panting journalists, wanting to know whether tougher measures were going to be taken, or whether the minister was finally going to throw the dangerous imams out of the country and what he was going to do to secure the safety of the country's citizens.

I listened to his yakking with half an ear while searching the files on my laptop for the report. I found it without difficulty, but when I scrolled to the pertinent information I felt as if my powers of reasoning had abandoned me. There, on the screen of my computer, were exactly the same conclusions that the minister was announcing to the world. The numbers were alarming: the threat was indeed much more serious than had been suspected.

My memory rose up in protest. I was certain that I had read a very different account less than a week ago, milder and more nuanced, but no matter how much I scrolled up and down, the report was still permeated with the same sense of urgency. I stared at the screen with dismay. Apparently my own memory was not to be trusted.

I collected my messages and looked for the e-mail I had sent to myself from Ina Radekker's apartment. Soon I had the list of web addresses on my screen. I saved the list in a text file and created a hyperlink for every address. All I had to do

was click on an address with the cursor and the browser would surf straight to it.

One by one I worked my way through the list, searching for the things that Ina had been dealing with from her own computer. It was a collection without any structure. I surfed from second-hand book sites to sites about the treatment of athlete's foot, recipes for bouillabaisse and a site from the city of Amsterdam on arbitrating a rental conflict. These were flashes from the life of a woman I had never met, flashes that might have had to do with someone else for all I knew, a girlfriend or a family member.

The last three addresses on the list were for HC&P itself: the Dutch site, the American site where our headquarters were located, and a subsite of that with an endlessly long address. I clicked on the subsite and the computer went to work. It took minutes before a dialog box finally opened up with the question 'Open or save file?'

I clicked on 'open,' and soon the depressing 'Insufficient memory' message appeared.

I stared at the screen. The internal memory of my laptop was too limited to open the site. Usually this meant that a program was included in the download in order to run the site, but in most cases this was no problem. Not now, though.

I closed all the programs I didn't need and tried again. The result was the same: not enough memory. Deep in thought I stared at the screen, and it took a while before I realized that my computer was downloading something. The hard drive was active, and in the lower right-hand corner of the screen there were two little green fields indicating intensive data traffic. I pointed the cursor at the x in the upper right-hand corner of the screen in order to close the web address, but the computer wouldn't respond. I clicked again. Still no response.

A couple of pop-ups then flashed across the screen in

quick succession. They disappeared just as quickly. All was quiet for a couple of seconds until the browser began working of its own accord. Then a series of web addresses began jumping into the address box at incredible speed. The computer was running through more than eight billion websites and God knows how many unknown, hidden sites, entirely on its own, and no matter what I clicked with the mouse, no matter what keys I hit, it had no influence on what was going on. The computer was executing a program, and as long as it was thus occupied it would not respond to any of my commands. The program had taken control of my laptop. Just like that. It wouldn't even let me touch my own stuff. I didn't know whether to be upset about it or not. I felt both resignation and anger.

It was a weird feeling, playing tag with myself.

Finally the screen settled down. A site was slowly being uploaded with a large photo in the background: the earth as seen from space. And across this a brief text appeared:

You have reached the home of Mr. Miller.
Welcome?

19

To see somebody, to talk

The home of Mr. Miller was less accessible than it seemed at first glance. No matter what I did, I was stuck on that start page. Finally I had to turn off the computer and re-start it in order to use it again. I was irritated and tired. The decision not to go home anymore and to sever all ties began to catch up with me. It had been an impulsive choice, quickly made. Based more on what I didn't know than what I did. It was an escape. I hadn't seen it that way until I checked in here, but that's how I saw it now.

I was so untraceable in the Novotel that I myself barely knew where I was. It was Friday afternoon, ten minutes to five. The end-of-the-week rush hour had been building up for more than an hour and the traffic on the ring road, which I could see from the window in my room, was bumper-to-bumper. In both directions. The big office buildings were emptying out, except for the ones with the consultants. I knew Gijs would be working late because of the rock-hard work ethic that prevailed at HC&P. No one ever went home on time. Everyone worked longer than the normal number of hours. In order to win the loyalty of its highly intelligent and talented workforce, HC&P placed strong emphasis on a sense of family. HC&P employees belong together and take care of each other. That was the flip side of the cutthroat competitive battles that were fought every day.

That's also why I was so certain that Van Waayen would think it over ten times before handing me over to the police. He couldn't keep me from being arrested, and if he were to speak to me he'd implore me to give myself up. But to tell the police, 'He's at such-and-such a place, and if you go there you can nab him'—not that. That wasn't how things were done at HC&P.

During my stint of temporary rest in the hotel room I could see how little space I really had. As long as the registration system maintained that no one else had been present in the building that night, no one could help me. I certainly couldn't turn to the firm's management for help. The question was why the system had registered me and not Huib Breger and the other men. It meant that certain people could go in and out of the building without the system taking note of their visit. Or that the registration of their presence was later erased. I kept going back and forth between both possibilities, unable to decide which was the worst.

The second was really the easiest to comprehend. Evidently there were people with access to the registration system, people who knew how to manipulate it. That wasn't good, but it happened so often and in so many companies that it was hardly remarkable. The person who did manipulate the system, however, and who had used it to eliminate a member of the office staff—both literally and figuratively—was on very friendly terms with at least one of the firm's partners. I was convinced that Van Waayen had nothing to do with the murder of Ina Radekker, but did he know that the registration system could be erased? I refused to believe it. That was one coincidence too many. So what was the connection between Van Waayen and this Breger?

The other possibility was much worse. A system that registers some of the people present and not others was quite conceivable. All you would need was a pass with a chip that ordered the system not to record it, and software that recognized and accepted such an order. It wasn't all that difficult, but the consequences were bizarre. It meant that the leadership of the firm had knowingly created a system in which certain individuals could enter and exit the offices without being noticed.

Simple.

But why? And if this was true, how could I ever prove it? The leadership of the firm would never admit it because they themselves were jointly responsible.

My thoughts were bouncing off the bare walls of the hotel room. The more I pondered this problem the bigger it became. In either scenario I had to get into the HC&P registration system because only there could I find something to prove that the system didn't work the way everyone thought it did or to demonstrate that it had been tinkered with. In either case I was up the creek, because I didn't know anything about software. I understood that you could do anything with computers, but I didn't know how that worked. I knew there was a program that registered the presence of people in the building, and I understood that it was run from one of the firm's big computers, but I had no idea where to look for that program, either physically or virtually. I didn't even know where the company's central computer was located. Maybe it wasn't even in our office, but somewhere entirely remote. With today's technology it could have been in India or China. Then no one would ever notice it.

Not only did I know nothing about information technology but I also knew no one working in that sector. Unlike other large consultancies, HC&P did not have its own IT department. So even if I could find someone who could help me, it would have to be someone outside the firm, and such a person would have no access to the company's internal network.

I still had access, although I had no illusions. It wouldn't be long before my own authorization was revoked. Being sought by the police in connection with a murder: that was reason enough to refuse me admission to the network. And when that finally happened, I hoped to be able to carry on with Ina's login data, which I assumed would remain active for a while. No one had any reason to hurry up and change it. On the contrary, things like that that sometimes got stuck in systems and stayed there for years. Cynical bureaucracy.

I checked my e-mail. Eleven messages. One was from Van Waayen. I read it.

Michael,
Since you're not answering your phone anymore (a distressing sign, incidentally), I'm forced to contact you in this rather impersonal way.
In the light of recent events, which not only have plunged this company into a period of mourning for the loss of one of its valued employees but have also filled us with deep despair, I think it would be better if you would get in touch with the police as soon as possible. There's no other way to clear this thing up. I personally cannot believe that you had anything to do with such a terrible murder. Nor do I want to believe it. But HC&P cannot afford to be naive. So I'm laying you off until you're able to convince the police of your innocence. I've already informed your clients of this change— including the Ministry of the Interior, even though it most probably means that the entire assignment will be terminated. You understand, then, how seriously I'm taking this. Please do whatever you have to do so we can quickly pick up where we left off.
Dries van Waayen

I tried to login on the office website, but my password and user name had already been invalidated. I cursed. So much for the warm HC&P sense of family.

Not only had the decision already been made, but it had already been carried out. This made the last sentence of his e-mail sound particularly phony. '... so we can quickly pick up where we left off.' I decided it would probably be wise not to count on it.

When I closed the message, a dialog box appeared. The sender wanted me to confirm that the message had been read. That confirmation could now be sent.

YES or NO?

I chose NO. Dries van Waayen could decide whatever he wanted but he wasn't getting any confirmation out of me. Nor would he get any answers to his phone calls—or any sign of life—until I knew what I was facing. And that could take a while.

I used the new cell phone to call my parents. Finally, much too late, of course, but for them every response was too late. They lived with assurances that were unknown to me: a built-up pension and a place in the hereafter. Their future was all sewn up until well beyond their old age. They had reserved seats in the realms of the eternal. All they had to do was to keep on paying their dues till they died. Every disruption of their well-ordered life was a direct attack on that scheme. Now my mother was beside herself. She couldn't take any more. First that business with Kurt and all the uncertainties that went with it, and now I was being accused of having murdered somebody.

'Is it true?' she asked. With her religious convictions she attached great importance to truth and honesty.

'No,' I said.

'Why do they say it then?'

The police, the press, other people. If 'they' are saying it, it must be a fact. What I have to say has suddenly become no more than an opinion. It was a familiar feeling. Distressingly familiar.

'They say it because that's what they think,' I said.

'Oh ... and why ...'

'Mom!' I said with a commanding tone. I didn't want to

talk this way, having to defend myself before my own family. I had already been afraid this would happen, but now that it had it was much harder to bear than I had expected.

'Are you coming to see us?' she asked.

'That depends,' I said. 'Maybe Sunday.'

'Sunday?'

'Maybe,' I said again. 'When do you get out of church?'

'Usually about eleven-thirty, but if you're coming I won't go.'

'Oh,' I said. 'Yes, that would work, too.'

And thus we felt each other out, trying to find small assurances, small areas of agreement that could give us something to hold on to. To that end my mother was prepared to give up her great mainstay, the Sunday church service—just this once, of course, but even so. What I would have to give up was something I didn't dare think about.

'Kurt is gone, too,' she said suddenly. 'Rented an apartment.'

'Where?'

'Well, where do you think? In Amsterdam of course, somewhere. I wrote it down ...' I heard her rummaging through some papers. '... here it is. Hondecoeterstraat. Do you know it? Is it a nice neighbourhood?'

'Hondecoeter is very decent, Mom. Don't worry.'

'Oh, I don't have to worry?' she snapped. 'Now I don't have to worry all of a sudden. It's a little late for that, if you don't mind my saying so.'

I tried to explain that I hadn't meant it that way, but I couldn't straighten out what was already bent. My mother had drawn a line.

'You know what, Michael? As soon as you can say something honest to me, something I can trust, then call me. If all I get from you is hot air, then don't bother. You understand?' She didn't wait for my answer.

One week ago I had known exactly who I was. My jokes were funny, my sense of humour was one of my strongest qualities, I was friendly, intelligent and considerate. And I was fast. My work rate was high and my insights had the unobstructed speed of intuition. I knew who I liked and who I didn't like. One week ago. Now I no longer knew what I wanted, and if I did know I didn't dare say it, or I didn't know how to say it.

I called Gijs. His voice boomed through the phone. 'Jesus, man, where are you? I've called you eight times! Ten times! More!'

'Send an e-mail,' I said. 'I'm not using that number anymore.'

But he wouldn't use e-mail out of fear that his messages would be screened and out of an acute lack of trust. 'Don't do anything by e-mail,' he said. 'Not with me or with anybody else in the office.'

'Are you home tonight?' I asked.

'I don't know.'

'Gijs, please,' I said. 'I have to see somebody, to talk. Too much is happening. I ...'

'Okay,' he said.

We agreed on a time that seemed safe for both of us. Way after midnight.

20

No, that's Kurt

By the end of the day I was back in the centre of town. I had put my laptop and all the papers and documents in the backpack, dragging everything around with me. All that was left in my hotel room were the rest of my clothes. I had turned over my pin-striped suit and shirt to the hotel's dry-cleaning service. They'd be ready in the morning.

I walked from the tram stop to the internet cafe, covering the ground with great strides. In the past few days a sense of urgency had crept into my body. No matter where I was, I wanted to get away as quickly as possible. I didn't want to be seen and I definitely didn't want to be found. I felt pursued by people I didn't know. I kept getting the idea that I had forgotten something, that something had slipped my mind. Hence the rush.

I bought one hour of internet use, entered the long web address in one of the computers and waited for contact with the site. The connection was made with dazzling speed and the computer went to work, effortlessly this time. The huge amount of information poured in through the cafe's high-capacity connections. The screen flashed a couple of times with strange information, unrecognizable to me, as if it had the hiccups, and then it turned a solid grey. In the middle of the screen was an hourglass telling me to be patient, that the system was at work.

I waited. For minutes I looked at the empty screen and the exasperating little icon. Nothing happened. I leaned back in my chair, folded my hands behind my head, and waited— my head empty, my eyes fixed on the screen.

After about four minutes the screen flashed a few more times, turned completely black and then completely blue. A beautiful deep blue.

In the upper right-hand corner of the screen was a chain of data:

b.ng-chn-infra/nat./051703/00.23—act.

In the lower left-hand corner was this:

User-id: pb***7?all**

At the upper left was a small menu:

Operate
Run
Link
Back

Using the mouse, I clicked to the last option on the menu, Back, and immediately the image flashed to a new screen. All the data disappeared. Now in the middle of the blue field were three lines:

User ID
Location

Log in

Following User ID and Location were spaces that had to be filled in. I cursed. By clicking Back I had shot out of the program and wouldn't be able to get back in without a login name. I typed pb***7?all** after User ID and Amsterdam after Location, and clicked on Log in. Without success. Entrance denied. Logical: the program automatically replaced a number of characters with asterisks or question marks, to prevent anyone else from seeing what the User ID was. I had accidentally picked up a web address from Ina Radekker's computer by which I could bypass the system's security in one go, as if I could get into a building through an open back window without anyone asking me for a pass.

I stared at the screen and at the words displayed on the deep, dark blue. After a couple of minutes I noticed the web address, 11121774.938/utilities/55618.222. The address no longer had anything to do with HC&P and was totally different from the address on the screen by which I had entered the site. I didn't get it.

Somewhere there had to be something, something that Radekker had done or failed to do and for which she was finally murdered. That was the only explanation. In view of her work, it probably had something to do with money, money belonging to clients or to the firm. All the transactions took place electronically, so anyone with the right codes could move a great deal of money from one account to another.

But what else? It was a possibility, but I didn't believe it. It wasn't logical, and even murders have to be logical. Perhaps even more logical than other things, or the motive wouldn't be good enough. That was certainly true in this case; Ina Radekker's death was no love story that had gone dramatically wrong. Not in front of the elevator doors on the third floor of the HC&P office building.

But what was it then? Even if she had made off with a couple of million, was that any reason to rub somebody out? Apart from the fact that you just didn't do that kind of thing, it didn't get you anywhere since you'd never get the money back. That was what didn't make any sense. Unless it was something else, of course. Unless Ms. Radekker had discovered that someone else was absconding with the company funds. Then there would be reason to step in. The larger the amount, the stronger the reason.

But there was still another question. What was this Huib Breger doing there? Why was he able to move through the building at will without being noticed? I spend one night hanging around in the canteen and the next day the computer spits out a nice little report about it. But he and a couple of his pals do away with a debt analyst and there isn't a trace of it to be found. The fact that someone is murdered, okay, not the done thing, but there was a level of organization at work here that was all out of proportion with what Radekker could have discovered. There were at least three men involved and it was the night before she was supposed to go on vacation, so it had been carefully premeditated. Not only did the men have access to the registration system, but they also knew about her personal plans. All that just to conceal financial fraud?

I could just imagine how much money was at stake.

The computer made a discreet little noise to indicate that my time was up. Within two minutes the computer would be disconnected from the internet, unless I bought more time. I took one last look time at the blue screen with the few words written on it. That didn't make any sense either. If Radekker had tracked down a case of fraud via her computer, I should have found something containing financial information: bookkeeping records or administration, at least something that showed that money was being moved around.

I hadn't found that kind of site or document anywhere, and this one had nothing to do with finances either. The purpose of this website was still completely unclear to me, but it certainly wasn't intended for managing money. Even I could see that.

I logged out and packed my things. Returning to the RAI by tram, I walked the couple of hundred metres from the terminus to the hotel. Once I reached my room I was overcome by fatigue. From the moment I sat down on the edge of the bed there was no stopping it. My whole body had a screaming need for sleep. Literally. I could actually hear my muscles. I called reception and asked if they would wake me at twelve-thirty that night. Then I showered, undressed and crawled into bed. It was a quarter after eight. With a little luck I could get in four hours of sleep. I can't remember what I was thinking at that moment, but it couldn't have been much.

At exactly twelve-thirty the phone rang. Half asleep, I dragged myself out of bed, heaved myself into my clothes and left. It was quiet in the hotel lobby and outside in the parking lot. Nights on the outskirts of Amsterdam are peaceful, even on weekends.

It was different in the centre of town, especially in the neighbourhood where Gijs lived. Friday nights there were full of activity. I squeezed the car into a spot between a streetlight and a bridge railing. The spot was so tight that I could hardly get out of the car.

Gijs came from a well-to-do family, so Gijs lived on a canal, the Keizersgracht. He owned a building on the strip between Utrechtsestraat and the Amstel. It wasn't big, but it was a whole building, three-and-a-half metres wide and fifteen metres deep. Four storeys high with narrow, steep stairs that he navigated by screwing his tall body into a ball. The rooms were narrow and smaller than you would expect in a canalside house. The stairwell in the middle of the building divided it into a front and a back with a narrow landing in between. The house had once belonged to some old aunt who died childless at the age of eighty-eight. It had been inherited by Gijs's parents and through them by Gijs, since the family never sold any of its real estate. Some buildings in the centre of town had been family property for more than two hundred years, from the end of the eighteenth century to modern times.

We walked in single file through the narrow corridor to the kitchen at the back of the building, and then out the back door and into the yard, just as narrow as the house and more than twenty metres deep. At the very end of the yard was a garden house, a little one-room structure, frugally furnished with a large desk and a couple of chairs, an old sofa pushed up against the wall, a little old table in the corner with an electric kettle and an automatic coffee maker on it, a small refrigerator and a minuscule sink. This was Gijs's lair. It was his favourite spot, cut off from Amsterdam and in contact with the rest of the world by means of the powerful computer under his desk.

Gijs said nothing. He dove under his work table and soon reappeared with a bottle of wine. He poured a glass for each of us and sat back, a glass under his nose, and only then did he want to know what in God's name was going on.

'Good question,' I said.

'This isn't the Michael I know,' he replied.

'Not the Michael I know either.'

He fell silent once again. So did I. We sipped our wine.

'Because you're always ... well, so normal ...' He looked at me. 'That may be a shitty thing to say, but I mean just the opposite. All those difficult so-called geniuses in the office have skin you can practically see through and you need an operating manual just to talk to them, they're that sensitive. All you have to do is look at them and they develop a complex. But not you. You're just ... normal ...'

We both fell silent.

'But not now,' he said. 'What were you doing in the canteen? Nobody does that.'

'I do,' I said. 'I was afraid I wouldn't be able to get in the next day.'

'Into the canteen?'

'No, into the building, of course. And that thought alone made me panic.'

Gijs nodded. 'Okay, I'm with you,' he said. 'Partly. Because even if they fire you, ...'

I knew what he was going to say and I knew he had no idea how ridiculous it sounded.

'Then what?' I said.

'Well, it's not the end of the world, is it?'

'Maybe not for you,' I said, 'but if I end up on the street it would only be a matter of months before I started scraping bottom. We don't all have fat unlimited bank accounts that we can draw on.' I was snarling, more sharply than I intended. 'My family doesn't have a nice collection of buildings. If I were to call my parents, I might get ten euros out of them, maybe a hundred, but that's all they've got. Okay?'

Gijs swallowed. 'I'm sorry,' he said. He felt self-conscious and waved his arms awkwardly.

'And right now I'm feeling a little sensitive, too, okay? Especially when my family is involved.'

Suddenly Gijs stood up and pulled me out of my chair so I was standing right in front of him. Without saying a word he threw his arms around me, pulled me close and slapped me on the back in a way that he was clearly unaccustomed to. It was as sincere as it was clumsy.

'Stupid of me,' he said.

Before I knew it the tears were streaming down my face. I lost all the self-control I had so fiercely struggled to maintain. In the middle of the night, in a garden house in Amsterdam, in Gijs's arms, I stood there bawling. And thinking about that made me cry even harder. There was no stopping it. Sniffling, I freed myself from his hug and wiped my eyes and cheeks with my sleeve. Gijs and I had known each other for about three years, no more than that, but from the first moment we understood each other as if we hadn't known anybody else. With Gijs every conversation was worthwhile, even if wasn't about anything at all. Especially then. That's the difference: not in the content of the conversation but in the way you relate to each other. I didn't know how that worked. Maybe it was a smell or a certain kind of electron cloud around the body, like an aura or whatever, but the basis of the contact was immediate. Not physical. Gijs and I didn't feel the need to climb all over each other, which is why his hug was so awkward. The contact between us was elemental, a kind of bedrock affinity, as if we both had the same bar code. Peep. Peep. Done. No need to take it any further.

That's what Gijs and I had. I dried my eyes and laughed.

'And what Van Waayen is saying about you, I don't believe that either,' Gijs said.

I grinned. 'I don't even know what Van Waayen is saying about me,' I said, 'and as far as I'm concerned I don't need to know.'

Gijs shook his head. 'Right,' he said.

Silence again. From this spot in the backyard you could still hear the sounds of Amsterdam, but they seemed far away.

'I'll tell you what I do know, though,' I said. 'I wasn't alone in the building. There were others, and one of the men is called Breger.'

'Breger?' Gijs repeated the name and his fingers flew to the keyboard of his computer. He did what I had already done, and with the same result. The name 'Breger' did not appear in the HC&P personnel listings.

'And who is this Breger?' he asked.

'Exactly,' I said. 'That's question number one, two and three.'

'What do you know?' Gijs asked.

'Not enough.'

Gijs shook his head. 'That's not what I meant,' he said. 'Come on, you're a consultant, aren't you?' He pulled me out of my chair and pushed me through the room. 'Get going, walk, move. As long as you stand still, nothing's going to happen.' He pushed me again and again, each time a couple of steps further. As soon as I stopped he was back. 'Let's hear it, where were you? What were you doing? What do you know?' With that combination of questions and movement Gijs forced me to shake off my despondency. You know more than you think you do, that's his basic premise. First look, then think. But it doesn't happen by itself.

With a faltering voice I told him what I knew, from the night in the canteen to the fight in Radekker's apartment. I didn't leave anything out, didn't skip a single detail, and the more I told him the less I understood, and the more the details began to predominate. As I talked, I pulled my laptop out of the backpack and turned the thing on.

'What did you use?' asked Gijs.

'A dumbbell,' I said. 'About two kilos.'

'In the middle of his forehead?'

I nodded. 'More or less, yes.'

'And is he still alive?'

'When I went to leave, he was still moving, so ...'

I shoved the laptop toward him. There was a list on the screen. 'These are web addresses,' I said. 'And it all has to do with one of them. But I have to access the site on your computer. My computer can't handle it.'

Gijs pulled up a chair and sat behind my laptop while I went to work on his computer. While the site was uploading, I could hear Gijs click through the e-mail and look at the sites. The laptop was zooming.

Click. Click.

'wow!' said Gijs. He leaned back in his chair and poured himself another glass of wine. 'It all comes down to this,' he said. 'There are beautiful women and there are very beautiful women. We all know that.' He rubbed his crotch unconsciously with his hand. 'And then you've got these kinds of women. Jesus, you've got some incredible babes on your computer, you know that?'

'Me?'

He changed the settings on the screen to get a sharper image. Suddenly he turned the computer so I could see the screen.

'Is this that Ina?' he asked.

On the screen was a photo of the woman who had thrown my life into disarray, the woman I knew better than any other but who had totally alienated me from myself. Because of her I no longer knew back from front, literally. Everything I thought I knew was gone. I thought things I shouldn't have thought but were impossible not to think. I tried to swallow, but my throat dried up from one minute to the next. My heart pounded, my breathing became so shallow that it seemed like it was stuck in my gullet. I had to force the words past it in order to speak.

'No,' I said. 'That's Kurt.'

21

Please reconfirm

For Gijs, Kurt was just a strange name for a woman. No more than that.

'Okay,' he said. 'Kurt. But otherwise Kurt is drop-dead gorgeous. I don't know how you know her or what she's doing in your computer, but Kurt is all right.'

'Kurt is my brother,' I said.

Gijs said nothing. His eyes darted from the screen to me and back again. Back and forth. He laughed. 'With a brother like that you don't need any sisters,' he said, laughing again awkwardly. 'What do you mean, your brother?'

'Kurt was my brother,' I said, 'until I went to pick him up at Schiphol last Monday and suddenly he turned out to be my sister.'

Gijs jumped to his feet. 'And you didn't know this?'

'No,' I said. 'He was gone for five years. For five years we hadn't seen each other, no photos, nothing. Then all of a sudden there he was standing in front of me ...'

'No, get out of here!'

'Think what you want, but ...'

'It totally blew you away.'

'Yes, that too,' I said, 'but what happened was ...'

'You think you know somebody and they turn out to be a stranger, an unknown quantity, a creature from outer space. Jesus, man, so what do you say then?'

I shook my head. 'No,' I said, 'no ...'

'Because that's what it's all about, right?' There was no stopping Gijs. 'He had himself altered. Because that's what we're talking about. And when somebody has himself altered you just can't wrap your head around it. At least I can't.'

I stared silently into the distance. Gijs had said a lot, but not what I was thinking.

'Or do you mean you *can* wrap your head around it?' he asked. 'That you completely understand it, or something like that. If you do, just say so.'

I shook my head again.

'No,' I said. 'But that's not it.'

'Oh, no? What is it, then?'

'Look at the screen,' I said.

Gijs turned the computer back towards himself and looked. Stared.

'What do you see?'

'A stunner, totally hot,' he said, without any hesitation.

'Exactly,' I said. 'That's what I think. Except for me that means something very different.'

It took a couple of seconds before what I said really sank in. Then he looked at me with wide-open eyes.

'Oh, fuck!' he said. 'Boy, are you ever confused.'

We both looked at the photo of Kurt, beaming on the little monitor. Eyes that knew me as no one else knew me. Kurt, with whom I had done everything for twenty years, learned everything, been everywhere. At least half of me had come into being along with Kurt. My memory was filled with connections to him that had come unglued in a flash. The longer I looked at the photo, the less I recognized myself. That was the real shock.

Suddenly the bookcase behind him began to move. At first I thought it was an excess of fatigue and alcohol, that I was hallucinating, but after the first deceptive little movement the entire cabinet slid noiselessly aside. Out of the darkness came the voice of a woman.

'I saw the lights were still on,' she said, and she came in. 'And I thought, surely the guy next door has an extra glass for a lonely ...' Then she saw me and recovered herself. 'Oh, hello,' she said. 'I didn't know you were ...' She stuck her hand out. 'Hi, I'm Emma. I live here in the back, and Gijs and I have a ...' She gestured behind her to the shifted bookcase, suddenly noticed our shocked faces and thought she had been the cause. '... Okay, this is not going well,' she said. 'Sorry, I ...' She was about to walk away but Gijs stopped her.

'No, wait,' he said, and he looked at me. 'I think we could use a little diversion. Don't you?'

I nodded. There wasn't all that much that I wanted to say. The most important things had been said and I myself didn't even understand the rest. I stood up and extended my hand.

'I'm Michael,' I said.

Emma looked at us. 'I think I've interrupted something,' she said. Then her eyes fell on the laptop and the photo of Kurt. 'Oh, now I get it. You guys are looking at dirty pictures on the internet?'

Gijs laughed. 'Sort of,' he said, clicking the photo away.

'Hey, it's all right with me,' said Emma. 'But then I want something to drink.'

There was plenty to drink. We polished off two bottles of wine in no time, and with all the wine and Emma's unabashed good spirits my panic disappeared. As the glasses were being filled and emptied it seemed to me that Emma was snuggling up closer to Gijs and not the other way around, but if that was the case he did nothing to prevent it.

While Gijs was opening the third bottle she suddenly leaned forward and laid a hand on my knee.

'I don't know what's eating you,' she said, 'but it's obvious that something is.'

With some difficulty I forced my face to assume an awkward smile. 'Well,' I said, 'you're right, there is, but ...'

Emma tossed back the rest of her glass, and before retreating behind the bookcase with a loud laugh she gave me a resounding slap on the shoulder. 'No, darling, you don't have to tell me. Tell the one who needs to hear it,' she said. Then she turned around and kissed Gijs full on the mouth. 'Someday I'll get you,' she said, and she disappeared into the dark hole behind the cabinet, laughing.

'Whoa,' said Gijs.

In silence we stared at the empty passageway, a hole in the room, a portal to another dimension, to the reverse side of life.

A little noise issued from Gijs's computer, a ping, like what you hear when a new e-mail comes in. Gijs looked.

'Do you know what this is?' he asked.

On the screen was the same blue website with the same short menu: Back, Operate, Run, Link, Log out. In the lower left-hand corner was the same text as before: User ID: pb***7?all**. And in the upper right was the same data chain: b.ng-chn-infra/nat./051703/00.23—act.

What was different was the bar in the middle of the screen, which had a flashing red box around it. In the bar were these words:

User please reconfirm with Mr. Miller. Log in location does not match current status.
Running server check.

Mr. Miller? I shook my head.

'I found this site in Radekker's computer,' I said. 'She was doing something with it, and of all the things I found of hers it's the only one I don't understand. So maybe it means something. I don't know.' I looked at the screen. 'But who's this Mr. Miller? Reconfirm with Mr. Miller, it says. Do you know any Miller?'

Gijs shook his head.

'And what's that?' I pointed to the last line. 'Running server check. I'm drawing a blank.'

'That's easy,' said Gijs. 'Computers always do exactly what

they say they're doing. So if it says "running server check," then that's what it's doing. Checking the server.'

'Okay, but for what?'

'For whatever it says,' explained Gijs, and he pointed to the lines on the screen. 'Identity and location. That's what it says. It's asking for identification, you have to supply that, and it says that the log in location doesn't match the current status. So now it's trying to figure out exactly where we are ... I think.'

'Can it do that?' I asked.

'Sure.'

I cursed, reached past him for the mouse and broke the connection with the internet.

22

The Sundance Kid

Early the next morning I awoke with a start. For a minute I didn't know where I was. The old three-person sofa I was lying on smelled familiar but unexpected. Saturday morning in Gijs's garden house, with plenty of alcohol still coursing through my veins, looked very different from what I was used to. Standing on unsteady feet I pulled on my pants and T-shirt and walked through the backyard to the house in search of a toilet. I opened the back door as quietly as possible and slipped inside. It was early, much earlier than I thought, and I didn't want to wake up Gijs. Upstairs I heard thumping, faint sounds of someone walking around. It was an old house. The floorboards creaked and sounded hollow. I smiled. Gijs was already up. With my hand on the handle of the bathroom door I looked down the hallway. It was daylight. The early sun was shining in, and not only through the panes in the front door. There was more. A long strip of light ran down the hallway, and suddenly I saw where it was coming from. The front door was ajar.

This surprised me. I walked to the front of the building, opened the door further and looked outside. No one was there. I turned around, went back inside and pushed the door shut. The lock fell into place with an unexpectedly loud click. At the same time the upstairs thumping stopped.

'Gijs?' I called.

A stifled curse came from upstairs along with an equally stifled response from someone else. For a moment it felt as if my body temperature had dropped ten degrees all at once. I shivered, trembled. One second later I began to glow, fear driving my temperature upward. From the sound of the voices it was evident that there were two men upstairs. Two men, I realized, and not one of them sounded like Gijs.

'There's a number two downstairs. GO!' said one of them, immediately followed by the sound of someone rushing down the stairs. I looked around in a panic. The house was too small to hide in. I had to make a snap decision beyond my range of experience. Outside I didn't stand a chance. If they came after me they'd be on me in no time. Inside my chances were even smaller, unless I could gain time. I opened the front door again, turned around, ran through the house and out the back door to the garden house. I grabbed my laptop and backpack, slid the bookcase aside a bit, slipped through the opening and pushed the cabinet back in place.

On the other side it was pitch dark. I found myself in a kind of shed, a closet without windows. The only point of light came through a small round hole located at eye level in the back of the bookcase. I pressed my face against it and peered through the hole. I could see almost the entire room, and through the glass door I had a view of the yard and the back of the house.

Carefully, almost hesitantly, a man came out through the back door. He looked to the left and to the right. The yard was so narrow and so scantily planted that there was hardly any place for a person to hide. Yet the man moved slowly, deliberately, until he was in the middle of the yard. There he turned around and looked up. From the gestures he was making I gathered that the second man had to be standing somewhere on a higher floor near a window. The man in the yard shook his head and quickly walked the last few metres toward the garden house.

Breathing deeply, I tried to calm myself, but no matter how hard I concentrated I only became more agitated. My head began to swim, I grew dizzy and I had to hold onto the wall of the shed to keep from falling over. At that moment I realized what was happening to me. It was the same oppressive feeling that had seized me at Schiphol: hyperventilation. The deep breathing I was forcing on myself was exactly the wrong way to deal with it. The pressure in my body kept rising higher and higher, as if my insides were swelling up and slowly but surely pressing against my lungs. Panicking, I tried to stop the process, but my fear only made it worse. My lungs were pumping far too much oxygen into my body, and in an attempt to rectify the imbalance they were working more instead of less. The male nurse in the ambulance had told me what to do. He had given me a small bag to hold over my mouth, to reduce the amount of oxygen I was getting and increase the carbon dioxide. Entirely simple, sensible and logical, but the bag was in the hotel. I knew just where it was, on the dresser next to the TV.

With tingling fingers I unzipped my backpack. Feeling my way in the dark I searched for the bag of liquorice I had bought earlier. Fiddling awkwardly and dizzily I pulled off the closing strip, shook the contents of the bag into the backpack and covered my mouth and nose with the empty bag. Behind my back I could feel the bookcase move a little as the man on the other side opened the door of the garden house. Breathing carefully, the bag still over my mouth, I looked through the peep hole once again. The man was inside. He was standing just opposite me, and I could see his face and his eyes. He was a bit shorter than I and somewhat broader, with heavy muscles that ran diagonally from his shoulders to his neck, giving his face a distorted look. His head looked like a bottle cap set on the top of his body. Deep-set, dark eyes surveyed the room. In his left ear was an earpiece. A wire ran along his cheek down to a small device in his breast pocket. A bag was hanging over his shoulder.

He spoke quietly: 'Unit is here.' He listened. 'Okay,' he said. He bent over and disappeared from sight. I could hear him rummaging under the desk, and soon he reappeared. He picked the computer off the floor and turned it upside down on the desk. Then he took a screwdriver out of his bag and opened the back of the case with practiced hands. He carefully removed the inner workings, unscrewed a couple of components and set them aside. From his bag he took out some new components which he installed in the computer. The man worked noiselessly and rapidly. He put the computer back on the floor under the desk, connected all the cables, put the old components in his bag and scoured the room once again.

At the last minute his attention was drawn to something in the cabinet. In three steps he was standing right in front of it and I saw his hand reach toward the peep hole. My breath stuck in my throat. I recoiled instinctively and struck a rake that was standing next to me. The slowly slipping handle made a tearing sound against the wooden wall of the shed. My hand shot out and caught the handle before it could clatter to the floor.

The man in the other room had heard the noise. He stopped and listened. His eyes scrutinized every part of the cabinet, shelf by shelf, and I realized that within a couple of seconds he was going to find the hole in the back wall. Feverishly I set my brains in motion. I couldn't get out; that would make so much noise that the man would come right through the bookcase if necessary to get at me. Going back was not an option at all. The only possibility I saw was to close the hole. For the man it was no more than a round black spot. Because there was no light on my side, he couldn't see anything through it. The most he could do would be to shine a flashlight through or stick something in. The hole was just big enough for a finger or a pen or his screwdriver. And if he were thereby to discover that there was an area behind the bookcase, he would start looking for a way to get in. So closing up the hole was the best idea.

Once again I began groping through my backpack and

found the portable hard drive that held the copied files. I pulled it out of the compartment and held it against the hole with the heel of my hand to keep it from moving.

I heard nothing and felt nothing, except for the fact that I immediately began itching in all the places I could only reach if I let go of the drive. Nervous itching. My breathing was even worse. Slowly it began to climb. I forced myself to keep my breathing as shallow as possible and to hold the air in my lungs as long as possible, longer than my nerves thought was good for me.

I heard the man's voice through the thin back wall of the bookcase.

'Okay,' he said, and immediately I felt something being stuck through the hole. The wood shook and in a few seconds something bumped against the drive. It didn't tick; it barely made any noise at all. It was probably his finger.

Keeping the drive still and in place was all I had to do, but it required all my concentration and attention. I knew the man couldn't see me, I knew he couldn't hear me, I knew he didn't know that I knew ... and all those things I knew didn't help.

My arm began to tremble. The hard drive seemed like the heaviest thing I had ever had to hold up in my life. Again the man pushed against the plastic. Once. Twice. He tapped his finger against the back wall of the cabinet. The hollow tapping sounded like claps of thunder in my ears.

'Okay, no, just a minute.' I heard his voice drift away from the cabinet. Quickly I lowered the drive and looked out. He was looking at the cabinet from a short distance. After a couple of seconds he walked over to one of the sides of the cabinet and disappeared from view. Soon he began to rock and jiggle the cabinet. He was trying to see behind it, but he was pushing from the wrong side. He was pushing it closed instead of open. If he had tried the other side, he would easily have succeeded. I heard him groaning and sighing, and with a shriek he put everything he had into it. Through all that screaming I heard a short, dry click on my side of the cabinet. The click of a lock.

The man on the other side gave up. I heard him panting and catching his breath.

'All clear,' he said. He looked around one more time just to make sure, and left.

I saw him walk to the house through the yard, go into the kitchen and close the door behind him. I waited a little while—not long, because I had to go back, I had to get into the house to see if Gijs was still there. To see how he was. Memories of Ina Radekker came flooding back in sharp focus. She had been a stranger to me. But I knew Gijs, and Gijs knew me. That was the difference. I held my hands against the back of the cabinet, found a vertical slat, clamped my fingers against it and pushed and pulled with all my might. Nothing happened.

Stumbling around in the dark I searched for the outer door of the shed and opened it. Light streamed in, and I saw the simple but strong mechanism that held the cabinet in place. At the bottom was a vertical rod, screwed against the back wall of the cabinet. The rod had fallen into a bracket, which could only be opened with a key. It was an old, simple lock that they probably never used anymore, but it made the cabinet immovable.

I searched for all the possible places where such a key could be kept. A nail on the wall was my first idea. I looked to the left and to the right of the cabinet. The shed was crammed full. There were things hanging everywhere: ropes, garden tools, sprinklers and a hose. There were step ladders, a folded-up drying rack for laundry, buckets and an enormous collection of old pots and cans, but nowhere did I find a key on a nail. I started turning the pots and cans over one by one to see if the key was under any of them.

Down on my knees, I groped around in the furthest boxes.

'Yes?' came a voice from behind. I turned around. Emma was standing right behind me with a sleepy face. In her hand was a bronze sculpture, an abstract sculpture that she was holding above her head on its tapered side.

Applied art.

'Oh, it's you,' she said. 'I thought you were making much too much noise for a burglar.' She lowered the sculpture. 'What are you doing on my side of the cabinet anyway?'

A few minutes later we stole through the back door and into the kitchen. The house was quiet. No voices or footsteps anywhere. We ran up the narrow stairs.

Gijs was lying on the floor next to his bed, and for a moment, perhaps a couple of seconds, Emma and I just stood there in the doorway. We held our breath and looked, hoping he would move or make a sound. Like Ina Radekker there was no blood to be seen anywhere, but like her, too, Gijs was lying motionless. We stared at him, as if radiation from our eyes could help him, could give him the energy or strength he needed to come back from wherever he was. Maybe that was true, probably not, but when thinking is the only thing you have, your thoughts become stronger than they really are. Emma was the first to see it.

'He moved,' she said. 'I saw it!'

She pushed me aside and knelt down next to him. Then she placed two fingers on his neck and closed her eyes. Her calm concentration seemed to last forever. I crept closer and knelt down on Gijs's other side, overcome by the fear that that strange elongated head of his—where numbers and computations were like images and landscapes, determining how he saw the world—would fall silent forever, closing off part of that world for good. Painful thoughts. Fear lodged in my body like a virus. The panic had another source. If I hadn't come to see Gijs and hadn't surfed to that website on his computer, none of this would have happened. There was no way around it.

Reconfirm with Mr. Miller.

Location does not match.

Running server check.

Who are you and where are you? they had asked, whoever they were, and they had figured out the answer themselves. Less than eight hours later there were strange people in the building, people who didn't ask questions but went straight over to the offensive—without warning, without explanation, without any interest in persons or reasons. Tough and efficient.

I stood up and looked around. A bedroom in a house on the Keizersgracht in Amsterdam. It was quite ordinary, neat, normal. These were things I was used to seeing. The fact that I was here, that I had come here yesterday—that, too, was normal. Obviously I couldn't do that anymore. I had been saved by the simple fact that I was sleeping in the garden house and that they hadn't seen me. So they ended up with Gijs instead.

'He's still alive!' said Emma. Suddenly her voice took on the urgency of a doctor at work. She rolled Gijs over on his side, prized his mouth open and stuck a finger deep down his throat. It took a while before he reacted, but the automatic reflex was still working. Gijs began to retch, and soon the first bit of fluid came up. I ran to the bathroom, pulled a towel from the rack and ran back. Carefully but quickly I placed the towel under Gijs's mouth. Emma pushed her fingers deep down his throat once again and this time he reacted violently. The contents of his stomach gushed out in waves. Emma took a corner of the towel and wiped his mouth. 'More!' she shouted. There were clean towels in the closet. I placed a stack of them next to her, removed the soiled one, tossed it in the bathtub and turned on the tap. For about ten minutes I ran back and forth with soiled and clean towels. I fetched and carried off and rinsed and wrung out until Gijs had nothing left to throw up. I stood in the doorway with a wet towel in my hand and watched Emma give him mouth-to-mouth.

Between gulps of air she called out, 'Call 1-1-2!'

One floor down, in the living room, I found a wireless phone. I grabbed it and ran back up the stairs. Back in the bedroom I punched in the number, looked at the phone in my hand and broke the connection before it had been made.

'Did you call?' Emma asked.

'No,' I said.

'What are you waiting for, you idiot!' She screamed at me and dived forward again over the body of Gijs, which she refused to release. Gijs was still there, that's all she needed to know.

I placed the phone next to her.

'Listen ...' I said. I didn't get any further. Emma's furious words cut mine off at the source.

'I don't need to listen! Do something!'

I seized her shoulders and pulled her up.

'Emma,' I said. 'I'm not here, okay?' I gave her a shake. 'I can't be here. I'm not here and I never was here.'

'If you keep on whining Gijs won't be here either.' I saw the restrained aggression in her eyes. She flailed her arm in an effort to knock my hands away. I didn't let go.

'This is my fault,' I said. 'I don't know who's doing it or why, but it's safer for you and for Gijs if no one knew I was here.'

'But you saw them, didn't you? You can tell the police what they look like. You ...'

'The police are looking for me already,' I said.

'Great.'

'For another murder.'

All expression drained from her face. She stared at me with wide-open eyes.

'Oh,' she said. 'Okay ...'

I picked up the phone and gave it to her. 'It's better if you call. You've got to believe me.'

She took the phone and for one second gave me a completely blank look, as if suddenly she could see what I saw. Then she turned away from me and bent over Gijs as if I was no longer there. As if I had never been there. Just as I had asked, but far worse than I could have imagined.

It wasn't until I was back in the hotel room that I began to function again. I showered, collected my clothes from the dry cleaning service, paid the bill and left. The less time I spent in one place, the smaller the chance that someone would find me.

I returned the car to the rental company and took the train to Schiphol. I was anonymous there in the national exhaust hood. Less than fifteen minutes from the centre of Amsterdam I disappeared into the crowd of travellers and vacationers. I booked a room at the Hilton and spent several minutes watching the planes take off and land, staring in silence, trying to piece together the facts as I knew them.

I had found a website on the internet that I didn't understand. That in itself wasn't very remarkable, since there were lots of things I didn't understand. But this website was deadly, and that was indeed remarkable. I had never come across a deadly website before, and certainly not one that was linked to HC&P, the company that I worked for, a company that didn't hire anyone until they knew everything there was to know about him.

Everything.

Until a couple of days before I would have found that reasonable and even appropriate. The company had grown prestigious by providing the highest possible quality for every conceivable situation, and it protected that status by following a few simple rules which it stringently applied.

Logical. But now I saw it quite differently.

Because the company knew so much about me, it could corner me at every turn. 'Man is the information he carries'—and as long as they had their hands on that information they could apply pressure to whoever it belonged to. Wherever they wanted. And eliminate them, if necessary.

As long as they had the correct information, that is, and that was where I could still make some changes. People no longer know who they're in contact with. E-mail is both easy and deceptive. Anyone can open any e-mail address they want. If I want someone to think I'm Winston Churchill, or George Bush, all I have to do is open an address under that name and send my message. It's that simple, except no one ever falls for it. Not if you get an e-mail from george.bush@ zonnet.nl, for example. Not then. But if one of the partners at HC&P were to receive a message from an acquaintance, he might not pay sufficient attention and might answer the mail.

At least that's what I thought.

Using Ina Radekker's user name and password, I logged into the HC&P network and searched for the e-mail addresses of all the partners of the firm. Then I surfed from the HC&P network to several provider sites and opened a number of new e-mail addresses, registered in my name. But the name in the address itself was the man I was looking for, whose identity was unknown to me: Huib.breger@ aol.com, h.breger@tiscali.nl and Huibbreger@hotmail.com.

Using one of those three addresses each time as the sender I wrote eleven e-mails, all with the same message, based on the notices that had appeared on the screen of Gijs's computer. In English.

Identity confirmed, but unavailable. Location NOT secure.
Please input Mr. Miller.
HBreger

That's all. The important thing was not the message but the reaction. Somehow I had to find a way in, a corner of the package I could pick at, and at that point a wild guess seemed better than endless brooding. 'I shoot better when I move,' said the Sundance Kid. He had to move in order to hit something. When he stopped moving, everything went wrong. That was my problem, too.

Do something.

The messages vanished through the data line, and in a little while the computer picked up new messages. Twenty-nine. I looked at them one by one. There were two that I really wanted to see. One because I was waiting for it. And the other because I wished it hadn't been sent.

23

Bellilog, June 19

Okay, where do I draw the line? That's a legitimate question. Where am I supposed to go? Wrong question. Where am I coming from? Here. I've almost reached that point right now. G has been caught. They've caught G. Who are 'they'? Someone. People. People who are looking for me. I can say less and less, while I've got more and more to say.

Miller?

Who is Miller?

Mail from: Jess
Subject: bad news
what are you saying?
xxxx
j

Mail to: Jess
Subject: Re: bad news
what are you asking?
Everything here 100% fucked. Tell you later, but it's not
good. Shit. When you are coming back? I love you. m.

Mail from: Miller
Subject: Confirmation
Dear Mr. Michael Bellicher,
You reached our website recently and failed to complete
the registration form. Also we understand you are no longer
at the Amsterdam Novotel.
Please reconfirm with us.
Sincerely,

Miller

24

Orange hands, white knees

Miller? Miller knew I had stayed at the Novotel and sent me an e-mail about some registration form I hadn't filled in. This was worse than I thought. That so-called innocent question meant that I had left that particular hotel just in time. Miller wanted me to know that he was right on my tail. If I wanted to stay ahead of him, I'd have to be more careful. I had no idea how he had found me there, but the fact that he had found me was clear.

It was busy in the main hall of the airport. Thousands of people were on the move, all with the same kind of passionate cheerfulness, in expectation of the journey that would begin in a couple of hours or in expectation of the person they had come to collect. As I had less than a week before. In those few days I had changed from a successful consultant to a tourist with a backpack, a globetrotter in the Randstad. My appearance was beyond recognition. I hadn't shaved in four days, my stubble growth had reached my ears. I was walking around in dirty clothes and in the wrong shoes. My suit had been dry cleaned and was hanging in the closet, waiting helplessly for a life that had been abruptly interrupted.

I needed money. I stopped at an ATM, stuck my bank card into the slit and keyed in my pin code. Noiselessly the machine processed my information and rejected it. The message that appeared on the screen was so harsh and so simple that I couldn't believe it. Didn't want to believe it.

Card invalid
Transaction terminated

That's all it said. The ATM switched back to its start screen and acted as if I didn't exist. As if I had never existed. My card had disappeared, never to re-emerge. The glorious anonymity of the ATM had turned against me. Now here I was, standing face to face with a machine, and I was powerless. A fully automated system had identified my card and ingested it. From one moment to the next I was cut off from my money. My property.

I cursed and kicked the machine. Hard. Senseless violence exploded in my body. I had an almost uncontrollable urge to hit somebody. I screamed. People standing nearby looked at me. One man came up to me and reached out with an imploring hand.

'You okay?' he asked.

I nodded, forced myself to calm down, swallowed my rage and felt it sink into my body like liquid concrete.

'Sorry,' I said. 'Don't mind me.' I straightened my jacket and walked away, into the main hall. No particular destination. Rage still in my head, in my guts. I walked aimlessly from one end of the hall to the other, past hamburger joints and coffee bars, past supermarkets and book shops, drug stores and clothing chains. Slowly my agitation slackened. Finally I sat down at a small table in a sandwich shop. A girl with an international sort of cheerfulness came up to me and asked me what I wanted.

Coffee.

While she went to get my order, I checked to see how much money I still had. Of the nine hundred I had withdrawn there was less than three hundred left. Enough for now, but the room at the Hilton would soon take care of that. If I were to stay there, my money would be gone in two days. And I still hadn't bought anything. No food and no personal stuff, no toothbrush, no toothpaste, no comb, no razor and no new chapstick. Things I needed. Badly needed.

The only thing I still had was a savings account in France.

I had opened it once after receiving a nice fat bonus. I had wanted to buy a small vineyard around Bergerac, an idea that never panned out. After an initial deposit in the account I hadn't done anything with it. I didn't need it here and it wasn't bothering anybody there. A little less than twenty thousand euros, deposited there in cash. Perfect. Except I didn't have a debit card or a credit card for the account. I did have a French cheque-book and an RIB, a relève d'identité bancaire. With that and my passport I could withdraw money. But I had to do it in France.

Both those things were still in my apartment.

Despondent, I drifted through the airport hall. I knew what I had to do and I knew I would do it, too, but my first reaction dragged on longer than I wanted it to. All around me was the sound of music, happy and energetic. The smells of fast food, fresh bread and French fries, fruit juice and coffee. In the various cafes and snack bars, TV sets were broadcasting noiseless news images out into the world. Wars and negotiations, dead people and sports. Riots in a city. Somewhere. People running. Men in helmets and carrying automatic weapons were shooting at someone who couldn't be seen. Blurred images. A blindfolded woman on her knees. Masked men with machetes dressed in black. Arabic letters. Subtitles: The infidels have gathered to attack us. They cannot attack us. Ministers in grey suits, sober faces.

'A double bacon burger and a diet Coke,' I said to the girl behind the counter.

She laughed at me the way only girls behind fast food counters ever laugh at me. Because they're supposed to. It's her job to like me. I'm paying for it. It's included in the price. 'Large Coke?' she asked.

'Large Coke,' I said.

Deurloostraat was only partly awake. I had a pretty good view of it from a side street. Parked diagonally across from my front door was a car with two men in it. It was the only car with people inside, and they didn't seem as if they were about to get out or drive away. They just sat there in a dark blue Kia, a nondescript vehicle that would never stand out anywhere if it weren't for those two men.

I lived at number 56, three floors up. Next to me, at number 58, lived Bert Vaasen, who was married to Francine and never went out before noon on Saturday. Bert had a key to my apartment in case I ever forgot mine. I had a key to his apartment, too, if he forgot his. The difference was that I had already come knocking at his door several times but he had never come to mine.

'Which is just as well,' he said then, 'because you're never there anyway.'

Bert never forgot his keys. It just wasn't in him. He was an accountant and he counted everything ten times before going out the door. He was fifty-something and had the face of a man who's always right because he's a man, with all the opinions that went with it. To him I was a ludicrous loud-mouth who never knew what he thought; he was the reliable bellyacher who knew all too well what he thought. Bert and I got on like a house on fire. He ranted at the government and the banks and insurance companies, and I did, too. A drink with Bert usually ended up with an exchange of prejudices that left both of us relieved and able to get on with life.

I took out my cell phone and called his number.

'Hey, Bert. It's me.'

'Yeah, I can tell,' he said. 'Forgot your key?'

'No,' I said. 'It's not that. But I'm out here a little further down the street, and ...'

'Thought so. You see the flatfeet?'

I laughed. 'Blue Kia,' I said.

'Jerks,' said Bert. 'See you in a minute.'

I retraced my steps down the side street, turned on to Rijnstraat and entered Deurloostraat again from the other side, approaching the police car from the back. Then I crossed the street to number 58-60 and rang Bert's bell. As I waited for him to buzz me in, I turned around and looked left and right down the street. The men in the car on the other side didn't respond.

When I got up to Bert's apartment, I wanted to tell him what was going on and why I had called on him, but he didn't even listen. Without saying a word, he picked up the previous day's newspaper, folded it open and laid it on the table in front of me. Murder in Amsterdam South, police are looking for Michael B. Photo of me next to the article with a black bar across my eyes, but *De Telegraaf* has mastered that art so well that anyone could see who I was.

'You need coffee?' Bert asked. He didn't wait for my answer. 'Francie,' he shouted to his wife in one of the other rooms, 'we have a murderer in the house. Make us a cup of coffee, would you?'

With a steaming mug under his nose, Bert told me how 'they' (the police) had searched my apartment a couple of days before. 'It was like they were moving you out,' he said with a curse. 'They must have had their paws on everything at least three times. Really, I'm not exaggerating. Am I exaggerating, Francie?'

Francine shook her head. 'They were at it all morning,' she said. 'Showed up at eight o'clock, downstairs. I don't know how many of them there were, but ...'

'Five,' said Bert. 'Five men. Jerks.'

'Until at least twelve-thirty. And they came back again once that night, but I think there were only two of them and they didn't take long. They were gone within the hour, right, Bert?'

'Less.'

Twice there had been people in my apartment. The police in the morning and others at night. I couldn't imagine what they thought they'd find there, but that hadn't stopped them from turning everything upside down.

'And now?' Bert asked.

'I've got to get in,' I said. 'Through the balcony.'

Bert looked at me. He understood what I meant and why I wanted to do it, but it took a while for him to accept it.

'Are you sure?' he asked.

'Sort of,' I said.

'Then it's okay.'

We walked to the other side of the apartment, through the kitchen and out to the narrow balcony running along the back of the building. Bert's balcony was adjacent to mine, separated by a low brick wall. I put one foot on the railing and one hand on Bert's shoulder.

'Give me a boost,' I said. Bert grabbed me around the waist, and before I knew it I was standing with two feet on the narrow masonry three floors above the ground. Bert's fist was clamped around my belt.

'You shouldn't think about these kinds of things too long,' I said. 'It only makes it worse.'

Bert laughed. 'Are you sure?' he asked again.

I nodded. 'No,' I said, 'but that won't do me any good. Now!'

Bert let go. In one long, sweeping movement I grabbed the top of the brick wall to my left, swung my right leg away from the balcony and around the wall and set my foot on the railing on the other side as far as I could reach. Then I threw my upper body over and dove onto my own balcony, head first. I scraped my hands open on the bricks and crashed onto my knees on the concrete floor.

'Well?' came Bert's laconic voice from behind the partition.

'I'm bleeding from three places and I'll probably be a cripple for the rest of my life.'

'Very good,' said Bert. There was a moment's silence. 'Are you coming back soon? What are you doing over there anyway?'

'I don't think I should try this again,' I said, rubbing the sore spots on my hands and legs. 'I'll get whatever there is to get and just walk out the front door. They won't be expecting that.'

Bert didn't respond.

'Okay?' I asked.

'Actually it would have been much smarter if *I* had gone inside,' he said.

'Maybe. But I also want to see how it looks inside. I want to see for myself.'

'Right,' said Bert. 'Call me before you go.'

There was less to see inside than I had expected. A few places had been rifled through, but most of the stuff was where it belonged, more or less. The greatest chaos was in my study and in the living room. Everything there was strewn all over the floor. Folders, binders, papers. The drawers of my desk were open, and most of the contents had been pulled out and simply flung in every direction. I couldn't understand how anyone expected to find anything this way. It didn't make sense. The mess was more an expression of fury than of furious searching.

I quickly checked the other rooms. The situation in the kitchen, the bedroom, the dining room and the bathroom was relatively normal. My clothes were in the closet and all the dishes were intact. The furniture had survived the onslaught, and they had left the floor covering alone. In the living room I went to the window on the street side and peered down from one corner. The two men were still in the blue car. They hadn't noticed a thing.

Back in the front hall I went to the wardrobe next to the door. I reached past the coats to the shelf above the fuse box and felt around with my fingers. The passport was still there, right next to the box of fuses. I smiled and slipped it into the inner pocket of my jacket.

That was one. Now the cheque-book with the RIB. In the living room I went to the bookcase to the right of the window. On the uppermost shelf I felt between two books, *The Thin Man* and *The Continental Op*, and pulled out the thin chequebook. Perfect. Untouched. I put that in one of the inner pockets of my jacket as well.

Done. I could leave, but I didn't go. A few minutes later I caught myself starting to pick things up and put them back, without being aware of it. I put a couple of folders back in the cabinet and straightened up some papers. I was standing in the middle of my study with a binder in my left hand and an archive box in my right when it suddenly dawned on me what I was doing. I was in my own apartment, and in a kind of reflex I wanted to get everything back in order. It was a logical reaction at the wrong moment. I put the two things neatly in their place in one of the cabinets and called Bert.

'It's me. I'm leaving.'

'Give me two minutes.'

I took the elevator to the ground floor and looked out through the little window in the front door of the entranceway. Soon Bert came out. He crossed the street and walked to the other side of the blue car. Then he bent over the window on the driver's side. I waited a couple of seconds until Bert had engaged the men in conversation. Then I opened the door and stepped outside. My hands were burning from the scrapes, and I felt my knees with every step I took, but I walked to the end of the street without limping or dragging my leg. On the corner of Rijnstraat I looked behind me. Bert was still standing next to the police car. He looked at me, raised his hand and waved. I waved back, just as easily, and disappeared around the corner.

By the time I got back to Schiphol everything hurt. My arms, my legs, my shoulders and my head rose up in protest against every move I made, as if I had wrenched every muscle in my body during the jump and the fall. Next stop was the drugstore, where I bought band-aids, iodine, analgesic cream and a large package of paracetamol. I took it all with me to my room and began an extensive round of self-medication. I washed the scrapes on my hands and dabbed them with iodine, applying band-aids wherever possible. I took three paracetamols and spread some of the analgesic cream on my knees. Then I stood in front of the mirror, orange hands and white knees. My head was spinning. I looked like a deadbeat delinquent who had just been beaten to a pulp. But in the Hilton. I would have to pay for this day anyway, so I figured I might as well make the most of it. I dropped onto the bed, exhausted.

That was all I could take.

25

The sterile light of the train

The Thalys glided peacefully out of the country into Belgium. Still early morning. Late June, the lovely weather of the past few days had disappeared. Grey clouds hung high in the sky. Every now and then blazing beams of sun broke through, but never for long. The farther we travelled, the thicker the cloud cover. Fine with me. It seemed to make me less vulnerable, more hidden.

My backpack had been stored at the Hilton's check-in counter. Everything I had was in it, safe in its enclosed space. If I wasn't carrying it with me I couldn't lose it. All I had in the train was a plastic bag.

With a notebook and a pen I sat at the narrow fold-out table and wrote. I had four and a half hours before arriving in Paris. During that time I wrote down everything that had happened. Not in my blog; this wasn't for others to read. This was for me alone, to keep from forgetting and to help me understand. To try to find the connection between the facts and the aggression. There had to be a reason for the violence. At first I had thought Ina Radekker had stumbled upon financial misdoings, fraud. She worked in Finance & Control, so that idea seemed logical. But since the attack on Gijs it seemed somewhat less likely. Gijs was a numbers genius, but he knew just as little about the administration of the office as I did. Nothing. Not only that, but the only reason they had tracked Gijs down was because I was there. They weren't interested in him but in me.

They. And who were 'they'?

Breger. And Miller. And who else? Van Waayen? And who was Ruud? Who had sent Ruud to Radekker's apartment? And who had taken him away? Because after getting conked with the dumbbell Ruud wouldn't have been able to go anywhere alone. Who were the American men in Gijs's house? Americans? Why Americans? Sent by Miller? So who was Miller?

And why me? Because I was demonstrably the only other person who had been in the building that night. The conveniently guilty party. The man no one would miss. Maybe, but why didn't they just leave that up to the police? The only other thing I knew was the web address, an address that was of no use to me and that had me utterly baffled. Except for the fact that it was linked to *The home of Mr. Miller*. Miller again.

I wrote and wrote. I kept re-ordering the same facts from different perspectives and in different hierarchies: chronologically, according to interests, contacts, money and the work. The work of HC&P. What were the firm's most important assignments? Strategic advice for large companies, policy development for government ministries, reorganizations, restructuring of public services—there was no aspect of society that HC&P didn't have some share in. All those assignments were important, but none of them could top the projects that the firm was doing for the European Union, and at the moment the EU Summit on Security and Integration was the biggest project of all. The firm was working on preparations in twelve different countries. Hundreds of consultants were trying to make some sense out of the chaos of rules and procedures, and at the same time trying to find an answer to the growing unrest in the countries of Western Europe. Reports and inventories generated endless quantities of numerical data, which could only be interpreted by means of the proper models. HC&P provided those models, supplied the frames of reference, worked out the interpretations and presented the results in handsome reports—each and every week, because each week there were new figures, new facts. And each week the tone became more forbidding, the politicians more nervous and the future more uncertain. The time pressure was enormous. The summit would be taking place in a couple of weeks but the negotiations were happening now. Day after day. What later would be adopted as new European policy in the areas of immigration, integration, refugees, antiterrorism and security was now being decided. Even I was working on it. The communication training I was providing to the Minister of Justice had everything to do with the persuasiveness of the Dutch point of view. And not just in the Netherlands.

That was where the interest of HC&P lay. The stakes were extremely high: bringing this project to a successful conclusion would guarantee the role of the firm in the EU for years to come. Even the corporate headquarters in America was following its progress. That's why Jess was there. She was one of the European consultants who had the ability to compare EU policy with that of the United States and see the points of connection.

With so much riding on this work, perhaps assessments were being made that were different from what I would consider normal. But what was the reason? What had Ina Radekker found that had to remain absolutely secret at all costs? What had I found? It wasn't fraud. I no longer believed that. It was the website. Something was happening on that website, and whatever it was, it had to do with the EU project. The longer I thought about it the more certain I became. I just didn't know why.

In Paris I emptied out my savings account, and with more than twenty thousand euros in my pocket I bought some new clothes. A pair of pants, T-shirts, a jacket with a gazillion pockets (all with zippers), underwear, socks, a cap and a pair of lightweight walking shoes. When I got back in the train at the end of the afternoon I looked like a commando on vacation.

As the Thalys tore through the landscape of northern France at three hundred kilometres an hour, I tried to reach Gijs. No answer. I let the phone ring endlessly until the phone company cut it off. He had probably been taken to a hospital, but I didn't know which one. I couldn't call his neighbour Emma because I didn't know her last name. At the office they might know something, but I didn't dare chance it. I didn't want to have any contact whatsoever with HC&P for the time being. Yet I did want to know how he was doing. I wanted information. Something.

I got out my old cell phone and called voicemail. There were more than two hundred new voice messages and almost as many text messages. It was the police, inundating me with calls to convince me to give myself up. After ten messages I turned the phone off. I wasn't available to anyone. Fine. Ultimately I had only one choice: I had to take care of this myself.

Late that evening I arrived in Amsterdam. I took the tram from Central Station to the Herengracht and walked east until I was level with Gijs's house but one canal further north. In the pale illumination of the streetlights I read the nameplates and found her name on the third door.

Emma Silverschmidt.

Couldn't miss it. I took a couple of steps back and looked at the building. It was big, much bigger than Gijs's—almost twice as wide. Basement, large front door and two tall windows on the ground floor, with two more storeys above that. There was still light shining in a few of the windows. I rang the bell, and soon I heard a bit of thumping behind the door. Then came her voice, quite unexpectedly, from a little speaker right next to my ear.

'Who's there?' she asked.

'Me,' I said, not realizing how stupid that sounded until after I had said it.

'That's good,' said Emma, "cause I'm here, too. Anything else you wanted to say?'

'Michael,' I said.

'Am I supposed to know you?'

'The shed guy,' I explained.

'Michael Shedguy?'

'You know. The guy in your shed, friend of Gijs.'

There was a moment of silence. 'Oh, it's you,' she said finally.

'That's what you said the last time.'

The door opened. Emma was not big, but she filled the doorway with her presence. 'Yes?' she asked, making it clear that I was not being invited in.

'How's Gijs?' I asked.

She didn't answer right away but looked at me again with that flat, empty gaze I had seen in her eyes before. Not cold but clinical, as if she were assessing me.

'Gijs is doing well,' she said.

I had to swallow the lump in my throat. 'You sure?'

She shrugged her shoulders. 'As well as can be expected,' she said, and fell silent.

'Thanks,' I said.

'Oh, that'll be a great help,' she said, and now her voice was bitter. 'If you can't stick around when it matters, don't show up later with your commiseration. Not the done thing, at least I don't think so.'

I avoided her glance and looked at the wall next to me, where I noticed another nameplate for the first time. A nameplate with its own bell.

E. Silverschmidt
Psychiatrist, practice

Suddenly I understood why she could be so distant, so blank. How she could be so totally invisible behind her own eyes. It was a professional glance that she used to observe me and to keep me at a distance. I didn't say anything, because everything I said was wrong. Emma had decided that I was an untrustworthy coward because I had let Gijs down. Because I had let her down. Then before my very eyes I watched her face assume a mask of friendliness.

'Will that be all?' she asked. Her hand was already on the door. 'Because I think we'd better end our conversation right now.'

'No,' I said. 'Wait a minute. Where is he?'

'He's at Prinsengracht Hospital, here in the neighbourhood. One more night, for observation. Tomorrow he's coming back home.' She looked at me, eyebrows raised. Suddenly she began addressing me formally. 'Shall we let it go at that? Then you can go home as well,' she said.

I sighed. With great effort I forced my face to smile. 'If only it were so simple,' I said, 'I wouldn't have had to come to your door.'

Central Station was a swarming mass of eating and drinking humanity. The passageway under the platforms smelled of beverages, pizza and French fries. A young guy on one of the stairs was throwing up and his friends were looking on from a distance and laughing at his misery. It wasn't midnight yet and many of the young people were already up to their eye sockets in beer, breezers and rum-and-cokes. There was an unreal atmosphere of spent pleasure, premature hangovers and heated opinions. Quarrels and shouted words reverberated throughout the tunnel under the platforms, Dutch, Moroccans, Turks and Surinamese raucously claiming the space around them.

Police and railroad personnel were patrolling everywhere. Here and there a fight was broken up. Some groups of young people dispersed of their own accord as soon as the uniforms came near, others stuck together in order to demand their rights with as much force as they could muster. The place was open to everyone, so that included them. Confrontation was in the air, on a small scale but intense and passionate. Small gangs formed border posts to secure their own territory. The dividing line between extravagant fun and untrammeled frustration was thin. This was the tough side of integration, the reality behind the figures and statistics, the feeling of people who had lost any understanding of what they were seeing. And to tell the truth, I myself no longer knew whether the facts were lagging behind the reality or vice versa.

There were ten or twelve young men moving through the train carriages with two conductors some distance behind them. The atmosphere was frightening. The group came very close in the sterile light of the train, shouting boisterously and whipping each other up. In groups of four or five they addressed the passengers, faces no more than ten centimetres away. Too close. Too loud. Straining for every wrong answer. Ten pairs of eyes that didn't miss a trick.

At Schiphol the night was still in full swing. I meandered through the airport's main hall and aimed for the exit, doing my best to avoid the patrolling security guards. There were guards on duty right up to the hotel entrance, and after a while I began to get used to it. Apparently they weren't looking for me, and as long as I didn't do anything to attract attention I had nothing to worry about.

I was so fixated on the guards that I failed to notice Breger until I was standing right behind him. I recognized the back of his head, his roughly shaved hair and his solid neck, and I recognized his voice with that strange, somewhat sing-song accent. He said, 'Okay, you guys go upstairs, I'll take care of the bar.' He pointed to the entrance to the bar opposite him.

I quickly turned around and hoped he wouldn't recognize me. In my new clothes I looked like a tourist, not a consultant.

Slowly, without making any sudden movements, I walked back to the desk. My head was seething with questions.

This wasn't possible! How could Breger know I was here? Here, in this hotel, at Schiphol. How could he find me so quickly? The spacious lobby had suddenly become oppressively small. The man on the other side of the desk looked at me with expectation.

'Good evening, sir,' he said. 'Can I help you?'

'I left my backpack here with you. Bellicher. I'm in room 517,' I said, and I waited.

The man smiled, said 'of course,' turned around, took the backpack out of a cabinet, handed it across the counter, and said, 'There was someone here asking for you, by the way. If you have a moment, ...'

'No,' I said, and put a finger to my lips. My heart was pounding in my throat. My breathing became shallow. I forced myself to remain calm, hoisted the backpack onto my back, pulled my cap down further over my eyes and turned towards the exit. Breger was standing right behind me. He stepped aside to let me pass. All went well, exactly as I had hoped. But when Breger turned around to gesture to one of his men he knocked the cap off my head. In a reflex action I leapt away. Breger responded, excusing himself. 'I didn't see you,' he said, and bent over to pick up my cap. He saw my face, and for a moment he scowled. His eyes narrowed, and I knew he was about to recognize me. It was unavoidable. The recognition only took a couple of seconds, maybe longer.

Long enough for me to get to the door of the hotel.

'Hey!' he shouted. I could hear the sound of bumping and cursing behind me. Breger was beating a path through the crowd. I ran outside and headed for the entrance to the main airport terminal, zigzagging through traffic. Racing at full speed, I tore into the hall and tried to disappear amid the masses. Breger was bigger and stronger than I, but I was nimbler, so I kept looking for the most densely packed crowds. Jumping and swerving left and right, I made my way through faster than he did. He was right behind me and was bound to catch up with me, since he was faster on the straightaways.

Turning sharply to the right I ran into a coffee shop. Without hesitating I threw myself among the clientele, jumping over chairs, tables and people and ended up back in the hall on the other side of the cafe with a couple of metres to spare.

Air was straining and hammering in my chest, acidosis pulling my muscles apart from the inside. I ran straight through the hall to the Burger King on the other side with Breger gaining on me. Heading for the counter, I raced between two rows of waiting customers and at the very last minute went in for a slide between their legs, ending up on the other side of the row. Breger crashed into the counter at full speed, gasping for air. I grabbed the first chair I saw, shot back along the line of people and rammed the legs of the chair into his back. Then I pounded away on him with everything I had. The people around me started to shout and scream. I grabbed Breger by his jacket and hurled him over the last bit of stainless steel counter. His jacket tore in my hands and Breger disappeared on the other side, beneath a rack of waiting hamburgers.

I turned around and walked away, ignoring all the shouts—as if I were just an innocent bystander. 'Sorry,' I said. 'Excuse me, pardon me ...' After reaching the end of the counter I went around the corner. With trembling legs and pumping lungs I slipped in with a group of passersby and walked with them back to the main hall. At the first entrance to the train platforms I shot down the escalator and boarded a waiting train. I didn't know where it was going, but anything was better than this. Unable to move, I waited for the doors to close.

Tucked into a far corner I pulled out the paper bag and held the opening over my nose and mouth. Then I breathed in and out, very slowly, until the tingling and the pressure in my body disappeared.

Only when the train began moving did I notice I had something else in my hand: a piece of Breger's jacket, a breast pocket that I had torn off in its entirety, complete with contents. There was a piece of hard plastic inside, some kind of card. I took it out slowly and looked at it.

Risk Containment Group
H. Breger
Operations manager
111.37vbr-599/00spm.002

Less than ten minutes later I got out at the deserted Hoofd-dorp station. Middle of the night. Last train. My lips were incredibly dry.

26

Gijs forever

Nighttime in Hoofddorp is total. No one ever goes there and no one ever wants to leave. They've all left already. The business district looks abandoned and silent between the railroad tracks and the highway. The station is made of concrete, glass, steel and modern tiles. Cheerful colours. Bare fluorescent lights keep the cheerfulness from getting out of hand. Another man got out of the train with me. He was wearing a dark suit and pulling a suitcase on wheels. The wheels clicked on the cracks between the tiles. It was the only sound to be heard. The man knew where he was going. He walked up the stairs resolutely and disappeared. I could hear the little wheels clicking into the distance. A car door slammed.

The hall of the train station was empty. The ticket counter was closed. Anyone who wanted to travel now had to rely on the ticket machines. Outside the emptiness was much vaster. There wasn't a single car in the parking lot, not a taxi to be seen at the taxi stand. The last one had probably just left.

For a minute I didn't know what to do. I was tired, my body was worn out, all my limbs were begging for a bath and a bed. And my head kept right on racing. When I stopped moving, my thoughts became even more agitated. So I hoisted my backpack onto my back and started walking. I followed the meandering new asphalt past dark buildings and beneath streetlights that were shining for no one but the security services, perhaps, and the night watchmen. And for the real estate agents, trying to sell off empty office space with signs printed in desperately enormous type. Instinctively I began to count. In one street alone I counted twenty-five thousand square metres of empty offices. I had come to a ghost town.

I walked and walked. The end of the street was further than I had expected. Fifteen minutes later I reached Crown Plaza Hotel. I trudged across the parking lot and finally found myself in front of a glistening check-in desk in a silent lobby. A man in a hotel uniform gave me a friendly look. It was one-fifteen. Even the muzak had been turned off.

'Good evening,' he said, and that sounded terrific.

I undressed and looked at myself in the mirror. There were a few scratches and black-and-blue spots here and there, but otherwise it wasn't so bad. It felt worse than it looked. I unpacked my backpack. Then I laid out all the papers on the small desk in a corner of the room, with my laptop beside them. With excessive deliberation I checked to make sure I still had everything. It wasn't much, but somewhere in the midst of those few things lay the answer I was looking for. Not now though.

With two painkillers and the contents of a mini bottle of whisky inside me I lowered myself into a hot bath. Slowly. I kept filling the bath with hot water so I could enjoy that strange state of semi-weightlessness as long as possible. Much later, deep in the night, I crept into bed.

The next day I was awakened by a single thought in my head: the laptop. If Breger had been able to find me so quickly, he must have had something that would enable him to find me. A device or a signal or something else. It couldn't have been my cell phone, because my old one had been turned off ever since I bought the new one. The only other device I had was the computer, which had been issued to me by the office and which I was now lugging around with me everywhere I went. If Breger had been receiving signals from me, they must have come from the laptop. There was no other way.

But how?

Gijs's address had been found in a snap as soon as he logged onto a certain website. I had never been there with my own computer so I assumed they couldn't find mine. Why would they want to anyway? They couldn't very well keep track of every computer.

Unless it was the other way around: that computers from the company had an automatic tracking system. HC&P had their own worldwide computer network by which a great deal of the company information was exchanged. It was quite possible that only employees had passwords for accessing the system, but perhaps the computers themselves had tracking codes as well. That would give HC&P a second line of security. And if that was true, then my computer would automatically report in every time I went on the company network. I had done that from the hotel at Schiphol. I had used Ina Radekker's password, but if my computer had its own code then all they had to do was to respond to that, which they had done with amazing speed.

I looked at the machine—lid closed, quiet and idle—with new interest. It was possible. I knew it was possible. Modern computers could do the strangest things without your being aware of it. But it didn't make any sense, because with my password I could log onto the company network from any computer. I could do it from a client's computer and even from an internet cafe if necessary. And if you could do that, what was the point of having computers that signed themselves in and out?

Yet I had been found by means of my computer and by connecting with the internet. I was sure of it. I cursed. Without the internet I was nowhere, and with the internet I couldn't stay anywhere. That meant I had to travel from one public internet facility to another until I discovered how they were tracing me.

I packed my things, checked out and took a taxi back to Hoofddorp station.

From the silent first class compartment I called Gijs. He sounded animated, almost cheerful. The whole thing had cost him one day and one night, and to tell the truth he hadn't slept so well in a long time.

'I ought to do that every weekend,' he said. 'They take everything away from you in the hospital, except the TV.'

He was very light-hearted about it. Too light-hearted, but that was his way. He was above all earthly cares, even if the earthly cares had tried to wrestle him down. Especially then. He did tell me that Emma and I had found him just in time. Emma had done the most important thing: empty his stomach as quickly as possible so they could treat him further in the hospital.

'Don't ask me how,' he said, 'because I was barely conscious myself. Emma knows everything.'

'Emma isn't speaking to me anymore, I'm afraid.'

Gijs laughed. 'Yeah, that'll happen,' he said. 'You just shouldn't have walked out.'

'I had no choice,' I said.

'I know.'

'No,' I said. 'You don't know the half of it. And it's only getting worse.'

'Oh, you think so?' Gijs remained laconic. 'Who ended up in the hospital anyway, you or me?'

'You,' I said.

'Exactly. But you know what *I* don't understand? Everything that was on my computer is gone. The programs are still there (and not all of them, by the way), but all my work, all my documents, my e-mail login—all the rest is gone. And what's there isn't mine.'

'Before they left, one of those guys took out your hard drive and put in a new one.' I told him what I had seen from behind the bookcase.

'But why?' Gijs asked. 'I noticed it right away. As soon as I turned the thing on I could tell something wasn't right.'

'That's true,' I said. 'But maybe they didn't intend for you ever to turn your computer on again.'

Gijs was quiet for a moment. 'And if I was gone, no one else would notice. They probably wouldn't even realize that it wasn't my disk.'

'Something like that,' I said.

'So I had to be eliminated because there was something on my computer,' said Gijs. 'Just breaking in and erasing the files wasn't good enough. No, I had to be erased myself.'

'Just like Radekker,' I said.

'That's what it looks like,' said Gijs. He thought for a moment. 'Where are you now?'

'I can't tell you,' I said. 'You'll hear from me. Open an e-mail address that you'll only use from internet cafes.'

'Gijsforever@yahoo.nl,' he said. 'What do you think of that?'

27

Reassuring bias

I really didn't know why I decided to go to my parents. Instinct, probably. Something that follows its own logic, whether it's logical or not. Family ties exert a force, even if there's hardly anything left to pull. It's a kind of nerve that keeps sending impulses long after the contact has been broken. Every now and then you have to give in to it to satisfy the impulse.

Addiction works the same way.

My parents' house is located in a residential area, at the end of a road that twists through the neighbourhood in an unpredictable way. No first-time visitors can ever find it. There's no longer any difference between the street and the sidewalk. In fact, there's no sidewalk at all. The fronts of the houses look like backs, and the whole thing is executed in that tasteless seventies building style. The house is almost as old as I am. We're just three years apart, but we have nothing in common.

This is where I grew up, in a suburb of Dordrecht. For sixteen long years I was able to see how the growing trees and bushes added not a hint of character to the neighbourhood. The aging greenery was more a disguise for the streets than a part of them. The best solution would probably have been to issue a ban on pruning and gardeners and to wait until the plants had overrun the entire area.

I stood at the end of the street for a moment and applied some chapstick to my lips. Calmly. I rolled my lips against each other to spread out the grease. My parents' house was not visible from where I was standing, but I could see a large section of the street. There weren't many cars, and the police car that had been posted there was so conspicuous that I didn't even have to look for it. Anyone who sits in a parked car in this neighbourhood doesn't belong here.

I walked past the street to the gateway that opens out between two houses a little further on, at a place where you wouldn't immediately expect it. The system behind the houses is just as whimsical as the design of the neighbourhood, with all its twisting streets.

I slipped in through the gate, walked across the yard to the back door and went inside. In a single step I was there, unannounced, among the tea and cookies.

'Michael?' said my mother.

'I said I would come, didn't I?'

'But it's not Sunday. You were going to come on Sunday, and on Sunday we were sitting here waiting, and …'

'We?' It was an unconscious question, a question that issued unannounced from my growing sense of distrust. My mother knew that the police were keeping the house under surveillance. My mother knew about everything that happened in the neighbourhood.

'Well, yes—we, here, the way we're always here, and you might have given a little thought to our situation. It hasn't been easy for us either.'

It was the three of them: my father in his chair and my mother in the doorway to the kitchen. Peter, my youngest brother, was slouched in a corner of the sofa, MP3 earbuds in his ears, TV remote in his hand. Fox Kids cartoons without sound for his eyes and house in his ears. He raised his right hand, palm turned toward me.

'Yo, Michael, cool.'

I rubbed the palm of my right hand against his. Soft contact, skin on skin.

'Pete,' I said.

My father heaved himself out of his chair and positioned his big body right in front of me. He slapped me on the shoulder and burst out laughing.

'I don't know what they think of you,' he said, 'but it seems to me those guys don't think at all.' It was his way of letting me know that he was behind me. Unconditionally. Brief and with reassuring bias. Exactly what you expect from your family. I was all right by him, but he wanted to know everything, such as who the murdered woman actually was.

'Girlfriend of yours?' he asked.

'No, somebody in the financial department. I had never seen her before.'

'You see!' My father turned to my mother and repeated what I had said. He had complete trust in me. My mother didn't. She thought I should obey the rules. If I was innocent, nothing could happen to me. That's what she thought. She sighed.

'I know that,' she said. 'A foreigner, no doubt?'

'Why would she be a foreigner?' I asked.

'Because she was there in the middle of the night. What was she doing there if she wasn't on the cleaning staff? They hire the strangest people. That's just a fact.'

'Radekker, Mom. Her name was Radekker. Okay?'

'Oh, a Jewish girl?' she asked, switching prejudices effortlessly.

'How should I know? And I was there in the middle of the night, too, remember!'

'Yes, but you had to work.'

'How come you know so much about it?'

Without even wanting to I had ended up in the quarrel I had wanted to avoid. My father used his prejudices to protect his family. My mother used hers to attack the rest of the world. It was insane. Peter looked at me from the sofa, eyebrows raised. He had withdrawn from these confrontations for good. The MP3 player was a wall he had raised around his thoughts. Thundering music hung around him like an electronic shield. Even my mother's steely opinions ricocheted off it.

My father walked over and stood between us, trying to put a stop to the absurd conversation.

'He says he had never seen her before.'

'Until she was lying there,' I said.

'Exactly,' said my father. 'And where was she lying?'

'In the corridor, in front of the elevator.' I nodded, picked up a cookie from the dish on the table and stuck it in my mouth. Sugar helped deal with the estrangement.

'But then other people must have seen her, too?' my father asked.

I shook my head, realizing how little they knew. They thought it was all about Ina Radekker, and it was, but in the meantime my world had been turned upside down, on its head, inside out, and I had ended up on the outside. The outside of my own life. Compared to them I was in another dimension. I saw things that didn't exist for them at all, and as I answered their questions I knew that everything I said needed ten times more explanation.

'No,' I said. 'No one else was there.'

'Oh. Okay. But why not? There are hundreds of people working there, right?'

'Yes, but not in the middle of the night.'

They didn't know anything, and the more I tried to find an opening the harder it became. 'Mom,' I said, 'I've ended up in a situation. I don't know what it is, but it's not what you've heard about it. Just believe me.'

'So you should go to the police,' she said. If the police were looking for me, then I had to cooperate. That's the way she saw it. She couldn't believe that the police wouldn't believe me.

I shook my head. 'I can't go to the police, Mom. Really. All the evidence points to me. If I were to walk into a police station they'd put me under arrest and toss me in a cell and that would be it. I wouldn't stand a chance. Forget it.'

I went to the kitchen and took a beer out of the fridge.

With the bottle at my lips I walked back into the living room. 'Kurt not here?' I asked.

My father shook his head. 'Kurt has way too much to do in Amsterdam,' he said. 'Don't ask me what.'

That was more than my mother could bear. She opened her mouth and started screaming. a high-pitched, shrieking sound that cut through the room. Then she stamped her foot and punched the air with her fists.

'HER NAME ISN'T KURT!' she shouted.

'Who cares what her name is?' said my father. 'She's still Kurt, right? Or have I got that wrong?'

Peter pulled the earbuds out of his ears and stared at the noiseless TV screen, where animal figures in clothing were chasing each other.

'Ah,' he said. 'Kurt is just a hot babe.'

The room was draped in silence. Peter had said the worst that could be said, the very words that my father, my mother and I had wanted to avoid. Forever. That's why the silence was so total. My mother was the first to recover herself.

'You shouldn't say those kinds of things!' she hissed.

'Yes, I should,' said Peter. 'You shouldn't make such a big deal out of it. Listen.' He stood up and walked over to us. 'I'll say it again: Kurt is a hot babe, okay? And any guy who doesn't think so has his cock screwed on backwards.'

'Her name is Kirsten,' said my mother. 'Kirsten. She won't know she's been accepted until we call her by the name she prefers.'

'Oh, give me a break! You call her Kirsten but she's still a guy with a problem. Come on! You've got to accept her body. If Kurt were to walk in here in a midriff top, I'd think: wow, cool. My sister! Then the name would come automatically.'

'Maybe for you,' I said. 'But it's different for me. Kurt and I used to share a bed.'

Peter laughed. 'Then you peaked too early, man. The world is cruel.'

It took a little while before I realized my mother had left. She had slipped away during the last few sentences and now I didn't see her anymore. I didn't hear her either, not in the kitchen and not anywhere else.

'Where's Mom?' I asked. My father reacted with as much surprise as I did.

'I thought she was here ...'

'I think she just went outside,' said Peter.

I cursed, ran through the room and yanked open the door to the hallway. At the other end of the hall I saw that the door was ajar, and in a flash I realized what she was doing. Maybe she could no longer save Kirsten, but there was still a chance for me. An abrupt calm descended over me. I turned around, went back into the living room and walked straight to the back door.

'I've got to go,' I said. 'Mom went to get the police.'

My father said nothing. He was standing in the middle of the room, immobile.

'I,' he said. '... but ...'

Peter uttered a curse that was new to me. My family was falling apart before my very eyes, too quickly for me to do anything about it. The glue had become unstuck. The changes that were taking place were exposing principles that had been hidden far too long for the sake of peace and harmony. Now that others had abandoned that peace, the cannons were being lined up, and my mother was bringing in live ammunition. Kurt's sex change was a frontal attack on the heart of God's order. My involvement in murder had hit her where she hadn't expected: in the flanks of her decency. My mother had withdrawn to the position she was familiar with, and she left my father behind, in the vacuum between his wife and his children. For all those years, his family had been the reference point for everything he did or thought. Now he was floundering in the darkness. For years he had kept us together. Now his wife was forcing him to choose: either her, his wife, his son or himself. I saw the hesitation in his eyes, and the fear.

'We may not be seeing each other for a while,' I said, 'but no matter what happens, no matter what they say, I didn't do it.'

He nodded. 'I know that,' he said. And at that moment I saw the familiar bias return. My father looked to one side. His eyes met with Peter's. 'We'll hold them off here. Okay, Pete?'

Peter responded immediately.

'GO!' he screamed, and he jumped over the back of the sofa and ran into the hallway. Even before I was out the back door I heard the front door lock click. I looked at my father one more time. I wanted to tell him everything, but all I could do was nod. Twice. I had nowhere else to go and no time to waste.

Not a second.

My advantage was that I knew the neighbourhood better. Their advantage was that they could call in as much help as they wanted. But before it got that far, I had to be gone. I ran out through the backyard and out the gate, and squeezed through a thick hedge into the yard of the back neighbours. Before I was all the way through I heard excited voices and footsteps come in through the gate. My backpack got stuck on a branch, and I pulled it loose with one clumsy tug. The bushes behind me waved back and forth.

From the yard I was standing in I could see into the house. No one was there. I looked around me. In the next yard there were people outside, the Janson family, who had lived here as long as we had. My pursuers were gaining on me. Faster. Closer. I scrambled over the fence and landed in the middle of their happy hour. They shouted and screamed, and as soon as they saw it was me they began to whoop.

'Hey, Michael, can't you find the door, buddy?'

I laughed at their joke because it was the appropriate

response, but in the meantime I sprinted to their back door.

'My father knows all about it,' I shouted. Why I don't know, but it seemed like the right thing to say. And it was true. I stormed into their house, through the back room, into the hallway and out the front door. Without turning around I shot through an alley between two houses on the other side of the street and ran as fast as I could to the far end. There the alley split. One side led back to the street, the other to a small park that separated our neighbourhood from the next one. I took the latter, and soon I was running among the trees and across the grassy fields that I had known for so long I didn't even have to think about where I was going. I knew every path, every little trail. I knew where they went and where they ended up. It was here that I had first discovered how big the world was. The woods and fields looked infinitely vast back then; now I dashed through as if it were a little city park.

On the other side of the woods I dove into one of the streets. Here the endlessly twisting and turning street plan worked in my favour, but any gain I made was temporary. I still had to get out of the neighbourhood. I walked and raced and ran until I found someone who was just about to drive away. A man, his car ready, the car door open. He came out of his house, kissed his wife, gave her one last hug. I crept to the other side of the car, opened the other door and sat down in the passenger's seat, backpack between my legs. What the man would think or how he would react didn't interest me anymore. This man was going to take me with him, except he didn't know it yet.

A few seconds later he got in. As he was lowering himself into the driver's seat, he saw me. His mouth dropped open to say something, but I beat him to it. I raised my finger in the air and held it in front of his eyes.

'Don't say anything,' I said. 'Drive.'

28

Leave the net alone

His fist hit me right between the eyes, on the bridge of my nose. I didn't even see it coming. My head flew back and slammed against the doorpost.

'What did you think, asshole,' he said. 'I'm supposed to be impressed by that finger of yours?'

He wound up to deliver another punch, but one was enough for me. I threw the door open and dropped out sideways. At the last minute I grabbed my backpack and crept away on my hands and knees. Then I heard him coming after me from behind, cursing and yelling. I scrambled to my feet and ran down the street, shot into the first alley I saw and wormed my way through another hedge and into a backyard.

The yards here were bigger than on our side of the park, and this one had a long path that twisted around a number of bushes before you got to the house. In the back, near the gate, there was a stone shed with the hedge on one side and a large, overgrown bay laurel on the other. I crept under the laurel and found a spot against the wall of the shed that was out of sight. There I sat down, dense green all around me. I pulled my legs up and rested my elbows on my knees. Cautiously I fingered my face and a felt a warm dampness. Blood was running along the side of my nose. The wound I had sustained in the fight with Ruud had opened up again, above my right eye. It wasn't bleeding badly, but enough to leave stains on my T-shirt and pants. I dabbed at my face with a tissue until the bleeding stopped.

Gradually the neighbourhood grew quiet. The screaming man left, and all that remained were people's voices. Distant voices. Every now and then there was a laugh or a shout, but after a while even those sounds died away. It was the end of the afternoon, around six o'clock. Dark clouds spelled rain.

I leaned against the wall and was startled by the painful bump on the back of my head. The more I relaxed the more everything hurt. I took the box of paracetamol out of the backpack and pushed two tablets out of the strip. I put them in my mouth, chewed them into a paste and swallowed them without water. Dry granules got stuck between my teeth.

I sank down onto my side and pulled the backpack under my head. The flat computer served as a kind of pillow, with only an extra T-shirt and underpants to soften the hard plastic.

In the middle of the night I woke up. The rain hadn't come, but dampness from the ground was seeping up into my clothes. I was stiff and chilled. Cautiously I pulled myself up. Then I crept between the hedge and the shed, out to the gate, and walked back to the street. I looked at my watch in the light of a streetlight. It was two-twenty. There was nothing there, no one. No bus and no taxi. I had no choice but to walk to the station. Not that there was anything to do there at this time of night, but staying here was pointless.

I took the first train to Rotterdam, sitting in an almost empty compartment, and from there I went on to Amsterdam. More and more people got in at every station, and by the time we pulled out of Leiden the train was full.

At Central Station in Amsterdam I bought a cup of coffee and a sandwich. I wolfed the sandwich down. Only then did I realize how hungry I was. Sitting on a bench in the hall, I took careful sips of the piping hot coffee and stared around me groggily. I was back in my city. That's just what it felt like. I was back where I belonged. Here I knew where everything was, and here I would remain until I had found a way out of the problems that were tormenting me. This was where it had to happen. I wasn't going to let myself be side-tracked again. If I was going to stand any chance at all I'd have to concentrate.

Here.

I took the tram to the Munt and walked the short distance to the hotel on the corner of the Flower Market and Vijzel-straat. I wanted a room where no one would come looking for me and where everything could be provided. Two hundred euros a night. The man behind the counter looked at me with a restrained but surprised expression. I glanced in the mirror behind him and saw what he saw: a dirty, unwashed, unshaven man with blood on his face and his clothes.

'Is ... everything ... all right?' he asked.

I put seven hundred fifty in cash on the counter and said, 'I think so,' and registered under the name of Richard Bakker.

'Three nights,' I said.

The man behind the counter repeated what I said.

'And do you have a passport or proof of identity?'

'No,' I said, peeled off another hundred and put it on the counter. 'I'm not even here. For no one.'

The man smiled, put the hundred euros in his pocket and gave me a keycard. 'There's never anyone in room 313,' he said.

'Except room service,' I said.

'Of course,' he said. 'Room service goes everywhere.'

I showered and shaved, put the dirty clothes in a bag for the laundry service and ordered a breakfast of scrambled eggs, bacon, bread, coffee and juice. Wrapped in a towel, I sat down at the little table in the room and polished off the meal. Then I put on the cleanest clothes I still had and went out.

At the internet cafe on the corner I logged in and began searching for whatever I could find out about the company on Breger's card, the Risk Containment Group. Google couldn't find anything and no other search engine gave me an answer. There wasn't a single mention of the company on the entire World Wide Web. More than eight billion pages of information, and the name of the organization didn't appear on any of them. Not only was that obscure, but it could only have been the result of a conscious choice to remain unknown.

From my bag I took the scrap of paper with the long internet address on it and entered it one more time. I waited until the connection was made, and while I was waiting I got out Breger's card. With the mouse I clicked to the first screen. In the middle of the blue field the three words appeared once again: *User ID, Location, Log in.*

On the card, beneath the name of Breger, were a number and letter code. I filled these in under User ID. Location: Amsterdam. Then I clicked on 'Log in.' The screen flashed, and soon the image appeared that I had seen once before: the earth from space. Superimposed over this the text: *You have reached the home of Mr. Miller. Welcome.*

This time without a question mark. A few seconds later the text disappeared and a brief menu appeared of its own accord.

Applications
Systems
Security

Log out

I chose 'Systems' and a new menu appeared:

Network
Embedded
Host

It meant nothing to me, but using his card from the Risk Containment Group, Huib Breger was authorized to enter the site. And if he had access here, then his card was probably good for the HC&P office buildings as well. That meant that the system did indeed recognize different passes and register them separately. And that meant exactly what I didn't want it to mean: that HC&P had intentionally installed a double system, one for ordinary people and one for secret people.

Huib Breger was one of the secret people. No more than that. There had to be others, but who were they? Every question led to more questions, and I kept ending up on the wrong side of the information.

I clicked to the first choice in the menu, 'Network', and waited while the computer downloaded a large file. A map of the world appeared on the screen, and with it a wildly complex pattern. Lines moved across the image, not in a swinging motion but as if their purpose was to make various currents visible. Points of connection in those currents lit up for a moment and then jumped. Around each point of connection a sort of local network formed which itself could suddenly expand, only to shrink again in a flash. What the whole thing resembled more than anything else was a large flock of birds that would fan out, then shrink back up and veer off, flying through the sky. It was a fascinating game of shapes that repeated themselves one moment and seemed to dissolve in the next. Sometimes the flock behaved like the centre of the network, but all of a sudden it would jump or shift or disappear from the screen altogether for seconds at a time, without the network seeming to take any notice.

I was totally baffled.

The screen was a way of visualizing the status of a network. An insanely large and complex network. Most probably the network of HC&P, but even that was uncertain. I clicked back to the first menu and chose 'Applications,' and went from there to 'Monitor.' Immediately the short menu I had seen earlier appeared in the upper left-hand corner of the screen: *Operate; Run; Link; Back.*

I chose the first option, 'Operate,' and clicked on it. On the right side of the screen an elongated text box appeared that ran top to bottom, with a scroll bar beside it. Inside the box was a row of country names, arranged in alphabetical order from Albania to Zimbabwe, with all the other countries in between. I clicked on the Netherlands and a new box appeared with a simpler choice: *National government; Local government; NGO; AEX companies; Other quoted companies; Other.*

By clicking 'National government' I found the full list of Dutch ministries. I chose the ministry with which I myself had had the most experience, Justice, and as soon as I clicked on it a new list appeared on the screen. Under the heading 'Choose project' a list appeared of all the projects currently being worked on at Justice. It took several seconds before I realized that this wasn't just an overview of the projects HC&P was carrying out for Justice, which at the moment were two, maybe three at the most. This was a list of all the projects the Ministry was working on, internal and external projects mixed together, neatly classified and accessible, and most of them strictly confidential. I had heard the names of some of these projects, but I didn't know what they were about or who was responsible for them. Everything was here, from the reorganization of the canteen to the criteria for financial cutbacks.

Using the mouse I scrolled through the list, with names and details shooting across the screen. I clicked on 'Coaching.' Under that heading a new choice appeared, 'Minister' or 'Summit.' I chose 'Minister' and was shown which activities were being undertaken to help the Minister of Justice communicate better and more effectively with his own department, his own party, his colleagues in the cabinet, with the Lower House of Parliament and the press. I read an explanation of everything that was being done with the minister and what had yet to be done. The monitor function of the program reported not only the status of the project but also its importance and its relationship to other projects, and to my own utter amazement I learned that the coaching of the Dutch minister had been assigned a high priority by this worldwide network. I clicked, and in a flash the network's map of the world returned to the screen. Now the lines ran from the Netherlands to the rest of the world, and the flock flew by way of France, England and Germany to all the countries of the European Union, to the Middle East and to North America.

On the right was a brief summary of the status. A little red ball began flashing next to the first point: *Coach out.*

That was me. I wasn't there. I laughed inadvertently, but the laugh felt wrong. It stuck in my throat, like old dry bread.

An orange ball flashed next to the following point, *Critical path.* When I clicked on it the map of the world disappeared and a kind of outline appeared on the screen. It was an overview of things I didn't understand. Dates, project names and places seemed to be arranged without any rhyme or reason. One of the names jumped out at me: RISC. I had seen that name on a document somewhere. I clicked on it, and a logo consisting of five words slowly took shape: *Roadmap for Interzonal Strategic Confrontation.*

The logo stayed on the screen for a few seconds and then

faded. It was followed by a brief introduction to the project, a combination of elements that could have been part of almost any policy document of any government, such as the increasing complexity of society, rapidly changing conditions, the interconnectedness of all economies on different continents and the shrinking influence that national governments have on conditions in their own country. To this a new notion was added: 'Interzonal Strategic Confrontation.' The idea was one of sickening simplicity. After the attacks in the United States, the world had been divided into a number of zones. Each zone played a role in the confrontation between Christianity and Islam. The War on Terror was being strategically carried out on three fronts: all-out war, hard negotiations and social confrontation. The first was occurring in the countries that were under direct attack, the second in the countries in the immediate vicinity of the war zones, and the third was taking place in Western Europe. It had to be Western Europe, because nowhere else were Christianity and Islam so strongly represented in one and the same area. There the confrontation had to occur within the bounds of democracy, but the fight was just as fierce. The roadmap sketched a picture of a war in which the Americans engaged in fighting from a distance, and we, the Europeans, had to drive Islam back in the streets and cities of our own countries.

That's what it said. Simple and hard, and inescapably clear. RISC was an ancient, time-honoured military strategy for overwhelming an enemy: ravage the homelands until the core is destroyed, then attack on the peripheral fronts. Finally they'll collapse, too, because there's no core left to keep them alive. And Western Europe was the peripheral front.

Suddenly the image on the screen split in two. The text was moved to a column on the left and the map of the world filled in most of the screen on the right. In the text, hyper-links and possible contacts to points all over the map began to flash. The computer was importing calculations that were completely unknown to me. This was a project on a scale quite different from what I was used to. After about a minute of calculating, the flock disappeared from the map of the world and a new network opened up, a network of lines that indicated the relationships between Europe and the United States, Africa, the Middle East and Asia.

The image solidified into a red outline. A second line was projected over this, a blue line, and suddenly it became clear what the flock was: an overview of activities and pol-icy in countries all over the world by which predictions could be made as to how the total effect of all those efforts would influence the balance.

This was some kind of scenario-calculating program, but on an enormous scale. It could be used to calculate the effect of decisions and events. The program was a cross between a computer game, a management game and a sim-ulation program.

The information density was unpredictable, but at the same time the information was presented in such a way that its significance could be clearly seen at a glance. It showed the details and the main lines and the relation between the two, so that important details became visible automatically, as it were. It was fascinating to see how the small details influenced the big ones, to follow the course of that influence and to see how the dealings of people all over the world related to each other. Everything is con-nected: not only did the screen prove that to be true but it also demonstrated how it all works. The image was intoxi-cating, addictive, and I was part of the scenario. The way I coached and supervised the Dutch Minister of Justice was reflected in the development of the entire world. The tougher he was in drawing the borders of Dutch tolerance, the more influential the radical conservatives in Europe would become. Because if the world famous Dutch tolerance failed, then there was no other option than confrontation.

The capability of the program was staggering, and the idea that it was linked to RISC gave me goose bumps. It was to protect this that Ina Radekker was murdered—I didn't doubt that for a second. There were interests at stake here that were infinitely greater than money. This had to do with belief, and belief has always been the deadliest human attribute. RISC had a goal, and the EC Summit on Security and Integration was one of the important steps on the way to that goal. The basic principles for the coming years were going to be laid down at the Summit. And somehow, this crazy bird-flock program of Mr. Miller monitored all the changes that were taking place and processed the results so the most effective policy could be dictated. The toughest policy.

Suddenly a dialog box sprang up right in the middle of my reflections. The message was simple. It said:

Do you wish to speak to Mr. Miller?
Yes—No

Did I wish to speak to Mr. Miller? What was this about? Of course I wanted to speak to the man, but he didn't know who I was. I had logged in with Huib Breger's login codes, and why would Huib Breger want to speak with Mr. Miller? That was the question. I could adopt Breger's identity and ask Miller anything I wanted. The temptation was great. At the same time I realized that I could only do that once. Before my virtual conversation with Mr. Miller was over they'd discover I wasn't Breger, and after that I'd never be able to use his ID again. I'd only get one chance and I'd have to milk it for all it was worth. But that wasn't now. I had to know more before I could go any further. Quickly I clicked

'No' and leaned back, unprepared for the chat statement that then popped up on the screen.

> *Huib, if you don't want control, then leave the net alone, will you?*

29

Automatic answer

This was for real! This was the world in a shoebox. This wasn't just power, it was omnipotence. *If you don't want control, then leave the net alone.* That could mean only one thing: I wasn't looking at an HC&P computer program, I was engaging live on a network. The changes and displacements I saw there were a reflection of what was happening in real time. *Do you wish to speak to Mr. Miller?* The question resounded in my head, louder and louder. The longer I looked at the screen, at the information flying in flocks all over the world, the more anxious I felt and the more improbable it became.

HC&P had offices in a hundred and twenty countries, and every office had its own computers that were all linked together in a single network. But the information I had just seen at the Ministry of Justice was not stored in an office computer. That would have been impossible. Only the Ministry had all that information. So if I could look into the data of the Ministry of Justice via that network, then I probably also had access to information from all the other ministries, and all the companies in the country that were quoted on the stock exchange. And that was only in the Netherlands!

Such a vast amount of information was more than one computer could ever process. The only way to do it would be to download the information directly from the systems of the companies and organizations themselves. But that was almost impossible. It would require disabling all sorts of security systems and firewalls. It might be possible for one company, or even two, or maybe three or four, but in order to gain access to all those organizations in all those countries you'd have to have an incredibly good code breaker at your disposal. Moreover, the access codes were all being changed on a regular basis, which meant you'd have to have an army of people on staff just to keep an eye on everything. Unless that, too, was computerized.

Yet it was the only way I could think of. If it was a real, live network, then it would have to have unlimited access to systems that were closed to outsiders. Hermetically closed.

Ina Radekker had landed in the middle of a system whose existence she wasn't even supposed to know about. That had been the end of her. And I had penetrated the system much further than she had. The only reason I was still here to think about it was because they hadn't been able to find me. They. Huib Breger. And who else? Who was Huib Breger anyway, other than being important enough to gain control of the network if he wanted it? From a certain Mr. Miller.

I logged out and wrote everything I knew in a long e-mail to HB2 in South Africa. I gave him the details of his disappeared namesake as well as the details from the card, and I sent him the web address where he could log in on the site of the network. I also told him that anyone who logged in would be monitored, that the system manager could find out where you were in a heartbeat down to the street name and house number, and that unauthorized use could lead to the permanent severance of every connection.

'I don't know what it is,' I wrote, 'and I don't know how it works, but somehow it has managed to get me on the wanted list for a murder they committed. Everyone is looking for me. The police want to lock me up, and your uncle wants to log me out for good. I'd be grateful for anything you can tell me, as soon as possible. Be careful!'

After I had sent the message I surfed to the various e-mail addresses I had opened in order to send mail in the name of

Huib Breger. It was time to see whether any answers had come in. There was one response to the Hotmail address, and it was short.

Message understood CU in Brussels. Talk there. CvdV

CvdV was Caspar van den Vogels. He was not only the managing partner of the office in the Netherlands but he was also a member of the European Board, which coordinated the activities of the firm in the various countries of Europe. 'In Brussels' meant at the regional conference, which this time was being organized around the theme of the approaching EU summit. Anyone who had anything to say at HC&P Europe would be there. Even partners from the United States and Japan were coming to make sure the right information ended up at the right place. So Caspar van den Vogels knew Huib Breger, and knew him well enough to make an appointment with him in such telegraphic language. Dries van Waayen and Caspar van den Vogels, two of the eleven.

I had sent e-mails to three others from this address: Klaas Nandringa, Wiebe Groothand and Sander Wispe. None of them had responded yet. I knew that Wiebe was in China, and maybe he wasn't checking his e-mail regularly. Klaas was up to his eyebrows in the re-structuring of one of the biggest installation companies in Europe—and in the Netherlands, too, obviously. The same was true for Sander. Neither one of them had responded yet to my message.

I surfed to the Tiscali site and checked the e-mail there, too. I had sent messages from that address to Rob Bank, Siem Kampen and Jan Willem Keizer. Rob and Siem had answered. Rob wrote:

Please inform when location is secure, Rob

In all its simplicity, the message spoke volumes about Rob Bank. He knew what was 'secure' and what wasn't, he knew what he should or shouldn't do as long as the 'location' was not 'secure,' and everything else was a piece of cake. Rob knew what it was all about. Deep in thought, I opened the mail from Siem Kampen and read a stack of messages with questions and answers, messages that clearly should not have been sent to this address but had ended up there by accident.

> —Huib, is this really from you? Siem
> —NO, IT'S NOT FROM ME! I DID NOT SEND ANY
> MESSAGE! HB
> —If it's not from you, then who's it from? Siem

Siem Kampen was on the ball. Sending the last e-mail to my Tiscali address by accident was a blunder, of course, but a blunder that worked in my favour. The Tiscali address had become useless. Huib Breger would be able to trace the spot from which I did my e-mail, and that was something I wanted to avoid. I quickly left the site and surfed to AOL. That was the address I had used to send the message to the last four partners. I had received only one answer, from Johan Wolfsen, the oldest partner and someone who tended to march to his own drummer. He had come to the firm after having built up an impressive practice on his own, with an extensive clientele. The firm kept bumping into him in their dealings with their own customers, and he had increasingly proved to be a competitor no one could ignore. When Johan Wolfsen spoke, his clients listened. HC&P had bought his company, Wolfsen Consultancy, and had paid far too much for it. Eight employees and an annual turnover of almost two and a half million: they offered him four times that amount plus a position as partner, everything guaranteed, gilt-edged and insured. Johan Wolfsen was sitting pretty at HC&P, and he wrote:

> I don't know any Huib Breger and I have no idea what this is all about. This message was probably sent to the wrong address. If that is true, this note confirms it. Regards, JW

That was him, all right.

I didn't know what would happen when I sent those messages, nor did I know what to expect. But as soon as I saw the response from Wolfsen I knew that he was the reason. I was looking for a partner, someone as high up in the company as possible, someone who knew as little as I did—someone who didn't know there were some very bad men walking around the company, men who were serving interests quite different from those of the company's clients, men who had no trouble at all considering interests that were unknown to the company staff. I was looking for someone who knew none of this, but who had so much to say in the firm that people would listen to him. And my first task was to make sure that he would listen to me.

I opened a new e-mail address with yet another provider, this time under another name. Not Huib Breger, but not under my own name either, which had too many associations and was too contaminated. My own name might actually keep him from listening to me (by e-mail anyway), and the beauty of the internet is that you can be whoever you want. You can build on your personality ad infinitum, all of it virtual, all of it sham, until it becomes a means of making contact. Then the virtual shifts and ends up influencing the actual because of the way you present it. I opened up an address with xs4all that contained the name of his boss, Caspar van den Vogels, a man he was supposed to listen to, and I wrote:

> Huib Breger is the new man at RCG, from America. Seems to be taking over everything here, extremely disagreeable. It's time for us to catch up, but somewhere else. Tomorrow, twelve-thirty, 't Kalfje, on the Amstel.

Wolfsen and I had met each other two or three times at meetings, but we had never had direct contact. So I didn't think he'd remember who I was. That's what I was counting on: that I would recognize him and he wouldn't immediately react to my being there.

I pushed the button and the message was gone. An answer wasn't necessary—as long as he showed up tomorrow. I had no idea what to say to him to convince him of my innocence and of the strange things that were happening at the office. I still had a little more than twenty-four hours to come up with a good story, and I knew I could use a little help. I called Gijs but there was no answer. Not even voicemail. I sent him an e-mail asking if we could see each other as soon as possible, and while I was sitting there thinking an answer arrived. An automated answer.

> Gijs van Olde Nieland will be unavailable for the next two weeks, until July 4.

I cursed.

30

Bellilog, June 19

The last time I spoke to anybody, I got room service. The time before that I got punched in the face. Nuances, details, minor differences in a world under pressure. I'm not a believer, but my lead is evaporating. Holiness is growing, everywhere, holy chair, holy stone, holy field, holy oil, holy light. Real holiness, the holiness of hardened men with a broad grasp of history and a deep knowledge of the Scriptures. Holy Scriptures, almost forgotten. Room service, send up a Bible, please. No, I've used up the Bible that was here. And a Quran. And throw in a Talmud while you're at it. And a diet Coke, for the digestion. A fight between parties, neither of which is mine. Did you ever have that? Forced to choose, just when you thought you'd entered the sixth dimension for good? Where that choice doesn't even exist anymore. And then the punch in the face. Because it turns out I'm in the seventh heaven, and everything is starting all over again.

Dry lips, always these dry lips. Words get stuck when I try to pronounce them. No matter how much chapstick I use. I'm keeping an entire chapstick factory afloat.

Mail from: Jess.
Subject: Re: Re: bad news
what I want to know is what the hell are you doing!? everybody here is talking about the Dutch Dirtball, and that's you. our relationship is really starting to make things shaky for me here. you know how they are: *you're either for us or against us*. the corporate family is sacred and i don't know what i'm supposed to say anymore. TALK TO ME, BELLI!
xxx

j

Mail to: Jess
Subject: Re: Re: Re: bad news
if you don't know what you're supposed to say anymore, be careful you don't say the wrong thing. jess, i miss you more than i thought. words cause pain. what are you trying to say? what do they know about us there? love you
the milk white kid

Mail from: HB2
Subject: spook
Uncle Huib has been gone for years. Big problems with everyone. All the time. My father, his brother, thinks he's a 'spook,' but that makes him sound nicer than he is. If I can believe what my cousins, aunts and uncles tell me, Uncle Huib is some kind of terrorist.
Huib

Mail to: HB2
Subject: Re: spook
Terrorist? With a beard? Haven't seen anyone like that around here.
Michael

31

No shaking

I was sitting at a small table in a corner of 't Kalfje cafe, nervous from waiting, strung out from too much coffee and dripping with water. Half an hour too early. Outside it was raining with enthusiasm, as if precipitation had just been invented. The scooter I had rented in order to reach this remote spot quickly—and to leave it just as quickly—offered me no protection whatsoever from the downpour. My hair was dripping and my lips were dry. Wiping myself with paper napkins, I tried to keep my nerves in check, but in the end it just made it worse. The longer I waited, the more significant the meeting with Wolfsen became. He was the only one inside the company with enough power to help me. There was no one else. Not for me anyway.

The people I hung around with were co-workers, occasionally someone I had come to know through a client, but always people with a direct or indirect connection to HC&P, the corporate family. And it wasn't until I was sitting at that small table in the cafe that I realized how total the absorption was. The company supported me and I lived for the company. The company was everywhere. From early in the morning to late at night, often fourteen hours a day, I thought about HC&P, talked about HC&P and did things for HC&P. Even my relationship with Jessica was twisted to suit it, or half twisted, because the harder I worked, the more the work swallowed me up, the more was asked of me, the more work came for me and, again, the harder I worked.

In South Africa, HB2 was sitting alone, fiddling around with a computer. I hoped he could provide me with more information, certainly after his last remarks. So Huib Breger was a spook—a spy? But who was he working for? The Risk

Containment Group? That would explain why the organization couldn't be found anywhere. And what was a secret service—any secret service—doing at the office of HC&P? And what did they want with Ina Radekker? The firm was involved in all kinds of confidential projects, even secret assignments. HC&P served as a regular advisor for the World Bank and the EU. Clients like these required the services of the firm's entire network. Naturally the firm had dealt with secret information before, and it had probably worked with its clients' security services as well.

But a spook?

Johan Wolfsen is almost two metres tall, and he wears his height well. Always erect, shoulders back, chin forward—a relaxed attitude marked by an easy balance. He let his eyes glide through the small interior. 't Kalfje cafe is on the very edge of Amsterdam, just outside the ring road, on the Amstel. It's not much of a place, a wooden shack with an extension built on, that's all. But the location is terrific. It's almost within walking distance of the city's futuristic offices and big money, but it's a relic of former times. Here the biggest issues could be reduced to their essence. Here you ate croquettes on bread and open-face ham-and-egg sandwiches at dark brown bar tables covered with little Persian tablecloths. Around you was nothing but fields, the river and the sky. A wet sky on that particular day.

Wolfsen slapped the drops from his coat and looked around once more. His face was stern, expressionless. He had expected to find his managing partner here for a meeting whose purpose was not yet clear. His sharp eyes flashed back and forth, failed to find the one he was looking for and came to rest at a small table next to the window. He took off his coat, hung it over one of the chairs and sat down.

He looked around expectantly, took his cell phone out of his pocket, tapped a couple of buttons, looked at the screen and put the phone away. Then he ordered a cup of coffee and waited. Two men came in, talking loudly, laughing, shaking the water from their clothes (pin-striped suits, shirts and ties). Bankers, from the looks of it. They searched out a place on the other side of the cafe and saw no one but themselves and the deal they were working on.

The waiter served coffee, a cup with a spoon, a little container of cream, sugar cubes and a packaged cookie. Wolfsen looked at it, carefully removed the foil from the container and poured the cream into the cup. Then stirred.

No one had come with him. I waited for almost five minutes, and as far as I could see he was alone. It was so quiet in the cafe that I could hardly have been mistaken. Wolfsen, the two men on the other side of the room, another older couple (also next to the window) and me. There simply wasn't anyone else there.

I stood up, walked to his table and placed a hand on the back of the chair across from him. Without saying anything I sat down. Wolfsen looked at me. He wanted to say something, but he swallowed his words. He looked around and then back at me. Neither of us spoke. I put him in control of the situation. I had too little going for me to take the lead in this encounter, so it was better for him to think he was in charge. And he was.

He squinted at me and turned his head away, looked outside at the pouring rain and didn't turn his gaze back to me for almost a minute.

'Michael Bellicher,' he said. 'That's you, right?

I nodded.

'Okay.'

He fell silent again and kept on staring. His gaze at rest was more active than the spinning eyes of someone in the clutches of panic. Wolfsen was looking for something, and he kept on looking until he found it. In the meantime he said nothing. Behind his eyes a lightning-fast selection process was taking place. I recognized it from him and from other partners. Dozens, hundreds of possibilities were shooting through his head, and every possibility was being identified, classified, set aside or retained and applied to this situation. He knew who I was. He knew what my problem was. And yet here I was, sitting with him. Under false pretenses, but here nonetheless. And he was here. He could have known that the invitation to have lunch had not come from his director. All he had to do was check, nothing more, that's all it would have taken, then he would have known for sure. But he didn't. He was here. The details of the situation were crystal clear, and I trusted that he would come to the same conclusion faster and better than I. His silent gaze kept me in its sights and refused to release me while he thought things through and positioned himself. Then he smiled.

'You look like shit,' he said. 'You look like you've been run over by a herd of couriers.'

I swallowed and said nothing.

Wolfsen was in no hurry. But he didn't need to pretend we were here for the fun of it, either. 'Okay, who is Huib Breger?' he asked.

'Huib Breger killed Ina Radekker.'

'And you didn't?'

I shook my head. 'No, I didn't,' I said.

'I don't buy it,' he said. 'Why don't you just say so?'

'Because I can't prove anything and because other people can prove that I did do it.'

Wolfsen nodded. 'Reality is the perception of reality,' he said. 'Truth is what people see, and what they don't see doesn't count. Is that what you mean? But you and Ina were the only ones in the building, right?'

I shook my head.

'No?'

'It can be proved that Ina and I were the only ones,' I said. 'In fact, it is being proved. But it's not true.'

Wolfsen said nothing. His attention was focused on the information he'd just been given. He hadn't the slightest urge to deny my claims or to dismiss them as nonsense. He listened to what I had to say without passing judgment. He was taking stock. He considered the consequences of what I said, jiggled the details and moved them around until they fit—or didn't. If something didn't fit, he had a question to ask. A consultant to the marrow of his bones.

'You realize what you're saying?' he asked.

'That Breger ...' I didn't get any further.

'No, no, no, it has nothing to do with this Mr. Breger. You're saying that HC&P, the world-famous, widely respected HC&P consultancy, has murdered one of its own employees. That's what you're saying.'

That was it. That was the rock-hard conclusion behind all the incomprehensible systems, computers and networks. That was the inescapable agony I was being confronted with. A powerful multinational, packed to the rafters with people flush with clients—politicians at every conceivable level, entrepreneurs, scientists, high-ranking officials in the armies and police forces of more countries than I could name—did away with an employee, just because they thought it was necessary.

'That's what you're saying,' Wolfsen repeated.

'Looks that way, yes.'

He nodded. 'Okay.' Still no judgment. 'Coffee?'

'No more for me,' I said. 'Make it something else—soup or something. Is that all right?'

'One more time,' said Wolfsen. 'Who is Huib Breger?'

'A guy from the Risk Containment Group.'

His coffee and my soup arrived and I ate. Nice thick Dutch vegetable soup. Lots of grey-green tendrils, orange-brown discs and plenty of tender meatballs. Hot and salty. Just what I needed. 'I've never heard of the RCG. Can't find the company anywhere either. But Breger has a pass that lets him in and out of our building without anyone being able to trace it.'

'And how do you know that?'

I put my hand in my pocket and put Breger's card on the table. Wolfsen picked it up and examined it from every angle. It was an ordinary plastic card, like hundreds of millions of others all over the world. It was printed with a logo in grey, silver and yellow. Simple, no fancy holograms. It did have a chip, though, and Breger's personal data.

'I can get into the HC&P building with this?' Wolfsen asked.

'And much more,' I said, and I held up my hand. He could examine and feel the card as much as he liked, but I did want it back. For the time being this card was my only access to the system. I wasn't leaving the cafe without it.

Wolfsen held it up one last time, as if he were trying to look through it, and then he placed it on the table. With an outstretched forefinger he pushed it over to me.

'Risk Containment Group,' he said, 'is HC&P's own security company.'

'You're kidding.'

'Listen.' Wolfsen waved his hands as if he were trying to make amends for something. 'HC&P works for so many highly-placed people that it needs its own security facility. Every time a chairman or a minister visits one of our offices, we have to be able to offer them security. And we also have to guarantee absolute confidentiality. And before you know it ...'

'The Risk Containment Group,' I said.

'Exactly. RCG. And RCG is a secret,' he said. 'Only partners are aware of its existence because only partners are in contact with those kinds of clients.'

'So that includes you,' I said.

He nodded. 'Yes, that includes me.'

'So you know who Huib Breger is?'

He shook his head. 'I've never heard of Huib Breger,' he said, 'and if he is what his card says he is, Operations Director, then that's impossible.'

I spooned in the last bit of soup and asked the only remaining question: 'If that is true, then why am I sitting here talking to you and not to one of the other partners?'

Wolfsen said nothing. He could come up with his own answer to this question, too—and he did—but he had very little influence over the situation that this answer gave rise to.

'That's impossible,' he said, but with a voice drained of all conviction. 'Do you mean that I'm the only partner who doesn't know this Huib Breger?'

I nodded. 'He's beating down the door of Dries van Waayen's office,' I said.

Wolfsen cursed, under his breath and with restraint, but his anger was palpable. The fact that he did not know one of the firm's employees, and a director at that, was not important. The firm was too big to know everyone. Even if Wolfsen thought he ought to know who the Operations Director of RCG was, it was still possible not to know him. But the fact that all the other partners *did* know this man, that he was present in the building the night of the murder and that absolutely no one knew anything or said anything about it—*that* he could not accept. That was absurd. *He* was the only one who didn't know, that was the difference, which meant that he was not the kind of partner he thought he was. His colleagues, the men he worked with every day, who were supposed to be treating him as their equal, had never told him that even at HC&P some people were more equal than others. He belonged to the others, to the same group I was in. For someone who had imagined himself on the other side, that was a lot to swallow. Wolfsen did it in style. He blinked a couple of times, rubbed his chin, scratched the back of his head and called for the waiter.

'Two young jenevers,' he said, and while he waited for his order he took out his cell phone and dialled a number. Looking at me with a gaze that both demanded my attention and ignored it, that made me feel distinctly insecure, he said nothing until the call was answered. For that brief moment neither of us spoke.

'Caspar,' he said without taking his eyes off me for a second. He had Caspar van den Vogels on the line, the company's managing partner. 'Caspar, Johan here. Yes. Listen, that e-mail from that Huib fellow, is that something I need to be concerned about or what?' He listened without moving, neither nodding nor shaking his head. A little while later he said, '... I thought so. Yes. No, exactly. That's all I need to know. Thanks a lot.' He ended the call and put the phone on the table in front of him. He said nothing and waited until the waiter came. The man laid down two coasters, and on each one he placed a small jenever glass filled to the brim and frosted due to the low temperature of the drink.

'Two young jenevers,' said the waiter.

Wolfsen placed the thumb and forefinger of his right hand around the stem of the glass and waited until I had done the same. We sat like this across from each other.

'What did Caspar say?' I asked.

He smiled, tightened his grip on the stem, raised the glass a centimetre from the surface of the table and held it still, arm outstretched.

'No shaking,' he said.

We raised our glasses in unison.

'Caspar told me not to worry about it and that he would take care of the business with Huib. No problem.' He lightly touched his glass to mine. 'Cheers,' he said. 'To everything I don't yet know.' He brought the glass up to his lips and tossed it back in one draught. I did the same. I felt the cold drink slide down my throat and for a moment I was back in the unthreatened world. This was Holland. Here the grass was green and the rain was wet. This was the korfball champion of the world and the inventor of the frikandel, where third-generation Moroccans were still regarded as foreigners and not as Arabic Dutchmen. Here it was safe and peaceful. Strange things never happened here. Not here. Two kilometres away from here they did, though. That's where the Netherlands fell apart and people were stumbling over the fragments.

Wolfsen brought things back into focus. 'Let's get this straight,' he said. 'The police are looking for you in connection with a murder, and by helping you I become an accessory. On that much we agree, right?'

I nodded.

'So why should I help you, instead of turning you over to the police?'

I said nothing. This was the question I didn't want to answer, that I couldn't answer. There were so many reasons—too many, perhaps—but all of them were my reasons. He had to help me because I was innocent, even though I needed his help just to prove it. He had to believe me because there was no one else inside the company who could, because the company—his company, our company—had apparently done something wrong. Apparently. It was all so vague and unconvincing.

Suddenly I realized what he was up to, and at the same time I realized why I couldn't answer him. He had withdrawn into the safe no-man's-land of the consultant, where everything is always the responsibility of the other guy, where every appeal to one's own commitment can be brushed aside by another question, another consideration, a new possibility or a forgotten aspect. But not now. Not with Radekker dead and Gijs just out of the hospital. Not now that everything had been taken away from me, now that nothing was mine any longer: no family, no home, no friends. I had nothing, except for the fear that I might lose that, too.

Now it was different.

'Why should you help?' I said. 'I don't know, and I'm not supposed to know. It's entirely up to you. If I have to convince you, then it's pointless. You can only do something if you yourself want to. For whatever reason. Because you feel like it or because you think it's important, it doesn't matter.' Just talking about it made me angry. I spat my words out with barely disguised rage. Why did I have to do everybody's thinking for them? I hadn't done anything wrong. 'It's your decision,' I said, 'so don't try to foist it on me. Okay? I've got enough to deal with.' We looked at each other. 'I don't care if you play the consultant,' I said, 'but please do it after you've made your decision. Not before. I'm not a client, I didn't bring an assignment, I don't have a budget and I don't have the authority to decide. I can use all the help you can give me, but you have to really give it. Otherwise we're just jerking each other around.'

Now it was my turn to stand up. I went to the bar and ordered two more drinks. I didn't doubt for a minute what Wolfsen would decide, but I didn't have to watch him do it.

I walked back to the table with two glasses on a small tray, without shaking, without spilling. Carefully I put down one for him and the other for myself. I said nothing. He said nothing. I sat down and raised the glass.

'What's it going to be?' I asked.

He smiled. 'Okay,' he said. 'You're right. I have to make my own decisions. But I do have a few more questions.' During the next half hour he led me away from the muddled profusion of details in my head to the questions I should be asking, and to the answers I was looking for. Not that he had the answers, but he knew how I should adjust my focus in order to see what I was missing. All the questions I myself had already asked came up as well. Wolfsen organized and analysed. For me, but mainly for himself. Who was Breger? What was his function? What was so secret about the work at HC&P? What was so secret that it justified calling in the firm's own secret service? He kept on asking until he had heard enough.

'So you've got to get into the software,' he finally said.

No matter what question he asked, it all boiled down to the same thing: no one at HC&P was going to give me any answers. No one was going to open his mouth. The proof I was looking for was somewhere in a computer, and the only way to get to it was via the software.

Wolfsen wrote something on a scrap of paper and shoved it across to me. It was a name: Vince Batte. With a phone number underneath it.

'Just call him,' said Wolfsen. 'I'll make sure he knows what he has to do.'

'And who is Batte?' I asked.

'Someone at WorldWare. They make all our programs. If anyone knows how to navigate our systems, it's Vince. He can also arrange to get you a pass so you can make use of the company network without setting off all kinds of alarms right away.'

He picked up his cell phone and punched in the number on the scrap of paper. He waited, but the call switched over to voicemail. 'Call him tomorrow morning,' he said, 'and I'll send him an e-mail right away. Okay?'

I nodded.

'Fine,' he said, shoving his chair backward. He stood up and paid the tab at the bar. While we were putting on our coats, he said, 'I'm not going to do anything until I hear from you again. And let me know how it goes with Vince. Take it easy.'

He gave me a brief slap on the back, pulled his head in between his shoulders and sprinted to his car in the little lane across from the entrance to the cafe. A few minutes later he drove away, windshield wipers sweeping back and forth. Then he turned left onto the dike, left again at the windmill and disappeared behind the bushes a hundred metres further on. I grabbed my scooter, strapped on the helmet and sat there in the pouring rain, staring into the distance.

32

Involuntary reactions

Water sprayed off both sides of the scooter. It wasn't even four in the afternoon but it seemed like nighttime. The cloud cover was so thick and the rain so heavy that it was hard to find any trace of daylight. The traffic circle in front of the RAI was flooded, and I had to brake and swerve here and there because the puddles were too deep for the scooter's small wheels. I looked left and right, in front of me and behind, to keep an eye on the rest of the traffic. In the pouring rain it was hard to tell which way the cars were going. I took a left at the bowling alley, shot past a couple of cars and was soon riding along the side of the RAI. The road here was practically empty. Almost everyone was driving straight on into Scheldestraat.

To minimize the effect of the rain I bent far over the handlebars. With my thoughts receding to the back of my helmet, I rode past the apartment building toward the bridge over the Boerenwetering. There was a big puddle on the road in front of me. I could pass it on the left, but that would mean swerving into the middle of the road. On the right was the sidewalk. I looked into my rearview mirror and saw a heavy black form quickly approaching. If I went to the left I'd be right in the path of the oncoming car.

I squeezed my brakes, turned the handlebars to the right, heaved the front wheel onto the sidewalk and was completely unprepared for the crash that came next, for at that very moment the car grazed the back of the scooter. I heard the thing crack beneath me and felt it topple over, despite my efforts to keep it upright. With dogged determination I held onto the handlebars and pulled my right leg out from under the scooter. Creaking and spitting sparks, it juddered across the paving stones until it hit the wall and came to a halt. I was lying on my stomach in the water, backpack on my back, helmet on my head. The scooter was beside me. The entire rear fender was torn off, right up to the saddle. The crash had left the front fender bent and torn as well. My whole body tensed up, and I felt all my muscles tingling and straining. I jumped up and looked behind me. Ten metres away the car was idling next to the sidewalk, its brake lights glowing red.

Cursing and roaring, I pulled the scooter upright, set it on its kickstand and walked up to the waiting car. I stepped off the sidewalk to get to the driver's side, and at that moment the brake lights went out. For a few seconds it was dark and silent except for the rain, which was still coming down in buckets. Then I heard the dry click of an automatic gearbox, and two blazing white back-up lights came on. All at once the roaring engine drowned out any other sound. The car was coming right at me.

I jumped—out of the path of the car and off the road, onto the sidewalk in a single bound. I raced to the scooter, climbed onto the remains of the saddle, pushed it off its kickstand and attempted to ride away. The torn front fender was dragging along the ground and part of it got stuck between the front wheel and the fork. I stopped, braced my foot against the frame, picked up the piece of plastic and jerked it loose. Then I climbed back on the stripped vehicle without a second to spare. The car had stopped and had taken up a position near an exit right across the sidewalk. I couldn't get past it, not by the road and not by the sidewalk. So I had to go the other way. I opened the throttle, leaned the scooter to the right, made a tight right-hand turn with a skidding back tire and tore off, back to the front of the RAI. Without fenders the scooter was a fountain on wheels. Behind me I saw the approaching car, slipping and sliding. It was a large car and it accelerated effortlessly through the rain. I gave the scooter full throttle, shot into Scheldestraat and continued riding down the middle of the street between the cars that were going to and from the RAI, where there was the most room. The little engine under me screamed as if I were trying to strangle it. Meanwhile, with bright headlights and flashing blinkers, the car stormed up behind me. The drivers on the right and left pulled over to the side, and in my rearview mirrors I could see him gaining on me. I had to do something. The distance was shrinking with every second. I squeezed the brakes hard, flung the scooter to the right, slid between two cars and up onto the wide sidewalk and turned the scooter around, front wheel toward the street. Gasping, I looked around. In the middle of the street was the big dark car, an Audi. I'd never be able to beat it. There was a side street to the right maybe two hundred metres farther on. Too far. The Audi would get there before I did. Going to the left would take me back to the RAI, to the big square in front of it and the street where he had already hit me once before. Feverishly I scanned the area. I was safe as long as I was on the sidewalk and the car was in the middle of the street. Or so I thought—until my reasoning process suddenly broke off. The Audi's side window slid down noiselessly, and between the passing cars I saw in a flash the barrel of a pistol. Instinctively I pulled the scooter to the left and accelerated. Behind me I heard a small bang, muffled by the rain, immediately followed by the tinkling noise of a shattered shop window.

The scooter leaped forward and rattled over the sidewalk. I saw the Audi next to me racing backwards down the street. It went almost as fast in reverse as it did going forward. I zipped between two parked cars and crossed the street, brushing past the back of the Audi, then tore up the other way to Churchilllaan. The sudden turn gave me a lead that I managed to maintain until I got to the corner. There the Audi caught up with me just before the curve to the left and hurled the scooter from the road. Again I pulled my legs up until I was almost standing on the saddle, hands on the handlebars, as the scooter bounced down the sidewalk and slammed into the wall, where it came to a stop. Upright. I heard the frame groan beneath me. And crack. But above it all I heard the unbroken sound of the little engine. Without even thinking I opened the throttle again and spurted away. Everything that could break off was already off. The scooter had been reduced to a bare frame with an engine, and it seemed to run all the faster for it. I tore off, down the sidewalk, down the shoulder and onto the wrong traffic lane, where I was safe. Until the next intersection. The Audi got there first. It turned left and ran the red light. With flashing lights the car stopped at the beginning of the roadway. I stopped too. We were a hundred metres apart, maybe less. There was no traffic between us and all the more around us. An accumulation of cars quickly formed behind the Audi, and they couldn't go anywhere. Flashing lights. Bleating horns. Pouring rain.

The Audi began advancing slowly, almost in slow-motion, creeping closer and closer. Its powerful engine was capable of building up enough speed to crush me, scooter and all, in five or six seconds flat. Somehow I had to make my way to the centre of town. It was the only thing I could think of. There in all the little streets and alleys I'd be able to shake him and disappear. But not here. In the broad streets of Amsterdam South the car had the advantage. The straight-aways were too long, the curves too wide. Not here, I thought, and stepped on the gas.

Cautiously I steered to the left side of the road, along the edge of the sidewalk. The Audi followed in my direction and blocked the way through, ready to rush onto the sidewalk and corner me. We crept toward each other with excruciating slowness, waiting for the moment when the other guy would make up his mind to go left or right, or straight ahead. We both put off the decision as long as possible, because whoever decided would be committing himself to one plan of action, precluding all other possibilities, trusting that with his speed at his disposal he had made the right choice.

I stopped, the engine chugging between my knees. Rainwater dripping from my helmet. I was drenched. My entire body was shaking in my dripping clothes. I couldn't keep this up. I could barely see what the other driver was doing. Every move I made was by feel and intuition, and that would have been fine if I had been shooting through the streets of downtown Amsterdam at top speed. There I knew every corner and every intersection. But here, face to face with a two-and-a-half litre V6 four-wheel drive Audi, that was out of the question. I accelerated, turned the scooter to the right, heaved it onto the grassy strip that separated the two lanes of traffic, and shot to the other side, spraying mud everywhere. This time the Audi responded immediately. Snarling and roaring, the heavy vehicle plunged into the low shrubs. Slipping on the smooth grass, turning and spinning to get itself aimed in the right direction, the monster came after me. I stayed on the grassy strip, riding as fast as I could, because there I could take the lead. If I were to choose one of the traffic lanes, either to the left or the right, the car would have the advantage. I rode to the bridge behind the Apollo Hotel. There I shot off the median strip and onto the right-hand lane, past the cars that were waiting at the traffic light. I turned right and crossed the bridge, then turned left onto the road running along the canal. The Audi took no notice of the one-way traffic and came after me at full speed. By the time I got to the last section, past the rowing club, my lead had already shrunk, but now I was at the edge of the Pijp and I knew that from the next side street on the advantage would be mine. I slid through the curve and across the sidewalk, the Audi less than ten metres behind me. A hundred metres further, then a sharp left. Two hundred metres, another sharp left. Another hundred metres, right-hand turn and immediately another left, across the Ceintuurbaan at full speed, left, right, and right again. I was riding as fast as I could, nothing to lose, yet the Audi was still too close. Street after street I managed to put more distance between us, but not enough. I took two more sharp, ninety-degree turns and flew toward Ferdinand Bol. Riding at top speed I arrived at the intersection, bounced over the tram rails, smashed the front wheel into a pothole that the rain had made invisible, lost control of the handlebars and succeeded in jumping off just in time before the scooter flew away, sputtering, crashed against the tracks of a big loading machine and burst apart. Apparently the fuel line had been severed, because a second later flames started shooting out. I ran away, looked around and saw a tram at the tram stop on the other side of the intersection. In a frantic sprint I squeezed out every bit of energy that was left in me. Stumbling and gasping for breath, I reached the front door of the tram and jumped inside.

'DRIVE!' I screamed.

The driver turned around and looked at me with big, astonished eyes. Another troublemaker in his tram, I saw him thinking.

'GO!' I shouted. 'DRIVE!'

I turned around and saw that the passenger from the car had jumped out and was running toward the same tram door. With one enormous kick I tried to slam the door shut behind me. Immediately the driver got out of his seat.

'Hey!' he shouted, grabbing me by the shoulder. 'Knock it off!' He was bigger than me. He pulled me away from the door with his huge hand and dragged me backward. Just then, the man from the Audi tried to kick the door open again. Provoked, the tram driver turned around.

'Ah, another comedian,' he said, and looked out through the window. He and I both saw the pistol that the man was trying to stick through the rubber door seal. I dove behind the driver and climbed into his seat. Pounding my fist on the bell button I pushed the handle forward, and with a jerk the tram began moving.

The steel wheels howled on the rails. People screamed and shouted, tumbling against each other. The tram pushed the Audi aside with a dull thud and began accelerating. The man at the front door tried to find something to hold onto, but ten metres further on he slammed into a lamppost. There was no room for him on the narrow sidewalk. With my hand on the bell I kept pushing the handle forward. The tram went faster and faster, down the Ferdinand Bol to the canal that ran past the Heineken Brewery. I couldn't tell whether the intersection at the bridge to the Weteringcircuit was free, and I had no time to worry about it. Clanging, rattling, cracking and squeaking, the tram flew across the intersection. The Audi was following at a distance. The right side of the car was crushed, but that didn't slow it down. My chances of shaking him were getting smaller and smaller. Even smaller than I thought.

'Okay, that's it!' With one violent tug the tram driver yanked me out of his seat and hurled me into the aisle. He assumed his rightful position and brought the tram to a halt in the middle of the Weteringcircuit. I crept between the passengers on my hands and knees, shouting at them to get out of the way. No matter what happened, I couldn't stay there. If the guy in the Audi managed to catch me, it would be all over. His partner was still lying somewhere on the sidewalk, and forgiveness was probably not high on his list of priorities. And if it were up to the driver of the tram we'd just sit there until the police came. That would be much worse, because I couldn't fight with the police. I screamed and flailed in every direction, pushing people out of the way without noticing who or what I was hitting. I had no choice. I had to get out of this trap. At the next door down I pulled on the emergency cord and the door sprang open. I rolled out, scrambled to my feet, ran across to the other side of the circle and disappeared into the narrow streets of the Weteringbuurt.

It was busy in Leidsestraat, drenched people everywhere. Everyone was trudging close together through the narrow street, snack bars were full of steaming, dripping groups of customers. Hamburgers, pizzas, bagels, ordinary sandwiches, French fries—food of every kind was being bolted down all around me, and in the crush of greasy smells, salty and sweet mixed together, my stomach pushed aside all my body's protests. With a cheeseburger and a large coffee in hand I searched for the most remote table at McDonald's and, hidden in the crowd, I promptly devoured the burger. The harsh flavours and soft texture were just what I needed. My hands shook and my teeth chattered, involuntary reactions of my relaxing muscles. My head was spinning. As I took tiny sips from the piping hot coffee, my first thoughts slowly began to return, and they were not encouraging. I opened my laptop on the small table, plugged in my cell phone and tried to make contact with the internet. With anyone. Anywhere.

33

Bellilog, June 20

Okay, if I had any doubts, I can forget them as of now. That in itself is something. No matter how little I know, I no longer doubt. This is real.

Mail from: Jess
Subject: return flight
at the airport, flight cancelled. terror warning. can you believe this? these people see attacks everywhere. so i'm back at the hotel. book new flight tomorrow, then soon in a'dam. where are you, because i don't think any planes are landing where you are
... love u, jess

Mail from: HB2
Subject: Re: Re: Uncle
No, no beard. Uncle is from the other side. Fundamentalist white. God himself with a gun. One of those. My family says you have to be careful. Discussing here what we're going to do. And where does that network come from? This is big, this is chaos. Mail. I'm waiting.

Mail to: HB2
Subject: Excuse me?
Fundamentalist white? And you're going to do something about it there?
By all means. M.

34

Defensive position

I couldn't go back to the hotel on Vijzelstraat. I had to find another address, another hotel in another part of the city. In one week's time I had been in more hotels in the Netherlands than in the thirty preceding years. I leaned back against the wall and closed my eyes, surrounded by the noise of voices and music. Dozens of school children were trying to outdo each other screaming for the attention they already had, wanting to confirm it every minute of the day. Tourists were calling to each other from one table to the next. In the steady clamour it was impossible to have two intelligible, consecutive thoughts. I picked up my cell phone and sent a text message to Wolfsen.

Meeting discovered. You're being followed. Don't do anything.

I pushed the buttons and sent the message. Two minutes later a message came back.

Okay. WorldWare is waiting for you.

I switched off my phone. Now that I had used it to make contact with Wolfsen it had become unusable. The 06 cell phone number could be recovered from Wolfsen's phone, and from that moment on I'd be traceable. I gathered my things together, walked into Leidsestraat and bought a new cell at the first phone shop I came to. I threw the old one away in a garbage can somewhere near a tram stop on a canal. Whoever found it could have it. At the Koningsplein I turned left onto the Singel and walked to the University Library a little further on. In the information centre were about fifty PCs, speedy things with a fast internet connection. Soon I was safely ensconced in the back rooms of Amsterdam academia.

E-mail, that's what it was all about. Always. Without e-mail and access to the internet there wasn't much I could do. The internet has become a part of our world that can neither be closed down nor monitored. It's a public logbook, anonymous and personal. Virtual society has become actual, not in the images and games and applications that can be found there but in the connections you can make through the internet from everywhere to everywhere. Not very long ago, the mail went either to your home or your place of work. You had two delivery spots. Now I could be reached at as many virtual addresses as I chose, all of which could be accessed from every other conceivable location. That was real, not virtual. I didn't know where Huib Breger lived in South Africa, but I had found him and he had managed to find me. That's what it was all about.

HB2 sent me the address of a website along with login credentials, instructing me to disconnect from the internet and to log in at that address on another computer. And to erase this e-mail. Dry. No nonsense.

I wrote the login on a scrap of paper, deleted the message from the folder of incoming e-mails and also deleted it from the recycle bin. Then I closed the browser and logged in again on another computer. The login I'd received from Huib took me directly to a chat program.

'Hi,' it said on my screen. 'Where were you? The chaos here is aggressive.'

I typed my answer: 'Busy.'

'This is safe,' he wrote. 'This is a secure server. No one runs it except me, and the identity of the server is hidden behind that of another one.'

'Then the other one is in danger.'

'Don't worry.'

'Too late,' I typed. 'I worry.'

Huib told me how he had shielded the server by hiding behind that of the Johannesburg police headquarters. 'By routing via Israel,' he wrote, 'we can get into the HC&P network without them being able to localize us.' Even if they did succeed in finding his computer they'd end up with the South African police, and if they tried to hack through that they'd find themselves at an address in Tel Aviv, where the contact would be scrambled before being routed to him.

'Everything you do, do it through this address,' he wrote.

Fine with me. The lower my chances of being found here again, the better I liked it. 'And what do you mean by chaos?' I wrote.

It took a while before his answer appeared, but once it did it came faster and faster, more and more of it. There he was, thousands of kilometres away, his fingers on the keyboard, and it was almost as if his fingers couldn't keep up with the thoughts in his head.

'The network,' he wrote, 'is the biggest I've ever seen. Millions of computers all over the world are connected to each other and are in constant contact with each other. The total computing capacity is beyond comprehension. Taken together, all those separate PCs constitute the biggest computer in the world. The network of the CIA in the United States pales in comparison. It's not only because there are so many of them, because even if you have a whole airplane hangar full of PCs and whatever else, you still don't have anything. What makes this so absurdly powerful is the way it's operated. The network operates itself. There's no heart, no centre, no monster computer that keeps everything under control and distributes, regulates and manages all the orders. The network regulates everything itself based on the flow of data going through it. And as the number of connected computers gets bigger—and it's growing by the day—the controls adjust accordingly. The greater the network becomes, the more effective its security is because the network provides its own surveillance. Its lead is constantly increasing. It's gorgeous and it's terrifying. And there's no stopping it. Even if you were to remove a million computers from the network, just pull the plugs and throw the stuff out the window, there would still be a couple of million left over and they'd keep on going as if nothing had happened. The only way to eliminate the network is to disconnect all the computers. ALL OF THEM! Do you realize what this is? This is beyond the internet. This is the new world, and it's a world no one wants. Whoever has this network at his disposal can do anything. He has control over all the information from all the governments and big businesses in the entire world. Look.' The screen split, and the chat line dropped to the bottom line of the screen. Above it appeared a web browser, and a little while later the website we were just discussing. Huib logged in and clicked through the menus as if he had spent his whole life doing nothing else. On the screen appeared the map of the world I had seen earlier, with the flocks of information. Huib kept on clicking and we zoomed in on the world map, then further to Europe, then to the Netherlands, and then to The Hague. The network of lines and dots became more and more subtle and distinct. Finally Huib clicked on one dot on one particular spot in one building, that's how detailed it was.

'This is a computer,' he wrote. 'Just a computer somewhere in a building in The Hague. The computer is on. Look.' He clicked again a couple of times and the map disappeared from the screen. Soon I was looking at an old-fashioned MS-DOS screen. Black. One line with three white characters—M:\—and a blinking cursor. It all looked completely innocuous.

'This is the M drive of this computer. I don't know what an

M drive is, but that's neither here nor there. A drive is a drive. And from this M drive you can just jump to the C drive, which everybody is familiar with.'

After the backslash he typed C: and a second line appeared: C:\.

'And from here you can enter the computer. Look.'

After C:\ the word 'exit' appeared. One second later Windows appeared on the screen, then Excel.

'Look. Someone's working here,' Huib typed.

I gazed at the screen in silence. Here and there numbers were being filled in or changed. The spreadsheet re-calculated the changes, and new totals appeared neatly at the bottom in the proper boxes. I couldn't tell what was being calculated, nor what the calculation was for, but what I did understand was that we were online looking into the computer of someone in The Hague who had no idea that two people—one in Amsterdam and one in South Africa—could see everything he was doing. Literally.

'But how is this possible?' I wrote. 'How can we look into someone else's computer? Does this mean that the computer has been hacked?'

'No,' Huib wrote. 'Not hacked. That computer is simply part of the network. Which means you can get in. Whenever you want. Even when this guy turns the thing off later on and goes home, you can still get in.'

'But how can we get in if this computer isn't hacked?'

'Through the M drive,' Huib wrote.

'And what is an M drive?'

'Who knows? Maybe a partitioned part of the hard drive. That's what it usually is. This computer has one at any rate, and it doesn't matter what point you click on in the network, they all have one.'

It was making my head swim. Millions of computers connected in a network that not only could export and import information to and from those computers, but could also change the calculating capacity of all those computers. Huib was right: this was taking place on a scale that far surpassed the powers of my imagination.

Man is the information he carries. Whoever controls the world's information controls the world. This network made it possible. And someone was at the controls. Uncle Huib Breger, for example. That's as far as my thinking took me, because at that very moment a heavy hand came down on my shoulder. In a split-second reaction I jumped out of my chair and tried to drop to the floor behind the table, but the hand wouldn't let me go. I lost my balance, tried to roll away and knocked my head on the edge of the table. By falling I slipped from the grasp of the man behind me. I turned around and crouched down, arms stretched forward, hands in a defensive position to fend off anything that might come at me.

The manager of the internet department looked at me with astonishment. 'Jesus,' he said. 'Take it easy. It's five to six. We close at six, so you only have five more minutes.' He took a couple of steps forward and came up to me, pointing to a wound above my eye. 'You okay?' he asked.

35

The reassurance of smooth skin

It still wasn't dry. It had been raining for two days straight—not very convincingly, to be sure, but it was still wet. Summer wet. I was standing outside on the sidewalk with a new band-aid above my eye. The most important questions had still not been answered. What I really wanted to do was talk to someone else from HC&P, to deliberate. I missed that, contact with someone who understood where I was coming from. HB2 helped, of course, but he didn't know the company, he didn't know what kind of work we did. The names of people, projects and places meant nothing to him. I needed someone else for that. Gijs, for instance. But Gijs was gone, and I couldn't even get near Wolfsen.

I wandered around, from fast-food joint to cafe, until just after eleven when I found myself in Gerrit van der Veenstraat, looking up. There was a light shining on the first floor. She was back, after almost a month and a half. I stepped up to the entranceway, rang the bell and waited. From behind the door I heard thumping and cursing from someone hurrying clumsily down the stairs.

We stood there facing each other, speechless.

'Hey, Belli,' she said.

'Jess.'

I don't know what was going through her head, but it was moving fast. She put out her hand, grabbed me by the wrist, pulled me inside and threw her arms around me. Her mouth on mine. Tongue against tongue. Moving together. Physical contact that finally made it impossible for me to think. Finally. Peace and quiet is the body of another. She let go of me and pushed me up the stairs. Without saying another word she set me down on the couch in the living room.

I heard her footsteps in the hallway, back and forth. Slowly the tension disappeared and domestic noises gained the upper hand. The longer it lasted, the more fatigue took possession of my body. I had been hacked. My legs felt shorter by half, my heels were up in my buttocks, my head hurt, both inside and out. I was sitting on the couch, a big, tightly upholstered, dark blue affair, with my backpack on my knees, my arms wrapped around it and my head resting on top. The two minutes became three, and after that all my ideas vanished. I woke up, lying outstretched on the couch, a pillow under my head and a blanket pulled up over me. I was still in my wet clothes. I no longer knew where I was or why I was there, but my backpack was gone. I began groping around in a panic. I couldn't see anything in the dark, but it wasn't next to me on the couch.

'Shit!' I said.

A lamp went on in a corner of the room. Jessica was sitting in the chair beside it. Her one hand operated the button on the lamp, the other pointed to a spot on the floor.

'You looking for that?' she asked.

On the floor next to the couch was my backpack. Intact. All the zippers shut. I picked it up and looked inside. Everything was still there (there wasn't all that much).

'Thanks,' I said.

'De nada.'

'I'm sorry, by the way, that I ...'

She laughed. 'Don't worry about it,' she said. 'Although you look as if you've got a whole lot to worry about.'

It was twelve thirty. I had slept for more than an hour, and that was only the beginning of the sleep I needed. My body was longing for unconsciousness, for a peaceful disconnection. The hour had been too short for any recovery and too long to just let go.

'Come,' she said.

She took me with her to the bathroom, helped me out of my clothes and put me under the shower. Hot water streamed over my body and for the first time I felt safe. All the weight seemed to drain out of my body and to dissolve. Clouds of steam filled the shower stall and shielded me from the rest of the world.

My clothes were gone, and laid out on a stool were some dry things, Jessica's, which I could wear in the meantime. Sweatpants and a sweatshirt. In the kitchen she took the band-aid off my eyebrow and examined the wound, cleaned it again and put a new band-aid over it. Then she looked at me from a short distance. She shook her head.

'Belli, my friend. Do you have any idea what you're doing?'

'No.'

'Because in the States they do.'

I looked at her. This was the beginning of the question, and Jessica had gotten to it faster than I had wanted. I would have been happier if she hadn't asked it at all. Asking it showed a lack of trust, something my mother had already exhibited. I couldn't take anymore. But now that Jessica had raised the question there was no going back. Pretending she hadn't said anything was not a solution. In the States they know. That's what she said, consciously or unconsciously, and that was also her opinion. Understandable, perhaps, because she only knew what she had heard from others, and that was something I couldn't accept.

'What do they know in the States?' I asked.

'That woman. The one you ...' She didn't want to say it, afraid that saying the words would make them true. What's said is said. Words only last a few seconds, but they hang in the air for years.

'What?' I asked. Going step by step through the minefield, and asking what's there at every step.

'You know,' she said.

'Maybe, but that's not what I asked.'

'Okay, I want to hear it from your own lips,' she said. 'You can understand that, right?'

That was a real kick in the soul. She was asking me to issue a statement, an oath, and she thought I'd understand why. But what I did understand was that I needed a statement from her now as well. Mr. Miller had made his way to the deepest layers of my life.

'And what was I supposed to have done to this woman?' I asked.

'You were supposed to have murdered her,' she said all at once, almost impersonally.

'Do you believe that?' I asked.

She acted as if she didn't have to think twice. It almost worked. 'No,' she said, 'but everyone says so.'

'Just what I need,' I said. Jessica had set out my problem with crystal clarity. Everyone said that I had murdered Ina Radekker, so I had. No one else was present that night, and that was sufficient proof. Plus the fact that communications people were not to be trusted. They said whatever came into their heads. Everybody knew that. I had been convicted and carried away. Perpetrator identified. Everybody happy. Except me.

'Do you know where Gijs is?' I asked.

'In San Francisco,' she said.

The main office. He had been called to the other side of the ocean without any kind of announcement.

'Since when?'

She hesitated, as if this was information not meant for my ears. 'For a while already,' she said, 'as far as I know. He's involved in the economic side of security. You know, coming up with systems for tracking and blocking the flow of money to terrorists, that kind of work.'

'And you?' Slowly it was dawning on me that the things

people around me were doing were very different from what I thought they were doing. Mostly that was my own fault, since I tended to overlook the obvious. But it was also the fault of the others. There was a double agenda at work here. Some people knew more than other people, a feeling I had had just a bit too often recently.

'Do I work for the EU? Yes, but at a very different level, more general.'

'RISC,' I said.

Never before had I seen such unambiguous proof of Jessica's devotion to power. She said nothing, but stared at me with a look I had come to know all too well, her nuclear look, the unfiltered look of the particle accelerator in her head, the look she used to split people open and mess around with their nuclei. Although I knew this about her, I had never been the object of the look until today. Now I was. Now I could feel her weighing me. Where did I stand in the hierarchy? Where did I stand with respect to her? If I knew about RISC, then I myself was also occupying a position she didn't know about. Who did I know? And who did I work with? What was my level? What was she able to say and what did she want to say?

Position and interests, influence and information. Power. Jessica couldn't get enough of it. Her body instantly began producing all the hormones she needed for combat. It made her sharper, faster and tougher. She dominated in every sense of the word, and that's just what she wanted.

'RISC?' she repeated. 'RISC isn't the European Union. RISC is an internal project, a sort of developmental prototype, a new analysis model we're testing.' She rattled off her story, which was not intended to answer questions but to keep them at bay.

'HC&P doesn't have any internal projects,' I said. It was a bluff. I didn't know a thing about it. But somehow I wanted to coax her into making statements she didn't want to make.

She laughed. 'You don't know what you're saying,' she said. 'HC&P *is* an internal project. Everything the firm does is internal.' She stood up and walked to the refrigerator. From the freezer she took out a bottle of vodka, put two glasses on the table and filled them to the brim.

What Jessica then told me took half a bottle to explain. RISC was a worldwide project. In all the countries where HC&P was active, inventories of strategic interests were being taken—not only the interests of individual companies but also those of governments, so they could be compared and so the firm could offer better and more focused advice.

'The trap we all find ourselves in,' she said, 'is that one person's strategy either enables that of the other or blocks it. Companies and countries keep each other in a kind of balance by not all wanting or being able to have the same thing. And if they do want the same thing, there's a limit attached to it. That's the trap. And it worked perfectly well until a couple of years ago. But because of recent events— the attacks and declaring the war on terror—the strategic interests have changed dramatically. Strategy always begins with yourself, taking others into account is second, not the other way around. Take you, for instance. You have to ask yourself what you're actually capable of. But you don't do that. You always ask yourself what other people are doing. And you respond to that. That's not strategy, it's running away.'

'Survival comes first,' I said, 'I'll see what happens after that.' What Jessica said made sense. But it also didn't make sense. I had different information about RISC, the strategic confrontation between Christianity and Islam, which she didn't mention. Maybe it was because she didn't want to say anything about it, or maybe because she *couldn't* say anything about it. The latter seemed more likely. 'Why do you think I've come here?' I asked.

'Because I was the only one you could turn to?'

'Partly that.'

'Any other reasons?'

'Because I love you and because my need to love you has been getting stronger and stronger lately.' I fell silent. She didn't respond. Just what I wanted. There seemed to be a delay in her reaction, as if she were assessing the situation first. 'And because the best hiding place is the one closest to your enemy,' I said.

'And that would be me? Thanks very much.'

Jessica was closer to me than she herself realized. That finally occurred to me as the night wore on. She wasn't the enemy, but she could be at any moment. Only when she had been drawn deeper into the HC&P network would she know why people were saying that I and no one else had murdered Ina Radekker. That would take a while, and until then I didn't have anything to worry about. As long as I was with her. I smiled.

'I've got to go to bed,' I said.

'It's about time,' she said. She pulled me out of the kitchen chair and pushed me into the hallway, turning out the lights behind me. Then she took me to the bedroom.

I undressed and got into bed, sliding between the sheets. Jessica followed. She stayed on her side for about thirty seconds, questions flying between us. Then we nestled up together. My body shook and trembled in her hands. Never had I needed sex so badly. I could no longer tell what Jessica was thinking, but judging from her body she was thinking as little as I was. The sex was hard and long, as if both of us were trying to postpone the end. Push it away. It wasn't until much later that I sensed the closeness of the other, of her—the warmth of her body and the deceptive reassurance of her smooth skin. I slept.

36

Bellilog, June 22

When my mother called in the police, my father left home. He left her. Three hours after I slipped out the back door, he closed the front door behind him. A weekend bag in one hand and his car keys in the other, that's all he needed to put an end to thirty-four years of marriage. That was a couple of days ago, and now he's gone. Dad is gone. Out of the house. He's left Mom. He had already left, but now he's left with his desk, his computer, his clothes, his books, his boots and his photos. Pete e-mailed to tell me. He was there. I wasn't. I wasn't even there when my family put an end to itself, took itself apart, dismantled itself. Since yesterday I've been a loose part, like a car bumper in a junkyard. Still a good bumper, but no more car. The whole is gone and now we're only the sum of our parts, if that, because what are the parts? Brothers and sisters—one sister, singular—and uncles and aunts, cousins—but where?—what? Parents?

This was between him and Mom, Dad said, says Pete. And God, probably, although I haven't heard anybody mention it. Better that way. But the questions are still being stripped down to their essence. Can I still go home? Is it still home? If all the parts have been replaced, is it still what it once was? Is my mother more a mother without my father? And vice versa? Because they don't interfere with each other's identity? Are the parts better without the whole? Is the bumper more a bumper without the car? Yes, of course, because then it's finally a bumper in all its glory. There's no hood or door to distract people or demand their attention. But there's nothing left to bump, either.

Something like that.

Mail from: HB2
Subject: Do you know where he is:

Mail to: HB2
Subject: Re:
In Amsterdam or Brussels. I think.

37

Be daring

Even before daybreak, the alarm began its piercing beep. Jessica's right hand gave the button a smack, and in the silence that followed she slid out of bed. I heard a couple of sounds, not many: a door, some footsteps. Then I fell back asleep and didn't wake up until Jessica squatted down next to the bed and tapped my forehead with one finger.

'Hello,' she said. 'Anybody there?'

She waved a couple of keys in front of my nose.

'Here,' she said. 'A new set of keys. To let yourself in and out. I'm going and I won't be back until about eight o'clock tonight. Maybe a little earlier. See you then, okay? Take it easy.'

I groaned and mumbled things that were supposed to sound like 'okay' and 'thank you,' but actually I was still asleep. I heard her moving around until the front door shut with a click. For the rest of the morning I was aware of nothing.

That afternoon I put her sweatpants and sweatshirt back on, went to the kitchen to look for something to eat, made some coffee and crawled over to my laptop, which I had set up in the middle of the night. Soon I was on the internet, surfing to Huib's secure site. He had shown me how to use the HC&P network to look into someone else's computer, and I wanted to give it a try. Preferably with someone I knew, one of my own clients, someone I could call while we were looking around in his computer. Using the chat feature I sent Huib to the computer of Erik Strila, head of communications at the Ministry of Justice in The Hague.

Huib found the computer without any difficulty. And faster than I expected, the documents and programs began rolling across the screen. A little while later I was looking at a document that changed on the screen as I watched.

'So he's working on it now?' I asked Huib.

'What you see on your screen is what is happening right now, at this moment, in his computer.'

'Okay,' I said. 'Give me a couple of minutes.'

I picked up my cell phone and searched for Strila's extension. He answered immediately, a little distracted at first, and surprised. He had understood from my boss that I was no longer with the firm, so he wasn't sure in what capacity I was calling him.

'You see what I'm saying?' he said.

I laughed and reassured him.

'I don't know what you've heard, but everything you've heard is true,' I said.

'Then you're really fucked,' he said.

'Probably,' I said. 'But let's not get into that. Listen, Erik, I have a couple of questions. Very simple ones. May I?'

'As long as they're not too personal.'

'What kind of computer are you working on?'

Strila responded immediately. 'Oh, on the computer I always work on at work, on my laptop. Everyone here works with them, so I do, too.'

'Laptop,' I repeated. 'Okay, what brand?'

'Datwell.'

'I thought so. Next question: are you working right now?'

'Yes.' Again without hesitation.

'Writing something?'

'Yes, a report on a meeting. Nothing special. Do you want to know what it's about?'

'No,' I said. 'I want you to type something. Just type the next sentence of your report. Don't say anything. Just type.'

'Does this have anything to do with your work, or ...?'

'Just do it,' I said. 'Please.'

For a moment nothing happened, but after a couple of

seconds the cursor began to move across the screen. Strila was writing.

'... is the most important target group,' I read aloud as the words appeared on the screen, 'and therefore ... cannot ... be ... limited ...' The more I read, the slower Strila typed, until he stopped entirely. He said nothing. I said nothing. Soon the cursor began moving again. I read: How do you know what I'm writing?

'Because I can read it here on my screen,' I said.

Strila cursed.

'And that's not all,' I said. With a couple of clicks of the mouse I opened a new menu and chose the program by which I myself could work in Strila's document. I changed a couple of sentences in his text and wrote a couple of new ones without him being able to do anything about it. Through the phone I could hear Strila's protests.

'That's impossible!' he shouted.

I saw on my screen that he had closed the document. It didn't make any difference to me. I could just keep on going. When Strila opened the document later on, he'd see that I had made a number of changes in the text. All that time, he'd never know that someone was working on his computer. There were no flashing LEDs, no additional sounds. With a highspeed connection his computer was continually on line. From the moment he turned on the laptop he was connected to the internet. That's why I could access his computer. It was normal, even though it wasn't right. But the fact that he had no way of knowing what was going on was not normal. Strila was furious, and he demanded that I stop doing whatever it was I was doing.

'Now!' he said.

'Erik, listen,' I said.

'Now!' he repeated. 'I want you to close that program now!'

'It's not my program,' I said. 'I can't close it. I wouldn't know how.'

'Okay, then I'll do it.' It was quiet for a moment. I could hear the laptop clicking and beeping through the phone. In the middle of my screen a small window appeared with the text:

Host computer shutting down.

A little while later a new text appeared in the window.

Host computer inactive.

The text in the window rolled itself into a ball that disappeared into the status bar at the lower right, where it reappeared as a small icon, a little computer with a red line running through it. But nothing else changed.

'Shit!' I said out loud.

'What's wrong?' Strila asked.

'You turned your computer off,' I said.

'Yes, what do you think? I can't allow ...'

'Erik, ERIK!' I shouted, 'you don't get it! You turned off your computer, but it doesn't make any difference! I'm still in!'

Strike cursed loudly. 'But that's impossible!' he shouted. 'I turned it off. I'll pull the plug out of the socket. There.'

No change.

'Oh, no? What about now?' said Strila.

In an instant his report disappeared from my screen and I was looking at an empty grey field. In the middle was a window with the text

Host computer unavailable.

'What did you do now?' I asked.

'Pulled out the phone cable,' Strila said.

'Okay, that helps.'

That's how the entire HC&P network worked. With today's

technology, all the computers were connected to the internet all the time. The only thing you needed was a way to get past all the security systems. That meant that all the computers, including Erik Strila's, had to contain some kind of program that would disable security. But try as he might, Huib could not find any dedicated hacking software. The M drive mainly contained the advanced program for running the network, but even that was based on the assumption that everyone could slip past security undetected.

'Try to get your hands on that laptop,' Huib wrote in the chat line.

'Why?' I asked.

'Because there has to be something in it, software or hardware, *something* that makes all the rest possible. If necessary someone will have to unscrew the thing and take a look inside.'

I could just see myself attacking the laptop with a screwdriver. I'd probably be able to open it—I could still turn screws—but then what? I was a technical dunce. I wouldn't be able to tell one part from another. I had seen a photo of a chip once in a magazine, but inside a computer it looked very different.

'You still there?' Strila's voice pulled me back to earth.

'Yes,' I said.

Strila was angry. This was an infringement of all kinds of rules. It was burgling, hacking, robbery, spying, you name it. Trying his best to control the tone of his voice, he told me he'd have to take this up with HC&P and that I'd be hearing a lot about it, even if I was no longer working for the firm.

'Erik,' I said, 'this is why I no longer work there.'

'Because you've been pulling these kinds of stunts?'

'No, because they have.'

'Oh, right. And I'm supposed to believe that?'

I explained it wasn't just a matter of pulling stunts, but

that it was an entire network, worldwide, and that inside the Ministry of Justice alone there were more than forty computers connected to it. 'And you think I'm capable of doing something complicated like this?' I asked. 'Do you believe it yourself?'

'No,' Strila said, 'I believe that even less.'

'Thank you.'

It was quiet for a moment. A new message from Huib appeared in the chat line at the bottom of my screen.

'This is taking too long. We have to get off the network.'

'Okay,' I answered, 'I'll be back this evening.'

'So you discovered this, and that's why you were fired from HC&P?' Strila asked.

'Almost,' I said. 'Someone else discovered it and she was murdered. And because I know that, I can't show my face at HC&P again.'

Strila didn't respond.

'You get it?'

'I don't want to get it,' he said.

'Good. That means you do.'

I racked my brain trying to come up with a way to get hold of his computer. I couldn't get into his office, I couldn't get into his house, and I could hardly ambush him somewhere on the street and take the thing from him.

'Erik,' I finally asked, 'do you take your laptop home every day?'

'Yes. Why?'

'Can I come over tonight and steal your computer?'

'Oh,' said Strila. 'How do you expect to do that?'

'Just ring the bell. About ten o'clock? Will that work for you?'

Clothes. I had to get some new clothes. Jessica's tracksuit was the latest thing in sportswear, but not something I could feel entirely relaxed in on the street. Light blue, pants tight around the butt and crotch, wide legs, sweatshirt emblazoned with the text *Be daring*.

It was an exhortation that actually meant something when Jessica walked around in it, but in my case it invited unwelcome attention. Now I had no choice. My own clothes were so battered that they were even more conspicuous. I put everything back in my backpack and went out the door. At Beethovenstraat I took tram 5 to the end of the line, to a shopping centre in Amstelveen. Music thundered around me at full blast while the salesman gave me a look of total amazement. His eyes moved up and down over my outfit, not once but three times. I wanted to say something but he raised his hand to silence me. He shook his head, pursed his lips and rolled his eyes.

'Hopeless,' he said finally.

'That's what I was afraid of,' I said.

'Afraid?' He shook his head again. 'What's that on your chest? The least you can do is set a good example.'

The man took me to a couple of racks all the way in the back of the shop, to the serious leisure clothing. Outdoor survival stuff. One hour later I was back outside, fully done up in the world's leading labels. I had two pairs of pants made from the same fabric that parachutes were made from, light and supple yet incredibly strong, and a Sympatex jacket that was both open weave and water-resistant, and with an endless number of pockets. I had shoes that incorporated the very latest discoveries in the science of walking, indestructible, with total traction on every conceivable surface. Not a bit of natural material was used in their manufacture.

At the Bijenkorf department store I bought a suit, ready-to-wear, no fuss, fit like a glove, brown with a yellow pinstripe, very modern and just what I needed to keep from standing out among my former colleagues and clients. White shirt, a stack of T-shirts and some underpants.

Everything disappeared into the backpack, as did Jessica's tracksuit. I bought new band-aids, a dark baseball cap, a pocket knife and cigarettes. I didn't care anymore. I wanted to smoke.

'You want a lighter with that?' asked the man behind the counter. He held up a plastic object, bright green. There were a couple of Zippos glistening in the halogen lighting one shelf higher. Accessories. I still didn't know why, but nice things often give you a certain sense of pleasure that you don't get from the cheap disposable models. I bought a Zippo, with flints and a little container of lighter fluid. There was plenty of room in the backpack, and pleasure was something I hadn't had nearly enough of lately.

I went to a sandwich shop in the middle of the shopping centre and sat down at an outdoor table off in a corner. I filled the lighter and waited for the wick to absorb the fluid. With a cigarette between my lips I flipped the little lid open and spun the wheel with my thumb. The soft yellow flame smoked for a few seconds, then calmed down. I held the end of the cigarette in the flame and inhaled. Smoke in my lungs, wonderful. I ordered coffee and called the number I'd been given by Johan Wolfsen.

'Batte,' said a rushed voice. 'Be right with you, just a minute ...'

The phone was put down and I tried to imagine what I could expect of Vince Batte. If Wolfsen was being shadowed, then theoretically any contact I had with Batte could be discovered, too. If I had the slightest suspicion that Batte was being approached by Breger and his men, in whatever way, I'd cut off the call without any explanation. The fact that he was having me wait felt wrong from the start. Yet I didn't hang up. No one knew my cell phone number so no one could know that it was me.

'I'm back,' said Batte. 'What can I do for you?'

I introduced myself, and that's all Batte needed. Wolfsen had indeed reached him and had filled him in as well. Batte talked fast, as thought he might forget his words if he spoke too slowly.

'Okay, great, your stuff is ready, so, uh, when are you coming?'

Now I hesitated. This was too easy. I couldn't tell whether he was just busy or whether someone else had told him to bring me in. 'Are you in a hurry?'

'Not me,' he laughed. 'Except for the fact that I'm always in a hurry. With software you're always on the wrong side of the time line. But Wolfsen said you had precedence, so ... whatever you want ...'

'Who else knows about this?' I asked.

'About what?'

There wasn't a bit of hesitation in his voice. None. He answered every question in the same rapid way. I asked him all kinds of questions at random to hear whether his reaction changed, got faster or slower, or whether he had to think longer about any one question.

'About the stuff?'

'Oh, that. Wolfsen and I know. And you. And Wolfsen doesn't even know what the number of your new pass is. I'm the only one who knows that.'

'What was your name again?'

'Batte. Vince Batte.'

'And exactly what kind of stuff have you got for me?' Every now and then in the background I could hear the gentle rattling sound of fingers racing across a keyboard.

'Well, *one* stuff, to be exact. Pass, complete with number, name (not yours, of course), and a code that can be recognized by the system but not registered. That kind of stuff. What we make for visiting senior officials, you know, people who are everywhere but never anywhere.'

'Are you working now?' I asked.

'Always. There's always something with that system of yours. Nice system, don't get me wrong, you can do anything with it, really, whatever you want, but it's so incredibly complex. Really, bizarre. Advanced tinkering. So what's it going to be?'

His rhythm and his entire way of doing things never varied. No matter what I asked him, he was always himself, cheerful, hurried, completely unhesitating.

'I'll come and get it,' I said. 'Where are you?'

I couldn't pick it up until the end of the afternoon, when he was back in Amsterdam. The company was somewhere on the outskirts of Amersfoort, and he was tied up for the rest of the day with meetings and testing new program components. We agreed to meet at a cafe near Central Station.

'You know 't Ponthuis?' he asked.

38

Batte

It was raining, and I was on the ferry to the other side of the IJ. According to the weather reports this was the wettest June week in I don't know how many years. Every day new storms swept across the land, supported by enormous, cocky atmospherics that had found a place to hang out above the North Sea.

The city looked quite different from the water—smaller, mainly, and lower-lying. The cyclists on the ferry and the water around it determined the proportions. Leaning on the railing of the afterdeck, I had the sense that Amsterdam had suddenly become a village, a city with a centre no more than four storeys high. It was a city built to human scale, and so unthreatening that I couldn't understand where the danger was coming from. And yet it was there, undeniably. There, behind the beautiful façades of the endless monuments, were people who wanted to do me in. Today rather than tomorrow. Yesterday would have been even better.

The ferry was moving across the water with the wind. The gusts kept overtaking us and blowing warm, fat raindrops in my face. I shook my head and felt all the places where my skin had tightened up on account of the healing wounds. The crossing took no more than five minutes, but it was long enough to chase away my agitation.

Batte was about my age, but that's where the similarities ended. He was tall and stylish, in a strange way. His dishevelled appearance was really a studied carelessness and was quite intentional, up to and including the last loose shirttail that stuck out in the back beneath his crooked black jacket. His glasses, with their heavy black frames, reinforced the impression of someone who attached no importance whatsoever to his appearance, except for the minuscule brand logo letting you know that his kind of nonchalance was not cheap. Batte was very cool and Batte was drenched. Just like me. Water was dripping from his head. There was little left of the gel composition he had created that morning. He stood beside the little table and hesitated.

'HC&P?' he asked finally.

I nodded.

'Okay,' he said and sat down.

'Not good?' I asked.

'Well, I had expected something in a suit, recent shave and all that—you know the type, someone with concept-free hair and a red tie with yellow thingies on it. Not, uh ...' He made a gesture that scattered drops of water everywhere. 'Whatever,' he said. He leaned forward and looked at the scratches and scabs on my face.

'How you doing with that?' he asked.

'Better than yesterday,' I said, hoping he'd drop the subject. I didn't feel like discussing my physical condition. It was bad enough as it was.

Batte was one hundred percent programmer, and it took a while before I realized that his head worked in a way totally different than mine. Batte thought in logical sequences, in mutually exclusive or mutually enhancing combinations, in ones and zeroes. He thought digitally. And he did it at a rate that I could scarcely keep up with.

Vince Batte could take on the computerized world. He understood how that world worked. He could build his own programs or dismantle them, whatever he wanted. He could use computers like a hammer or a pair of pliers. That was the difference. The people who are masters of technology are constantly increasing their skill set. The people who aren't fall farther and farther behind. That's the dichotomy between the makers and the users, and the disparity between them is getting bigger and bigger. In the past a journalist could still fix his own pen or typewriter if he had to, but not anymore. He can use the stuff and that's it. I myself belonged to the class of people who couldn't do anything. Communications advice had nothing to do with the way the world worked. It was the spice in a restaurant kitchen, one of the many little jars on the shelf that the chef had only occasional need for. What I did could improve the flavour, but no one could make an entire dish with it. Sitting across the table from Vince Batte made me feel small. Batte had the world at his fingertips. If he did this, then that happened. If he did that, then this happened. Logical consequences. He knew what was going to happen, and so it did. While I blundered my way through a minefield, jumping aside just in time to avoid the explosions that were going off all around me, Batte could decide where the mines were located. Up to a certain point.

'But can you get the system to tell you all the people who were present in the HC&P building on a particular night?' I asked.

'Yes.'

'Can you do it for Wednesday night a week and a half ago?'

'The night that woman from financial administration was murdered.'

He said it without hesitation. Without judging. He was the first one to leave me out of the picture. Just the events, logical and simple. Liberating.

'Her, yes,' I said.

'Already did it,' he said. 'At least, we did it.'

'You did it? Yourselves?'

'No, operations are in India. For the whole group.'

The consequences of what he said took a while to get through to me. 'Is the security system for the whole group in one place?' I asked.

Batte nodded.

'HC&P has a hundred and twenty offices all over the world, and the records of who is present in what office are all kept in one place?'

He nodded again. 'Doesn't make any fucking difference,' he said, 'whether you do it centrally or decentrally. That's all a load of crap. Words from a different era. Everything you do decentrally is linked together in a network, which makes it central, too. If you have the right codes. The only reason it's all in India is because it's much cheaper there. And those guys are amazingly good.'

'Big Brother,' I said.

'HC&P,' said Batte.

We looked at each other. 'HC&P is Big Brother?' I asked. I wasn't altogether sure what I was asking, but Batte's remark fit in too neatly with the hunted feeling I had and with the network the company maintained.

'In our world you can't get around them,' Batte said in a matter-of-fact tone as if it were common knowledge. 'At least WorldWare can't. If we weren't working for HC&P, we wouldn't be half as big as we are. And the same is true for Datwell. Maybe even more so.'

Datwell had experienced a boom in recent years. PCs, laptops, servers, entire automation systems, all of it high quality and at a price no one thought possible. Datwell had launched a price war, and so far they seemed to be winning that war on all fronts. WorldWare and Datwell had a lot in common in that regard. Apparently they had both emerged from nowhere to secure a dominant position in an extremely competitive market. HC&P worked with Datwell products and WorldWare programs. Thousands of companies all over the world did the same.

'Whatever,' said Batte again. The subject wasn't part of the discussion he was having so he set it aside. 'We worked it out the same day, zippity-zip. No big deal. Code goes in, authorization, you're done in ten minutes. Really. You and that Radekker were the only ones. And security. Nobody else.'

'Yeah, I know all about it,' I said. All these people who were certain I was the only one in the building were driving me nuts. 'Can you also find people in the system who were in the building but weren't registered? As I would be with this pass?' I held up my new plastic card.

'Of course not,' said Batte.

'Why not?'

'Because they're not registered. And you can't call up what you haven't registered. Right? Are you still with me?'

I was playing with the pass and staring at the drinks on the table. Batte was drinking a Bacardi and Coke, I had a mineral water. I had a long evening ahead of me and I wanted to hold onto whatever meagre view I had. Batte's words were spinning around in my head. What he said was logical yet I didn't feel comfortable with it. Earlier he had said that the HC&P system could do anything, yet the first thing I asked about was something it couldn't do.

'That doesn't make any sense,' I said.

'No, not when you put it that way,' he said, 'but you can't take out what you don't put in.'

'If I were to enter with this pass, I wouldn't be registered. Okay, I understand that. But doesn't the system have another place for registering the entrance of a non-registered person? In other words, isn't there something else in the system that you *can* take out as long as you know it's in there?'

Batte fell silent and began thinking. He drank his Bacardi and put the glass down, very slowly and with great control.

'Go on,' he said.

'I was there and Radekker was there. The two of us are known quantities and we come rolling out of the system as neat as you please. But I know there were at least two and probably three other people in the building. They don't show up in the system. At least not when you ask the standard question: who were the registered individuals present? But they were there! I know it, and if I know it, then the system knows it, too.'

'You better believe it,' said Batte. 'What that system doesn't know isn't worth knowing.'

'Exactly,' I said. 'Except the system only gives you an answer if you ask the right question.'

'That's the basic principle of every system.'

'Okay,' I said, 'so the question is: what is the question?'

'Very good,' said Batte. He smiled. 'And are you asking me?'

'Am I asking you? I have no idea what I can and cannot ask.'

'You have an unregistered VIP pass. I think you can ask a whole lot of questions.'

'Just don't send me a bill,' I said.

'I'll jiggle the hours in between some other shit,' he said, and I thought I sort of understood what he meant. I figured that anyone who used that kind of language would never let himself be taken in by Huib Breger. 'Where can I reach you?' he asked.

'You can't,' I said. 'I don't exist and I'm not here. And I'd like to keep it that way.'

I wrote down his home address, somewhere on one of the islands east of the station. Java Island. 'I'll find you,' I said. 'How are you with hardware, by the way?'

'Hardware is peanuts,' he said. 'Even you can do it.'

With that misunderstanding fresh in mind I took the train to The Hague. Erik Strila lived on a lovely, spacious street, the two sides divided by a wide green strip running down the middle. Big trees gave the avenue the character of a park. The bus stopped on the corner of the street, and as darkness approached I searched for the house number. There was silence all around me. In this neighbourhood there were no cafes or restaurants, no snack bars or discos. The bus was the most exciting thing around, and it was only passing through. The whole area was pervaded by the deep security that came with permanent appointments and Swedish cars amidst a generous use of Dutch bricks. It felt strange, almost unseemly.

Strila opened the door and let me in. He was curt. There was no trace of his usual easy manner. Without a word or a question he led me to the dining room. His laptop was on the table. He stood in the doorway and pointed at it.

'There,' he said.

I walked over to the laptop and picked it up, held it in my hands, turned it over and over, looked at the top and the bottom and put it back down. It was indeed a Datwell. Very similar to my own laptop.

'Have you spoken to anyone about this yet?' I asked?

Strila shook his head.

'You sure?'

'What's sure?' he said, in an attempt to inject his own insecurity into the conversation. I understood why he would want to do that, but this wasn't the right moment.

'Yes is sure and no is sure,' I said.

'No,' he said, 'I have not spoken to anyone about this.' It was as if this forced pronouncement served to free him from his self-imposed silence. 'And what if I had spoken to someone about it? Because that's what I should have done, you know. You know I should have reported it immediately. This is a serious violation of our ...'

I raised my hand in the air as a sign of surrender and to let him know that he didn't have to continue.

'I know,' I said.

We stood side by side, staring at his computer. It held our attention captive, like a strange, half-dead beast. It seemed to have a life of its own. The outside looked familiar, but there were things happening inside that were not supposed to be happening. There had to be something in there, something that could be found. I didn't know what it was, but I hoped Vince Batte could succeed in finding it with a couple of different kinds of screwdrivers.

'And you say there are more computers in our department that you can just break into from the outside?' Strila asked.

'About forty, yes,' I said, 'but you can't just break into them. First you have to have access to a certain network.'

'And you do?'

'Yes,' I said, 'but that was not my intention.'

I quickly explained to Strila what was going on. I had to tell him something, but at the same time I was eager to leave. The sooner I could get his laptop out of the house, the better I'd like it. I wanted to get out, get moving. As long as I was in motion I felt safe. In a bus or in the train. Fine. The longer I sat still anywhere, the more nervous I became.

39

Fucking eyes

The tram began its ride across the Damrak with a shriek. I was almost alone in the carriage, staring blankly out the window at the passing city, happy that for a moment there wasn't anything I had to think about. I got out at Beethovenstraat and walked the last few hundred metres to Jessica's upstairs apartment. Lights were on. That meant she was home, and that made me feel good. Jess and I were too important for each other. Any doubt I had felt yesterday had more to do with me than with her. I was the one being hunted, not her. And no matter what she said, when I was with her I no longer felt threatened. I went inside and bounded up the steep stairway to the second floor, taking two steps at a time.

Just before I reached the top I saw Jessica's long blond hair hanging down from the uppermost step. She was lying on her side, her head half turned, eyes wide open, staring at the ceiling and seeing nothing. Her mouth hung open as if she were still gasping for air. Too late, much too late.

'JESSICA!' I screamed, and jumped up the last steps.

'Fuck, he's in!' someone shouted from the kitchen, and just then a man came storming into the hallway. He grabbed me and tore me away from Jessica. With his arms clamped around my chest he beat on my back with his head. I heard bumping in one of the other rooms. This man wasn't alone, and if I didn't do something fast I'd soon be lying next to Jessica. I had to get out, as fast as I could. All my senses were concentrated on the next moment. All my thoughts, all my reflections, all my interests merged here. I saw and heard everything just before it happened. I thrust my foot backwards and kicked the man hard in the shin. At the same time I rammed my elbow back into his chest. He loosened his grip somewhat and I dropped down. I rolled over and tried to get to the stairs, but he was faster. He slid around me and took a swing. I ducked down, away from his fist, and kicked his knee. He cursed and dove onto me. Then he grabbed me from the front, his arms locked around my chest, but before he could immobilize me I jumped up, grabbed the wide ornamental frame at the top of the stairwell and pulled my legs upward, ramming my knees into his stomach with all my might. The man groaned and let me go, just for a moment. He gasped for air, and in that half second I planted my feet on his chest and shoved him down—two feet at once, suspended from my arms, all my muscle power free to let him have it. And I did.

He went down the steep stairway in an arc head first, crashing onto his back. Two other men came into the hall behind me. I looked around and in a flash I saw Breger's face, grinning behind the monolithic head of a massive, well-trained figure.

'GRAB HIM!' shrieked Breger. The man dove onto me, fists flying like a battering ram, and he hit me right under my backpack in the middle of my back.

The pain spread from my spine to every part of my body. For a minute I thought it was all over. Finished. End of story. The punch sent me sailing. I let go of the frame and jumped, right behind the first man. Free from the wall, free from the floor, I glided at top speed down the steps in a perfect line to where the first man was trying to right himself.

I landed in the middle of his chest, ramming him back down with my falling weight, and under my feet I heard his ribs crack. The big body sprang up in a spastic response, and the next moment he went even further down the stairs, shrieking with pain. I jerked the front door open, flew outside and slammed the door behind me. Then I groped around in my pocket for the keys, and as I listened to the men racing down the stairs behind the door, I stuck the key into the deadbolt and turned it. My body trembling, I stood at the door and waited, but no matter how hard the two men on the other side tugged and pounded, the door would not open. The only way they could get out was by opening the deadbolt from the inside. Cursing and shouting, they stamped back upstairs. I leaned forward, stuck the key back in the lock and left it there. Then I turned around and walked to the end of the street, where it ran into Olympia Square. Every step I took was a misstep. I walked as if my feet were no longer mine. Every time I put my feet down, it wasn't the hard paving stones I felt but the man's chest cracking beneath my soles.

Pain was shooting from my back to my legs and neck. I kept on walking, unsteadily, stone by stone. In those silent, wide streets I was suddenly further from home than ever. In all that time I had thought that sooner or later, somewhere, I would find the evidence I needed to prove that I wasn't the only one in the HC&P building and that the problems would disappear one by one. Just prove that I wasn't the murderer and that would be that. Not too ridiculous a hope, right?

But now it would scarcely solve anything. I had sunk so low that I figured I might as well give myself up to the police. At least there I'd be safer and there was little chance that I'd be making my situation worse.

The dark Audi on the corner of the street looked like so many other luxury cars. First I walked past it, until I recognized the damaged front fender. It was Breger's car. Cautiously I walked around it. No one was inside. The doors were locked. Tiny red alarm lights blinked on the doors. I lowered myself onto the edge of the sidewalk and took the little container of lighter fluid from one of the side pockets of my backpack. I flipped the nozzle up and squirted a good-sized jet of fluid over one of the car's rear tires. Then I took the lighter from my pants pocket, pushed the cap open and spun the wheel. With great caution I held the little flame up to the tire and immediately the fire began to envelop it. From a distance I squirted on a bit more fluid until the fire took hold. Then I walked around the car and lit up the other rear tire. It wasn't until I had gone around the corner, leaving the car smouldering and burning behind me, that I knew how helplessly angry I was. I wanted to strike out, kick, bite if necessary. Suddenly the fact that I had hit one of them hard didn't matter to me anymore. At the very most it hadn't been hard enough, and that realization struck me like an incoming tidal wave. I had ended up in another world, where life was not an unquestioned right. If I wasn't careful I'd be handing in my own life before I knew it.

Limping, I hurried on to Stadionweg and just managed to catch a late tram bound for Central Station, dropping into one of the seats in the back. As the tram rode away I could see an orange fire blaze up in the distance. Soon the fire disappeared from sight. The tram moved on. The hard little bench was an uncomfortable place to sit. No matter how much I shifted back and forth, I could find no position that would alleviate the pain in my back. I clasped my arms around the backpack on my lap and rested my head against the stiff synthetic fabric jabbing my cheeks. Tears ran from my eyes.

Jessica.

I cursed, very loudly, and my voice boomed through the carriage. The few other people in the tram looked around, annoyed. I was the umpteenth Amsterdam loony riding in a public conveyance, nothing more. I saw their reaction. I knew their reaction. One week ago I would have done the same thing: look around, eyebrows raised, provoked expression. It was counterproductive. What do you mean, provoked? Annoyed?

'KEEP YOUR FUCKING EYES TO YOURSELF!' I screamed at

a man who had turned around, and I kicked the seat ahead of me, harder than I thought, probably because my brain was completely disengaged. The seat cracked but remained intact. Soon the tram came to a halt at the corner of Stadion-weg and Beethovenstraat. The driver got out of his seat and walked the full length of the tram, stopping at the seat right in front of me. He placed a hand on the back of that seat and bent forward toward me, only very slightly.

'What's this all about?' he said. 'You can get out here if you want.'

I tried to say something—I no longer remember what—but my lips trembled uncontrollably and suddenly the only sounds I could produce were gibberish. My arms still clamped around my backpack with the two laptops as the hard core of my existence, I began rocking slowly back and forth. Jessica was dead. She was no longer there. Her crazy, free-spirited way of life, searching for extremes to keep the remorseless precision of her brain in check, was no more. Not because she wanted it (this was the last thing she wanted) but because someone else had decided it was enough. She was dead, not because I didn't trust her but because she had done something she shouldn't have done. Thoughts grinding circles in my head, like ruts in a road. The tram driver leaned a little further toward me.

'Okay, we all have a hard day every now and then,' he said. He put a hand on my shoulder and pushed me gently so my back was pressed against the back of the seat. I almost jumped out of my skin from the pain. My face contracted into a grimace and I clamped my jaws together. There would be no more screaming here. Control was what I needed, and this was the moment to get it back.

'Hard day,' I said, squeezing the words out between my lips. Tears streamed down my cheeks. This was beyond the reach of my powers of control.

'Right,' said the driver, and he let go of my shoulder. I

immediately leaned forward on my arms to take the tension off my back.

'So we're going to calm down?' he asked.

I nodded. 'Calm down,' I said.

'Great,' he said, and he looked at me. Something wasn't right. He saw it, too, but whether it was the nighttime or the late hour or problems with his wife or something else, he didn't take it any further. 'You see now?' said the man. 'It's not so hard.' And with an encouraging pat on my back he returned to his seat.

Slowly I dropped down even further. The pain was unbearable. The comforting pat was more than my vertebrae could bear. I noticed that it was growing darker. Darker and quieter. I couldn't drop forward any further because I was jammed against the back of the seat in front of me. The two laptops in the backpack on my lap were keeping me upright, though I myself was incapable of realizing it.

40

An unnatural angle

It wasn't until the tram made its turn crossing the bridge in front of the station, wheels shrieking, that I came to. The shrill sound tore through everything and jerked me out of my stupor, back to my conscious state, where the first thing to be registered was pain. I was still alive.

Just barely.

I heaved myself upright, got out of the tram and looked across the square in front of the station. It was busy. The police were patrolling in pairs, checking people everywhere. Groups here, single individuals there. Confrontation hung in the air like a scent, sharp and hard. Opinions were being shouted like weapons in an endless battle. Boys, men—always men—in search of the punch they're eager to deliver and the punch that hits home.

There were puddles on the dark square from an earlier rain. Now it was dry, but the air was so saturated that it still soaked you through. I dragged myself listlessly to the other end of the station. I don't know why. I walked for the sake of walking, the backpack pushing against the sensitive spot with every step I took. After a couple of paces I hung it from my shoulder.

On the other side of the square was the big Ibis Hotel. Slowly I walked to the middle strip with trams on the left and the right, the triangular area that extends to the bridge, and there I stopped. I had been walking around for at least ten minutes and hadn't gone one step further. This was the tip of Amsterdam well past midnight, the city I wasn't going to leave until I had solved my problems, and I hadn't gotten any further than the front door. Or the back door. A couple of steps further back and I'd be floating in the IJ, tossed out of the city, washed out to the IJsselmeer—or the North Sea (I didn't even know what direction the water flowed in).

My city. My life. I could preface everything with 'my' without having to know anything about it. My country, my job, my work, my family, my brother. Each time it seemed that nothing and no one really cared about me at all. My job was gone, my work wasn't what I was told it would be, my family had fallen apart and my brother wasn't even a brother. My life was no more than a memory. A vague memory. Every day more details disappeared, things I still thought were immutable two weeks ago. Permanent. My life was shaped by people and by who they were. Because of them I knew who I was. Where I was. Without people all that was left were things, and things never become friends.

And my Jessica, I thought, even though she wasn't my Jessica anymore. It was the knowledge that she could never be my Jessica again that made her my Jessica, in my head, where suddenly everything was going on. I sat on a bench and looked at the Damrak, dressed up like a party without a purpose. The ugliest street in the Netherlands, ruined forever by cheap cafes and bad urban design. The party was fake. In fact there was no party, at least not any that I had noticed.

The rain resumed its duties and fat drops began falling on my head, my shoulders and my legs. I knew what I had to do. Of course I knew what I had to do. It was the last thing I wanted to do, but I had no choice. What Jessica had told me about the assignments she was working on and the significance of that work was too scanty, too thin. She had confirmed my suspicions, but no more than that. It was beginning to look more and more like RISC was HC&P's main project. When I looked around on the internet I found references everywhere. If I wanted to learn anything about it I'd have to go to the office now, as soon as possible, before her things were cleared away and before every trace of Jessica Polse had been erased. The best time would be the middle of the night. The night watchmen didn't know who was who, and with my new pass I could get into the building without anyone thinking anything of it. All I had to do was to act as if I belonged there, and all I needed to bring it off was a suit and a shirt. Which I had.

I checked into the Ibis, paid in advance, and went up to my room. Once I got inside, in the safety of the closed space, my functions began to break down. Moving became increasingly difficult. Without painkillers I couldn't do anything. My back was a wreck. I chewed five paracetamols into paste, one by one, and swallowed them down with plenty of water. Then I carefully undressed and folded the damp clothes into a small packet. I threw my underwear away (I had no desire to walk around with dirty laundry). In the bathroom I took the old band-aids off my face, washed, and dabbed my face dry, very carefully. I did as little as possible. No shower, no bath, no shaving, nothing. I had to avoid any form of relaxation, because if I were to unwind now there would be no energy left.

With the little scissors that came with the pocket knife I cut band-aids into tiny strips and stuck them over the wounds, straight and neat. I took a clean change of underwear from the backpack and a pair of clean socks, the suit and the shirt. Then I slowly dressed. The new clothes were dry and clean and soft. I put cigarettes and lighter in the pockets of my jacket, put my pocket knife in a pants pocket and my wallet in an inside pocket. I stuffed the damp clothing in a separate compartment of the backpack. Then I put the dark baseball cap on my head and pulled the visor down over my eyes. In the mirror I looked very slick. All of it fake.

I went downstairs, put my key on the counter and left. It was way after one o'clock by the time I climbed into a taxi and gave the driver the address of HC&P. The car glided through Amsterdam to the strange sounds of Arabic disco. The driver left me to myself, which suited me fine. Every few minutes he barked something into a microphone and received a scratchy response. I slumped down in the seat beside him, my backpack between my knees, and thought I could easily spend the rest of the night there. Just driving, into the city, out of the city, funky whining coming from the speakers, man at the steering wheel who was fine with everything as long as I paid my fare. And money was no object.

I had the taxi stop on the Parnassusweg access road. After giving the driver a hundred euros I told him to wait until I was back.

'This might take a while,' I said.

The man flipped the two fifty euro notes between his fingers and said, 'For a hundred and fifty I'll wait until seven o'clock tomorrow morning.'

'No longer than that?' I asked, as I gave him a third fifty-euro note.

'I go off duty at seven.' He laughed. 'After that you're on your own.'

I stepped out of the car with caution, leaving my backpack behind.

'Before you go off duty, I'll be back,' I said. 'Don't go away.'

I crossed the street, walked under the overpass and continued along the back of the Atrium building to the new towers next to the World Trade Center. Without hastening my steps I proceeded to the entrance. For a moment I was afraid sirens would start wailing all over the place and I'd be overtaken by security guards. For a moment. I dismissed the thought from my mind, took out the pass Batte had given me and held it up to the scanner. The scanner emitted a brief peep, the red light turned green and the glass doors slid open. Wolfsen had kept his word and Vince Batte had delivered the goods. I took a deep breath, tightened all my reluctant body parts and walked into the entrance hall.

The night watchman was looking at the TV screen behind the counter. My heart was in my throat. If I could get past this, the rest would be simple. Everything depended on my ability to act normally. I put my left hand in my pocket, waved with the pass in my right hand and sauntered to the security gate as if I didn't feel a thing, as if the pain in my back wasn't there at all. With the new suit and the cap, I was just eccentric enough to pass for a midnight consultant.

'Evening,' I said.

'Late one?' responded the man. I had never seen him before. So far so good.

'And it'll be even later before I'm done,' I said. I held my pass up to the next scanner with an experienced gesture. The gate peeped and let me through.

'Take a fall?' asked the night watchman, pointing to the band-aids on my face.

'Marital abuse,' I said. 'Why do you think I'm here so late?' He laughed and I passed through the gate and into the hall where the elevators were. In four more steps I was out of his field of vision, so he didn't see me get in the elevator with much less nonchalance, dragging my leg behind me.

What I didn't see were the instructions all the security personnel had been given, which included reporting all unplanned visits by personnel outside normal office hours. At HC&P that was eight o'clock in the evening. I didn't see that, and I certainly didn't see that my visit was actually being reported.

What I did see were the cameras that were aimed at the most important areas of the building. They registered persons in the elevators and in the hall directly in front of the elevators on every floor, as well as a couple of other places. No matter how good my pass was, the night watchman didn't need to know where in the building I was going. I took the elevator to the fifth floor, got out, walked down one of the corridors all the way to the end, beyond the reach of the camera, and took the stairs up to the ninth. Before I began climbing I took a strip of paracetamols out of my pocket and popped two more into my mouth. I chewed them without water, swallowed them and began limping up the stairs.

I finally emerged four floors higher in the corridor I was aiming for. No cameras there, either. Even if someone were to come looking for me, he'd have to check every floor, and the building was large. As far as that was concerned I wasn't in a hurry, but the sooner I was able to get back outside the better I would feel.

The office was deserted. I left the lit corridor and entered the dark work area, the large room filled with hot desks. Next to the door were the carts, all lined up neatly. I didn't turn the lights on in the room or everyone outside would immediately see where I was. Gazing into the semi-darkness, I examined the carts by the light of the corridor. There were sixteen of them and they all looked exactly the same. The lowest part of each cart, right above the wheels, was a compartment with a door that could be locked. That was meant for work materials. All the documents containing information about clients were supposed to be kept behind the little locked door. Above that was a shelf where all kinds of office supplies were kept: pens, pencils, paper-clips. And above that was a bookshelf that was tipped slightly backward to keep the books from falling out. Most people kept reference books on those shelves and usually a couple of folders and binders related to their work, simply because the locked compartment was too small for all the things you might accumulate over the course of a project. It was like the whole idea of the hot desk, which didn't take into account the fact that you needed to have all your project-related materials close by, within reach. Or at least more than you could fit on your desk.

The carts had nameplates on the handles. Gijs's was there. Mine wasn't. As childish as it may seem, I felt this as an unjust snub, a wound I didn't deserve. Against my better judgment I looked one more time to make sure I hadn't missed it. Idiotic. And stupid, too. I had to keep from being tempted by such trivialities. I didn't have time for it, and if Breger got his way I wouldn't have the breath for it, either. Priorities were more important than ever.

Jessica's cart was there. I took the handle and pulled it over to the closest chair. Then I took a desk lamp, bent it down and turned it on so the light shone directly onto the cart. Seated, I took a quick look at the uppermost shelf. Two folders, one with information on an assignment for an oil company and the other with reports of the steering committee meetings of a health care facility. The rest were books and old reports, reference material. Nothing interesting. I felt the door of the lowest compartment. Locked. Logical. Most of us kept the key on the shelf among the pens and other paraphernalia. I pulled it forward and looked. Jessica had placed a kind of cutlery organizer there so the various things had their own compartments, but no matter how hard I looked I still couldn't find any key.

I opened my pocket knife and stuck the point between the compartment door and the side of the cart. The lock was small, more a design element than something to provide protection. I pushed the blade in as far as I could and began prying. The cracking and scraping sounded ridiculously loud in the silent space. Instinctively I stopped to listen. I heard nothing. It was quiet in the corridor, and the only sounds were vague noises from outside making their way in. So vague that it took a minute before I realized just what I was hearing. A slamming car door. Not something you'd expect at this time of night. I was here, and if anyone else were to come into the building I wanted to know who it was. I jumped out of the chair, cursed my back and rushed to the window. Standing off to the side I looked down below to the road running along the front of the building. It was difficult to see in the dark from nine storeys up, but I could identify the makes of cars from great distances. Parked along the sidewalk was a dark Audi. It couldn't have been the same one whose tires I had set fire to a couple of hours before. Evidently the gentlemen weren't short on cars. A man was standing on the driver's side, slightly bent over and talking to the man behind the wheel. Soon a third man came out of the front door of the building. He made a beckoning motion. The man next to the car walked to the front door and they both went inside. The last man parked the car right in front of the building.

Wherever I was, they were there, too, each time with greater confidence and an even clearer sense of mission. There was little wrong with this team in organizational terms. The only thing they lacked was success, and I wasn't about to sit around and wait for that to happen. I crept back to the cart on my hands and knees, hoisted myself onto the chair, set one foot against the pocket knife, and with one kick the little door sprang open.

The compartment was crammed with folders and papers, far too many to peruse at my leisure. Every second I stayed in this room was too long. The night watchman might not know where I was, but Huib Breger would make a beeline for this floor and this room. If he had stopped at the desk and had seen the images of my entrance, he'd know it was me and he'd also know where I was. I had to get away, and in order to take the documents with me I needed a bag. I looked around, but all I saw were the empty desks and the carts standing in a row beside the door. I tried to visualize the owners of the carts. Which one of them would have a plastic bag. Thomas? No, too fashionable. Not Frans, either. Gijs? Yes, Gijs would. Of course Gijs would have one. He had come to the office more than once with a plastic bag.

I grabbed his cart and pulled the shelf open. In the back was the key to the lower compartment. I quickly opened the door, and there to the right, in a corner next to the folders, were three plastic bags, all neatly folded up into little squares. One from the Albert Heijn, one from the Edah and one from the Bijenkorf. I hurried back to Jessica's cart and jammed as many papers into the bags as I could. Then I turned off the desk lamp and stepped into the corridor. The painkillers worked as long as I didn't make any exaggerated moves, but now I had no choice. I ran, raced—not to the elevators, because any minute now Breger could come walking out of one of them, but back to the stairwell at the corridor's end. The bags were hanging heavily from my arms. Every step reverberated down my spine. I leaned against the door, pushed it open and slipped out of the corridor, and as the door closed behind me I heard the polite ding-dong sound of the elevator. I had a headstart, but I wouldn't be able to hold onto it for long. This was the same route Breger had taken with the body of Ina Radekker. He knew exactly how to get in and out of the building, and he wouldn't need more than five minutes to be on my tail.

I couldn't stay in the stairwell. It was too far down and I was too slow. I had to get out before they came in, so they wouldn't know what floor I was on. The sooner I got out the better, so I went down to the eighth, and back into the corridor. I raced to the central hall, pushed the elevator buttons and waited. As soon as the door opened I leaned forward and pushed the button for the top floor, but I myself stayed out in the hall. When the door closed I ran into the next corridor and down to the far end of the other wing of the building. The handles of the bags were cutting into my hands. Bumping and bouncing, I went down the stairs. More and more urgently, faster and faster—or so I thought. Actually I no longer knew what I thought. I needed all my concentration just to stay upright. Then on the floor below me I saw the door swing open, but it was too late. I was half-way between the fourth and third floors, and suddenly the man from the security service was standing in front of me. In the middle of the stairwell. He looked up, his expression blank and hard.

'I thought so,' he said, and his right hand slid over to the blunt club on his belt.

Without even thinking I turned around and began limping up the stairs. It was a no-go. I hadn't taken three steps before I realized I had made the wrong decision. Going up was a dead-end street, in every respect. I turned around again and looked down. The guard was coming after me, his movements calm and controlled. Here I had no more to lose. Anything was better than Breger, I thought. Anything. And then I thought some more. I thought that when I was in the hotel I should have shaved, for instance, that I should have taken a bath. I thought that, too. Nice, warm, gentle thoughts, while I pressed the bags to my chest, bent my knees slightly and took off. In one smooth curve I dove down, right on top of the man. The bags and papers broke my fall, but my whole body was creaking and tearing. I ended up a couple of steps below him, my feet pointed down. I had let go of the bags. The man above me jumped up with a resilience that I could only remember from a former life. I couldn't even work in a seated position anymore.

Half hidden under one of the bags beside me was the club. I grabbed it, held it in a concealed position and waited until he came down to the step just above me, the big shoes in front of my nose, the dark grey pants with piping along the side seams. I saw every detail with crystal clarity, and then I struck. With all the strength I had, I hit him on the ankle just above the opening of his shoe. The club landed right on the protruding bone. It cracked. I heard it crack. In the silent stairwell with its bare concrete walls it sounded loud and clear. Shattering bone. For a fraction of a second nothing happened. Deadly silence. Then the man started bellowing as the pain surged through his leg. He grabbed onto the banister. At that moment I completely lost all control. All I could see were the feet of the man above me. My powers of observation were reduced to what I had to break, what I had to smash through in order to get away. My life depended on someone else's ankles, and I had no problem doing something about it. So I laid into the other ankle like a wild man. Three, four times I bashed the club against the man's ankle joint. I kept on beating until the man let go of the railing and toppled over. He lay diagonally across the stairs, wailing and shrieking, both feet hanging at an unnatural angle at the far end of his body.

I quickly grabbed the bags, swept up the papers and stuffed them back in. Then I carefully stepped over the man. I didn't even recognize him. He didn't know me, either. It didn't look as if we were about to become great pals. His walkie-talkie began crackling.

'Rob?' came a voice that I would gradually learn to recognize anywhere. Breger was looking for his man. 'Rob, where are you?'

I grabbed the device, pulled the wires out and tossed it away. Then I went downstairs, stumbling and staggering, past the ground floor and into the parking garage. Using the pass, I opened the gate at the back and went out. No one was there. I walked to the side of the grounds, climbed over the barrier to Strawinskylaan, crossed the road and slid down the slope on the other side, through the wet earth and thick bushes. Then I followed the bike path back to Parnassusweg, opened the door of the taxi and dropped onto the seat.

'I'm back,' I said.

The driver looked at me and said nothing. The jacket of my suits was in tatters, the pants were torn from front to back, all the buttons on the shirt were gone, my eyes were so swollen that I could hardly see, I'd lost the cap and the mud from the slope was everywhere.

He looked at the little clock on his dashboard. It was three-twenty.

'With time to spare,' he said.

41

Deeper and deeper under my skin

If you want family, you've got to be family.

It may not have been the best moment to start, but it was the only moment I had. I didn't want to go back to the hotel. The thought of a closet of a room with a reproduction of some painting screwed to the wall and a printed card for writing down your complaints and suggestions was more than I could take. The room had no mini-bar and there was no room service. There was no service at all, in fact, and without service in a hotel you're very, very alone. I didn't want that. I didn't want to be alone, and I was in serious need of care. Lots of care. Ten minutes later the taxi pulled up to Hondecoeterstraat. The driver helped me out and set the backpack and the plastic bags down next to me on the sidewalk.

'Okay?' he asked.

We both knew the answer was 'no' but I said 'yes,' because what are you supposed to do in a situation like that? I had what I wanted and I was where I wanted to be. Even that was a lot. I could have started complaining, of course, and to be honest I really felt like a good gripe, but I just didn't have the energy. Moaning was all I could manage.

The taxi slowly drove away trailing snatches of song, a bungee-jumping voice sawing away to a steady beat. I looked around. Hondecoeter was one of those streets you could be directed to a hundred times and still not be able to find, a respectable street in a respectable neighbourhood, a street that makes no impression whatsoever. Between Nicolaas Maes and Frans van Mieris. The houses seemed taller because the street was narrower. Optical illusion.

For the zillionth time I was standing in front of a door. I

hadn't known I had it in me, but calling on other people turned out to be one of my basic skills. I lugged the backpack and the bags up to the door, and in the dimness of the streetlights, which were just a little too far away, I searched for the names next to the doorbells.

Third floor. Kirsten, it said, without any last name. No one would ever be able to find me here. Because I don't have a sister.

I rang the bell and had to wait a long time for a response. Didn't matter. I wasn't in a hurry. Hesitantly the door opened a crack.

'Yes?' I heard. 'Who's there?'

'Me,' I said. Totally indistinct, but evidently just the sound of my voice was enough because the door slowly began to open. Kirsten looked at me, and what she saw bore no resemblance to what she knew. I was no longer the same man who had come to meet her at the airport. I was no longer the brother she thought I was. She recognized me immediately, but it thinned out after that. I saw it in her eyes, that dizzy about-face that I had felt once myself. One-one, I thought, grabbing onto the door frame.

That was all I could manage.

She lugged me inside and dragged me up the stairs. Three floors up was higher than I thought it would be. They built the ceilings higher in the respectable neighbourhoods, so the stairs were steeper. Amsterdam at its narrowest is always a stairwell. It was endless. Up we went, step by step. Every few steps I had to stop, lean against the wall and release the tension from my back. I was living around a core of pain. Colours were dancing before my eyes, colours that weren't really there, green and yellow, purple. Blue stripes on black. Or was it white? If it turned orange I knew I was done for. I knew it for sure. Orange made me dizzy, always did.

When we got to the third floor she pushed the door open to the front room, and very carefully, step by step, she led me to a large couch.

'Just sit here,' she said.

I sat down in silence, searching for words so I'd have something to say.

'Dad's gone,' I said. I don't know where that came from, but it was the only thing I could think of. Typical.

'About time,' she said, and with those two words I knew I had come to the right place. The only place. Kurt wasn't gone. He was still here. He just wasn't Kurt anymore.

With her hands on my shoulders she pushed me gently to the side until I was lying on the couch. Then she pulled off my shoes and socks and straightened my legs. Now I began losing touch, and it happened so quickly that I had to struggle just to wrench a few words from my flickering consciousness.

'Backpack,' I said. 'Bags.'

'What bags?' she asked.

'Sidewalk.'

'Okay, I'll get them. Don't worry.'

Don't worry. That was just what I wanted to hear. Kurt and I understood each other. We always had. Eyes shut, still all those colours flashing wildly through my head. I heard her go out of the room and down the stairs.

The couch wasn't working. The cushions were too soft, and after just a few seconds my back began hurting so much that I knew I couldn't stay there. I rolled onto my side and gingerly tried to slide myself onto the floor, but the displacement of weight caused the cushions to shift and I landed right on the planks, my chin on the wood and my teeth clenched, and not by choice. I was lying on my stomach. Carefully raising my arms, I pushed my hands under my face. I was lying flat on a hard surface, and although my knees, arms and face were not in full agreement, my back felt blissful. The colours stopped, and finally it began to grow dark. I think I may have heard her coming back upstairs, but it also could have been the beating of my heart. As familiar as climbing stairs.

I woke up with a thin pillow under my head and a stiff body. Everything was locked. My arms and legs no longer responded to my commands. Even my fingers didn't seem to understand what they were supposed to do. A thin blanket had been drawn up over me and I couldn't get it to budge. I was probably groaning, because a little while later Kirsten came and sat beside me on the floor. Daylight all around her.

'Are you still there?' she asked.

'Barely.'

'Can you stand up?'

I shook my head, and even that was almost impossible.

'You're going to have to get up anyway,' she said.

'Wait. Just a minute,' I said. 'Before you start pulling me, my back ...'

'Your back? Does your back hurt?'

I nodded.

'Whereabouts?'

'In the middle. My vertebrae.'

She disappeared from my field of vision and pulled off the blanket, and soon I felt her fingers sliding across my back, cautiously exploring, feeling, and occasionally pressing down slightly. Every other centimetre she asked me, 'Here?' and as soon as I said no she let her fingers slide further.

'Here?'

'No.'

She was barely touching me. Between her fingertips and the spot on my back there was still a shirt and jacket, or what was left of them, but when she touched the spot I screamed.

'Okay,' she said. 'So it's here.'

'Yes.'

'Fine. Don't move.' She stood up, went out of the room and came back with a pair of scissors. She cut my jacket and shirt open up to the collar and pulled the two halves back so she could see what was going on. Nothing happened. She didn't say a word and she didn't touch me. She just looked.

'And have you had this long?' she finally asked.

'Since last night.'

'Hm mm,' she said, and once again she disappeared from sight. Her fingers glided around the centre of the pain. Every now and then she pushed lightly, squeezed a bit. It felt good. The dominance of the pain subsided somewhat.

'Very active after that?' she asked.

'Reasonably.'

'Is that all?'

'That was more than enough.'

She stopped and sat down next to me again, where I could see her. 'Okay,' she said. 'Are you going to tell me what's going on or what?'

'As if you've ever told me anything,' I said, which was exactly what I knew I shouldn't have said because it was so stupid. I was taking a swipe at her and she couldn't answer back. What was she supposed to say? I didn't want to go into detail either, certainly not now that I could hardly move, being nailed to the floor. The ideal position for saying stupid things. But these moments choose themselves, and you have to trust them up to a certain point.

'That's true,' said Kirsten, 'but there are some things that are best talked about when you can show what you mean, otherwise it's just a lot of theoretical hot air. And I'm not like that. I'm not theoretical.'

'No,' I said.

'Otherwise, you're right.'

'Great,' I said. 'Just the kind of right I need to be.'

Neither of us spoke.

'Pills,' I said.

She left the room and came back with two paracetamols.

'More,' I said, and put the first two in my mouth.

'I do realize that you had nowhere else to go,' she said after a while, 'but even so, I'm glad you're here.'

'Me too.'

'Definitely.'

'It may not look like it,' I said, 'but I'm gladder than you think.'

More silence.

'Partly, at least.'

'And the other part?'

'Everything there is wrecked.'

'Here, you mean?' She pointed to my back.

I shook my head. 'No,' I said, 'that just hurts.'

'You have to accept who I am,' she said.

'Yes.'

'Otherwise we're going to have problems.'

'Tell me about it.'

'I'm serious.'

Gradually my limbs began moving again. Our hands brushed against each other. 'I do know who you are,' I said, 'but when I look at you, I don't know who I am anymore, you know what I mean? You haven't just changed yourself. You've changed me, too.'

'And I shouldn't have done that?'

'No, that's not it.'

'Are you sure?'

'Sure I'm sure, don't even think about it. You are who you are. But since you've stopped being Kurt, I've stopped being myself.'

'That's exactly the kind of theoretical hot air I was talking about,' she said. 'What do you mean?' She squatted down next to me and grabbed my arm. Then very carefully she rolled me on my side. 'First of all, you have to sit up.' She folded my legs and pulled me up to a sitting position. Then she stood in front of me, planted her feet on my toes, grabbed my hands and pulled me to my feet. Pain shot through my body. I knew she was right, that I had to do something to counteract the stiffness, but my body just wanted to remain prone. Finally I stood up and my divided shirt and jacket dropped to the floor. I was covered with scratches and black-and-blue spots. I was filthy and I stank. I groaned.

'And now into the shower, please. I can't do anything with you this way.'

She supported me, guided me, actually just dragged me down the hall and into the bathroom. In a few minutes we were standing face to face in the small, white-tiled cubicle and she began to loosen my pants.

'Hey!' I shouted, knocking her hands away. The sudden movement made me lose my balance. I grabbed onto the edge of the shower stall.

'Not good?' she asked.

'No, of course not.'

'I've seen you so often, so why ...'

'Because back then you weren't ... like this.'

'Oh, and now that I'm ... like this ... I can't look at you any- more?'

'No. Jeez.'

'Why not?'

'Why not, why not, yeah, why do you think?' It was an impossible conversation. Kirsten was pushing me irrevoca- bly to say things I had not yet said. Not out loud. Because I didn't know how to say it until someone forced the words out of me. And that's what she was doing.

'What do I think?' she asked. 'If there's one thing I've learned, it's that you should never do somebody else's thinking for them because nine out of ten times you'll be off base, and the one time you get it right it'll come out wrong. So come on. Why not?' She was less than ten centimetres away. I could smell her, feel the warmth of her body. And no matter how much I blinked, I couldn't get her eyes out of mine.

'Because ...'

'Because you don't want me to be ... like this. But what that "like this" is, is something you don't even dare to say!'

'A woman,' I said.

'Exactly. Because I'm not what you think I ought to be, that's why not.'

I shook my head. Pain in my back. 'No,' I said. 'No ...'

'Oh, no? What is it then?' She was angry, with an injured viciousness. She had chosen this particular moment, and the moment had chosen me. Here on the tiles in front of the shower. I could barely hold my body together and I had to tell her what it was, here. Every explanation I could think of seemed blunt and crude. Harsh.

'WHAT?' she screamed.

'Okay, what? You want to know what?'

'YES!'

'Because I'd end up standing here with this massive erection, okay?'

Her mouth fell open. 'Oh,' she said.

'Or is that theoretical, too?'

She shook her head. 'No,' she said.

I leaned against the wall with one hand and dropped onto the edge of the bathtub. 'Can you picture it?'

She laughed. 'At least then I'd know the operation was a success.'

'You don't know by half,' I said.

'And there's me thinking you didn't love me anymore.'

I groaned. 'Give me a break!'

She cupped my face in her hands. 'Don't you worry about that organ of yours. In your condition it's probably the only body part that can't get stiff.' She kissed me, gently and not long enough for it to be anything else but a kiss. In a few rapid movements she ripped the band-aids from my face. I closed my eyes in shock. She grabbed my hands, helped me back up, unbuttoned my pants and pulled everything down. Then she turned me around and pushed me into the shower stall.

'You can find the tap yourself,' she said, shutting the door behind me. 'When you're done, just call me and I'll come and get you.'

She was right. The pain in my back made any kind of arousal impossible. I showered with difficulty. Every time I moved or turned in that slippery, confined space I expected to lose my balance. With a towel wrapped around my waist I stumbled into the living room. She had pushed the table a little to the side and had placed a mattress on the floor. It just fit. I laid down on it carefully, on my stomach. It was a good mattress. Not too hard, not too soft and wonderfully flat. As soon as I was down she began rubbing my back with salves and creams I didn't even know existed. Arnica salve for the scrapes and the bruise, Advil cream for the pain and Tiger Balm to relax my stiff muscles.

'You don't have any shaving equipment,' I said.

'No, it took a while, but eventually I didn't need it anymore. It's one of those things that ...'

'That's not what I meant,' I said. 'I meant that that's why I hadn't shaved yet.'

'You think I didn't know that?' she said.

'I'm starting not to know what I'm supposed to think anymore.'

'Common problem,' she said.

I told her everything, starting with her arrival at Schiphol and the total chaos I had ended up in. 'If I hadn't known who you were, I would have hit on you right then and there,'

I said. 'Really.' I said that for several minutes I had thought and felt and realized everything at once, and that when she finally came out through the sliding glass doors I was so caught up in contradictory emotions that there was only one place to go.

'Down,' said Kirsten.

'Carried off in an ambulance,' I said. 'Wasn't even really necessary, but it was fine with me. As long as I was gone. And then I spent days hanging around in a drunken stupor in my apartment. No one knew where I was. I didn't even pick up the phone, or check my e-mail, or open the door. The only thing I opened were bottles. Vodka, whisky, jenever, cognac, you name it. I had a pretty good supply and in a couple of days most of it was gone.' I told her everything, from the threatened dismissal to the death of Radekker and to the hunt for me that her death had touched off. I told her about my escape, about making sure I didn't disappear somewhere without a trace, where no one would ever be able to find me. Up until last night, when I ended up on her doorstep at three-thirty in the morning. I told her about everything, except Jessica. I went out of my way to avoid talking about Jessica. I wasn't ready to deal with that yet. Not by a long shot.

'So it's really all my fault,' said Kirsten.

'Actually it is.'

'Sorry.'

After that she said lots of other things, but I don't remember what. I fell asleep in the middle of a sentence. Deeper sleep this time, and more peaceful. For the first time in I don't know how many days and nights I relaxed. When I woke up at the end of the afternoon I was still far from rested but the pain was less intense.

'It looks worse than it is,' she said. 'A couple of more days of salves and creams, I think, and then I'll be able to help you.'

I spent the whole weekend with her, on the floor in the dining room, halfway under the table, flat on my stomach. Kirsten massaged my back, gently, with fingers that sometimes barely seemed to touch me but that felt everything. Every bruise, every battered muscle, every pinched nerve.

'Because it's no more than that,' she said. 'As soon as I can see where it is, I'll be able to rub it out and the pain will go away.'

'That's what you think.'

'That's what I know. I had other things to occupy my time in America all those years.' She was straddling my thighs, leaning forward slightly, rubbing and kneading. Further and further, deeper and deeper into my skin. Under my skin. The pain was killing me, but I said nothing.

Bellilog, June 26

I've lost my inner core somewhere along the way, my heart, my soul, whatever. All I have now are cracking joints and aching muscles. I'm physical, nothing more, and even that is in pretty bad shape.

Mail from: HB2
Subject: online
Tomorrow morning, ten o'clock your time. Okay? Till then.

Viruses in a favourable climate

I was lying flat on my stomach behind my laptop. I surfed to Huib's secure server, and before I could type a single word his questions started flying off the screen. Where had I been? Why hadn't he heard from me in such a long time? What was going on? Had I looked on the network? Had I seen how incredibly busy it had been? The data flow that was getting more and more frantic? Had I ...

Patiently I waited until he was finished before typing my first comment. It was the beginning of a sober chat.

- yesterday second victim, myself almost third
- by uncle?
- Yes.
- SURE?
- 100%
- Fuck
- and I have the computer
- ....
- what do you think?
- I have to discuss this with my father first
- what?
- about HB
- what does your father have to do with it?
- he's his brother

From that moment on there was no talking to Huib. He was stuck in a family situation that was totally beyond me. My own family was a scattered little group of people. I had just gotten to know my sister, I still had to find my father, my mother had reported me to the police and my brother had plugs in his ears. Huib was talking about his father, his uncles, his brothers, his grandfather and his cousins as if it were an indivisible unit. The entire male division of the Breger family was getting involved.

The increased data flow probably had to do with the upcoming EU Summit on Security and Integration. Government leaders meeting at the summit were hoping to draw up agreements on taking joint action against extremism and religious fundamentalism. The contrasts were getting fiercer by the day. HC&P was involved in preparations for the summit at a number of levels, and it only seemed logical that they would coordinate their efforts in all the countries they were working in. HB2 disappeared from the network and left me with a lot of open-ended thoughts.

Kirsten gave me some exercises to do. As I bent and stretched, I clamped my jaws together so hard that my teeth started grating. She felt my back, letting her fingers glide over the injured areas once again.

'It's still too black-and-blue,' she said, 'still too dark. I can't really see it yet.'

She rubbed on more salve and cream and left me alone. Exhausted by the pain and the endless treatment, I fell back asleep. I didn't sleep long, a couple of hours, but when I woke up Kirsten was gone. I pulled the telephone towards me and called Vince Batte. Strila's computer was still in my backpack, and it was about time someone with a bit of know-how had a look at it.

'Bring it over,' said Batte cheerfully.

'Bad idea,' I said, and I really had to do my best to convince him that he'd have to give up his Saturday night and come to me instead. The consultant in me was working overtime, and on my stomach at that. I had a cramp in my neck and jaw from talking in that position.

'And one more thing,' I said. 'That pass I got from you is

probably already invalid. Last night I was detected, and if I'm right about the registration of non-registered people it won't work anymore.'

Batte was silent.

'You still there?' I asked after almost half a minute.

'Yeah, yeah, just hold on.'

More silence.

'Okay, I can only finish the pass at the office, which means Monday or Tuesday. When do you want me to come?'

'Whenever you want,' I said. 'I'm not going anywhere.'

Kirsten came back with food and shaving gear. She helped me to the bathroom, and with lots of shaving cream and hot water I was able to scrape off my days-old whiskers. It felt good. Being shaved is cleaner than being washed. I looked at my face in the mirror and carefully fingered the scratches and bumps. The wound above my eyebrow was really closed now. Soon the scab would loosen. Kirsten came over and stood next to me, and together we looked at each other in the mirror.

'Hey, Kurt,' I said.

She smiled and shook her head. 'I've never been Kurt.'

'That's not what I meant,' I said. 'But I'm starting to understand.' We continued to stare at our mirror image, neither of us speaking. Just when I opened my mouth and was about to say something, the doorbell rang. Whatever I had wanted to say disappeared. It had something to do with family and with brother and sister, and lots of thoughts that Huib had put into my head. But I didn't say any of that. What I did say was, 'Oh, that must be Batte.'

At first Kirsten was angry that I had given her address to an unknown person. She brought me back to the living room with an injured look on her face. In the hallway she pulled on the cord for the front door and shouted 'Third floor!'

down the stairwell. By the time she had me back on my stomach on the mattress, Batte's footsteps could be heard on the top steps. In the hallway.

'Okay, where is it?' he asked.

'Here,' Kirsten and I called out in chorus.

Kirsten turned to the door, and one second later Batte's fashionable nerd face appeared from around the corner, sunglasses shoved up on top of an almost clean-shaven bald head. No more than a few millimetres were left of the soggy, gel-enhanced spikes. He saw Kirsten and froze in his tracks, his arms extended oddly from the left and right sides of his body.

'wow!' he said. 'Reboot all systems!' He looked as if he was about to drop to his knees but he straightened himself up, stiffened his arms spastically, turned around in a wooden, wobbly pirouette, slammed the door and grabbed his head.

Kirsten shot forward to support him. 'What are you doing?' she asked.

'This program has encountered fatal beauty,' said Batte. 'Don't let go. Whatever you do, don't let go.'

She held on to him and waited. Nothing happened. Batte stopped twitching, and it looked as if he wasn't going to fall over after all. All he did was stare at her, with a look in his eyes that seemed to soften gradually.

'And now?' Kirsten asked after about a minute.

'And now it's time for eternity.'

'Oh, sure, and you're going to be part of it, right?' She let him go and gave him a punch on the arm. Batte groaned and winced, but Kirsten didn't respond.

'Kirsten,' I said, 'this is Vince. Vince, when you regain consciousness, my sister.'

In two more or less normal minutes they shook hands and exchanged the conventional greetings, and Batte managed to find me on my mattress. He cursed.

'What did you do?' he asked. He pointed to my back and turned to Kirsten. His eyes flashed back and forth a couple of times, but before I could answer he had already forgotten me. 'Or did you do this?' he asked Kirsten.

'What do you take me for?'

'Well, now that you mention it, ...'

There was no stopping them. Batte circled around Kirsten and spoke a language that she seemed to understand better than I did. The room was bristling with life, but not where I was. In the same room, but beyond the reach of my mattress, Batte and Kirsten began behaving like a pair of viruses in a favourable climate. It was as if they were duplicating themselves every second. And everything they said was obscurely witty. Kirsten laughed and giggled. Suddenly she threw her head back, her long hair fanning out around her face. She made two or three small gestures with her hands, and then somewhere between those moments (I can't say exactly when) Kurt disappeared.

Just like that.

'VINCE!' I shouted.

He turned around with a theatrical movement and looked at me. '*Oui, mon Général?*'

'Knock it off.'

'But I'm not doing anything.'

'That's why.'

My anger surprised me, but I had ground to cover. The more Kirsten and Batte became interested in each other, the more rushed I felt. That was unfair. What they were doing had nothing to do with me, except for the fact that it was all taking place on my time, which I didn't have much of. It was a bizarre situation. I couldn't go anywhere, I was completely dependent on the people who wanted to help me, yet everyone was doing whatever they felt like doing. I pointed to Strila's laptop.

'Right,' said Batte. He made an apologetic gesture towards

Kirsten and flipped the laptop open. 'What was the problem again?'

He started up the computer. I gave him Strila's password, and soon he was clicking through the files on the hard drive. He ran a couple of system checks and did a system inventory, then he shook his head. 'Perfectly normal little computer,' he said. 'What were you saying about some kind of M-drive?' He clicked to the ms-dos prompt and typed M: and a return.

'Station designation invalid,' it said on the screen.

'This thing doesn't have an M-drive,' he said. 'Here.' He pointed on the screen to the system properties list, which I couldn't see. 'Forty gigabytes partitioned in a C-drive and a D-drive. What are you yakking about? This is a standard Datwell 4120, the most popular laptop in the world. There are millions of them. I have one myself.'

'Where?'

'At home. It's at home.'

'Connected to the internet?'

'No, it's off now.'

'But with all the cables attached?'

'Of course.'

I pulled up my own laptop, clicked onto the internet and, using Huib's secure server, surfed to the HC&P network.

'You know this?' I asked.

'What?' Batte was sitting with his back to me.

'This. Here. If you don't look, you can't see it.' He couldn't take his eyes off Kirsten so I had to drag him away. 'Here,' I said.

Batte sat down on the floor next to me and looked at the screen. In less than two seconds his attention was completely absorbed by the program. He looked at the pulsing image, information moving around in flocks. Huib was right. The network was more active than I had ever seen it before. The greatest activity was between Brussels, Amsterdam and San Francisco.

'Is this a game?' asked Batte. 'Because it's new to me.'

'No, it's no game,' I said. 'Look at this.'

I clicked through the menus at great speed, as I had seen Huib do, until I found WorldWare in the Netherlands. Since the company was so intimately involved in everything HC&P was doing, I guessed it would be almost fully contained within the network. I clicked to the company's project list, and soon almost all of WorldWare's activities were shown on the screen. All Batte could do was whistle.

'Fuck,' he said quietly.

I clicked the list away and entered via the departments.

'Where do you work?' I asked.

'Registration Systems.'

A list of employee names appeared on the screen, with Batte's almost at the top. I clicked on his name and in a few seconds a dialog box appeared.

    Host available. Proceed 'yes' or 'no.'

I clicked on 'yes' and the box disappeared. On a dark, empty screen the simple prompt of an MS-DOS environment appeared—M:—followed by a blinking cursor. I typed C: and a return. A new dialog box appeared:

    Host switched off. Proceed 'yes' or 'no.'

Again I chose 'yes' and the spinning hourglass appeared.

    Please wait while booting host.

Batte was utterly silent. His eyes seemed to be peering right through the screen and into the wires and digital movement of the information behind it. The Windows desktop appeared on the screen. A lovely blue, almost serene. I shoved the computer towards Batte.

'Go ahead,' I said.

Hesitantly, his fingers drew near to the keyboard and the touchpad for moving the cursor.

'Is this my computer?' he asked.

'You know that better than I do.'

He clicked on Windows Explorer, and no sooner did the overview appear on the screen than he pulled his hands away from the keyboard.

'This can't be!' he said. 'Nobody knows my password! Nobody can get into my computer without my password, and ...'

'There wasn't even a request for your password,' I said.

Batte cursed. He gazed at the screen in bewilderment. 'But how do you get in?'

I pulled the laptop towards me and closed Windows. The computer switched back to MS-DOS.

'By way of the M-drive,' I said, and I pointed to the laptop on the table. 'And you can tell me a hundred times that it's not there, but what's that then?'

Now I pointed to the dark screen of my own computer, showing that one inescapable prompt. M:

Batte jumped up and stared at the computer with a look of grim determination. Hands on his hips, lips pursed into an outpost of his face. His eyes shifted back and forth between Strila's computer and the M-prompt on my screen. Slowly he shook his head.

'It's not possible,' he said. 'You can't access a computer that's been turned off and bypass all the safeguards as if they didn't exist. I know anything's possible. A computer that's connected to the internet has more than sixty-five thousand points of entry. But it has to be turned on. This is impossible! Not with *my* computer!'

Suddenly he made a decision. He turned Strila's computer off, slammed it shut and turned it over. 'Do you have a screwdriver?' he asked Kirsten. 'Phillips?'

'My name's not Phillip,' said Kirsten. She was playing with him, and it took Batte a few seconds to catch on. She was playing the dumb broad who doesn't know anything about tools and other guy things, and was challenging him to be the equally dumb guy. Batte smiled. He was quick on the uptake. He switched effortlessly between his own concentration and the joke she was making.

'If your name was Phillip we'd be talking football. So what do you think?'

'Hmm,' said Kirsten. 'What does a Phillips do?'

'A Phillips screws, I guess,' said Batte. 'May be best to leave this for later.'

She took a box out of the cabinet and put it on the table. 'If I have one, it's in here.'

He pulled the cables out of the computer, took out the battery, turned a couple of screws in the lower plate, pulled on a panel, clicked away two of the sides and carefully removed the entire lower section. Then he stared at the inner workings with concentration.

'That's all it is,' he said. 'Hard drive, DVD drive, floppy ...' He pointed with the screwdriver to the various parts as he mentioned them. Kirsten looked over his shoulder. 'Modem,' said Batte, 'communication ports, it's all so simple. I mean, you don't even look at them anymore. These models are so compact. That's the beauty of them.'

'And what's this?' asked Kirsten. She pointed with one long fingernail to a minuscule connection on the input side of the modem.

'That is ...' Batte tapped the thing with the point of the screwdriver. 'That is ... I have no idea what that is.'

'Looks like a splicer,' said Kirsten.

'And how would you know that?'

'We Phillipses get around,' she said, raising her eyebrows. She pointed to the device. 'Or do you have a better idea?'

Batte nodded. 'A much better idea,' he said, and he turned to me. 'May I?'

'Please do,' I said. 'Under one condition. That you do it on the floor so I can see what you're up to. I'm starting to feel left out.'

They sat across from each other right in front of my nose with the computer turned upside down between us. Batte used the screwdriver again to point out the various parts, finally tapping on the connection attached to the modem.

'This thingamajig does something we don't understand,' said Batte, 'and when you don't understand something, you have to do some more looking.'

'First look, then think,' I said.

Batte put his hands in the computer and pulled out one component after another. Almost everything was secured by means of a click system. There were no more than three little screws in the whole thing.

'It's not hard,' he said. 'You just have to follow a certain order.' Finally he got to the hard drive. It was attached to the back of the computer with just one screw. He loosened the screw and slowly prized the hard drive from its contact points. 'The processor is underneath,' he said, 'so you have to be a bit careful.' At that very moment the thing popped loose. Batte took it out and placed it on the floor next to the computer. The three of us were looking at two identical processors, lying neatly side by side in the computer's heart.

'What have we got here?' said Batte. 'A double processor?'

'For more speed, maybe?' Kirsten asked.

Batte shook his head. 'I don't think so. They're not connected in any way. Here, look, this one operates the computer we just took apart, and this one seems to be linked to something else. But what?' He tried to follow the connections with the point of his screwdriver. 'And there's also this weird steel plate on the bottom.'

'It looks like the thing you just took out,' I said.

Batte picked up the last component he had removed and

held it up. 'You mean this? This is the hard drive, this is ...' He shook his head. 'Oh, no,' he said, and he put the drive back down. Then working at terrific speed he began taking the rest of the computer apart, and five minutes later there were not only two processors but also two hard drives lying side by side on the carpet.

'This isn't just one computer,' said Batte. 'This is two computers in one case. The M-drive isn't a partition at all. It's a second hard drive with its own processor and its own link to the modem. Always available, whether the computer is on or not, because you can't turn this drive off. Look.' He pointed to the separate power supply connection that bypassed the on-and-off switch. 'And it wouldn't surprise me if the software on the M-drive is engineered in such a way that you can go from M: to C: and back again, but never from C: to M: if you started in C: ... May I?'

He picked up my computer, where the M: was still waiting for a command. Batte typed a couple of things, and lists and directories rolled across the screen. He stared with concentration at the cryptic data, his eyes moving in cadence with the information racing past, his fingers ready to stop or move the data stream at any given moment. 'Here,' he said suddenly. 'Here, here, look at this ... FUCK!'

He pulled his hand from the keyboard and stared at the screen.

'What is it?' Kirsten asked.

'This is a registry of all my work,' he said. 'Even the things I haven't reported. If anyone wants to know how you got into that building yesterday, and where your VIP pass came from, they can trace it to me.'

No one said a word. My physical state was clear enough.

'And can't you erase that file?' asked Kirsten.

'Immediately.' Batte's fingers flew across the keys, but the commands he typed had no effect. He kept getting the same message.

File access denied.

Feverishly he tried to cancel the security protocol so he could remove the file in its entirety. Finally he came upon the right codes. He typed the command again to erase the file and hit the return. A box appeared in the middle of the screen.

User please re-identify. Login location does not match current status.
Running server check.

'GET OUT!' I screamed. 'GET OUT, GET OUT!' Fear seized my entire body, my guts began to writhe. The last time I had seen that message was with Gijs, and he had barely survived the consequences. I snatched the computer from Batte, clicked through the menus like a maniac and logged out. Seconds later the screen was solid grey.

Kirsten and Vince stared at me.

'And now?' Kirsten asked.

'Now?' I said. I repeated the question, feverishly searching for an answer, but all I found were more questions. Had Huib's server been hacked? Had they located him? Had they located us? If they had, Kirsten's apartment was no longer safe. They must have located Batte's computer. That was the host and it was part of their own network. That's what had disabled Batte's address. Where were we supposed to go? I didn't dare take a chance and hope that the address on Hondecoeterstraat hadn't been found. If two or three men were to come in here, we'd be powerless. But what then? I had used up all my options, I was at the end of my family, my network.

'Now I don't know,' I said, 'except that we have to get out of here. As fast as we can.'

44

No way back

The end of my family was the beginning of the rest of the world. Kirsten and Vince took over for me. After asking a couple of questions they had enough to go by, and they began making preparations for the joint move of two people who barely knew each other and a semi-invalid. Batte made three phone calls and stood up.

'Fifteen minutes,' he said. 'We have fifteen minutes to do everything we have to do before our ride comes to the door. And I have a place we can go to. Okay?'

Kirsten nodded. Her facial features had hardened. There was nothing left of the playful woman. She had turned inward and silent. I was still lying on the mattress on the floor.

'So what do we do?' Batte asked.

'Pack up the computers,' I said. 'And all my stuff. Anything that can be traced to me has to go. And anything with your name on it has to go, too,' I said to Kirsten.

It only took a couple of minutes to pack. Everything I had was already in stored a backpack and three plastic bags. Kirsten crammed her bank statements and some other papers into a bag. She grabbed the salves and creams she was using to treat me and some clothes for herself, and she was ready. In the meantime I sent e-mails and chat messages to South Africa to warn Huib that his secure serve may no longer be secure. Usually I had an answer within five minutes, but not this time. Huib didn't respond to any of my messages. Anxious, I shut my laptop and gave it to Vince. He put it in my backpack. Then Kirsten and Vince came over to me, one on either side.

'And now you,' said Kirsten. The two of them helped me to

my feet. That went well, but getting dressed was more difficult. The suit I was wearing had long been consigned to the garbage. Kirsten took some other clothes out of the backpack. Every movement or twist I made was more than my back could bear. Now that I was rested the pain seemed sharper, more intense, no longer masked by fatigue or excitement. My body had stopped producing enough adrenaline to shift the pain threshold. Now all that was left was the pain.

It took all the remaining time to go down the three flights of stairs to the front door. Every move made the next one more difficult. A car outside beeped its horn. Batte ran on ahead and opened the car door. He waved to someone Kirsten and I couldn't see and came back upstairs. Then the two of them carried me the rest of the way. Finally they put me down on the sidewalk next to a mid-size camper. The door to the back was open, and while Kirsten went upstairs to get our things Batte helped me up the three small steps.

The camper had everything. A little kitchen, a toilet with a shower, a sitting area and a dinner table, lights on the walls and ceiling, carpet on the floor and, most important, a couch I could stretch out on. On my stomach. My demands became fewer and fewer. With a sigh of relief I felt the pain subside to a manageable level.

Kirsten came out laden with bags and my backpack. She put everything in the back of the camper, turned around, walked back to the front door and tore her nameplate away from the bell. Then she got into the camper and closed the door behind her, stuffing the nameplate into the back pocket of her pants. She came over and sat down next to me.

Vince tried to restore the flirtatious atmosphere between himself and Kirsten, but she cut him short every time. Now that she suddenly didn't know where she was going to end up, she refused to get involved in anything that didn't interest her. She informed Vince that she wasn't interested in anything and certainly not in him. This may have put a damper on things inside the camper, but at least the relationships were clear.

'If everybody's more or less comfortable, maybe we can take off,' called a melodious voice from behind the enormous driver's seat. The thing was so big that it was impossible to tell from the back whether anyone was actually sitting in it. A man with a blond ponytail hanging between his shoulders leaned over to one side. Kirsten and I were seeing him for the first time. He was wearing rings and necklaces and pair of glasses with lenses way too thick for a normal person to see through. Dangling between his fingers was a huge joint.

'This is Bernie,' said Vince.

'Hi,' said Bernie.

'Bernie and I have known each other for ...' He thought a minute. 'How long have we known each other?' he asked.

'Real long,' said Bernie. 'From when my mother was still buying underpants for me.'

'Exactly, and Bernie is the owner of this ... uh ...'

'Spaceship,' said Bernie. 'By which I can reach any solar system I want.' He raised an index finger and pressed a large button on the dashboard. With a deep snarl, the diesel engine started up. The camper shook a bit and calmed back down as soon as the engine began to idle.

'Hyperdrive,' said Bernie, holding the joint up invitingly.

'Toke, anyone?' he asked.

The joint was passed around, from Batte to Kirsten to me. Everyone took a couple of hits, holding their breath as long as they could and then exhaling the disarmed smoke. The fragrance filled the camper, and it didn't take long before I began feeling the weed's effects.

'And where exactly are these distant reaches?' I asked.

'Amsterdam North,' said Vince.

'Always wanted to go there,' I said, and I stuck the joint

between my lips, inhaled deeply a couple of times and passed it on to Kirsten. What happened after that I no longer remember. Bernie drove away slowly, very cautiously, at Vince and Kirsten's express instructions. The languid, rocking movement of the camper and the deep hum of the diesel engine encircled us like a protective shield. The journey into space had begun.

Bernie stopped the camper on a street corner somewhere on Java Island. He and Vince exchanged a few muttered words, then Bernie got out.

'Cool, be right back,' he said. He closed the door gently behind him. I raised myself up and looked out through the window. I could see the island's new canals in the early evening light. Bernie swaggered away.

'This isn't North, is it?' I asked.

Batte shook his head. Kirsten stared at the street we were parked on with strained concentration.

'So where are we?'

'Come to get my thing,' said Vince.

'Oh,' I said. My problem was just the opposite of Kirsten's. My concentration was nowhere. 'What thing?' I asked.

Batte looked around with a glazed expression and rubbed his eyes. 'You know,' he said.

'Oh.'

Bernie stopped halfway down the street and went into a doorway. Slowly it began to dawn on me that we were at Batte's apartment and that Bernie had gone in to pick something up.

'Fuck,' I said.

'Cool,' said Vince.

Kirsten stared out the window and said nothing. Actually I should have been exploding with rage, I should have been screaming and shouting that they were totally out of their minds to come here, that they had no idea how dangerous it was, and on and on, but the only thing that came out of my mouth was a kind of rolling giggle.

'Wow, scary!' I said.

Now Vince started giggling. The weed had wrapped itself around our funny bones and was making them do very unusual things.

'Oh, Bernie's just going inside,' said Vince, 'and ... nobody ever asks Bernie to do anything, really. He's just not the kind of individual that other people ask to do things ... which is weird, by the way, because he does whatever you want, but nobody knows that, so actually he's got the perfect disguise ...' Vince was silent for a moment. 'Fuck, this is strong weed,' he said suddenly, and I couldn't hold it any longer. I lay prostrate on the couch bed, hooting with laughter. Vince was in his seat, laughing so hard that the tears trickled down his cheeks.

'Jesus, what is it with you two?' said Kirsten. Our laughing fit had disturbed her concentration. She was angry, but her anger had the opposite effect.

'You know,' I said, 'if this goes wrong, we're all goners.' My body was shaking with laughter.

'Oh, now that's really funny,' said Kirsten.

Vince howled. He slid off his seat and disappeared under the dashboard. His arms were wrapped around his knees and he lay like a little ball on the floor of the camper. I tried to stuff one of the couch cushions into my mouth to stifle the rapidly spreading internal goofiness.

'I'm trying to see something here,' said Kirsten peevishly. Vince and I were out of control.

Bernie rode from the island back to the Piet Hein Tunnel. The big camper hummed peacefully, as if we were in a private room, traveling through an unfamiliar world of concrete, asphalt and artificial lighting. A spaceship with a diesel engine, slowly and imperturbably making our way to a new solar system.

The laughing fit disappeared as it had struck, bit by bit. By the time we got to the ring road to Amsterdam North we were silent. Kirsten looked out the window as the night glided past. Vince searched through the things Bernie had retrieved for him from his apartment. I was still lying on my stomach, head on a pillow, arms wrapped around it. My body was completely relaxed, thanks to the weed. No pressure on my back, no frenetic attempts to keep my limbs under control, to prevent any unexpected or stupid movements from stirring up the pain again. All I did was lie there.

Thoughts drifted through my head of their accord, big and intangible, as happens in a head that's stoned. Everything crystal clear and unavoidable. Jessica's long blond hair hanging from the top steps of the stairway. The look in her eyes that I'd never see again. Only pictures of her. Photos, memories. And a feeling I couldn't find a picture to illustrate. A feeling that I was no longer who I was. Like when Kurt turned out to be Kirsten and I lost part of myself. Now I had lost something again. Something more fundamental, because Jessica was the link connecting everything I did, the link between the hard work and the absurd obsessiveness. She was the logic between the lust and the chaos. Without her my organizing principle was gone and I was no more than an accidental collection of data. Unstructured data. That was me. There on the little couch in the camper I felt permanently unstructured.

'We're systems that we ourselves don't understand,' Jessica always said, and now I saw that just the opposite was true. We aren't systems. We need other people to give us direction. Other people aren't just other people. We all fit together, literally. Family, friends, lovers, enemies. Without Jessica I had become someone else. Now I was alone, or what was left of me, and the prospects were none too good.

Cautiously I shook my head to break that line of thought.

I couldn't think about Jessica. Not yet. What had happened in her apartment was too threatening. Too dangerous. Death was too immediate. Around me and within me. Hard-nose to hard-nose. Aggression instead of arguments. I had landed in a world I only knew from the news and from the reports that HC&P produced non-stop. Reports I had worked on myself. The cultural confrontation. The difference that having a God makes. Everywhere there were warnings of growing hatred. Violence was already there, on the streets, unexpected. Fear was growing, it was taking possession of our thinking, our actions, slowly but surely. And now I was right in the middle of it all, dragging others along with me. Gijs, my parents, Jessica, Kirsten and Vince. The circle was getting bigger and bigger, the violence worse and worse. But it wasn't coming from the quarter that everyone was warning us about. I wasn't being chased by Muslims. The violence came from the people who were always pointing out the nuances, who made the inventories and wrote the reports. This violence came from HC&P, from the consultants, from the party that was no party at all.

Or was it?

That was a question that wouldn't go away. The question was brief but the implications were overwhelming. If HC&P was not an independent consultancy then the firm was definitely partial. The elaborately detailed projects were not the firm's advice but its opinions, the opinions of HC&P itself. That meant that the confrontational policies being adopted by more and more countries had not been chosen by the countries themselves but by HC&P.

You have reached the home of Mr. Miller.

My breath caught in my throat. Apparently very different rules applied in Mr. Miller's house, rules that only a small, select group were aware of. Rules that were brutally enforced.

People make decisions based on facts. Data. If you want to influence those decisions, then you have to make sure you control the data. The facts. That's what Mr. Miller did. With an enormous network of computers it was possible not only to steal information but also to change it. Manipulate it. Adapt it. I had done it myself with Strila's computer. I had used the network the other way around without even realizing it. And if I could do it, then others could do it, too. Far better than I could. *If you don't want control, then leave the net alone.*

Even my advice to the Minister of Justice on the best way to address the press: that he ought to be firmer, clearer, less circuitous, that he shouldn't be afraid of calling a spade a spade, that he should offer people security without losing sight of the facts, that he didn't have to give in to the growing call for harder measures, but that he did have to have ready answers—all that advice was based on facts that I had never called into question, on figures and data produced by the Ministry itself. Inventories, research and reports that were all open to manipulation.

By Mr. Miller. By HC&P. And it wasn't until that moment that that it finally dawned on me that my own computer must have an M-drive, too. My laptop itself was part of the network. The reason Huib Breger and his men had been able to find me so quickly was because they could look into my computer via the M-drive. They knew what I had written and what I was reading. What I had been looking for elsewhere had been with me all along.

That's how stoned I was.

The camper drove through an abandoned industrial park in Amsterdam North. This was the part of the city that was on the brink of being 'discovered.' Dilapidated warehouses, half-finished new buildings alternating with vacant lots. Here the old businesses had left and the buildings were waiting for new plans. New people. The advance guard was already here. Artists and performers had moved in, and it was just a matter of time before the wealthier studios and creative agencies discovered the neighbourhood. Now it was still dark and abandoned. The street lighting was minimal. There was hardly a soul to be seen.

I reached over to the other side of the seat and tapped Kirsten on the knee. Annoyed, she turned her head toward me.

'Yes?'

'You okay?' I asked.

'No.' Then she turned away again and stared out the window into the dark neighbourhood.

'I ...'

'Forget it,' she said. 'Anything you might say now would only make it worse. Apparently you have no idea what I had to leave behind tonight. My apartment, okay? You just drop in, and before I know it I'm ripping my nameplate off the door. Why? Because his highness says I have to. Because his highness has done something that suddenly I'm supposed to be part of. But nobody ever asks what *I* want. You never asked what I want.'

She fell silent. Her accusations were older and bigger than our helter skelter flight from Hondecoeterstraat. She was shouldering years of misunderstandings.

'There's no way back,' I said, and my intentions were good, just as my intentions were always good. But good intentions didn't count. Not anymore.

'YOU THINK I DIDN'T KNOW THAT?!' Kirsten screamed. 'Did *you* really think that *I* didn't know there was no way back? ME? What did you think I'd been doing all those years? The only difference is that I thought long and hard about it before going down that road. Real long. And you? You take a left-hand turn without even bothering to look. And now there's suddenly no way back. How dare you?!'

Vince had turned around and was looking at the quarrel with wide eyes. 'Hey,' he said.

'What? You got something to say, too?' Kirsten spat the question out at him.

'No,' said Vince. He shook his head. 'No, I don't know what's it's all about. I only wanted to say that we're almost there. That's it.' He pointed to a building in the dark on the edge of the neighbourhood. Behind the building glistened the water of the IJ.

Bernie carefully manoeuvered the camper onto the yard through a half-open fence. He drove around to the back of the building at a snail's pace. Light was shining out of the tall windows and was being reflected on the water. This was the glistening we had seen before. A couple of small boats were tied to a long dock. Bernie turned the camper around with its nose facing a large sliding door and honked, once, short.

Slowly the door slid to the side. Behind it was a large open area, a huge shed. Two men pushed the door further open until the camper was able to drive through. Bernie accelerated and the camper rolled in. The sliding door closed behind us. I heard the lock clank shut.

Bernie turned the engine off, opened his door and got out. Vince got out the other side. In a little while the side door opened and he came back in. He extended his hand to Kirsten.

'Here,' he said. 'Come on.'

That's all he said. Kirsten climbed off the bench and followed him inside. From one moment to the next I was lying alone in the camper. On my stomach.

'Hey,' I shouted.

No answer.

'Hey, how about me?!'

Vince's crazy face appeared again in the door opening. He smiled.

'I'll be right back,' he said.

I slept. In the silence of the deserted camper, on the narrow bench, my arms folded around my pillow, still enough weed in my body to fall into a deep and dreamless sleep. Only when someone began to tug at me did I wake up. There were three men standing around me. Kirsten was sitting backward in the driver's seat.

'Take it easy,' she said. 'Keep his back straight, whatever you do.'

Caution didn't help. The pills and salves had worn off. All that was left of the weed was a thick, fuzzy head. Every movement cut right through my back. They lifted me from the bench and helped me out of the camper, where a makeshift stretcher awaited me. It was made of a couple of steel pipes and a pair of old blankets. As soon as I was settled on it, each of them picked up a pipe at the far end and carried me through the shed to a door on the other side.

Behind the door were the old offices of the former commercial premises. They carried me down a long corridor, up a flight of stairs, around a corner, up another flight of stairs and around another corner until we finally entered a room. It was a room with a bed, a table, a chair and a closet. There was a door to the corridor and a window with a view that I couldn't see, because I was flat on my stomach again.

Bellilog, June 28

Okay. Not okay. It's not okay. I'm lying here in a room some-where (it is doesn't matter where) and K comes in and asks how I'm doing. Just like that, the way people do. A normal question. And she looks at me, at my eyes. She doesn't look at the bare room, or the old mattress, or the mold on the walls or the paint coming down from the ceiling in strips. She doesn't look at the total absence of facilities. There's no heat, no water and no electricity in the room. There's one lamp that's connected to an extension cord that gets its power from another part of the building. But she doesn't look at that. Or at my body, which is so stiff and miserable that I can barely move without piercing pain. No, she looks at my eyes, as if she could peer through those little round balls and see deep inside me, at the havoc I've left behind there. Because I'm living outside myself. It's safer out there. And that's not okay.

The Pattern

'Where am I?'

No one responded to my question. Kirsten checked to see if I was comfortable. She pulled my shirt up and felt my back. Her fingers slid down my vertebrae, almost without touching them.

'Okay,' she said, 'this is something I can work on.' She turned to Vince. 'Do you have that bag somewhere? The yellow one with the pink handles?'

They both left the room behind me. I heard their footsteps going down the hallway. Silence. In a little while Kirsten came back. She put a glass of water on the small table next to the bed. Vince brought the bag and dropped it on the floor beside her.

'You mean this one?' he asked.

She nodded, zipped the bag open and took out the tube of analgesic cream and a package of paracetamol. She gave me a couple of tablets. I swallowed them with water one by one. After the last tablet she took the glass from me and put it away. Then she picked up the tube and began to rub the cream into the spot on my back. Very slowly, very gently, she rubbed the cream into the pain. I shut my eyes, bit on the edge of my pillow and waited until she was finished.

'Fifteen minutes,' she said. 'I'll be back in fifteen minutes.'

Vince was sitting on a straight back wooden chair next to the bed.

'Hi,' he said.

'And to you.'

'You doing all right?'

'Let's not overdo it,' I said. 'Where are we?'

'At The Pattern.'

'Never heard of it.'

'Actually it's a commune. An IT commune.'

'An IT commune? Sounds like a contradiction in terms.'

'Because you don't know anything about it.'

'Right. Less than I'd like to know.'

'Seventeen people live and work here,' said Vince. 'All of them involved in high-end software design. Not games or other fun stuff that only keep people further away from technology. No. Systems. Operating systems. Content management systems. Security systems. Specialized. The Pattern picks up where WorldWare leaves off. That's how you have to see it.'

'Friends of yours?'

'More than that.'

'But you yourself don't live here.'

'I do now.' He laughed. 'Kirsten may be mad that she had to leave her apartment, but I'm not. I was just about to move here anyway. All I needed was a kick in the butt, so, uh ...'

'You're welcome,' I said.

'Exactly. And if they can't hack that network here, then I don't know who can.'

A jolt of fear ran through me. I saw my newly found peace and quiet disappearing once again. In less than an hour they'd discover this place, too, and Breger and his men would be back on my trail. I didn't want that. Not ever again. From now on, all channels were closed. That was the only way to keep from being found.

'Whatever you do,' I said, 'wait till I'm there. Don't go near the network without me.'

Vince looked at me with pity.

'Don't worry,' he said. 'These guys are the best in Holland. We really do know what we're doing.'

I shook my head. 'Maybe you do know what you're doing, but you have no idea what the others are up to. And I do.'

47

If we're free, we're lost

The Pattern worked in one enormous room. Long tables, banks of computers, monitors, a jungle of cables. Keyboards with colour codes to tell you which computer they were connected to. Everything mixed up together. There wasn't even the appearance of order in the placement of the equipment. It was more like something that had grown organically, an enormous technological fungus with wires, cases and surfaces.

'I thought information technology was all about order,' I said.

'It's all about imposing order,' said Batte. 'That's something different. And precision. Not neatness. The important thing isn't understanding the system. If we were to start in on that, nothing would ever happen. The important thing is that the system works.' He pointed to the tables and the jumble of paraphernalia. 'And that works,' he said.

We walked past the equipment to a group of five men and women standing around a separate table. As we got closer I saw two dismantled laptops lying there. Mine and Vince's. Like dead pets. I felt a flash of unexpected pain somewhere in my chest. This was my little computer. In the past weeks it had been my only remaining possession. I had slept with it and worked with it. I had leaned on it, literally, and cradled it in my arms. That night in the tram it had kept me upright. It was my contact with the rest of the world. It was by means of this laptop that Jess and I had talked to each other, when that was still possible. By means of this laptop I had found Huib Breger 2, I had forced the partners of HC&P out of their hiding place and had ended up with Vince Batte. It wasn't just any old thing, it was a buddy, a friend (although it did have a rotten spot).

'This is Karl,' said Batte.

A small man in his late forties turned to look at me. Deep-set eyes. Forehead like a duplex, brains on two floors. He shook my hand.

'And you're the owner of this victim,' he said, pointing to my laptop. 'Vince says we're not supposed to do anything unless you're around.'

'I'd rather you didn't,' I said, and I told him what they were dealing with. The network, and mainly the network's pernicious ability to locate users and eliminate them. 'There's a certain Mr. Miller, who personally sees to it that unauthorized users are done away with. And not just here, because I'm afraid that my contact person in South Africa has disappeared, too. I haven't heard from him in days, and that's unusual.' I told him how I had found Huib, what he had done and the secure server he had created, which I wasn't sure was secure anymore. 'If they've got Huib, they're not far away.'

'A secure server is no problem,' said Karl. 'That's technology, we'll take care of that here. No, the real problem is why. Why does this happen? I myself can think of a hundred different reasons, but there's always only one that's the real culprit. And you don't know what to do next until you find it.'

I said nothing.

'So that's the question,' Karl repeated. 'Why?'

'Did you google my name?' I asked.

He shook his head.

'Do you mind if I do?'

Karl took me over to a keyboard and a monitor. He clicked the mouse a couple of times and the familiar icon of the search engine appeared. I typed my name into the search field. 'Michael Bellicher.' Within a second the search engine had come up with 14,978 internet hits containing my name.

'Popular guy,' said Karl.

'Depends on how you look at it,' I said. I slowly scrolled down the list of hits. Each and every one was a report of violence, murder and the fact that I was on the run. Comparisons with *American Psycho*. The respectable consultant turned brutal murderer. 'That's me,' I said. 'Apparently.'

Karl took over the mouse and scrolled down further. 'And you didn't do this?' he asked. 'None of these things? So not this either. Here. Woman raped and murdered in Amsterdam South. A Jessica Polse. You didn't do this either?'

My eyes found the report on the screen and I stumbled over every word I read. I was being sought for the murder of Jessica. Forensic evidence connected this incident with the murder of I. Radekker, administrative assistant at the same firm. Everything matched, from my hair on the handle of Ina's bag to the traces of my blood found in her apartment, from my fingerprints at Gijs's place to my semen in Jessica's body. Everything I had done proved that I had done something else.

Karl's eyes went back and forth, from the reports on the screen to my face. He saw the bewilderment, which slowly turned into rage. Then he reached for the mouse and clicked the page away.

'Okay, somebody's manipulating information. Is that what you mean?'

I nodded.

'To provoke you?'

'No,' I said, and I shook my head. 'No, I'm nothing but a glitch, a speck of dust.' I paused. 'I don't know why they're doing it. And I don't know how they're doing it, either. It has to do with those things,' I pointed to the laptops. 'But what I don't understand is how they can tamper with so many files without anyone catching on.'

'It's easier than you think,' said Karl. He put his hand on a monitor. 'Because this is God.'

'Excuse me? Are you starting in on that, too?'

'No, listen. We used to have God for everything we didn't understand. All we could do was scratch the surface, like chickens in a pen. But no more. All the deeper stuff, like the creation and the natural order of things—God did that. He was there for all the really complicated things. Right? Well, very little has actually changed in that relationship. Except the complicated things are now the complex structures and technological systems that govern our daily lives. We are still human beings with a free will, but the systems decide whether it's time to renew my passport, or whether I'm even going to get a new passport or not.' He pointed to the monitor. 'We, the human race, devised and built all those systems, but now they're surpassing us in terms of strength. There's little that you or I alone can do about it, and whether we like it or not, the systems are controlling our lives more and more. Determining our fate. In the end, most people trust that what comes out of the system is good. Without that trust we can't go on. We have to trust, in the depth of our being, that the systems have our best interests at heart. Just like God,' said Karl. 'Or whatever you want to call it.'

'Evil.'

Karl laughed. 'Yeah, maybe, but that's for another discussion,' he said. 'Why do you think we're working here?'

'To earn money?'

'That, too. But mainly because the only chance you have is with a system of your own. The only way to keep the complexity under control is with your own structure. At least if you know what you're doing.'

One month ago I would have found that subversive at best, but mainly extremely uninteresting. A lot of esoteric mumbo jumbo. Yammering by people who didn't matter, who weren't important. Now what I saw was exactly the opposite.

'Okay,' said Karl. 'Two things: this Huib Breger in South Africa and the Roadmap. In that order.'

'Maybe it would be better to set up our own secure server first,' I said, but Karl shook his head.

'That's technology,' he said with a laugh. For him it wasn't even a subject of discussion. He slapped me on the shoulder. 'You can't help it,' he said. 'Most people think it's all about technology. But it's not. It's about people, like this Huib. He was from the same family as one of the bad guys, right?'

'Namesake, actually.'

'Very good. Very good. Vince, give Michael a hand, will you? Right away, if you can.' He turned around and walked over to another table. There he spread his arms, wide, as if he were trying to encompass the whole room. 'Family,' he said. 'Without family we're free, and if we're free, we're lost.'

48

Mail from: HB2

Subject:???
WHERE ARE YOU???
ALL SET TO GO HERE.
MAIL!

49

A genetic directive

The whole group gathered around the computer screen. All of them had taken an interest in the e-mails I had sent to Huib, and all of them had something to say about the messages I had received from him—what he should do and especially what he shouldn't do. All of them seemed to know better than he did himself. I typed and mailed until my fingertips were black and blue. And until Huib had had enough.

'NO NO NO!' he wrote. His agitation erupted from the screen. 'This is Breger business. This is my family, okay? When one of us takes a wrong turn, it's up to the whole family to bring him back ... as a group. If the family wants Uncle Huib to do something, Uncle Huib does it. Make no mistake.'

'Very good,' said Karl. He smiled. 'Very good. When are they coming to get Uncle Huib? Ask him that.'

I typed the question and sent it. The answer came a couple of seconds later.

'Next week Monday.'

'Where?' I asked.

'Brussels.'

'In Brussels? Since when is HB in Brussels?'

'Hello! Is anybody home? Don't you guys get CNN?'

Karl picked up a remote control and pushed a button. A large TV set was hanging from a brace mounted to the ceiling. The image flashed and kept on jumping until it got to CNN. The news network was reporting on the EU summit in Brussels. Images showing the arrival of government leaders, smiling and shaking hands, of our own prime minister entering the building with the chancellor of Germany.

Laughing for the cameras. Pointing to each other. At people who couldn't be seen. Microphones being pushed forward from left and right on the waves of shouted questions that were no laughing matter.

'Are the borders going to be closed?'

'Is the EU going to adopt the ban on headscarves?'

'Are the radical mosques going to be closed?'

'Is freedom of religion at issue?'

Appealing hands, vague expressions. The prime minister stepped forward and spoke into the microphones. 'One thing,' he said. 'The problems are serious and no one denies it, but this is an integration summit, not a disintegration summit, and we intend to let the facts and figures speak for themselves, not the emotions.'

The CNN commentator took over and spoke of the enormous responsibility these leaders now faced. The task was to find a new balance in Europe. The challenge was to find a place and a role for the growing number of Muslims, one that would not threaten democracy. 'Defining the future' was what they called it on CNN, but the driving urgency of the American voices betrayed something very different. A threat. I pointed to the screen.

'We're going to let the facts and figures speak for themselves,' I said. 'But which facts and figures?'

Karl looked at me. 'Do you mean somebody's tampering with the social and political data? Nothing special about that. It's been going on for centuries. Everybody fudges his figures.'

'*His* figures, yes. People fudge their own figures all the time. But this is someone else who's been tampering with *our* facts. Interzonal Strategic Confrontation,' I said. 'I don't know exactly where those zones are, but one of them is here. Look.' I pointed to the TV. 'When you're out on the street or in a store or wherever, have you ever felt the threat and the danger that everybody today says is there? The threat that's in all the reports and that forms the basis of the facts and figures that they're talking about? Ever?'

'Impossible,' said Karl. His tone was decisive, almost abrupt. 'That would mean an extremely deep form of infiltration. It's just impossible.'

'That's what you think because you don't yet know about the network,' I said. 'Vince?'

Via the routers and Huib's secure server we went on the internet. I typed the domain name in the browser's uppermost field and in a flash the computer jumped to the virtual address.

Black screen. White type.

You have reached the home of Mr. Miller. Welcome?

Behind these two simple sentences appeared the slowly revolving earth. Green and white and blue, bathing in the unfiltered light of the sun in space. The home of Mr. Miller looked like a peaceful planet. The website was unchanged since the last time I had visited. With Huib's help, who was looking on from South Africa, I guided the people of The Pattern through the bizarre network. The first smug comments and jokes soon died away. Within just a couple of minutes they were all staring breathlessly at Mr. Miller's incredible reach. Karl needed about fifteen minutes to take it in and to comprehend the consequences. 'You have no life anymore,' he said. 'Whoever gets on the wrong side of this system may as well give up.'

'Thank you,' I said, happy that finally someone had put into words what I had been feeling for a couple of weeks.

From that moment on things started happening fast. Karl began organizing his people. A couple of men took over the M-drives from my laptop and from Vince's, removed the network program and began to extract the software, code by code. Others went onto the network and tried to gain access to the underlying data. Each one focused his attention on a part of the system, and soon the big room had turned into a workshop. People disappeared into their various tasks, into the minuscule space between bits and bytes, and each time it was amazing to see how much was possible by gaining control of the tiniest components.

Vince and I withdrew to a separate room to work things out with Huib. If the Bregers were going to go to Brussels the following Monday to restore the prodigal uncle to the bosom of the family, then I wanted to know how they were going to do it. When. And where. And I wanted to be there.

The European headquarters of HC&P was right outside the city in a business district designed along American lines, with broad lawns and manicured parks. I had been there a couple of times, for meetings and once for internal training.

It was the perfect place for the Bregers to strike. Secluded, spacious and easy to reach. The only real problem was access. No one could get in without an HC&P pass—unless they wanted to storm the building.

Huib mailed his pithy answer a couple of minutes later. 'We will if we have to. We went to fetch a cousin of ours once, someone who had been ... uh, how shall I put this ... exploited by her husband, okay? And then, too, we didn't just stand on the sidewalk and wait for him to come out. Didn't want to, either. We're not going there for the view. It's prettier here anyway.'

That thought alone cheered me up quite a bit. Nothing could bring Jessica back and nothing could restore the life I had before that night, before the day I left myself behind. But the idea of Huib Breger being hauled out of the HC&P building by his own flesh and blood brought a smile to my lips.

'I don't know how you think you're going to do this,' I mailed, 'but if you show up at the door with three guys,

HC&P is not going to be impressed.'

'You don't know my family,' Huib wrote back.

'We'll take care of the passes at our end,' I said, ignoring the surprised look on Vince's face. 'How many will you need? Ten? Fifteen? Twenty?'

Vince disappeared into the workshop. Producing twenty untraceable passes was much more difficult than I had let on. After the stunt I had pulled that night in the office here in Amsterdam, Vince had been identified as the maker of my new pass. Now he would have to find a way to erase the automatic registration of his work, and so far he had not been successful. Security measures had been taken that blocked every form of interference. If those security measures couldn't be hacked, then all the passes he produced would be spotted immediately—making them unusable. So he sat in the back of the big room, plugging away with one of the other programmers from The Pattern. Everyone was working with the same single-mindedness, with the same determination. For these people, the internet and information technology were the biggest achievements of individual freedom, symbols of man's ability to make information available and to decide what he did or did not want to know. The presumptuous statement by Mr. Miller, that it was *his* home and that he was the one to decide who was welcome and who wasn't, was an outright declaration of war.

A couple of hours later Karl came up to me. He told me how they were getting along. The security measures for the passes had been hacked. The network operating system on the laptops had been identified, and now they were trying to create a sabotage program, a sort of computer virus that would knock out the entire network.

'It's not as easy as it sounds, though,' he said. 'You can't just disable a couple of parts here and there. That has no effect whatsoever. The system simply overrides the defective part and makes itself a replacement. The controls aren't located in a single computer, either, so you can't just disconnect them. If only that were true. And not only that,' he hesitated a moment, 'but the whole thing is beautiful to behold. It's software with a kind of genetic directive. It would almost be a shame to disable it.'

'That's where you cross the line,' I said. I wasn't in the mood for his techno-romanticism.

'Probably,' he said. 'And that's not what I came here for anyway. In all the commotion we still haven't gotten to the second point.'

'What was that again?' I had forgotten his list of important things.

'The roadmap,' he said. 'What did you call it again?'

'The Roadmap for Interzonal Strategic Confrontation.'

'Right. Where can I find that thing? I've looked everywhere, but ...'

I shook my head, shrugged my shoulders and spread my hands. 'I have no idea,' I said. 'Where have you looked so far?'

Everywhere. He'd looked in every place I could think of. Every corner of the internet. The few references to the roadmap did not provide links to other pages or other sources.

'If it already exists,' said Karl, 'then it's not on the internet. And if it is on the internet, it's not in a place where search engines can reach.'

'What are you suggesting?' I asked.

'Intelligence services. Pentagon. Guys like that.'

If the information was tucked away in an organization like Huib Breger's or some other kind of secret service, I wanted to avoid it like the plague. Karl's confidence in his own safety measures was encouraging, but I wasn't totally convinced. For the time being no one knew where I was, and I wanted to keep it that way.

If possible.

'Wait a minute,' I said. Suddenly I remembered Jessica and Ina's papers and documents. 'Be right back.' I raced through the corridors to the shed and found the plastic bags in the camper. There they were, side by side in a corner between the little countertop and one of the benches. Bernie kept his spaceship neat and tidy.

Mail to: Jess

Subject: forever
I don't expect an answer, but I really miss you.
belli

The chessboard

Everything was all mixed up. After my fall in the HC&P stairwell I had gathered up all the papers that had been arranged in folders according to subject and simply stuffed them into the bags. All semblance of order was gone. I laid the sheets out on the floor one by one, side by side. Three bags full. There were hundreds of pages.

I examined the pages for identifying marks, connections, typefaces, anything I could find that would help me determine which papers belonged together. My eyes ran down the endless numbers of words. I didn't read. I scanned the pages, looking for an overall picture, a verbal image.

Many of the pages could be eliminated right away. As soon as I saw the name of a client, I knew I didn't have to look any further. HC&P would never entrust a client with what I was looking for. I made slow but steady progress, and at the end of the day I had three pages, three solitary pieces of paper, each one with a reference to RISC. That's all. All the references together did tell a story, but it was far from complete. It didn't explain what RISC was, or how it was constructed, or where it came from. Or who was behind it. Disappointed, I dropped the papers on the floor. Karl picked them up and gave them another look, but he couldn't see any more in them than a vague description of something we had no use for.

'And what's that?' he asked, pointing to a fourth plastic bag that was leaning against the wall untouched.

'That's some stuff from the other woman,' I said. 'Radekker, the woman from the financial department, but it doesn't amount to much, either. Bookkeeping, that's all. And I have no idea whose.'

Karl picked up the bag and took out the few thin folders, paged through them and shook his head. 'I'll show it to Sacha, she's good with figures.' With the papers in his hand he left the room, and from one moment to the next all was silent. I was standing there alone in that big space, surrounded by heaps of clutter. I dropped to the floor and began gathering it all together again and stowing it away.

Kirsten came in. 'Hi,' she said, and she sat down on the floor next to me. We both worked on straightening up the mess. Silent hands. Sounds of rustling paper. Stretching plastic.

'That woman?' she asked.

'Jessica?'

'Her, yes. Was that a girlfriend of yours?'

I nodded. 'I don't have that many,' I said.

'I'm sorry,' she said, and threw her arms around me. She rocked me back and forth. Slowly. A movement of mercy. 'I didn't know,' she said.

'There's so much we don't know about each other.'

'That's true. But you never told me.'

I shrugged my shoulders. Pressed my lips together. 'I don't know what to say,' I said. There was too much. Too much violence to clear the path for grief. I was still in too much of a hurry to allow it.

'Here,' said Kirsten. She pulled out my chapstick. 'Is this yours?'

I looked at the little plastic cylinder with surprise. For years I hadn't been able to do without it, and now I hadn't missed it in days. I rolled my lips together. They were supple and soft. No cracks or flakes of skin anywhere. I took the stick from her and dropped it into my pocket. A reminder. Of something.

Not at all sure of what.

The night was a constantly interrupted attempt to get more than an hour of sleep. Work went on in shifts. At two-thirty Vince came to get me. He had organized the passes. The entire process, from application to completion, was automated. The only thing we still had to do was to get the passes in our hands.

'Every day a courier goes out to deliver new passes. Not only for HC&P but for other companies, too. And that's where it gets sticky,' he said. 'Because I can make and order just about anything, but I can't get the courier to drive to a different address. The passes are for HC&P and they have to be delivered to HC&P. He'd never drop them off anywhere else. It's all part of the security procedures.'

'So?' I asked. Sleep was still fighting for the right to take over my body.

'So we have to think of something else.'

'You're kidding.' I stared at the computer screen. If I had to look at many more of those little menus and programs I'd go nuts. 'Then we have to intercept the courier somewhere,' I said.

Vince looked at me. 'How did you plan on doing that?'

'You know, force the car off the road, pull the guy out, grab the passes. How should I know!'

'Bad plan,' said Vince.

'Do you have a better one?'

He shook his head.

'Can you use the computer to find out the courier's route?'

In the middle of the night, Vince, Bernie, Kirsten and I were sitting at a table somewhere in the building. I was looking through the room's big windows out over the IJ. With a mug of steaming coffee in my hand I sauntered from one window to the next. Then to the adjacent room, a big, empty space. The linoleum on the floor was worn, the walls were drab and filthy and the woodwork was half rotten. Overdue maintenance was putting it far too mildly, but the space was unique. On the water with a view of the station, the city and the opposite side. I took pleasure in the space and the distance.

Vince handed us print-outs of the courier's route. Bernie explained the plan. Kirsten nodded and apparently knew what she was supposed to do.

Karl stuck his head in the door.

'L.G.? Does that ring a bell?' He was looking at me.

'Low grade?' I said.

'I think it's a company, but not any company you know?' I shook my head. Karl was already gone.

So was I.

The next morning I found Kirsten in the kitchen with toast, fried eggs and more coffee. We ate in silence. Daytime, today in particular, was more important than I was willing to admit. This weekend all the parties concerned were meeting in Brussels. Not only the EU leaders but also everyone at HC&P who had anything to do with me. With Mr. Miller. If ever there was a chance to exonerate myself, to free myself from the madness that was hunting me down, it was there. This weekend. After Monday everyone would be leaving. Going back to America, to all the countries from which the firm obtained its people.

There was nothing else for me to do in Amsterdam. Nor did it make any sense to wait any longer. If I couldn't make a breakthrough now, with all the help I was getting here, then all I could do was throw up my hands.

Kirsten and I walked together to the workshop, the big room with all the hardware. The people there were working in groups of three, trying to find a way to disrupt the network. Paralyze it. But so far they had nothing.

'The software is so elusive,' said Vince. 'No matter what we stick in, it gets isolated and defused. Just like that. Plop! As if we hadn't even tried anything.'

The network was visible on a big screen. Its gently pulsing streams, the flocks. It looked stronger than ever. More focused.

'Maybe it doesn't have anything to do with the software,' Kirsten said.

Karl reacted with irritation. 'It's always the software,' he said. 'Anybody who knows anything about it knows that it has to do with the software.'

Acting as if she hadn't even heard his sarcastic tone, Kirsten pointed to the monitor. 'The network,' she said. Her fingers slid across the screen. 'Why is it so elusive?'

'Because we don't know where it is. It's everywhere. In parts. And all those parts form a whole, not according to a fixed structure but according to a need that's determined second by second. It's as if you had a wound on your arm or your leg, and your body responds in different ways. First there's the stuff that gets sent through your blood vessels to the wound in order to close it. At the same time, the functions and tasks are redistributed so you don't have to use the wounded arm any more than necessary. Where does all this take place? In your brains, in your spinal column, in your nerves, your muscles, your heart. Everywhere.'

'Exactly,' said Kirsten. 'It's everywhere. So what is it then, that "everywhere"?'

'Computers,' said Karl. 'Millions of computers.'

'Hardware, you mean.' Kirsten turned around and walked to the table with the two dismantled laptops on it. 'That elusive software will only work on a network containing millions of computers. If you want to get at the software, you have to cripple the computers. Look.' She pointed to the parts on the table. 'All those computers have an extra drive. How they got it is something we haven't even talked about yet, but the extra drive is there. The network works because all the computers sign in as soon as they go on line. That signing in is automatic. It's in the software of the extra hard drive. What you need is a program that will sign the computer back out and clear the extra drive. And that's it. Done. Down they go. One by one.'

'Times who knows how many million,' said Vince.

'Ah, what's a few million these days?' said Kirsten. 'You know the story of the Egyptian chess player? He had saved the country, and the pharaoh asked him to choose his reward. The chess player pointed to the chessboard and said, "Sire, this is the reward I choose. Put one grain of wheat on the first square of my chessboard. Put two grains on the second. Four on the third, and so on. On every square put double the amount from the previous square, until you've covered all the squares on the chessboard." "Is that all?" asked the pharaoh, who couldn't imagine he'd be losing more than one bag of grain. "That's all," said the chess player. Well, we all know what happened.'

Karl looked at her, eyebrows raised. 'By the twentieth square you're over a million,' he said.

'In twenty-four steps you'd have hit more than ten million computers. And the only thing you need to do is to instruct every computer to find two other computers that have signed onto the same network before that computer knocks itself out. Two. No more than that. That's nothing for a bit of virus.'

'That's right,' said Karl. 'But how do we get such a virus into the first computer?'

Kirsten pointed to the two laptops. 'You've got two right here,' she said. 'You can experiment with one until you get it right. Then you inject the virus into the other computer and reconnect it to the network.'

'That means we only have one chance,' said Vince.

'One chance, yeah.' Kirsten laid a finger in the middle of his chest and tapped it a few times. Long fingernail, light blue on his black T-shirt. 'But that's always the way it is, right, Vince?'

He laughed. 'I only get one chance,' he asked. 'That's all?'

She shook her head slowly.

'I wasn't talking about you,' she said. She fluttered her eyelashes and walked away. 'In an hour and a half we have to be out of here,' she said. 'Don't forget.'

Vince and I watched her go.

'How many squares does a chessboard have, anyway?'

'Sixty-four,' I said.

Vince closed his eyes and tried to work out the answer. After a couple of minutes he gave up.

'So tell me,' he said. 'How many grains of wheat did this guy get?'

'The entire national harvest for one year.'

52

The interests of the Lord

Kirsten walked down the sidewalk. Tight knit top, bare midriff, gleaming, supple sweatpants, small bag over her shoulder, orange Pumas. Every step she took was a good one. Beautiful morning. Sun on the canal. Not a breath of wind. June at its best. Keizersgracht in Amsterdam. Lots of people on the street. Lots of traffic. The courier's car was parked in front of a large building. A bank. The courier himself had just gone inside. Small package in his hand. Car in the middle of the streets, hazard lights flashing. He'd be gone for a couple of minutes. Kirsten walked slowly up to the car.

Vince groaned. The camper was standing in a parking spot a little further on. We followed Kirsten's movements through one of the windows in the back. Vince couldn't help himself.

'Boy, that sister of yours.'

'Some other time, Vince.'

The courier came back out, quickly, taking the entrance steps two at a time. He looked down the canal to the right, to the left, to the row of cars that were backed up behind his. He gestured his apologies. Laughed. Fantastic day. And ran straight into Kirsten, who with two well-timed strides had manoeuvered herself right onto his path.

Vince groaned. 'If I don't get her soon, bad things are going to happen.'

'Vince.'

'You're no help.'

Kirsten scrambled up and looked around, dazed. Grabbed onto the courier for a moment and laughed.

The courier laughed, too. Concerned, afraid she'd broken

or bruised something. Kirsten felt her head, moved her neck back and forth a couple of times, swung her hips left and right, to see if everything still worked.

Vince closed his eyes.

'It was your idea,' I said.

'I know. I'm a genius.'

The courier said something. Kirsten pointed. The courier said something else and Kirsten nodded. She opened the door on the passenger's side and got in. The courier ran around his car and got in on the driver's side. In a few seconds the hazard lights went off.

'Pay attention,' I said. 'Now!'

Bernie steered the camper onto the road. Behind him the courier was able to break just in time. 'Ready?' he asked.

'Go!' said Vince.

Bernie shifted the camper into reverse and backed the thing up with agonizing slowness. The courier began honking his horn, but Bernie paid no attention and backed the camper up further and further until it hit the courier's car with a clear jolt. Nothing dramatic. Not hard enough to make any dents or cause any damage, but an unmistakable hit nonetheless. Just to make sure, Bernie gave the camper a little more gas, effortlessly pushing the courier's car one metre backward. The courier leaned on his horn, threw open his door and came running up to Bernie. At the same time, Vince and I opened the side door of the camper and painstakingly began to unload a bookcase. While the courier shouted at Bernie and demanded that he get out of the camper, we put the bookcase down in such a way that Kirsten was blocked from his view.

Kirsten worked with breakneck speed. She pulled the key out of the car's ignition, went through the rest of the keys on the ring and found the one to the courier's valise, opened it and took out the order list and the pack of passes. She pulled a new order list from her bag, scribbled an initial in one of the boxes, put the new list in the valise, locked it back up, put the key back in the ignition and got out of the car. In less than a minute she was lying on the floor of the camper under the table, Vince and I on the benches on either side. Bookcase back in. Side door shut.

The damage to the car proved to be no more than a scratch on the bumper. After a couple of minutes the tension turned to relief and Bernie calmed the courier down.

'I just didn't see you,' he said. 'You have such a tiny little car, man, I didn't even feel it.' He laughed. 'Here.' He gave the man a card. 'If it turns out we missed something, just give me a call. You can always reach me here.'

They shook hands, patted each other on the shoulder. What's a little scratch between two men? Bernie turned around once more. 'And make sure you call, okay? If anything's wrong. You make sure now!' Laughing, he got into the camper and started it up.

'And if he does call, who's going to answer the phone?' Vince asked.

'Kitchen supply wholesaler, I think. Oven gloves and coasters. Nice stuff. I got that card last year from a guy at the automation show.' He shifted gears and drove away. 'And?' he asked without looking back.

Vince peeked out of the little curtain running across the back window. The courier was about to get in his car. He bent down and looked inside, straightened up again and looked around.

'He's looking for Kirsten,' said Vince.

'Who isn't?' Kirsten said from under the table. It sounded tough, but only she knew whether she meant it that way or not.

Bernie drove down the Rozengracht and the Nieuwe Zijdsvoorburgwal in the direction of the train station. In front of the station he turned onto the Prins Hendrikkade and took the IJ Tunnel back to the shed in Amsterdam North, with twenty unregistered passes to the HC&P building. Vince had cleared all the information concerning the passes from the system. After the courier had picked them up and left, Vince had altered the order list in the computer. The passes for HC&P were no longer there. He had then erased the old list from the computer of the courier company. Kirsten had put the print-out of the new list in the courier's valise and taken the old list with her. The courier wouldn't miss it because he had been given the whole valise, passes and all, at the beginning of the day. WorldWare had no record of the passes in its archive: no record that they were made and no record that they were delivered. These twenty passes didn't exist. But they worked.

Karl was waiting for us in the shed and took us to the workshop, to a table where a woman was sitting behind a computer in total concentration.

'This is Sacha,' he said. 'Sacha is working on L.G.' She reached out her hand and glanced at me. Not too long. She was focused on her work.

'L.G., from Radekker's records,' I said.

Karl nodded. 'What those records actually are is still unclear,' he said. 'But at least now we know where they come from.'

'L.G.?'

'Larkowl Group.' It took Sacha some time to extricate herself from her work. Her eyes kept drifting back to the screen, and her right hand to the mouse. She felt more at ease with the computer than with people she didn't know. She was the kind of woman who's ashamed of her intelligence and of being interested in systems instead of fashion. She wore black pants and a black sweater. Her dark hair kept falling down over her eyes, and every other sentence she turned her back to us to point to something on the screen or to click to another field. She spoke in short sentences, and each sentence was meant to convey information. Sacha was not one for descriptive prose.

'The Larkowl Group is a foundation,' she said. 'An organization of pious Christians. Mainly in North America. Set up to ...' she turned around and read from the screen, '... "defend the interests of our Lord Jesus Christ and to safeguard them in a world that is turning further and further from holiness and that no longer accepts holiness as a guiding principle." Their words.'

'A church, you mean?' I asked. 'A sect?'

'No. Just the opposite, actually. They have no form of liturgy or service of any kind. No buildings, no centres. Nothing. As far as I can tell, the foundation is an alliance of rich businessmen, politicians and military officers. That's less unusual there than it is here.'

'Larkowl Group,' I said.

'There are nine people on the board of the foundation. Names that don't mean anything to me, except for Ralph Well, the owner of Datwell Computers.'

Everyone knew Datwell, the company that within the space of five years had captured more than forty percent of the PC and laptop market with good merchandise for less money.

'I still have to look up the rest of the names. There they are.' She leaned back a bit and turned the screen so we all could read the list. Alphabetical. Ralph Well was there, all right, almost at the bottom. But my eyes were drawn to the second name, Herbert Colland, co-founder and owner of the largest consultancy in the world, the 'C' in HC&P.

'The foundation is based in Houston, Texas,' Sacha said, 'and it has a small office there with a few staff members. Not many. The Larkowl Group itself is small and avoids any form of publicity.'

'Except the internet.'

'What do you mean?' Sacha gave me a puzzled look.

'Apparently,' I said, 'because you were able to find all this information there.'

'Oh, this,' said Sacha. 'This didn't come from the internet. You won't find anything about the Larkowl Group on the internet. We looked ourselves silly, but you can't find anything about this organization through the normal channels. Nothing. This,' she said, and she tapped the monitor with her finger, 'is from Mr. Miller. I'm in their computer. It's from the M-drive.'

'How long have you been there?'

She looked at her watch. 'Half an hour. Maybe a little longer.'

Too many thoughts were crowding into my head. Questions, concrete questions and vague uncertainties. What were Herbert Colland and Ralph Well doing on the board of this foundation? What did the foundation itself actually do? How much time would it take for them to find us here? And what then? What was this all about, anyway? The Larkowl Group? Safeguard interests? For Jesus Christ? What was going on here?

'What kinds of interests do you mean?' I asked.

'I don't know yet,' said Sacha. 'You need a password and user name for most of the information, and we still have to get around that.'

I thought for a minute. 'And who is Mr. Miller?' I asked. 'Is he in the foundation, too?'

Sacha shook her head. 'Not that I know of.'

I cursed. 'Why should these people have anything to do with me? That's what I want to know. Why should they want me ...' These were questions without answers. I wanted to know too much all at once. 'Okay,' I said, 'another question. What kind of computer do they have there at the Larkowl Group?'

'You mean type and specifications?'

'No, what brand?'

She clicked the mouse a couple of times and a window appeared on the screen. She read what it said. 'A Datwell Pro 8100. Big brute. Not the very newest, but very, very good.'

'Datwell,' I said.

'Yes. Almost everybody has a Datwell, so there's nothing unusual about that.'

'You, too?'

Sacha and Karl laughed. 'No, we don't,' said Karl. 'We buy components and put them together ourselves. It's cheaper and better and you can adapt the equipment to your needs faster.'

'But does this mean that all the computers with an M-drive are Datwell computers?'

There was silence. That was another question waiting to be answered. I could guess, and I did, too, but it was no more than a guess. 'Because somebody's got to handle that end of the business, right? On a regular basis. Without anyone knowing.'

'I could point out a few at random,' said Sacha. With a click of her mouse the image on her screen changed faster than I could keep up with. 'Datwell,' she said. 'And here's one, too, Datwell. And this one. And this. That's only five, but ...'

'But all five are Datwell,' I said. 'And then the next question. How do they manage to sell the machines at a lower price than anyone else while there's twice as much stuff inside? My laptop had two hard drives, two CPUs and who knows how much extra circuitry, and it cost a hundred and fifty euros less than the laptops from other companies that don't have all those things. How do they do it? How can those guys make so much money? Datwell is pretty much the biggest in the world. There are almost four and a half million computers on Mr. Miller's network. Four and a half million! Considering the cost price alone these things ought to be fifty euros more expensive. Not less! I mean, we've all seen how a business works on the inside. So why didn't this outfit go bankrupt long ago?'

We stared at the computer screen in silence.

'Maybe it's not a sales organization,' said Kirsten.

'What do you mean?'

'Well, maybe we're not seeing it because we're looking at it the wrong way. Say you want to build a worldwide computer network. Four and a half million units linked together. Units that offer you access to all the information you might want. And that also make it possible for you to change information at will. Say that's your objective. How much would that cost?'

'To build?'

'Yes. Approximately. Doesn't have to be accurate to the last euro.'

'It's incalculable,' said Karl. 'A hundred billion? Five hundred billion? You tell me. You can buy four and a half million computers for four billion, a thousand euros apiece, and that would go a long way toward covering the costs. But then you have to place them all over the world. And all the rest.'

'So,' said Kirsten slowly, as if pondering every word, 'if you were able to buy such a system, such a network, fully assembled, operational, fully loaded, for, well, let's say nine hundred million?'

'You'd be crazy not to,' said Karl. Instinctive reaction. He turned around and looked at the screen. 'Huh?'

'It all depends on how you look at it,' said Kirsten. 'You can see Datwell as a company that sells computers below cost, which means they ought to be bankrupt. Or you can see it as a company that buys something priceless for a song.'

'So it's not selling but buying,' said Karl. 'You add two hundred euros to every Datwell computer. Probably less, because part of the price advantage is genuine. You deliver

the stuff with every order, all over the world, and the customer does all the work. All you need are a couple years'
patience.' He whistled softly. 'That's why Datwell hasn't
gone bankrupt. They're making the deal of the century
here.'

'But who are they making it for? And why?' Vince asked.
'To safeguard the interests of the Lord? That's a load of crap!
How am I supposed to understand this?'

'Literally,' I said. For the first time I saw the logic of the
whole nightmare scenario. For the first time I understood
why a human life could be ended so easily. For the first time
I understood why I was no longer welcome in the home of
Mr. Miller: in the interests of the Lord I had been written off
ages ago.

53

Mail from: HB2

Subject: check-in
first group has left, checking in one hour from now, late
afternoon flight, feel just like a travel agency, hardly ever
go on the internet except to order tickets, do the planning,
duh, give me hard data every time, huib

Mail from: Peter Bellicher
Subject: Dad
K, Mike, dad's in the hague. Since yesterday, 21b
Trompstraat. I'm going there saturday morning—where are
you guys anyway, because this basically sucks, not being
together
cu pete

54

Everything we have is here

I saw what I thought I was seeing. Or what others wanted me to see. Actually there was only one thing I knew for certain: everything I saw was somehow being manipulated. To a certain extent that wasn't so bad; it may have been unavoidable. No one knows what reality is. What hurts one person is barely felt by another. My reality was a battlefield, a great chaos of grief and misery. But for others it was almost the end of a clean-up campaign. Just one more good sweep and the job would be done.

But what was I seeing? A strange organization on the other side of the ocean. Rich men who invested their money in a bizarre and incomprehensible computer network. Men for whom a few hundred million was nothing. I saw things that were too far away. That was it. I had to look closer to home. Dries van Waayen, Huib Breger. Johan Wolfsen. Gijs. Where was Gijs? He'd gone to the corporate headquarters in America, Jessica had said. But what did she really know about it? Did I hear what I wanted to hear, did I hear what someone else wanted me to hear, or was he really there? Someone was bound to be in touch with him. I picked up the phone and called his backyard neighbour.

'Silverschmidt.'

'Emma?' I said. 'It's the shed guy.' And this time she knew exactly who that was. I waited to see whether she would stay on the line or cut me off.

'Yes?' she said.

'I'm calling for Gijs.'

'He's not here.'

'No, but I was wondering if you had heard anything from him?'

'When?'

'Last week.'

'No.'

'And before that?'

'The day he got out of the hospital was the last time. I haven't seen him since then.'

'No phone call? No card?'

'Nothing.'

'Me neither.'

'Not surprising, after what happened here.'

'Maybe not,' I said. 'But that's the whole point, right? Maybe I don't think it's strange, but why do I think that way? Why are you talking to me now when you didn't the last time?'

'Because I read the newspaper, and nothing there matches the picture of you I'd come to know. You've really lost your way somehow, but hey, who hasn't, you know what I mean? As far as that's concerned you're a perfectly normal human being.'

'So?'

'So I call on my own experience. On what I know. That's something I can trust. Or no, I said that wrong. I know how far I can trust it.'

'You know the limits?'

'Yes, I know the limits of my own trustworthiness. That's it. And I can use that to assess the trustworthiness of other people. Not whether something is true or not. When you get right down to it, I don't really know whether you killed someone or not. I'm sorry I have to say it, but as long as I don't know, I can only look at the likelihood of its being true. And that's easy. The trustworthiness of the media pales in comparison with mine.'

'Okay,' I said. 'Gijs and I talked to each other every day. For three years straight. About nothing. About everything. Work, women, cars, houses in France, loneliness, orgasms, shoes ...'

'Shoes?'

'And now I haven't heard anything from him in almost two weeks.'

Emma Silverschmidt was silent.

'My own experience tells me that that is very, very odd,' I said, 'regardless of what I did or did not do.'

'I agree,' she said. 'But you probably didn't call to hear me tell you that I agree with you.'

Suddenly I had to laugh, because that was exactly why I did call. No matter how strongly she insisted that you have to base your judgments on your own experience, I had an enormous need for someone who agreed with me. Certainly as far as Gijs was concerned.

'Would you do something for me?' I asked. 'Go into Gijs's house through the shed and see if you can find anything. A note, a message, a letter for the cleaning lady. Something.'

'Will do,' said Emma. She became practical from one minute to the next. She wanted a number where she could reach me. Apparently she was just as eager to know Gijs's whereabouts as I was.

Gijs had turned my head upside down. Suddenly I was looking at the people who were closest to me. In my immediate vicinity. Gijs had disappeared, and the more I thought about it the more convinced I became that he wasn't in America at all. It didn't make any sense. I had believed it because Jessica had said it. Once again I had seen what someone else wanted me to see. Gijs was in the States. Working on a big project. International level. Nothing could be easier to believe, especially because the person who told me was someone I trusted. Someone I wanted to trust. Jess.

And this brought me to the one place I didn't want to be, the place I had been avoiding so carefully all that time, sidestepping with my eyes closed, with my head averted. To Jessica. Jess. Golden Jess. To the question that had stuck with me long after her death because I didn't want to hear the answer. Jessica was dead and there was no room for doubt. Emotion is a tough director. Tough as nails. Whatever doesn't suit his purpose gets the boot. Ruthless. Questions? What do you mean, questions?

These, for instance.

Why was Huib Breger in her apartment?

Because I had gone on the internet from her apartment. That was the easy answer. I had made contact with Erik Strila's computer via the secure server and had stayed in contact with him for half an hour. At least. Since bumping into Breger and his men in her apartment, I had assumed that the secure server had been hacked. That they had cut through all the ingenious defenses and had found me. After all, HB2 in South Africa had disappeared, too. The conclusion seemed logical—until I got back in touch with him and learned that his server was still secure. HB2 hadn't disappeared at all. No one had tracked him down. He was as safe as anything, so Jessica and I should have been safe as well.

Why were those men in her apartment?

Because Jessica herself had let them in. That was the difficult answer. The answer I had been afraid of all that time and for which there was no longer any alternative. Jessica had reported that I was in her apartment. She had told Dries van Waayen, perhaps, or another one of the partners. I didn't think she had ever had direct contact with Huib Breger. But she had reported it herself, and in doing so she had called in the clean-up team of the Risk Containment Group. There was no other explanation. What had she e-mailed me from America? 'Our relationship is really starting to make things shaky for me here. You know how they are: you're either for us or against us. The corporate family is sacred and I don't know what I'm supposed to say anymore.'

The limits of trustworthiness could only be seen in one

way. And if Jessica had said that Gijs was in America, I now had every reason not to believe her.

My head was spinning. I was dizzy with betrayal. Even though Jessica and I had often toyed with the border between our careers and our relationship, and taunted each other with the loyalty that the company demanded, we still assumed that the balance would always end up in our favour. Tacitly. Maybe I was the only one who thought so, and I was too quick to take it for granted that Jessica would agree with me.

One minute I was relieved, the next minute I felt deceived. The new certainty I had found came with a high price tag. The old one I had traded in for it had left a hole, an absence that was bigger than lost property. As if the surgeon had amputated a leg to save my life. I was alive, I was healthy again, and that knowledge made me stronger than I had felt in a long time. But there was no denying the handicap.

Vince, Bernie, Karl and Kirsten were staring at the screen with eyes agog. Next to the keyboard was a digital camera, and on the screen there were photos of an apartment. It had been a modern place once, but now the interior was in ruins. Chairs were lying on the floor with shattered legs. A table was broken in two. The couch had been cut open. In the kitchen the exhaust fan was hanging crookedly from the wall, doors had been pulled out of the cabinets and the contents were scattered all over the floor. The mess was mind-boggling.

'Look,' said Vince. 'My CDs!' He pointed to the twisted and warped plastic boxes and disks. Black streaks of soot ran up to the ceiling. The wooden shelves were scorched. 'It looks like somebody took a flame thrower to it!'

'And you haven't even seen the bedroom yet,' said Bernie. He pushed a button on the camera and the image changed. The bedroom was beyond all recognition. 'This is where the fire department went to work,' said Bernie. Water lay on the floor in puddles. Everything was black, charred.

Karl turned around and looked at me. 'And this is all because of you?' he asked.

'This is nothing,' I said.

'Oh, no?' He stood and walked up to me. 'I'll be the one to decide that, if you don't mind.'

'You?'

Karl nodded. This was his place, his world. He was spoiling for a confrontation that I wasn't the least bit interested in, but now I realized that I couldn't step aside.

'And why would you be the one to decide that? Nobody's been here yet. There are three other people here who have some deciding to do, and that's Vince, Kirsten and me. You've only seen a few photos. No more than that!'

We faced each other in silence, not sure of the next step. I had no intention of taking the blame again for whatever happened. At some point it had to stop. I understood Karl, all right. He had opened his door to Kirsten and me. He was fascinated by Mr. Miller's network, by the technology involved, by the software, which he was opposed to in principle but found so beautiful that he wanted to learn all about it. Now suddenly the world was more than virtual. Physical threats came closer to the bone, and he hadn't counted on that.

'If anything happens to these people ...'

'It already has,' I said.

'Hey, it's just stuff,' said Vince. He walked over and stood between us, putting an arm around Karl's shoulder. 'Now I don't have to move. That's one way of looking at it.'

'Okay,' said Karl. 'But it's not my way of looking at it. This is my place. Our place. Everything we have is here. This site is our haven, literally and figuratively. On the banks of the IJ, in the heart of Amsterdam. If we let someone in, we expect them not to abuse our trust.'

'*You have reached the home of Mr. Miller.*' I didn't know why I said it, but it was just the right thing to say. On another scale, and with other people, but the meaning was the same. Everyone drew a line somewhere to determine who he was. My mother drew the line between herself and her family. She no longer recognized herself in her husband and her children. No, it wasn't recognition, it was stronger than that. In order to stay with her family she would have to change, and if she did that she wouldn't be herself anymore. That's what drove her, the protection of her identity. *The home of Mr. Miller.* Kirsten had to look deep inside herself and choose between her body and her spirit, between what she knew and what she was. My father hadn't known who he was for years, but when my mother threatened to break the bond between him and his children, his choice was made, too. If you know who you belong with, then you know who you are. It's a topsy-turvy world, but the world has been standing on its head for so long that we aren't used to anything else. Jessica chose power, the road to the top of the international business community. That road was open to her, but the power didn't want her because she was tied to me. Mr. Miller drew the line somewhere else. Right through the middle of her. And me? I had never made a choice. Not one like that. For ten years I outpaced my own time. Late nights blended seamlessly into early mornings. Sleep was a lost moment between projects. Deadlines sucked the life out of the love I was supposed to be feeling, which slowly but surely degenerated into nothing more than an arrangement. Just another arrangement. The pressure of work was always a valid reason for not choosing. Not today. Not now.

Until a couple of weeks ago, when it was decided that I no longer belonged there. It. Was. Decided. Maybe I hadn't had much experience in making decisions, but this was a decision I didn't agree with. I had to start somewhere.

'Karl,' I said, 'what you guys do here is terrific. Really. Without Kirsten and Vince and without you all I'd be wasting away in some hotel. I wouldn't know what I know now. And I'm very grateful to you all for that.'

'So behave yourself if you're so grateful.'

'That's what I'm doing.' I pointed to the photo of the gutted room. 'I didn't do that. I know who did, though, and I know they did it to catch me. Or Vince first and then me. It doesn't matter. So what are you asking, really? That I pick up my stuff and leave? So you guys don't have to be afraid anymore of the people who are looking for me? Is that what you're asking? And should Vince leave, too? And all the people here who've been connected to that goddamned network—do they have to leave?' My voice cut through the big room like a knife. Not a keyboard or a telephone could be heard. Only the constant hum of dozens of computers, the murmur of technology that has replaced silence almost everywhere.

'What we do here is safe,' said Karl.

'I was safe, too,' I said. 'I was the safest person I knew.' I saw Sacha get up from her work table behind him. Noiselessly she approached us until she was standing right behind Karl. She tapped him on the arm.

'Karl?'

'Not now, Sacha.' He was about to turn away. Sacha grabbed his arm and held him back.

'Karl,' she said. 'I'm in.'

55

The world is too small for us

Behind the scenes at the Larkowl Group the power was there for the taking. It was a foundation in which the biggest companies in the United States had combined forces. Construction companies, weapons manufacturers, oil companies, information technology, computer manufacturers, private security firms and many more saw it as a platform for defending their interests. The foundation maintained contact with politicians and military officers who lent their names to various commissions, joint ventures and trade delegations, for a great deal of money. It was a cartel of power and capital that asserted its influence without the slightest bit of restraint. The archives showed activities taking place all over the world. And wherever it went, the group displayed an unparalleled drive.

'Here, this was what you were looking for, right?' said Sacha. She clicked her mouse and the request for a password appeared on the screen. She typed something and eight stars appeared in the field. She clicked on 'next' and two new fields opened up. In the first was an eight-figure number. The second was empty.

'This was the hardest part,' said Sacha. She typed the eight figures into a laptop that was next to her standard keyboard. The laptop made a quick calculation and soon produced a new code consisting of five numbers and two letters. Sacha copied that code into the second field, and soon a new image appeared on the screen. A text. No more than two lines.

Roadmap for Interzonal Strategic Confrontation
Forward Defense program

Sacha clicked with her mouse. The text disappeared and a new one took its place.

Never fight a war at home if you can fight it somewhere else.
M. Miller

What followed was a description of RISC, a program for the active defence of Christianity against the advance of Islam and the threat of radical fundamentalism. In silence we read what the plan entailed and how it was being carried out. It was crystal clear, far too clear. Not only because of its smug self-assurance but also because of its scale. A strictly controlled information war was being carried out to ensure that the strategic confrontation did not take place in the United States. To avoid such a scenario, the polarization in Europe was being intensified. Research studies and reports were being manipulated in every conceivable way so that governments would always opt for the toughest policy. These policies provoked violent reactions from Muslims. Minor and major attacks in France, Germany, England, Spain and the Netherlands had steeled these countries in their decision to adopt the hardest line possible.

The confrontation was already taking place, and Mr. Miller made sure we were kept sufficiently frightened. Terrified. Because without fear the confrontation doesn't work. Time and again, the most alarming figures were chosen as the basis for policy. Factions of the Christian political parties were given reports that they could use to lambaste every moderate opinion. Mr. Miller was the linchpin in an information war and Europe was the theatre of operations.

'Everything is always different than what you think,' said Karl. 'How in God's name did you get mixed up in this?'

'Here we're all mixed up in this,' I said. 'The only difference is that now we know. But don't worry. I'm leaving the day after tomorrow. I'm going to Brussels.'

'Brussels,' he said. 'Right. And what do you think you can accomplish there?'

'I can get my life back. Because the man who can prove my innocence is in Brussels.'

'How's he going to do that? By furnishing you with an alibi?'

'No,' I said. 'By confessing to the crime himself.'

Karl said nothing. He pressed his lips into a tight frown. His forehead looked more expansive than ever. 'Solid plan,' he said, and without waiting for my response he turned to Bernie. 'How many UMTS lines do you have in the camper?' he asked.

'Three. And a dish.'

'Can you be ready to leave by the end of the day tomorrow?'

Bernie nodded.

'Great. Sacha, can you expose the Larkowl Group website to the press?'

'With a couple of minor alterations.'

'Vince, how's it going on the anti-software for Mr. Miller?'

'It's not,' said Vince. He shook his head. 'No matter what we write, there's always a new security layer.'

Karl cursed softly. 'We still have forty-eight hours to do something about that, which is more time than we've ever needed. Okay?' With that he turned back to me and poked his index finger into my chest. 'We'll talk again tomorrow at the end of the day. I don't want to see you until then.'

Emma called. She had searched the whole house. The only thing she could find was a small, rolled-up note in the peep-hole between her shed and Gijs's garden house.

'A note in that particular spot, it must mean something,' she said. 'It's got to. No one knows about that place. I almost overlooked it myself. He must have put it there the one day he was home. After the hospital. Except I can't make head nor tail of the message. Here, listen ...'

I heard her fiddling with a scrap of paper. The faint rustling sound was clear over the phone. She read.

'W. is available.'

She paused. 'Do you understand that?' she asked. 'Because I certainly don't.'

'Maybe,' I said. 'I think W. is his Uncle Walter. He's at the Ministry of the Interior. I met him once. Apparently he's in contact with Gijs. Or Gijs with him. Or whatever. I'll figure that out later on.'

'Let me know,' she said. 'As soon as you learn anything. Because I'm really starting to miss the boy next door.'

Bernie was in the shed, converting the camper into a high-tech communication centre. The little countertop had disappeared and had been replaced by a workbench. Three flat screen monitors were hanging on the wall, and next to them was a panel with telecom connections and a stack of headsets. Bernie was lying under the workbench with cables and cords all around him.

'Be with you in a minute,' he said. He fastened the cables somewhere with a click, plugged in the cords and tucked everything away in a ready cable holder. Then he reappeared, sliding out carefully on his back. The interior of the camper had been radically changed. All traces of domesticity were gone. Now it looked more like a conference room, and even the dining table and benches seemed to fit in.

'Plug and play,' he said. 'All the connections are in the wall. The entire countertop with everything included. Taps, drainage. Just click 'em out and click the workbench in. Easy peasy. The computers are already installed.' He opened the kitchen cabinets. Cleaning supplies to the left, and on the right three identical PCs side-by-side, tightly secured in a plastic frame. On a shelf above was a battery of modems.

Broadband. Red and green LED lamps flickering. 'Standard camping gear,' he said. 'What can I do for you?'

'I have to call someone,' I said, 'but I don't want anyone to know where I'm calling from. Not even afterward by tracing the number.'

'Okay.' Bernie nodded and looked at the equipment he was installing. 'Now?'

'Can you manage it?'

'I think so. A couple of minutes.' He reached under the workbench, pulled out a kind of fold-out stool and sat down at the keyboard. He clicked casually through several menus and created connections that only existed in computers. I watched Bernie in silence. He was a heavy-set man in his early thirties. Big hands and fat fingers that obeyed his every command with remarkable speed and precision. His touch on the keys was light, lighter than mine. I hammered away with far too much force, as if the energy I was pounding in would be reflected in what I typed. Not him. He didn't fight with the equipment. Nor was there any reason to do so, since he and the machines were on the same side. He knew the world that existed behind the buttons, so he never had to get rough with them.

That's what I thought, and that's what I felt here all around me: the will of people to bond together, both with each other and with the invisible systems that control so much of our lives.

'Oh, no, sorry,' said Bernie, not to me but to the screen, and with nimble fingers he remedied his mistake. 'There, is that better?' From behind the little door came a satisfied hum. Bernie looked fixedly at the formulas and codes flashing by on the screen until the computer finally settled down, producing a tiny, discreet little noise.

Beep.

'I thought so,' said Bernie. He picked up a cordless phone. 'What number?' he asked.

I gave him the number of Walter Eberhuizen, Secretary-General of the Ministry of the Interior.

Bernie keyed in a much longer number. 'Satellite connection, onto the internet via the secure server of that friend of yours in South Africa and then off again and onto a landline to The Hague. Not all that complicated, but it has to be good enough. Here.' He handed me the phone.

I listened to the connection being made, its progress marked by a series of clicks and peeps, via a mechanism that was orbiting the earth to a country on the other side of the equator and then back to the Netherlands. Amsterdam—The Hague. The world is too small for us.

'Eberhuizen.'

I jumped. I had not expected to get the man himself on the line but his secretary. After a bit of spluttering I regained my composure. I explained who I was, that we had met a couple of weeks earlier in connection with a possible assignment for HC&P and that subsequent events had unfortunately made any further contact impossible.

'I know very well who you are, Mr. Bellicher. Even without the explanation.'

'I was afraid you might.'

'The question is whether talking to you is such a good idea. We can't talk about the work. The assignment is moving along, the first phase is almost completed and as I understand it you are no longer associated with the firm. And that's not surprising considering the things you're suspected of having done.'

I barely heard the last comment. I was stuck with the third sentence. 'The assignment is moving along?' I asked.

'Yes, of course.'

'You haven't cancelled it?'

'No. It was quite unclear for the first few days, but later I discussed it at length with Van Waayen, and Gijs told me how things stood, so ...'

'Gijs?' I asked. 'Is Gijs in charge of the assignment?'

'No, what gave you that idea? Frans Stutman is here, nice fellow. Gijs is gone, by the way. He's with the whole EU team in Brussels.'

'In Brussels,' I said. So Gijs wasn't in the United States after all. He was a couple of hundred kilometres away. If his Uncle Walter was right, then I knew exactly where to look for Gijs. The European headquarters of HC&P was not just a sterile building with work stations and conference rooms. It was the European heart of the company. People from all over the world went there for training and projects. The big EU assignments were contracted out and divided there. Parts of them were farmed out to offices in other countries, but occasionally international teams were assembled, with specialists who sometimes spent months in Brussels. To avoid having to put everyone up in hotels for their entire stay, HC&P had had a new tower added on to the main office with small apartments and suites, a restaurant, a movie theatre, a bar, a fitness centre and a swimming pool—all the facilities a modern consultant needed. The entire building, including the offices, had even better security than the office in Amsterdam. No one got in without the right pass. For Gijs the opposite was true: you couldn't get out without that pass, either. Everything was equally luxurious, but in practice the building was as effective as a prison.

'When was the last time you spoke to him?' I asked.

'Less than a week ago, last Monday.' He hesitated. 'Why do you ask?'

'I can't find him,' I said, 'but now that I know where he is, I'm reassured.'

'So should I be reassured as well?'

'I don't know what you've heard,' I said, 'although I can guess most of it.'

'Mr. Bellicher, you're charged with two counts of murder. You're the most wanted man in the Netherlands. I would very much like to be certain of seeing Gijs at my fifty-ninth birthday party in two weeks.'

'You will, if I have anything to do with it,' I said.

'Splendid.'

'But actually I'm not the one to ask,' I said. 'Mr. Van Waayen is.'

There were a few seconds of silence. I waited for him to speak. I didn't know what he was waiting for (everyone has his own procedure for dealing with these things).

'I can tell from the tone of your voice,' he finally said, 'that I probably shouldn't do that. Or am I hearing you wrong?'

'No, you're hearing me just fine.' I felt a smile spread across my face. Eberhuizen was holding the door open for me. 'Personally I have a couple of questions for Mr. Van Waayen myself,' I said. 'Maybe I can include yours while I'm at it?'

'Mr. Bellicher, as long as you give me sufficient reason, I'm man enough to ask my own questions. I think that's a better way of going about it. If I knew where you were, I'd have to alert the police. So I think our conversation is over now. Don't you?'

Eberhuizen had been clear about what he expected of me. The door wasn't open that wide, not yet.

Kirsten was sitting on the back deck of one of the little boats moored to the dock behind the building. I cautiously clambered on board and sat down beside her. Wordlessly, we both looked at the water and the heavy traffic running between the northern part of the city and the centre. Boats of all shapes and sizes were going in every conceivable direction, some fast, others strikingly slow. Unhindered by streets or sidewalks, parks or buildings, everyone chose the most direct path to their destination. People were free on the water, they could go wherever they wanted, and the result was a swarming, teeming mass. All the routes intersected. There were a couple of simple rules, but otherwise everyone kept an eye on everyone else. It wasn't that hard.

'You going to see Dad tomorrow?' Kirsten asked.

'If you're going, I'm going.'

'And if I'm not going?'

Silently I looked out at the boats, at the satisfaction people got out of steering a vessel. Taking their lives in their own hands. Setting their own course. 'Then I'm going anyway,' I said.

'Then we'll go together,' said Kirsten. She laughed. 'And we're going to Brussels together, too,' she said. Before I could respond she continued. 'Because I'm not hanging out here in this shed all by myself.'

'Not with Vince?'

'Vince is also going,' she said.

'Together in the camper?' I asked.

She laughed. 'Why not?'

I looked at her, eyebrows raised so high that they made wrinkles in my forehead. 'Does he know about you?'

'That's none of your business.'

'No, of course it's none of my business. Duh, I get that, too, you know.'

'So why did you ask?'

'Because I want to know,' I said.

We looked down in silence at our legs, dangling over the surface of the water. Kirsten stared out at the far side of the IJ.

'Yes,' she said.

'Intense,' I said.

'Not so bad,' she said. 'His first reaction was good. Very good.'

'But?'

'No buts.'

'What, then?'

'Well, in a couple of months there'll be other reactions. From his family. From his friends. From other women. And that can be hard going.' She smiled. Subdued.

'Been there?' I asked.

'Hm.' She nodded.

56

Meaning is history

'Burger?'

'Ew, God.'

'Slice of pizza, then? You were always one for pizza.'

'Come on, it's ten-thirty in the morning!'

'Good time for pizza, right?'

'Normal people want coffee at about this time.'

'Since when are we normal people? Watch what you say, because they have a Burger King here.'

'So?'

'So the King is better than the Mac. Everybody knows that.'

You could get anything at The Hague Central Station. Sunlight was pouring into the main hall through the tall windows. The rain from a few days back was gone for good, and the beginning of summer had barely enough patience to wait until the weekend. The air was getting warmer by the day, and the closer you got to the coast the clearer it was. You could even see that inside the station hall. Thick beams of light cut through the space like spots on a stage. On one side were the platforms and the trains, all of them standing with their noses facing the station, and on the other side were the doors to the centre of the city. Nowhere do arrivals and departures join together so beautifully as in a main train terminal. The city receives the train as its final destination. This is no intermediate station along the way, no five-minute stop. When you travel by train it isn't a grazing shot, it's a direct hit, and I felt that with every move I made. The Hague station may have been a bit chaotic because of the renovation, but it managed to retain that special atmosphere.

I slipped my hand behind Kirsten's arm and pulled her along to the Burger King entrance. It was peaceful there, too early for the big onslaught. A girl not more than twenty years old greeted us, her uniform still clean at the start of the working day, cap on her head, smile still fresh.

'Whopper and a coffee,' I said.

She repeated the order, put a cup under the coffee machine and pushed the button, and while the coffee was pouring she took a packaged hamburger from the warming rack. Everything was ready in less than a minute and a half.

'Anything else?'

I shook my head. Kirsten took the coffee, I took the burger. I had the wrapper off before we even got through the door. I held it in two hands and lifted it to my mouth. The smell of grilled meat, onions, tomato and sauce curled up to my nose and brought my feet to a halt. I sighed, waited a second and inhaled the aggressive aroma once more. You can prolong pleasure by postponing it. Then comes the gratification, but that's always momentary.

I ate.

The pulpy, soft substance of the bun and the burger itself slid through my mouth. The fat and the salt clung to my taste buds as if that was their natural home. I wolfed the burger down. Five, six bites, that's all it took. I remember stuffing a small hamburger into my mouth all at once a while back, jamming the whole thing in. When I tried to chew, streams of sauce and fat squirted from between my lips. Bits of onion and tomato fell out of my mouth. Junk food had nothing to do with eating. It was the gratification of a whim, a way of surrendering instantly to an impulse. Eating was no more than a means to an end.

Delicious. I had been violently shunted aside recently, and the longer it lasted the hungrier I got. I couldn't help it. I was drawn to hamburgers and they were drawn to me. I wiped my mouth and tossed the napkin into the trash can.

'Now we can go,' I said.

The Zeeheldenkwartier is just outside the downtown area of The Hague. This was where my father originally came from. His parents had lived here, in a house that was long gone. He had grown up in the narrow streets between the Waldeck Pyrmontkade and Anna Paulownastraat. And that's where he had returned, within biking distance of the insurance company where he had survived three mergers and countless reorganizations with greater ease than the marriage with my mother.

The tram stopped at Elandstraat, and from there Kirsten and I entered Zoutmanstraat and turned onto Piet Hein-straat, back toward the Royal Stables.

The little street was busy. Nothing but stores on either side. Lots of second-hand shops, a few antique shops, a big office supply store, one hairdresser after another, a green-grocer and a shop for bathroom fixtures, a bike shop, coffee shops, a shoe store and a shop for recycled goods. Lots of Turks and Moroccans at the beginning of the street. Russians further on. Empty businesses and renovations all mixed up together. Fighting dogs and art nouveau. Hash and borscht.

It felt good to be out with Kirsten. For the first time in weeks I pretended nothing was wrong and no one appeared to be holding me back. The most wanted man in the Nether-lands, Eberhuizen had said, and that Saturday morning, there among the shopping crowds, I wasn't even aware of it. No one was looking for me. Kirsten didn't ask me any ques-tions about my guilt or innocence. For her the matter was beyond doubt. After her initial anger she had come to accept the rough disruption of her new life on Hondecoeterstraat. For the time being, that is. For her, my back injury had been the decisive reason for coming with me. She was the only one who could help me, and the thought of leaving me in the unskilled hands of an enthusiastic software fanatic sim-ply never occurred to her. No matter how much she liked Vince herself.

But now that my vertebrae had been realigned, her reasons had also changed. She had found her own way among the people of the commune in Amsterdam North, and much to my surprise she had stopped talking about her apartment or about the desire to go back to it. She observed me and Vince and the others, and more than once I suspected that for her the forced evacuation was a temporary suspension of an approaching solitude. At the same time I wondered why I recognized that solitude so accurately and even so willingly. It was mainly the willingness that turned me back to myself. I understood that now better than ever.

'It was Trompstraat, right?' I asked.

'Add one, subtract two,' said Kirsten.

'Excuse me?'

'A language Pete and I made up,' she said. 'From when we were kids, if we wanted to agree to meet somewhere without letting anyone else know where it was. One street further, two numbers less.'

'Did you actually do that?'

'Sometimes. It was more for the kick. If I had to pick him up somewhere, for example, and he didn't want Dad and Mom to know where he had been. Add one, subtract two. Here,' she said, 'Barendzstraat.' She looked on a little scrap of paper. 'Twenty-one minus two is nineteen.'

We stopped in front of 19B. Two identical front doors side-by-side. Ground-floor apartment and upstairs apartment. I looked up. It was a large, straight-walled building with tall windows on the first floor. It didn't look anything like our old house in Dordrecht. The neat suburb, dominated by modern proportions, seemed cramped compared with the spacious dimensions of this city dwelling. The paint was flaking off the window and door frames and the mortar between the bricks was worn and eroded, but poor maintenance had not affected the building's character.

Kirsten rang the bell, and in the short time we stood there

waiting my world began to loosen from its moorings. As soon as my father opened the door, Dordrecht and everything I had experienced there would be consigned to the past for good. Until that moment, this was no more than an address in a neighbourhood somewhere in The Hague. I knew my father lived in this house, but not until I saw him there, until we stood together in the kitchen or sat at the dining room table, would the old images be replaced by new ones. The difference between knowledge and experience is the role other people play. I heard the footsteps on the stairs, and in a little while the door opened. My father was beaming.

'Kirsten,' he said. 'Michael. Jesus.' Tears ran down his cheeks. He wiped them away, trying to keep his face dry.

Kirsten threw her arms around him and kissed him. Awkwardly he returned her embrace. Dad had never been very physical, and even now, when he probably needed contact more than ever, it still wasn't easy for him. He could be boisterous and warm-hearted, but touching others was something he did as little as possible. Kirsten let him go, wiped another tear from his cheek and stepped aside. I stuck out my hand.

'Dad,' I said.

Upstairs, Peter had just come out of the kitchen with a pot of coffee and four mugs. 'Hey, sis,' he said. 'Yo, Mike.' He went into the back room and put everything on the table.

Kirsten stuck her arm under his and leaned against him. 'Are you making the coffee these days?' she asked.

'I don't do anything,' he said, 'but waiting for him is just as bad as being with the nuns. You don't get anything there, either.'

'I'm still finding my way,' said Dad.

'Your way,' repeated Peter. 'Your on-switch, you mean.' He walked out of the room.

Kirsten laughed and followed him. My father and I looked at each other somewhat sheepishly and moved restlessly around the table. I picked up the coffee pot.

'Shall I?' I asked.

'Why not.'

I filled up four mugs, and soon Peter and Kirsten returned, Kirsten with milk, sugar and spoons, Peter with an apple pie, four plates and a knife. While he sliced the pie, we stirred our coffee. Spoons ticked against pottery. My father looked at his children one by one and his happiness seemed to intensify, to sink deeper within him.

'You're allowed to say something,' said Peter.

'So are you still with Mom, in Dordrecht?' I asked.

'Looks that way.' He placed the slices of pie on the four plates and handed them out. 'I don't see you two there.'

'No, but I mean ...'

'I don't care what you mean, Mike. Everybody means something, you know, and meaning is history. It's old. Last century. Fuck meaning, okay?' He pointed to the pie. 'You got enough?'

I nodded.

'Because Mom is always talking about what she means, too, okay, and she always means well.' He turned to Dad. 'True or not, Dad?'

'She means well,' he said.

'Exactly. But it still sucks! Am I saying that right, Kirsten?'

'What are you asking me for?'

'Because you know where I stand.'

Kirsten said nothing. She looked at Pete, the younger brother with the big mouth. Screaming and cursing, he had retreated between both Dad and Mom, who had become more and more entrenched in their ideas. Not to hurt them but to protect himself from their megalomaniacal misunderstanding.

'Add one, subtract two,' she said.

'Yeah, there.'

'I think I'd use a different word.'

'Whatever.'

'And how's it going there then?' I asked.

'It's a fight,' said Peter. He took a bite of his pie and washed it down with a mouthful of coffee. 'No choice, really,' he said, 'because there's nobody left to hide behind, right, Dad?' He laughed. 'Say something, Dad?'

'Living with your mother has never been simple.' He said this without reproach, without putting the blame on anyone. At most he was astonished that he hadn't made that observation until now.

For the first time I realized how much our family had changed. All its members and all the relationships had been turned on their heads, all the compromises that had been made over the years, consciously or unconsciously, had been scrapped. No matter how many experiences we shared, it had now become apparent how little we knew about each other, if only because we didn't know who we were ourselves until now.

Peter was still himself, but we had changed him. Suddenly he was the constant and no longer the superannuated adolescent who was always against everything. He had been moved from the edge of the family to its very heart. He had a new position, and this gave everything he did and said another shade of meaning. He cursed as much as he used to do, but now we couldn't get enough of it. I saw my father, Peter, Kirsten and myself. I saw the family that we had never been, that we now could become, and I knew I wanted to be part of it.

57

Bellilog, June 30

V, this afternoon in the kitchen, head in the fridge, searching for Coke. 'No more Coke?' he said. Three bottles right in front of his nose. I pointed and V looked surprised. His surprise was wonderful, artless. Like sunrise in a nature reserve, the first light of day. He put a hand on his forehead and straightened up. 'Déjà vu,' he said. I thought he meant the Coke, which I could understand. 'Okay, reboot,' he said, and he shut the fridge door, took two, three steps backward and started all over again. Walked up to the fridge, opened the door, looked in. He felt the door. Shut the door again. And opened it. His eyes shut so he could feel every motion, every movement. Shook his head. Looked in the fridge again. Put a hand on one of the Coke bottles. 'It wasn't this,' he said, 'because I didn't see this.' He picked up a chair, put it in front of the fridge and sat down, staring at the cartons of milk, the cheese, the vegetables, the meat and everything else in the fridge. 'I didn't see it, and then I did, and I can't imagine not having seen it.' He picked up a bottle, took off the cap and put the bottle to his mouth. He drank greedily (computers make you thirsty), quarter of the bottle gone in an instant, screwed the cap back on and put the bottle back in its place. 'And after that I had déjà vu,' he said, 'that I couldn't imagine not having seen it.' He closed the fridge door, turned the chair around and sat down across from me at the kitchen table. 'So the déjà vu is that I overlook something that's staring me right in the face. Okay, now I only have to find out what's staring me in the face.' And satisfied, he walked out of the kitchen.

Half an hour later V came back. He sat down next to me. 'Okay, this is it,' he said, and he put a list with five points down in front of me. 1. passes, 2. antivirus, 3. k, 4. Brussels, 5. apartment. 'These five things are staring me in the face. Which of these five am I not seeing?' And that question filled my heart with terror. The realization that even if you're able to list them all, there are still things you overlook. Maybe there was something I wasn't seeing, either. So I asked him. 'You have no proof,' he said. I knew that. 'Yes, but you don't see it. Look, whatever Mr. B. is or isn't going to say may be interesting to you, but even if he confesses, all he has to do is hesitate once and everything points back to you. Your name just keeps rolling out of the computer. Not his. So ...' And at that point he suddenly looked at me with a glassy look in his eyes. 'If you can get at something one way, can you also get at it the other way around?' he asked.

By which I simply mean: I don't know where the virtual world begins and the real world ends. Or has the real world been virtual all along? Are only the wars real? And the disasters?

Mail from: HB2
Subject: see more, know more
okay, second group is gone. i'm with the last group, night flight, in brussels monday morning early. server still clean. link with pattern very nice, wow! thanks, thanks! want to see more, know more. but first uncle.

Mail to: HB2
Subject: Re: see more, know more
men with passes wearing suits and carrying attaché cases. look for the camper.

58

A language I haven't mastered

Sunday, middle of the night, the camper was ready to leave. Bernie in the driver's seat. Me in the passenger's seat next to him. Kirsten and Vince in the back. All the members of The Pattern standing at the gate. It was a gorgeous night. Under a clear night sky noises sound louder than normal. Bernie had rolled his window down and was still talking to Karl. A few words. Karl gave the body of the camper two rapid smacks with his hand and took a step backward. Bernie shifted, responded to Karl's signal with two brief honks of the horn and drove away. The big vehicle rolled slowly through the gate. All the way to the corner a few hundred metres further on we kept looking in the mirrors and through the rear window at the people waving behind us. It was the departure from a base camp, a departure in which the return was part of the destination right from the start. As soon as Bernie turned the first corner and the shed disappeared from our sight, silence descended on the camper. It was a charged silence. All four of us were imprisoned in our thoughts. Memories and expectations were woven together. Past and future were linked in the moment of choice. This choice. For the first time since the death of Ina Radekker I was taking the offensive. No more reacting to what others did, but bent on getting what I needed. With your back to the wall, they say, and it's true, but it's also nice to have something behind you. The wall also covers your back. If you can no longer trust the people around you, you're worse off. I had passed that stage. Back to the wall. Fine.

We crawled through Amsterdam North. All the normal streets were small for the camper, so as long as we were driving through residential areas Bernie kept the speed down to thirty kilometres an hour. He went even slower on the curves. He reached for the dashboard and turned the radio on. The voice of a news presenter sounded calm and trustworthy. Reports of a pile-up on the A12, dissension in the coalition, quarrel between cabinet ministers, a demonstration in Brussels. It took a while before the contents of the report registered with me.

> ... the previously banned demonstration was held anyway. Thousands of Belgian, Dutch, French, German and British Muslims took to the streets to protest discrimination and the unequal treatment they say they are experiencing. It was the first time European Muslims held a mass demonstration to make their dissatisfaction known. Images from Brussels today are reminiscent of the emotional marches in the Middle East. The police were present in full force and were able to keep the demonstration from reaching the centre of the city. After a number of brief, sometimes fierce charges, the demonstrators were dispersed. Disturbances continued into the evening but took place far beyond the range of the visiting government leaders. The police arrested nineteen ...

Bernie switched to another channel, classical music, Mozart piano sonatas. Fleeting notes of a melody that sticks in your head, keeps coming back until it, too, exists without sound.

At two-ten in the morning we stopped for a red light. The road was five lanes wide, not another car to be seen, the camper alone at an impressively large intersection.

'Why are you driving a camper, anyway?' I asked. 'It's very conspicuous, isn't it?'

'Maybe,' said Bernie. He laughed. 'But I've never had to hide myself until today.'

The light turned green and he pulled out, bearing right

onto the approach to the ring road. The camper sped up. There was no traffic on the ring and Bernie drove onto it without a care in the world. Instinctively I began thinking about the Breger family and the gravity with which HB2 spoke of it. I thought of the groups of people who were now on their way, one coming from Amsterdam (that was us) and three from South Africa. Later we'd find ourselves in Brussels, twenty of us standing at the door of an immense office building. And then what? I had to laugh to myself, my smile reflected in the dark windshield. An empty asphalt expanse stretched out before us, yellow light from the streetlights on the black road surface, white lines in the night. Bernie stepped on the gas and the monster accelerated with indescribable slowness from sixty to eighty-five. Accelerate wasn't the right word. Evolved. Five thousand revolutions.

'Okay, warp speed,' said Bernie, and he shifted to the highest gear.

Somewhere between Antwerp and Brussels I woke up, the deep roar of the diesel engine like an accompanying substructure supporting the peace and quiet of the car, Bernie's motionless hands on the great steering wheel, his eerie face bathed in an astonishing combination of light: the green of the dashboard and the light blue of the little GPS route planner screen.

'Almost there,' said Bernie.

In the back, Kirsten was lying on one of the narrow benches. Vince was sitting at the workbench on the fold-out stool, his glance no more than a stare. There were codes on one of the monitors and commands on the other, neither of which I understood. I unbuckled my seat belt and climbed between the front seats and into the back. I took two cans of Coke from the little fridge, one for myself and the other for Vince.

'What are you doing?' I asked.

'Something I should have done three days ago,' he said. He tapped the top of the can with a fingernail. 'Thanks.' He pulled the tab up, folded it back and drank half the contents all at once. Then he pointed to the screen on the left. 'This is the program operated by the pass registration at HC&P: who has which pass and who's using it when and where, that kind of thing. Somewhere in this program is the order not to register certain passes. If only I could find that part of the program ...'

'Then you could disable it,' I said.

Vince looked at me. 'Yes, that's a possibility,' he said, 'but it's not very interesting. If I could find it, then I could figure out which passes were not being registered. Those passes have a collective code, otherwise the computer can't recognize them. If I had that code, I'd be able to find them, see what I mean?'

'Not really.'

'First I have to know what I'm looking for. If I ask the computer: look for unregistered passes, I'd have the answer in no time, because the computer doesn't know of any unregistered passes. For the computer nothing is unregistered. That's only true for us, because we don't pay attention three-quarters of the time. But a computer doesn't work that way. A computer always pays attention.'

'And?' I asked.

Vince shook his head. 'Nothing,' he said. 'No matter how hard I look, I can't find any routines that regulate exceptions.' He typed a new command on the right-hand screen, and on the left-hand screen codes began slipping across the image area at high speed.

'How can you see what's there?' I asked.

'I don't have to,' said Vince. 'The computer is searching. As soon as it finds something, it stops. Then I take a look.' He took another sip of his Coke.

Mesmerized, I stared at the flashing numbers and letters. For me it was meaningless information, it was a language I hadn't mastered, and for the first time I realized how much I had lost contact with the world. For years I had thought that English, Spanish and Chinese were the great languages of the world, that mastering at least one of those language was a condition for understanding what was happening around us, for joining in the conversation, at whatever level. Now I saw that there was only one world language, a language that was spoken everywhere, in every country, and that was the language of computers, of information technology. All the rest, the languages we speak and have found so essential to our identity, was folklore, an amusement for people who had nothing else to contribute. It was culture, and that was the wrong level. The wrong program. Vince's words came back to me. Three-quarters of the time we aren't paying attention. If you're looking at the wrong program, you're not paying attention a hundred percent of the time, no matter how hard you look.

'Wait a minute,' I said. 'What exactly are you looking at?'

'What I just said. At ...'

'No, I mean how?'

'Well, like we always do when we have to modify or update something, via the WorldWare operating system. By plugging in directly.'

'Maybe that's the problem,' I said. 'Maybe you're approaching it from the wrong angle, from the angle of the manager.'

'The only other angle is that of the user, and they don't get to see anything.'

I shook my head. 'No,' I said, 'there's still a third angle. The angle of the owner.'

Vince stared at the screen.

'You mean Mr. Miller.'

59

Searching eyes

A business park at night is a confrontation. It's as if the neutron bomb had finally been tested and the buildings had been left to their own devices. Perfectly feasible, since everything is computerized. The heating system turns on when it gets too cold, the awnings come down if the sunlight is too bright, when it gets dark the lights go on, air conditioning maintains a pleasant climate. The supply of electricity and gas can go on forever because without people energy doesn't have to cost anything. Not only that but the consumption of energy is also drastically reduced. All the systems are in place and working on their own, and even the most basic computer can understand that if the electricity gets shut off the computer alone will suffer. Buildings are happier at night.

You can feel it.

Slowly the camper rolled through the wide, empty streets, followed by the ever-suspicious logos in every shade of neon that keep watch high up on the gleaming façades. It was four-thirty in the morning and there wasn't a soul to be seen in the entire area. We crept further and further, street after street, until we finally came to a stop at HC&P's main European office. It was deathly still. A minimum of lighting in the office buildings. You could see a smattering of lights in the residential tower next door, the first sign of human presence. Gijs was in there somewhere, behind one of the hundreds of windows.

Bernie turned off the headlights and drove into a parking lot on the other side of the street, opposite the entrance to the office. He backed into the first space along the side. Through the back window we had an unobstructed view of the main entrance. He turned the engine off and rolled down his window. Silence, and the irresistibly fresh smell of a summer morning just about to begin, swept into the camper.

I could hear Kirsten moving behind me. She yawned and turned over on the bench, muttered something unintelligible and kept on sleeping. Vince worked steadily on. His pace had slowed considerably over the last hour but he wasn't giving up. His fingers could be heard again and again tapping the keyboard, the little clicks of the mouse, the short beeps when the computer finished an operation or wanted an answer to a question.

Bernie opened his door and stepped out. 'Leave Vince alone,' he said. He stretched and went to the front of the camper, where he sat down on the bumper.

I got out, too, and I walked over to him. Together we sat on the bumper and stared at the empty parking lot, and at the light of dawn cautiously spreading upward behind the heavy buildings. Bernie took a joint out of the breast pocket of his shirt and lit it. The thick sweet fragrance of weed curled up in the silent morning air.

'You?' he asked, offering me the joint.

'No,' I said. 'I have to make sure I'm still good and angry later on.'

'Aggressive,' said Bernie. He nodded, took another hit, held the smoke deep in his lungs and slowly let it escape. 'So you have to know what your limit is.'

'Or not,' I said, 'but then I'd have to know that, too.'

Bernie laughed. 'It's always something,' he said. He paused. The joint crackled a bit between his fingers. 'Fuck,' he said. 'What an absolutely beautiful parking lot.'

I went inside the camper and made coffee. Bernie had taken out the counter, but otherwise everything was just as it was. There was a toilet, a shower, a fridge, there were plates, mugs, silverware, a cabinet full of food and an industrial-size pack of Nuts candy bars. I opened the pack of Nuts and took out three. Kirsten was still sleeping. Vince took the mug I offered, tore the wrapper off the Nuts and took a bite. With his mouth full he mumbled something, a cross between a groan and a word. I went outside and gave Bernie a mug and a candy bar and sat down next to him again.

'Very good,' he said. He laid the Nuts down beside him on the bumper and enclosed the steaming mug in his big hands. 'I don't know what's going to happen later,' he said, 'but before you go inside, I'm going to give you a cell phone with an open connection to the camper. From here I can put you through to Amsterdam or to whoever you want. I can organize a conference call, you name it. I'm operating the phone from here. Make sure you don't break the connection with the camper, whatever you do. We're here. Vince can get anything you're looking for from a computer, and I can make any connection you need. And Vince and I are on the same wavelength. We've known each other since grade school in Alkmaar. What we don't know about each other isn't worth knowing.'

'That's why you're here,' I said. 'Because Vince wanted it.'

'Because Vince wanted it,' he repeated. 'Because let's be honest, what do I know about you?'

'Nothing.'

'That's why,' he said. 'Even so, it's important for Vince.'

'For me, too,' I said.

A car drove into the parking lot in the early morning light. It was a quarter to six. The first consultant had arrived for his work.

'Time to go in,' said Bernie. We picked up our mugs, Bernie grabbed the wrapper from his Nuts and soon we were closing the little door behind us.

In the confined space of the camper everyone moved more slowly. Kirsten was awake, and while Vince continued working, she, Bernie and I sat at the table. From behind the curtains we watched the parking lot slowly fill up. Between six and seven o'clock hundreds of people went into the building. Bernie made another pot of coffee, took a carton of milk out of the fridge and put bowls, spoons and a box of Cruesli on the table. We ate and drank in silence.

At seven-forty Vince straightened his back and stood up.

'Done,' he said. He looked at the screen as if he couldn't believe it himself. Laughed. Sighed. Turned to me. 'You want to see this?'

All the codes and program language had disappeared from the screen. All that was left was a small, neatly organized menu.

'What do you want to know?' he asked.

'Who was in the HC&P office building in Amsterdam on the night of Wednesday, May 25th to Thursday, May 26th?'

Vince clicked on the menu, selected the date and the office and filled in the times, and in less than a second three names appeared on the screen. And an automobile license plate number. Time of arrival. Time of departure. A ruthless logbook.

I couldn't take my eyes off the screen. This was the proof I needed: a digital record that I had not been the only one in the building. I wanted to laugh and cry at the same time, trapped by strange, contradictory emotions, overtaken by the longing that had been hounding me for weeks and was now racing past me and disappearing like a fading siren. Vince had worked uninterrupted for a day and a night, and this for him was a breakthrough. He had deciphered a code. Beautiful, even tremendous, but for me it was something quite different. For me it was a new beginning.

From that moment it felt as if time was being compressed. I took a shower in the little stall, shaved and dressed. Shirt and suit. Tie. Shining shoes. Attaché case.

'What's in there?' Kirsten asked.

'Nothing.' I put it on the table and opened it up. The attaché case was empty.

'Why do you have it then?'

'It's a disguise,' I said. 'A consultant without an attaché case is no consultant.'

Bernie gave me a belt with a cell phone in a leather holster attached to it.

'It has an extra powerful battery,' he said. 'It'll go for at least six hours. Probably seven.'

'I'll have to be back outside long before then,' I said. 'Otherwise it doesn't matter.'

'It always matters,' said Bernie, and he ran a wire across my back and under my shirt. The wire reappeared behind the collar. Then he pushed an ear bud into my ear.

'That feel okay?' he asked as he straightened my shirt.

I pulled the wire forward a little so the microphone hung closer to my mouth.

'Fine,' I said.

The telecommunication connections were shown on one of the monitors. Bernie could turn the phone on and off with the computer. He put on a headset, clicked the mouse a couple of times and began speaking softly.

'Okay, Michael, this is a test. Speak softly and speak straight ahead.'

His voice resonated deep in my ear. He was calm. For the first time it struck me how much control he had over the volume and tone. What he said was free of judgment and opinion. His intonation was neither upbeat nor serious. It was neither an order nor a command, but it wasn't an off-hand suggestion, either. It was logical, straightforward, which made it immediately trustworthy. 'I have Amsterdam here for you.'

I watched Bernie move the mouse around and heard two clicks.

'Michael?'

It was Karl.

'Yes?'

'A bug is born,' he said. In Amsterdam they'd hacked the security system for the M-drive and had written a virus that could spread throughout the network. It consisted of a nice little program that would immobilize the security system, a program that would send itself to two other computers in the network, wait to receive the confirmation that it had lodged itself in the next two computers, and then carry out a stunningly simple series of commands: format the M-drive.

'It's ready to go,' said Karl. 'In just over an hour and a half the whole network could be down. Twenty-one steps, each one taking about five minutes. You say the word.'

'Not yet,' I said. 'I want everyone to be here before we do anything. In the meantime Vince has found something here that has to go to the police and the press today. Can you guys take care of that?'

I wrote a brief report to go with the data. 'New development in the Radekker murder case.' Vince pasted the summary below it along with instructions on how journalists could access the information themselves. We sent this to Amsterdam.

Then the waiting began. Vince used Mr. Miller to keep an eye on who was entering the Brussels building. Every time someone held his pass up to a scanner, his name would appear on our screen. I had drawn up a short list of names and put it on the workbench next to Vince. The names of the people who had to be there.

The first partners began arriving at nine-fifteen.

'Vogels is in,' said Vince. Caspar van den Vogels, managing partner of the Amsterdam office. Van Waayen followed five minutes later.

'No Olde Nieland yet?' I asked.

Vince shook his head.

'Can you see who's in the tower?'

Vince clicked through the screens until the logo of HC&P Residential Facilities appeared. He scrolled down the guest list and shook his head. No Olde Nieland. I could have expected so much, but even so I was disappointed.

'Can you print that list?' I asked.

Vince nodded and clicked a couple of times with his mouse, and soon I had three A4-sized sheets of paper in my hand. Seventy-four names. Not one that I knew.

'Breger's in, too,' said Vince. 'That was the last one. What now?'

I was silent. I looked around me—from Vince to Kirsten to Bernie. 'I don't know,' I said.

'You wanted to go inside, didn't you? What are you waiting for?'

'For the Breger family. Ten or fifteen of them were supposed to be here to pick him up.'

'Breger's family? What do they look like?' asked Bernie.

'I have no idea.'

Every minute seemed longer than the last. Under the pressure of steadily building expectations, plus all the planning and effort everyone had made just to get us here, time was becoming distorted. I had to wait. Without Breger's family I couldn't do a thing. They had to neutralize Huib Breger so I would be free to focus on the firm's partners. As long as Breger was still at large the partners would be inaccessible.

'At least let's shove that virus into the network,' said Bernie. 'The sooner we do that, the sooner we'll shut it down.'

I shook my head. 'No. No. No,' I said. 'If we release the virus too soon, they'll know there's something wrong, they'll block our way and Breger will be beyond reach. You have to wait until we're in. Not before.'

Adrenaline was surging through my body. It took an enormous effort to control myself. If I were to start ranting like a lunatic I wouldn't stand a chance. I'd be picked up by the security service and locked up somewhere within ten minutes. That would be the end of me. The whole operation rested on the simple fact that later on, in that building, I would have to act as if I belonged there, calm, controlled, smiling, without rushing and without dawdling, with the self-assured decisiveness that is second nature to every consultant. If I couldn't manage that, I didn't belong there.

Back to the list. Seventy-four names. Still not a single one that was familiar to me.

'What are you looking for?' Kirsten asked.

'Gijs. Gijs van Olde Nieland. Buddy of mine.'

'Is he in there?'

'I think so, yes. I think he's being held, in that tower.' I pointed through the window.

'Held? Doesn't he have a pass?'

Vince leaned across the table. Towards Kirsten. 'What did you want to know?'

'Whether he didn't have a pass.'

'Interesting,' he said. 'That means I should also be able to look for someone without a pass ...' He turned around. His hand on the mouse. Click. Click. Click. 'A Mr. Gold doesn't have a pass,' he said. 'Room 506. Suite. Extension 506.' He picked up a phone, entered the number and handed the phone to me.

Nervously I waited for the connection to be made, but as soon as the call was answered I knew it wouldn't work. I was put through to the phone exchange and got a polite woman on the line who told me with a musical voice that room 506 was not picking up. I ended the call.

Still nothing. I didn't even know whether Gijs was in immediate danger or not. Probably not immediate. The danger didn't matter anymore. Today, here, I had reached my limit.

I wanted my life back. And I wanted the same for Gijs. If I thought about it too long, I'd never get anywhere. The enormous power of the company and of the Larkowl Group was way too much for me. Only by concentrating on people, individuals, did I stand a chance of puncturing their line of defence. By removing Breger I hoped to hit HC&P in such a sensitive spot that it would undermine their confidence. And if the network imploded on top of that, I hoped that enough partners would decide to make a clean sweep of things in order to save the company. It was a one-two punch, and both punches had to hit home or I'd be left with nothing.

'Must be a company outing,' said Kirsten. She was leaning against the back window, pulling the curtain aside. 'Look.'

One by one, in closed formation, five identical, dark blue touring coaches had turned languidly into the street. They continued on slowly until they came to the office entrance. There they stopped. Bumper to bumper.

'Looks like the riot police,' said Vince.

After a few minutes the door of the first bus opened and a young man stepped out. Dark blue suit, black shoes, white shirt, red tie. In his hand an attaché case. Blond hair. Searching eyes. He took a few steps to the side and looked around, until he found the camper.

60

Bug on the move

I opened the door even before he had a chance to knock. He was somewhat younger than I. Blue eyes looked at me with a cheerful indomitability that I had never seen in anyone before.

'Sorry we're a little late,' he said, 'but before we had everybody in the bus ...' He shook his head. 'I thought I was losing my mind.'

'Who've you got in there?' I asked.

'Family.'

I looked outside, at the five buses that were standing motionless along the roadside.

'There were going to be about fifteen of you, you said?'

Huib Breger 2 laughed. 'No, I said I needed fifteen passes, but that I was coming with the family. If you take a good look at this company Uncle Huib is with and at everything he's done, you'd see we had no other choice.' He paused for a moment. 'Do you people know Uncle Huib?' he asked.

'From close range,' I said.

'Of course,' he said. 'But you don't know who he is. Uncle Huib is an uncompromising white man. You don't have that here. What you call extreme right is moderate where we come from. And Uncle Huib is not moderate. Never was. Apartheid is in his blood. After the changes he couldn't live in South Africa anymore, so he left for America. There's still plenty of room there for the white Christian heart.' He laughed. 'So we're not talking about some two-bit little pimp who's run off with his niece. That's why.'

'How many people are in those buses?' Kirsten asked.

'Two hundred thirteen.'

'Men, women and children?'

'No, just men.' Huib answered every question with a casualness that continued to astonish us. We couldn't help but turn our heads to the window, to the enormous numerical supremacy that was peacefully waiting for the signal to take action.

'Uncle Huib is going back to South Africa with us this afternoon,' said Huib, almost carelessly. 'The flight leaves at one-thirty. Check-in two hours before departure.' He looked at me, and the indomitability in his eyes hardened to a deep, unbreakable core. 'No other flavours available,' he said.

'Okay,' I said, 'the logistics are a little different for more than two hundred people, so ...'

Huib shook his head. 'Fifteen men are going with you. We'll do the rest ourselves.'

'That's just what I was afraid of,' I said.

'No need. Nothing untoward is going to happen. The whole gang is going to go in and report at the desk, one by one. As visitors.'

'Whose visitors?' I asked.

'You tell me. Who's the one most likely to get so nervous that he says the wrong things?'

I smiled. Some things are suddenly just so simple. I gave fifteen passes to Huib and one to Bernie. I kept all the rest myself.

'Your uncle isn't the only one who has to be brought out,' I said.

Huib nodded. 'Another bad guy?'

'No, on the contrary.'

Huib looked at me. 'Right,' he said. 'You know the building, you know where we have to be, so you lead the way. As soon as we have my uncle, there'll be ten men to bring him and my grandfather back outside.'

'Your grandfather?' I asked. 'Is your grandfather going inside, too?!'

Huib nodded. 'Willem is coming along.'

'But that's insane!'

'It's his son,' Huib said resolutely. 'He's the only one who can get him. The rest of us are here to reduce his options. See you in ten minutes at the entrance.' He got out of the camper and walked back to the first bus.

We went inside in groups of two and three. Through the entrance hall, nodding amiably to the receptionists, running passes across the scanner, through the security gate, on to the elevators. I was in the first group of three. As soon as I passed through the security gate, I contacted Karl in Amsterdam by phone.

'Now,' I said.

'And ... click,' said Karl. 'Bug is ... on the move.'

'Keep me informed,' I said. 'At every step I want to know how far we are.'

The attack had begun. Six men now inside. The virus in the network. There was no turning back. I saw old Willem Breger approaching through the hall. Eighty-three years old, his stark white hair waving in thick locks around his craggy face. He did not walk quickly, but he walked as if the world was his. And it was, I thought. Willem Breger had eight sons and thirty-six grandsons. His seven brothers together had thirty-five sons and a hundred and twenty-seven grandsons. He was the oldest, the pater familias of a family that was big enough to enforce its own values. Willem Breger greeted the receptionist, smiled, showed his pass and walked to the security gate. His walking stick tapped on the smooth marble floor. He held his pass up to the scanner, waited for the beep and kept on walking, as if he came here every day.

A couple of minutes later Huib came into the entrance hall, the last one to do so. He, too, walked straight to the security gate, pass in hand, and as he greeted the receptionist a wall of men appeared behind him, all of them with friendly smiles on their faces, no pushing or shoving. As Huib joined us we heard the first man reporting to the reception desk.

'I've come for Mr. Van Waayen.'

'And you have an appointment?'

'He's expecting me.'

'And your name is?'

'Breger.'

'Mr. Breger. If you'll just take a seat, I'll pass this information on.' She picked up the phone and made a call.

There were already almost a hundred standing in the entrance hall. The area was fully blocked.

'Additional benefit,' said Huib. 'Nobody else can come in or go out—until we're gone.' He laughed. 'As soon as we have Uncle Huib, Rob and I will go off with Michael. The rest will bring Uncle Huib and Grandfather downstairs, outside and to the bus. The group stays in the hall until Rob, Michael and I are back. Okay?' He turned to his grandpa. 'Everything all right, Grandfather?'

Breger the elder tapped his stick on the floor and pointed to the elevator. 'Let's get going,' he said.

We needed two elevators to take everyone up all at once. I held the door of one elevator open until a second had arrived.

'Four,' Karl's dry voice sounded in my ear. 'Add that to the previous steps.'

'And how much is that?'

'The number of the last step minus one.'

'So we're now at seven?'

'Exactly.'

The elevator stopped on the third floor. I led the way into the corridor. To the left were the offices of the partners and their secretaries. To the right, around the corner, were the conference rooms, and at the far end of the corridor was the big boardroom. That's where I expected to find everyone.

I heard a second signal a few metres away and Huib stepped into the corridor. At the same time a door flew open across from us and a woman came running out, a cell phone in her hand.

'Then just interrupt the meeting,' she shouted. 'I'm breaking in on it now. Stay on the line.'

She went around the corner and I listened to her footsteps fade as she ran down the corridor. I motioned, and all fifteen Bregers came out of the elevators. One of the men took a wedge out of his pocket and slammed it into the channel of the elevator door with a loud smack. I pointed to the right and the group moved off in silence.

'Thirty-two,' said Karl.

'What happened to eight and sixteen?' I asked.

'It's going faster than we thought.'

The door to the boardroom at the end of the corridor was ajar and sounds of shouting were emerging, Van Waayen's above all the others. He was hysterical.

'But why is he asking for me?'

As he spoke, a second secretary rushed toward the room. She gave our group a questioning look.

'Can I help you?' she asked. At the same moment, Breger's loud voice came booming from the boardroom.

'DRIES! See for yourself, God damn it! There can't be a Breger at the reception desk because I'm here. You can see that, can't you?'

The secretary reacted with shock. 'I'm afraid I have to go ...'

'Don't worry about us,' I said. 'We're almost there.'

She shot into the boardroom closely followed by a third woman. There fell a lull in the tumult. For a moment. Then the deep voice of Caspar van den Vogels broke the silence.

'Huib, what is this all about? There seem to be twenty Mr.

Bregers in the reception area, and all of them are asking for me ...?' He paused. 'And now there are thirty, I've just been told. Is this a joke of some kind? Or a test? Or a coup?'

Uncomfortable laughter could be heard. Not the best time for a joke.

'Apparently you still think I'd need such a thing.' Breger's voice was icy, condescending. Unconcealed aggression. 'There's only one man here who controls Mr. Miller,' he said, 'and without Miller this company is nothing.'

'Two-hundred fifty.' Karl's voice in my ear.

Then I heard the sound of someone standing up. 'I'm going to go see what this is all about,' said Breger. 'In the meantime, no one leaves the room!'

It was at that moment that I pushed the door open. With fifteen Breger men behind me I stepped inside. Every seat in the luxurious boardroom was filled. Partners from all the European countries were sitting shoulder to shoulder at an immense table. Hanging at the short end of the table was a large screen on which the network was being shown. A few hundred downed computers didn't make the slightest difference. They weren't even discernible. Huib Breger was halfway to the door. I held my ground in the doorway.

'It might be better if you stayed as well,' I said.

Breger cursed. Loudly. 'Michael Bellicher! You should have been eliminated three times already!' he shouted, and for a minute he lost his self-control. He stormed around the table, his hands ready to squeeze the breath out of my body once and for all. Frightened partners began jumping up left and right. Some of them screamed, which was probably what caused Breger to regain his control. In one rapid motion he pulled out a cell phone, pushed a couple of buttons and began speaking into it.

'Security, two men to the boardroom. Now!' He listened to the answer, and slowly his face drained of all its colour. 'Then get two from the hall!' he shrieked. 'What do you mean, it can't be done?!' With a gesture of annoyance he flipped the phone closed and stuck it back in his inside jacket pocket. 'All right,' he said, 'then I'll do it this way.' With the same motion he pulled a pistol from a shoulder holster and aimed it at me. No one said a word. The silence in the room was palpable.

'One thousand,' said Karl in my ear bud.

On the screen behind Breger's back I watched the network swing into action in an attempt to neutralize the downed computers and to work around them. A thousand was still nothing, but from now on every successive step would hit harder. No one saw it. Everyone was looking at me. Breger came one step closer and was about to take another step when he seemed to freeze up in mid-movement.

Behind me his family appeared and came further into the room. His brothers and his cousins. One by one they stood beside me.

'Jesus, Rob,' said Breger. His pistol hand hesitated. 'Peter? Chris? Where did you all come from? Hey, come on, fellows, I'm working here. This isn't the time to ...' All the confidence drained from his voice. With every name he named, he seemed to grow smaller. I was being surrounded by a shield made up of his family. Firing his gun was out of the question. His arms hung limply at his side. 'Those people downstairs?' he asked.

'Yes, what about them?' said Rob.

'So they're real?'

Rob nodded. He was more than a head taller than me. A few slight movements were all Rob Breger needed to get someone to proceed with caution.

'Are you all here?'

'Almost,' said Rob. 'Niels couldn't make it.'

This last comment, the name of the one person who hadn't come, shattered Breger's remaining resistance. He shook his head and stared at his family in disbelief. Then pandemonium broke loose all around us, everyone screaming at once, and it seemed as if the situation really was going to get out of hand. The fifteen Bregers blocked the exit from the room, but the blockade couldn't last long. The partners demanded an explanation. Shouting and screaming, they tried to call each other to order. Without Breger the authority evaporated from the room. Consultants can never accept each other's leadership. The very idea that someone else knows better than they do themselves is foreign to them. With all these men yelling and jumping up and down around me, I feverishly kept an eye on one individual: Van Waayen. I needed him on my side.

'Four thousand,' came the voice of Karl. 'Now we're getting somewhere.'

Behind me I felt the closed rank of Breger men open up. In the midst of all the tumult old Willem Breger appeared from behind his sons. He held his stick high in the air and brought it down on the wooden conference table with a jarring crash. He put all his strength into that smack, all his rage. The lacquer sprang from the table's surface.

'If you all would just shut up for a minute, we could be out of here in no time,' he said. He didn't even deign to look at the assembled group, but turned around and walked up to his son.

In the oppressive silence one man stood up at the other end of the table. A small man, who up until then hadn't said a thing. It was Herbert Colland, co-owner and CEO of HC&P, the driving force behind the Larkowl Group and the self-appointed guardian of the interests of the Lord. He allowed the silence to intensify until he alone could break it.

'And who do you think you are?' he asked. His caustic tone cut through the room with unconcealed aggression.

Willem Breger didn't even look at him. The authority that

Colland was trying to lay claim to failed to reach the other end of the table. Willem placed a hand on his son's shoulder.

'Huib,' he said, 'that dwarf down there wants to know who I am.'

It seemed like minutes before Huib Breger could utter any intelligible words.

'This is my father,' he said.

Colland changed his approach to accommodate this new information. The look in his eyes softened, his intonation shifted to a higher register, warmer, the vowels longer. 'Mr. Breger,' he said, 'what an honour to meet you. Your son is a phenomenon, a genius.'

'You don't know anything about it,' said Willem. He was not impressed by sweet talk. 'And if you can call this monster here a genius, then I know where you're coming from.'

'You underestimate him.'

'I don't underestimate anybody.' Old Willem had obviously had enough. 'And now it's time to go, Huib. Come.'

Colland wouldn't give up. 'But you can't just walk in here and ...'

'Oh yes, I can. This is a family affair. It doesn't matter where I handle it. Huib, tell him I'm right.' Willem poked his son with his walking stick.

Huib Breger nodded.

'Good,' said Willem. 'Then that's taken care of.' Two brothers stepped forward, took Huib by the arms and dragged him down the corridor behind his father.

From Colland's icy stare it was plain to see that he had already taken leave of the man who had provided his security for so many years and had run Mr. Miller for him. Easily replaced.

'Sixteen thousand,' said Karl. 'It won't be long now. Six more steps and the network will be obliterated. You'll have to be gone before then, because we won't know what's still working and what isn't.' The network on the screen began to behave eccentrically.

With Rob Breger and young Huib at my side I ran over to Dries van Waayen, pulled him up out of his chair and tried to take him with us.

'What the hell is going on here?!' Herbert Colland exploded, and now his rage was directed at me and the few remaining Bregers. Far down the corridor I heard the others step into the elevator and leave. I was standing there alone.

'Mr. Van Waayen is expected in Amsterdam,' I said, 'in connection with the case of murder in the office there.' Van Waayen cowered beside me.

'I'll decide who is being expected and where,' answered Colland. 'And I don't think you realize exactly what that means.'

61

A camper doesn't need a pass

No one moved. Colland had reappropriated his authority. He may have had little to contribute to the Breger's family matters, but this was different. This was his domain, his company. He came around the table and walked up to me. He walked gracefully, almost effortlessly, adding power to his words with small, stylized gestures. But once he got closer I saw that his eyes were cursing.

'The only one who's wanted for murder in Amsterdam is you,' he said. His mouth twisted up crookedly into a disturbed sort of smile.

'There's a difference,' I said, 'between the ones who did it and the one who is wanted for it.'

'We make that difference,' said Colland. The man's arrogance was devastating in its simplicity. Supported by the most successful consultancy in the world, Colland no longer needed to explain things to people who didn't agree with him. His success was the only proof he needed. His power did the rest. 'We protect things of value. Companies, organizations that otherwise might not make it. Interests that are in danger of being forgotten.'

'Like modern knights,' I said.

Colland nodded, satisfied. 'You might call us that, yes.'

'Then this must be the round table?'

'One of many,' said Colland.

'For a new crusade,' I said.

'Against the threat to our values. And that is something you should take to heart. We have a special responsibility in this world. You take it far too lightly.'

'Why?' I asked.

Herbert Colland looked at me as if I were some kind of

obsolete implement. 'Why?' he repeated. 'Because the world is too complex to be handed over to the good care of elected nitwits with an average IQ of somewhere between eighty and a hundred and twenty,' he said. 'It's all quite charming, you understand, but they don't see the big picture. Everywhere our values are being frittered away in spineless negotiations. Politicians keep thinking about the next election and they're only willing to take action when they have hard, indisputable information, when they can prove that things have gotten out of control, when it's actually too late. Otherwise they do nothing. And it can't go on like that. They're just plugging holes. The time for waiting is over. Finished! The governments of Western Europe must seek confrontation based on the firm belief that they have no other choice. The Christian faith has already made that choice. What's missing are the right facts.'

'And Mr. Miller's job is to supply them with those facts?'

'Everyone gets the facts they need,' said Colland. 'That's what it's all about. That is crucial. Actually I don't even have to keep you here. You want to leave with Mr. Van Waayen? Go right ahead. Before you're back in Amsterdam I think everyone will know the facts about this meeting.'

'Oh, yes?' I asked.

'Yes, because we are the new elite, the new intelligentsia. We combine insight and knowledge, and we have the power to influence choices. Some half-baked conservative might think that public transport should be privatized, but we make the analyses. We generate the arguments and supply the facts that determine feasibility. If we don't want something, it can always be corroborated by facts. By our facts. And our facts are always better than anyone else's. We control the facts, Mr. Bellicher, and no one can escape them.'

On the screen I could see how the network was slowly falling apart. Now there were so many downed computers that the program was beginning to falter. Little blinking lights indicated that something was not right.

'Two hundred sixty thousand,' came the voice of Karl. 'Can you see it, too?'

'You bet,' I answered.

'You bet what?' asked Colland, still standing with his back to the screen. Everyone was looking at me. Only Van Waayen and I were looking the other way. Van Waayen said nothing.

'First look, then think,' I said, and pointed to the screen. At that moment a shrill beep sounded, an alarm. A red window with a warning text lit up. Everyone turned around and looked at the screen. Large sections of the network were breaking down before their very eyes. With frantic signals and shrill squeals, Mr. Miller was trying to rally. Speechless, Colland stared at the fight between software and hardware. Two hundred sixty thousand computers had each found two other computers and had now begun to immobilize themselves. Then the next five hundred thousand computers began searching for two new ones in order to pass the virus on. Every step was twice as big as the last. Every subsequent step therefore took a little longer, but you could still count on it happening. Mr. Miller's very existence was based on the idea of computers constantly seeking contact with each other. To pass on the destructive file, all they had to do was to replicate the operation that kept Mr. Miller going.

As the virus continued along its path, the network recovered from the last blow. With a quarter of a million computers fewer it was still fully operational. It redistributed its capacity and came to rest once more, somewhat smaller than it had been, but stable. The signals regained strength as the minutes passed. Colland laughed.

'I don't know what just happened,' he said, 'but it's not very interesting. Mr. Miller is the first intelligent, self-directing network ever created. It searches for the solution to every problem it encounters, and the calculating capacity of the network is so vast that no problem can defeat it.'

'Of course,' I said. I turned to Van Waayen and pulled him with me. Huib squeezed past me and pushed Colland aside, thereby creating an opening by which we could reach the door. Colland reacted with fury.

'I don't think so!' he screamed. He shouted for the security service, but no one came. Stamping his feet with rage, he picked up his cell phone and called a number. Even before his call was answered, a cry of dismay went up in the room. The virus had completed the next step, and it was as if the screen had been hit by a dark wave. Connections went down everywhere. Alarms went off again, but this time they didn't stop. Colland shrieked. With flailing arms he threw himself on us, throwing punches with the force of someone who no longer knows what he's doing. The three of us struck back until Rob Breger grabbed him and flung him across the big wooden table in an enormous sweep. With nothing to stop him he sailed over the gleaming polished surface. Cups and glasses went crashing. When he reached the other side of the table he slid over the edge and landed in the lap of one of the partners. The chair tipped backward and both of them fell to the floor with a crash.

'Soon Mr. Miller will be no more,' I said to the assembled partners. 'Maybe it's time to think about your own interests.'

That's all they needed to hear. Everyone began screaming, and in all the commotion we raced out of the conference room. With Van Waayen, in search of Gijs.

The passage to the residential part of the building was one floor lower. There, too, movement was controlled by sliding glass doors that could only be opened by means of a pass. We shot through. Van Waayen was moaning and groaning, but he made no attempt to escape.

'What do you want with me?' he shouted.

'I want you to testify on my behalf,' I said.

'And why should I do that?'

'Because if you don't you'll be going to South Africa with your little friend Huib. It's up to you.'

Van Waayen stared at me.

'This is kidnapping,' he said.

'Not if you decide to come on your own,' I said, and we dragged him further.

'One million,' said Karl in my ear bud.

On the fifth floor we raced down the corridor until we got to room 506. I tried the door handle, but it just moved loosely up and down. The door remained locked. Below the handle was a combination lock. I cursed.

'Vince!' I shouted into the little microphone on my cell. 'Combination lock, room 506. Can you find the code in the system?'

'Forget it,' said Vince. 'The whole network is down. No one can get in anywhere.'

I turned around abruptly.

'Okay,' I said to Van Waayen, 'then you give it to me.'

'I'm not saying anything,' said Van Waayen, demonstratively clamping his jaw shut.

'If you're going to testify on my behalf, you're going to have to say all sorts of things that you don't want to say. So think of this as practice.'

Van Waayen said nothing.

'WHY NOT?' I screamed. 'What in God's name do you have to gain by keeping your mouth shut now?'

Still he refused to respond. He looked at me with big, glassy eyes.

'I have nothing to do with those murders,' he finally said.

'Oh. Great! Terrific! Dries, if you're so sure about that, then what are you complaining about? I'm also sure that I have nothing to do with those murders, but I have to prove it because all of you destroyed my credibility. Give me a break!'

He didn't answer but stepped forward and quickly keyed in a number, and in a few seconds the door sprang open.

Gijs was lying in bed, wearing some kind of sweatsuit. He was anesthetized, or at least so full of pills that he barely knew where he was or what he was doing. His own clothing was hanging in a closet, but the prospect of getting him dressed seemed hopeless. I quickly began looking for the most important things—wallet, keys—and put them in my pockets. Huib and I picked Gijs up and tried to carry him between us. It was hard going. His long body refused to cooperate. His muscles were so limp that every time we took a step we were never sure we'd be able to continue. After two steps we stopped. It wasn't working.

I tried feverishly to figure out how to get away. As long as the Bregers were keeping the security men occupied in the entrance hall we could more or less do what we wanted. But that wouldn't last forever. As soon as Colland regained control of security, things would get very difficult very fast. We didn't have that much time. I cursed.

'Allow me,' said Rob. He let go of Van Waayen, dropped to his knees, lifted Gijs across his back and stood up. 'Ready,' he said.

Huib and I pushed Van Waayen down the corridor to the elevator. Rob followed with big, heavy strides.

We got out on the second floor and hurried to the gates separating the residential part from the office building proper. From there it was still two floors down and then a long straight line to the exit.

'Michael?' Bernie's voice came through my ear bud. 'You can't get out the front door anymore. Employees wanting to leave the building are trying to clear a path through the Bregers. You'll never get through.'

We stopped in the middle of the corridor. While I told the

others what was going on, I tried to come up with an alternative.

'Through the parking garage?' suggested Huib.

I shook my head. This building had no parking garage. The space around it was so big that everyone just parked their car outside. I cursed again. 'The rats are abandoning ship and we're up here somewhere on the second deck. It's like the goddamned Titanic.'

'There's still a VIP entrance,' Van Waayen said suddenly. 'At the back of the building, next to the house printing office. We can't get out through the service entrances because they work with a different system. But the VIP entrance works with the ordinary passes.'

I looked at him. 'A VIP entrance?' I said. I didn't believe it. The back of the building was not the place to receive a VIP.

'For people who don't want to be seen,' said Van Waayen. He was becoming impatient and he began pulling Huib and me after him.

'Why are you in such a rush all of a sudden?' I asked. 'Because a couple of employees want to get out of the building?'

'Think about it,' he snarled. 'They aren't employees. The employees don't know anything about this. They're the partners. That's the cream of the company that wants out, and I don't want to be the only one left behind!' He dragged Huib along with him, and soon we were racing through the corridors to the back of the building. While I was running I gave Bernie instructions on how to get to the service entrance. He could gain access to the grounds by using the pass I had given him.

'And Bernie,' I said, 'tell the Bregers to clear the entrance hall. Everyone has to be able to get out of the building. As fast as possible.' If the company leadership wanted to leave, we shouldn't keep them a second longer. I didn't want to give anyone the opportunity to change his mind.

Through the ear telephone I heard Bernie talking to one

of the Bregers. Car doors slammed, and a second later all I could hear was the deep sound of the diesel engine.

There seemed to be no end to the corridor running to the back of the building. Rob Breger trudged on under the half-conscious body of Gijs and fell further and further behind. Van Waayen pointed ahead to where the corridor made a turn to the left.

'Almost there,' he said.

'Mike?' This time it was Kirsten's voice coming through the ear bud. Agitated. 'We're here at the boom barrier and the pass doesn't work.'

'That's impossible!' I shouted. 'That thing has to work! Try it again.'

'Nothing happens,' said Kirsten.

'Then Vince will know what to do. Ask Vince.'

But Vince wasn't there. He had gone with the Bregers to make sure everyone got out of the entrance hall quickly and back into the buses.

'Aw, fuck it,' I heard Bernie say in the background. Kirsten screamed, and her scream drowned out the other sounds of cracking, splintering wood. Soon Kirsten was back on the line.

'Okay,' she said, 'we're through. Now what?'

We dashed around the corner. At the end of the corridor was an ordinary glass office door in a metal frame. Door handle and an electronic lock. Hanging on the wall was a small cabinet with a little red light. Van Waayen got there first. He held his pass up to the scanner, a short beeping signal sounded and the door sprang open. Huib went out first and Van Waayen next, followed by me. Both of us held on to him. I didn't want him to make a last-minute run for it.

We waited outside for Rob, who had just rounded the turn in the corridor with Gijs over his shoulders. Suddenly two other men appeared behind him, Colland and his chauffeur.

I shouted to Rob. Too late. The chauffeur pushed him aside and Rob lost his balance. He was unable to prevent Gijs from sliding down. Rob stayed upright, put Gijs on the floor and ran after the two men. He grabbed the chauffeur, and with a rapid, violent movement he slammed the man against the wall and pinned him there—his left arm across his throat, knee high up in his groin, his right fist ready to put out the man's lights.

'ROB!' I shouted. 'DON'T DO IT! Leave him alone. Let him go.'

'No, no,' Van Waayen hissed beside me. 'Don't let him go! This is your chance. This guy is a maniac!'

I shook my head. 'There's nothing else to be gained here,' I said.

Van Waayen groaned. 'Jesus, what a wuss,' he said. 'Then I'll do it myself.'

He walked back into the corridor and screamed at Colland, hurling every kind of abuse he could think of at him. Colland was now alone, and he shouted back. There wasn't much else he could do. Rob was behind him, holding the chauffeur in an iron grip. Van Waayen was in front of him, and Huib and I were behind Van Waayen. Sweat was dripping off his face. The confined space was filled with the smell of his fear. The two men stood nose to nose, screaming at each other with increasing violence and intensity, until Van Waayen took aim and kicked with unbridled ferocity, burying one of his highly polished, russet loafers deep in Colland's crotch.

In an instant the man fell silent.

He buckled over and reached for his balls, which were now probably somewhere in his abdominal cavity. He must have felt the pain all the way up to his ears.

The camper pulled up behind us and stopped. There was a deep, horizontal dent running straight across the front, just above the bumper. Wood splinters were sticking out from underneath the windshield wipers. Kirsten threw the side door open and Huib got in first, pulling Van Waayen in after him. I shot past Colland, who was still doubled over, and helped Gijs make his way down the corridor and out the door. Rob was last. He let go of the chauffeur, took three or four steps backward without losing sight of the man, turned around and ran the last stretch to the car.

Bernie was hanging over the steering wheel. The heavy camper bounced around the building and back to the exit, tires squealing. There was a line of traffic backed up in front of the boom barrier because the fleeing cars could only go through one by one. Bernie drove around the cars and stepped on the gas, heading for the entrance on the other side.

'Forget that shit about the passes,' he said. 'A camper doesn't need a pass.' He drove through the broken barrier and left the grounds.

Vince was waiting at the door of the first bus. All the Bregers had gotten in. They were waiting for the last two. Rob got out of the camper and we shook hands on the street. For the first time.

'We haven't even been introduced,' I said.

'That's not the way I see it,' he answered. He laughed. 'All the same, very nice to meet you.' He leaned past me and stuck his head back in the camper. 'Huib, you coming?'

Huib hesitated. 'I ... uh ...'

Suddenly I remembered his last e-mail. 'Want to know more. Want to see more.'

Huib wanted to come with us to Amsterdam. He had told me this and I still hadn't responded.

Details.

So important. And I wasn't ready to say goodbye to the man who looked at the world and understood it from the perspective of his family. He had a lot to teach me.

'Huib,' I said, 'they're counting on you in Amsterdam. You're not going to run away now, are you?'

62

BON

Most of the HC&P partners slipped away from Brussels quietly. Without their constant input and without the manipulated facts produced by Mr. Miller, the government leaders were suddenly incapable of agreeing on anything. On the last day the European Summit on Security and Integration collapsed. The declarations that had been drafted earlier seemed too severe. Too harsh. Too confrontational. The EU retreated to the safe position of calling for more research, more analysis and more coordination.

Back in South Africa, old Willem Breger and his eight sons reported to the police. Huib Breger confessed his complicity in the murders in Amsterdam, provided the names of the men who had helped him and revealed the identity of the organization behind it all. HC&P, the world's most powerful international consultancy, suffered the heaviest blow in the company's history. Herbert Colland stepped down. He continued to swear that he was not involved in any way, but no one believed him. The fallen commander is always misunderstood.

The office in Amsterdam was the hardest hit. Almost all the partners were aware of what Huib Breger had been up to, and the police hauled them in for questioning one by one. As the only partner without any connections to Colland and the Larkowl Group, Johan Wolfsen took over the leadership of the Dutch office. He launched a drastic cleanup operation and made it a top priority to arrange for the firm's complete independence by means of a management buyout.

And he made sure that Dries van Waayen cooperated with the police investigation of the murders of Ina Radekker and

Jessica Polse. Inspector Pletting called me personally to tell me I was no longer a wanted man.

The bank was less cooperative. It took weeks before my accounts were unblocked and I was able get at my money again. No one understood why the accounts had been blocked in the first place and everyone agreed that they had to be unblocked as soon as possible, but for some unaccountable reason it didn't happen. Finally Gijs's father called an acquaintance of his on the board of directors and asked what on earth was going on in that bank of his. One day later the problem was solved.

That's banking for you.

HB2 stayed for a few more weeks. He fit right in at The Pattern as if he had never been anywhere else. He'd disappear for days in the digital fun park, where power and subversion are never far removed. Information and communication technology constitute a worldwide system that's being increasingly perfected in the hands of anarchists and freaks. The law-abiding citizen just doesn't have the brains for that kind of work. Huib found what he was looking for, although I'll never really understand what that intimate attraction to technology is all about. Maybe computers have become what motorbikes and cars used to be. What was once the cubic capacity of an engine block is now the number of gigabytes. It's all just another kind of tinkering. The paraphernalia has changed but the magic is the same.

After three weeks he left and went back to South Africa, to his family. 'Sometimes they drive me nuts,' he said, 'but there are so many of them that I always end up missing one or two. Even so, you shouldn't take them for granted.'

Johan Wolfsen did what he could to keep Gijs and me with the firm, but finally he understood that too much had taken place. We rented the rooms on the water, in the annexe to one of the wings at The Pattern's huge premises, and after a few weeks of painting and furnishing we opened BON Consultancy (Bellicher Olde Nieland), complete with letterhead, business cards and a secretary. Wolfsen came to the festive opening with a fat binder, which he solemnly handed over to us.

'A small gift,' he said, 'in lieu of flowers. You seem to have enough of those already. Work begins Monday morning, eight-thirty.' He tapped the binder with one finger. 'The briefing is in here. If you're so intent on striking out on your own, I'll just have to hire you.'

It was our first job.

Vince gave us an M-drive that he had turned into a work of art, dismantled and mounted between two pieces of Plexiglas. *Mr. Miller* was engraved in the plastic, and just looking at it reduced me to silence.

The fear was still there. Even without Mr. Miller everyone was trying to out-shout the rest, claiming that the world was their world, or that it belonged to a higher power who would not be contradicted. The facts were less distorted, less aggressively manipulated, yet the old facts remained. People believe what they want to believe. They quote their own theories and defend their own position, even long after it's been disproven. Rightly or wrongly, abandoning their own position is always the last step.

There's still a lot of communication to be done.

Kirsten and Vince had a couple of difficult weeks—why, I don't know. Kirsten went back to her apartment on Hondecoeterstraat. Vince stayed at The Pattern. They didn't say anything about it, and Vince acted as if nothing was wrong. Now they seem to be doing better. Like old times, actually. Maybe they needed to take some distance after their bizarre beginning. Maybe it was something else entirely. Maybe I should stop trying to interpret things and just ask her if I have any questions.

My parents don't talk to each other at all anymore. They communicate through us, which is probably better. The house in Dordrecht has been sold. Pete and I helped Mom with the packing and moving. That was strange. I still feel betrayed by her, but I lost the ability to be angry at her somewhere along the line. Now I know how careful I have to be with my anger.

After the move, Pete moved in with Kirsten, and since she's spending more and more time with Vince he pretty much has the whole apartment to himself. He still hasn't been able to explain to me what he's going to do here in Amsterdam, except that he just wants to be here. And I understand that.

Dad has a new girlfriend. Now that's taking some getting used to. It's the first time I've ever seen him in love, and even though I'm happy for him, I can't bridge the gap between this and the past. My fault. They like to travel. As soon as they get the chance, they're off. Now they're in New York. Next week San Francisco.

Gijs is visiting a client. An industrial baker somewhere around Spakenburg, the heart of Dutch fundamentalism. He can deal with that better than I can.

It's Thursday afternoon. I'm sitting in the back room, the window open, the sun reflecting off the surface of the IJ. The summer reaches a new high point every day now. Leaning against the wall behind my chair is my backpack, red and dark grey with black straps. Hasn't been used in weeks, but it's filled with everything I need and ready to go at a moment's notice. I'm working on my blog.

63

Bellilog, July 19

I'm back.

On the Design

As book design is an integral part of the reading experience, we would like to acknowledge the work of those who shaped the form in which the story is housed.

Tessa van der Waals (Netherlands) is responsible for the cover design, cover typography and art direction of all World Editions books. She works in the internationally renowned tradition of Dutch Design. Her bright and powerful visual aesthetic maintains a harmony between image and typography and captures the unique atmosphere of each book. She works closely with internationally celebrated photographers, artists, and letter designers. Her work has frequently been awarded prizes for Best Dutch Book Design.

The photograph on the cover is taken by Thomas Schlijper, also known as the 'Amsterdam City Chronicler.' On a daily basis he photographs Amsterdam (and, frequently, Tel Aviv and Paris as well) and publishes the images on his website (http://schlijper.nl). This photograph, taken on April 6, 2011, features a school in IJburg, a new suburb of Amsterdam. In Schlijper's words: 'I always love it when there's still a bit of light in the sky and when buildings are lit from inside.'

The cover has been edited by lithographer Bert van der Horst of BFC Graphics (Netherlands).

Suzan Beijer (Netherlands) is responsible for the typography and careful interior book design of all World Editions titles.

The text on the inside covers and the press quotes are set in Circular, designed by Laurenz Brunner (Switzerland) and published by Swiss type foundry Lineto.

All World Editions books are set in the typeface Dolly, specifically designed for book typography. Dolly creates a warm page image perfect for an enjoyable reading experience. This typeface is designed by Underware, a European collective formed by Bas Jacobs (Netherlands), Akiem Helmling (Germany), and Sami Kortemäki (Finland). Underware are also the creators of the World Editions logo, which meets the design requirement that 'a strong shape can always be drawn with a toe in the sand.'